HER CLOSEST
FRIEND

BOOKS BY CLARE BOYD

Little Liar
Three Secrets

CLARE BOYD

HER CLOSEST FRIEND

Bookouture

Published by Bookouture in 2019

An imprint of StoryFire Ltd.

Carmelite House
50 Victoria Embankment
London EC4Y 0DZ

www.bookouture.com

ISBN: 978-1-78681-770-9
eBook ISBN: 978-1-78681-769-3

'A drunk mind speaks a sober heart.'

CHAPTER ONE

As we walked through the snow up the final hill to Sophie and Adam's house for their son's eighth birthday party, I took a moment to look around me, wanting to be present in the here and now. I tried to capture the scene playing out before me, to press pause, to set it into slow motion, to see every detail before it became the past. A reel of true beauty: the sun sparking from the snow-piped branches, the joy radiating from my daughters' smiles, my husband's laughter lines as he ducked and darted from the girls' snowball attacks. Their shared glee resonated deep within me, as though I were laughing and playing too.

Our dog skittered about at my feet, his shiny black coat speckled with snow. He tugged on the lead. I didn't want to move on. If I zoomed out from that moment, millions of miles into the atmosphere, I could look down at me and I would be too small to be seen, insignificant in the grander scheme of things. The worries of tomorrow, or even a second into the future seemed far, far away. I thought, *If I died today, I would have had the fullest, luckiest life I could ever have wished for.*

Now, Sophie and I stood side by side at the kitchen counter, buttering white bread, chopping cheese slices and drinking Prosecco too quickly. As we chatted, I tried to savour this good moment, just as I had done in the woods earlier, but I couldn't. I was agonising over whether or not I should relay to Sophie what *my* husband had told me about *her* husband.

'When are the others getting here?' I asked, already choked by incense smoke and overheated by the fire glowing in the wood burner.

'They all cancelled.'

I hid my surprise. 'Very sensible of them. The roads are like ice rinks,' I said, rapping my fingers on the countertop, tapping out a rhythm, relieved that we had made the effort to get here. Not for Dylan's sake, so much, but for Sophie's. If my information about Adam was true, Sophie would need me more than ever.

'It doesn't matter. All we need is you lot,' she said, holding up her glass. 'To us! Forever friends!'

'Forever friends!' I said.

She grinned at me as she took another sip, adding, 'This is yum. What's the grape again?'

'Incrocio Manzoni,' I answered, raising my eyebrow at her, waiting for her to contradict me.

'No, it's not!'

'You tell me then.'

'Is it… Glera?'

'Spot on. Top of the class.'

She looked down to the floor, laughing. 'Never.'

'Don't be daft,' I said, chinking my glass again with hers. 'Happy Birthday to little Dylan.'

'I can't believe I've kept him alive for eight whole years,' she sighed, half serious.

'It is quite miraculous.'

We chuckled, but I had noted the 'I've kept him alive' rather than 'we', wondering if this was relevant. The information that was gnawing at me had the potential to pull Sophie's life down on her head. I wanted to hold the happy times up for her, for one afternoon longer, to allow her to enjoy her son's birthday party, to hold on to this present moment a little longer.

My plate of sandwiches was growing bigger. The neat, crust-free squares were arranged in a chessboard pattern of brown and white, sensible and boring. Sophie's plate was a hodgepodge of over-buttered doorsteps. I smiled to myself, amused as I watched my friend's long fingers, decorated with a series of delicate gold rings, tearing holes in the bread. She was distracted in her task, as though her eyes were turned inwards to other mysterious thoughts. I decided to leave a few crusts on and mess up my plate a little to make the contrast less stark. We then cling-filmed them and put them in the fridge, where I noticed a supermarket caterpillar cake, more suitable for a four-year-old than an eight-year-old.

'Candles! I knew I'd forgotten something! Shit,' she cried, slamming the fridge shut.

She began opening various kitchen cupboards in their tiny, jumbled kitchen, swearing under her breath as packets of tea or pasta fell on her head. 'We must have some old ones somewhere.'

'Do you want me to pop out to get some?'

Sophie laughed at me. 'You walked, remember?'

'Oh. Yes. Ice rink roads.'

The kitchen cupboards were rammed. One object removed would cause an avalanche of mess. 'There's bound to be one left over from some other birthday,' I said, daring to pull out a saucepan to see underneath.

A clash of pots cascaded onto the floor. 'Whoops,' I said.

'Bloody hell,' she cried, yanking open the top half of the stable door on to the garden. A freezing blast of air sent a shiver through me.

'Adam!' she called out, waving her long arms, flapping her billowing sleeves. 'Adam!'

Outside, Adam and Charlie sat at either end of an iced bench, wrapped in scarves, cradling cups of coffee. They looked formal, yet engaged with one another, like the famous bronze statue of Franklin D. Roosevelt and Winston Churchill on New Bond Street. If I hadn't seen the plumes of condensed air as they talked, I would have thought they were frozen solid. Past them, a trail of welly boot and paw prints wove down the bank into the trees, from where I could hear playful yelps and screams.

'Adam, do you know where there might be some cake candles?'

Charlie immediately stood up, frowning. 'Do you need some help, you two?' His concern sent a rush of love up through me. I shook my head, shrugging, not sure whether two more bodies in the hot house would help.

'Candles, Adam?' Sophie repeated, pulling her white-blonde, waist-length straggles of hair around and down over one shoulder.

'Why would I know?' Adam snapped at her.

'Er, because you live in this house, too?'

Adam's mouth straightened.

Sophie slammed the door and screwed her face and fists up. 'He's driving me mad.'

Behind her, through the window, I saw Adam bent over his knees with his head in his hands, while Charlie reached over to give his shoulder a squeeze. A brown patch of snow melted at the mouth of the flask, fallen from the bench.

'How is it between you two?' I asked, checking the drawers Sophie had already looked in.

Sophie plonked herself down on the stool at the small kitchen island, knocking back the last of her drink, pouring us two more. She pushed away the Batman paper plates and napkins and played with a balloon at her toe, drawing it back and forth across the ball of her foot. I braced myself for the pop, but she then released it and kicked it into the air lightly. 'Everything I do is wrong.'

'Like what kind of thing?'

'Like Dylan's school shoes aren't polished, or the car smells of old crisps, or the carrots are too rubbery or the house is too messy.

It's all my fault, apparently. I mean, why couldn't he have thought about the bloody candles? He's his son too! Why is it always my responsibility?'

I looked around us, at their home, which Sophie affection-ately called The Shack, wondering where else I could look for some candles. Pot plants and cacti crowded the high sill of the picture window, which stretched across the length of their tiny one-bedroom self-build. A pile of logs tumbled loosely from the wall next to the wood burner. Up each ladder-step to the galley room – where Adam had his office, where Dylan slept on a futon crowded by files – were stacks of books and toys, barely leaving enough space for a foot on each wooden plank. Torn wrapping paper took over the two-seater sofa that sat in the middle of the room, nose up to the oversized television. The door to the built-in wardrobe behind the sofa was wide open, revealing a clash of uses. Towels on the top shelf, muddy boots flopping out of the next, waxed jackets and 1970s maxi-dresses vying for space along the rail.

I opened a small cabinet. 'Could they be in here?'

As though she hadn't heard my question, Sophie stared out of the window across the driveway to her grandfather's run-down cottage. The clearing of trees that encircled both the cottage and this little cabin was like a secret clearing, a hideaway protected by dense woodland that sloped down to the main road. But some-times I sensed the trees were inching closer every day, encroaching on Sophie and her family, stealing back their space.

'When do you think you'll be moving into your grandad's?' I asked.

'I'm still not sure I want to.'

'I thought your grandad...'

She cut me dead. 'Naomi, Grandad's savings won't stretch to a new boiler, and Dylan's skin will get much worse again if we live in a damp...'

'Found some!' I cried, holding an opened packet of red candles high in the air like a trophy.

'Eight of them?'

'He won't notice that he's only seven and a half, will he?' I smiled, waving one snapped candle at her.

'Don't think so. Adam might, though,' she tutted.

In the early years of their marriage, Sophie could do no wrong in Adam's eyes. He had loved her chaotic, hippy ways and her bijou shack in the forest which had promised a simple life of low overheads and cosy nights in front of the fire. Her flirtations with him in her cotton print dresses and wellies, soil dusted over one cheek, had persuaded him to reject his London upbringing in favour of chopping wood, picking mushrooms and taking photographs of her in the dappled light. I had been envious of their love affair. Charlie and I had been rather stiff and conventional by comparison.

'Maybe you and Adam need a night out somewhere,' I suggested, handing her the candles.

She brought out the cake and began ripping open the packaging.

'We don't have the money for babysitting, let alone a restaurant.'

'I'll babysit, and I've got some vouchers for that pizza place in town. You can have them, if you like,' I offered desperately, knowing how critical it might be for their relationship.

'I don't want to put you out,' she said, and stabbed the blunt end of each candle into the cake, cracking the chocolate icing.

'Honestly, I'd love to. I know you'd do the same for me.'

She lifted her pale, cornflower-blue eyes up to mine and twirled a piece of her almost-white hair. 'Yes, that's true, I would.'

'Go on, then. Let's find a date,' I said, reaching for my phone.

She stared at me, scrutinising me for sincerity. 'That's really sweet of you, but we're fine. We're just going through a bad patch.'

I bit my lip, wishing I could shake her into action, but deciding I did not have the power to save their marriage. For the same reason, it did not seem appropriate to pass on a second-hand conversation relayed through Charlie, whose ability to glean detail and nuance about important emotional situations was not good at the best of times. 'Let me know if you change your mind.'

'I will.' She dropped the paper plates out, leaving the plastic wrapping in the middle of the table next to the cake box and the supermarket bags. I supposed the presentation shouldn't matter, but somehow I minded that she wasn't putting more effort into Dylan's small party. Her lack of energy did not seem to come from a low mood; it struck me as belligerent and deliberate. While her back was turned, I began organising the tiny kitchen island by placing the flowers I had brought into the centre, folding the napkins into triangles and throwing some streamers across the plates.

'I'll call the others in,' I said, suddenly wanting to go home. The sad red half-candle that drew the eye, in spite of its seven intact friends, seemed to warn of trouble ahead.

A few minutes later, Izzy and Diana came traipsing in, rosy-cheeked and exhilarated, shaking off snow from their all-in-one waterproofs, mimicking Harley, who then trotted wet paws into the kitchen. Their eyes were wide for chocolate cake and they launched into Sophie for a cuddle.

'Hello, girls. Here, have some of these, before Dylan sees,' she whispered, stuffing a handful of chocolate buttons into their fists.

'Thanks!' they cried gleefully, giving her an extra cuddle.

Adam and Charlie stomped their boots on the mat, and Dylan, the birthday boy, slipped through his father's legs. His lips were wet, hanging open, and his round blue eyes were doleful, framed by white-blond lashes and black smears of exhaustion, looking hangdog at his mother as he lay down at her feet, snow and mud melting everywhere.

'Oh, hello, Mischief, look at that handsome face,' Sophie said, letting go of my two. 'Did you have fun with the girls? You didn't get cold, did you?'

'I got snow down my neck,' he replied in a baby voice, blinking his big eyes at Izzy and Diana.

Sophie immediately lifted him up under his armpits and onto one hip, and stuck her hand inside his jumper. He looked too big to be carried.

'You're soaked through!' she cried. 'Adam, you were supposed to be watching them!'

'He's fine,' Adam sighed, hanging both his and Charlie's coats up in the packed closet.

'Come on, Dylan, let's go and get you changed, come on, love,' Sophie said, as though he were an invalid. She put him down, adding, 'I'm sure you didn't mean it, girls, but Dylan's skin has been very bad lately.'

Dylan's face was triumphant as he passed the girls, who had both snuggled into my middle, and he skipped out of the room at Sophie's heels.

'I'll just get more wood,' Adam said, taking his phone from the counter.

I glanced at the huge pile by the wood burner.

'Girls, get the sandwiches out of the fridge, will you, darlings?' I said, pulling Charlie away, out of their earshot.

'What did Adam tell you outside?' I whispered urgently.

'He wants to tell her this afternoon!'

'Are you *serious*? On Dylan's *birthday*? I hope you told him…'

Before I had a chance to finish my sentence, Sophie returned, followed by Dylan, who sloped in, reclothed in a onesie. The children sat down to eat the sandwiches and Sophie lit the seven and a half candles. But Adam remained outside in the cold on his phone.

'Happy Birthday to you! Happy Birthday to you!' Sophie chimed, presenting the cake without waiting for Adam.

'There are only seven and a half candles!' Dylan wailed, waving a knife in his mother's face, stabbing a finger into the side of the cake. The singing stopped.

'Daddy forgot to get them, sweetie. But look, there are still eight flames.'

His white eyelashes were covered in chocolate like mascara as he cried, 'Where *is* Daddy?'

Sophie stormed outside. We could hear shouting. I could see puffs of air shooting back and forth between them, but the words weren't discernible. I had an urge to gather my family up and take them away from here. At the same time, I felt mean for thinking it.

'I'll cut you a slice, Dylan,' I said, prizing the weapon out of Dylan's sticky hands, handing out doorsteps of cake to keep them occupied for as long as possible.

When their plates were licked clean, Sophie and Adam came back inside.

They both looked sombre and wan, but they were holding hands, knuckles whitened. I exhaled, relieved for a moment that they had managed to talk without an explosion.

Adam pulled his hand from Sophie's. 'Let's play musical statues.'

Charlie joined Adam by the iPod station and the children crowded round with requests.

The music blasted out. While the two dads and three children danced, Sophie and I began clearing away the paper plates.

'Everything okay?' I whispered at the sink.

'No.'

'What's happened?'

Sophie clutched the washing-up brush and glared at me. 'Don't pretend you didn't know.'

I looked down at the cake-smeared Batman, with his black mask, and wished I could hide my blush behind it. 'I didn't know how to tell you.'

'When did you find out?'

'Adam rang Charlie last night.'

'Do you know her?'

Now I was confused. 'Know who?'

'The woman he's been sleeping with,' she whispered, her eyes watering.

'What?' I gasped, looking over my shoulder briefly. This was not what Charlie had told me about Adam. I dropped my voice. 'I didn't know anything about that. Are you serious? There's another woman?'

'She's that young stylist he's worked with on a few trips recently.'

'On that job in Spain?'

'That's it.'

'I swear I didn't know. Charlie only told me that Adam was unhappy, and he'd asked him if he knew anyone with a flat in London to rent.'

Sophie's face crumpled, and she stifled a sob behind her hand, 'Apparently, he's in love with her.' Her tears splashed straight into the sink.

I wrapped my arm around her shoulder, smelling that familiar musty tang of incense in her hair, feeling protective and full of hate towards this young stylist. As I thought about what Sophie faced now, I feared for her. Deep down, she still loved Adam, in spite of how challenging their marriage had been recently. I imagined she might unravel without him. The terrible burden of responsibility hit me. Twelve years ago, Adam had taken her off my hands, supported her and looked after her, for better and for worse, and now he was abandoning her. She would be untethered.

'What am I going to do, Naomi?' she asked, begging me for help.

Guilt tumbled into my heart. Everything I had felt grateful for earlier had been a lucky throw of the dice. It seemed I had too much, while Sophie's life was about to fall apart.

'It's going to be okay,' I soothed, feeling that it wasn't.

'Maybe it's just a midlife crisis,' she added, under her breath.

'It must be. He loves you. You're beautiful and gorgeous and lovely in every way.' I gave her hand a squeeze. 'I'm here for you, don't worry. You're not on your own, okay?'

Sophie's future spread out before me like a burnt-to-nothing dystopian landscape. The here-and-now became brittle, ready to disintegrate. If she suffered, I would – more. Every happy twist in my life would become a twist of unhappiness in hers. I couldn't be content, I couldn't be still, I couldn't press the slow motion button unless I knew Sophie was happy. We were interlocked, like fingers holding hands; her needs were mine and mine were hers. It had always been the same.

I resolved to do everything in my power as her friend to help her through this. I would prioritise her and step in as her support, as I had done many times in the past, as she had done for me. That's what best friends are for.

CHAPTER TWO

At the window, Sophie rolled the focus rings of her binoculars, watching Naomi and her family trudge away through the snow, fearing, as always – somewhat illogically – that it might be the last time she saw her.

Their snow clothes were matching, in navy blue. They were a close unit, an amorphous mass of love, walking side by side, hand in hand.

Sophie picked Naomi out, training the lenses on her, getting glimpses of her dimpled smile and full cheeks and spring of blonde curls as she turned her head every which way. Her small, bright eyes were darting about, checking her girls were safe, perhaps; her hands were jammed in her pockets, probably fiddling around with some trinket of Izzy or Diana's left there. Her thoughts would be about others. About Sophie and Adam's troubles.

As Sophie studied her, she imagined she was making upbeat suggestions to Charlie about how to solve the problem of Sophie and Adam. 'She should tidy that house, for starters!' 'And make sure Dylan sleeps in his own bed!' 'They should definitely move into the cottage!' As though she knew better. Positivity and optimism came easily to Naomi. The thought of her do-gooding chatter provoked a stab of anger. Sophie changed her mind about her lines of dialogue, and imagined her making crude, sexually explicit suggestions to Charlie. It gave Sophie a much-needed laugh.

She replaced the binoculars behind the line of cacti, holding on to the pretty images of her friend in her mind. Her fingers brushed over the tips of her arid pot plants. Some spines were left in her skin. Enjoying the prickles of pain, she plucked them out and mulled over the authenticity of Naomi's promise to love and support her now that Adam was leaving, sceptical that she had been ignorant about Adam's affair. Neither was she wholly convinced by Adam's declaration of love for this stylist woman. None of it rang true. She wasn't sure anyone was saying what they really meant.

'Adam?' Sophie called out to him in the galley.

Upstairs, in the galley office, Adam was sitting at his computer, ignoring her. She hoped that he was regretting his ill-timed confession as he moped at his screen, editing photographs from his latest shoots. She did not like to think that he might be emailing the stylist woman, looking online at rentals in London, wishing he could be with her, longing to be rid of this life with Sophie. Her insides twisted. He said he would stay until he had found somewhere suitable to live. She was no longer the focus of his love. It was unbelievable. Shocking even, like a blow to the head.

'Adam!' she bellowed.

Still no reply.

'Dylan, will you tell your dad that I'm just going over to Grandad's?' Sophie said.

Dylan, who was engrossed in a film on the television, nose to screen, did not reply. She felt invisible, worthless to them both. But her son's white-haired beauty struck her down, as it did every time she looked at him, and she forgave him in a way she would never forgive Adam. Before she put her boots on to go out, Sophie covered Dylan with kisses, aggressively demanding his love, overwhelmed, smothered, suffocated by a cloying, desperate, almost edible adoration for him.

'Get off, Mum!' he cried.

She laughed at Dylan and then, to Adam, she mumbled scornfully, 'Bye, *Adam!*'

As she was closing the door, Adam piped up. 'Sophie?'

'Yeah?'

'You're not going out, are you?'

He still cared? She could climb the steps to him, rest a cup of tea by his hand, sit on his lap, become his beautiful distraction again. Change the course of today. She wouldn't give him the satisfaction.

'I'm popping over to Grandad's. Dylan's pie will be ready in ten minutes. Don't forget the peas.'

'For fuck's sake,' he hissed.

'You can't handle taking the peas out of the freezer on your own?' she said, darting outside into the cold, too rapidly to hear his retaliation.

She crunched across the snowy drive into her grandfather's cottage, pulling her coat collar up, stewing about Adam, looking forward to some wisdom and advice from a real man, who would never lie to her.

'Hi Deda!'

She slammed the door, which would wake him up if he was snoozing. The snow from her boots melted into a damp patch by the door and she padded into his kitchen in her socks.

'The usual?' she shouted through, twirling the duster around the glasses and plates on the shelf, spraying the bleach cleaner and rubbing away the grime.

'Yes, Sophia!'

His bottle of vodka and their two special tumblers were there, as always, in the right-hand cupboard next to the teabags. In her grandfather's eyes, vodka was no different to tea.

She checked in the fridge for his meat pasties. There was one left. Sophie sliced it in half and resolved to make some more for him later.

The glasses rattled on the melamine tray as she brought them through.

As always, he sat there in his winged chair, clean shirt, brown trousers, a paperback resting on the arm.

Sophie kissed his bare, liver-spotted head, turned the lamp on and drew the curtains closed. The room was cold. She turned up the bar heater in the fireplace.

'I must have nodded off,' he said, as though this were a surprise. 'Thank you,' he said, taking the glass she handed him.

His nose stretched as wide as his moustache when he smiled, either side of which there were grooves as deep as crevasses. Underneath the untrimmed mass of eyebrow hair, Sophie could see that the shine in his eyes was still there. Every day, she looked for it.

She pulled the stool close to his slippers and tapped the top of her glass with his. The warm liquid stung her throat, but soothed her mind. If the whole world, and all its ills, had melted away around her while she sat with her Dedushka, eating meat pasties and drinking vodka, she would not have cared.

'Did Dylan have a good birthday party?'

'Wonderful. I made *Medovik*, and we danced and sang. We missed you.'

'You look so pale.'

'I had some bad news today.'

'Tell me.'

'Adam wants to leave us.'

Dedushka leant forward and screwed up his eyes. 'Why, my Sophia?'

'He is in love with someone else.'

'A man?'

Sophie laughed. 'No. Not a man, Deda.'

'You never know these days. He has long hair like a girl.'

'She's not pretty. I don't know why he wants her and not me.'

She had looked up the stylist woman, Natalie, on her Instagram page. Or was she a girl? A girl-woman, whose body was exposed regularly in her Instagram posts, with her large hips and flat chest.

She was no beauty. And Sophie wondered if it would have been easier if she had been. What man could resist a young, beautiful woman? Of course he would stray! But Natalie was plain and dull, judging from her posts: a photograph of her manicured wonky toes against a backdrop of a white, sandy beach; a series of selfies of her dull outfits in front of a mirror; a black Labrador running through the snow. Yawn. Yawn. Yawn.

Yet, Sophie had been gripped by her. Gripped by the concept of Adam's love for her. Their relationship lurked in an alternate universe to the one Sophie and Adam had shared together for twelve years. She seemed to have that undefinable quality that men fell for, that marriageable ordinariness – or was it safeness? – that Naomi certainly had, that Sophie did not. Marriage had not suited Sophie. Their chaotic, last-minute wedding day in Marylebone register office had been their first mistake. Even then, she had known it, having forced the event, wanting to get married before Naomi, who had recently said 'yes' to Charlie's proposal. When Naomi, as Sophie's maid of honour, had stood next to Sophie in front of the registrar, Sophie remembered feeling like an impostor bride in her white trouser suit. In her mind, Naomi had been the real bride.

'Boff!' Deda raised his hands, spilling his drink. 'He's a pig.'

'I have not been very nice to him.'

'You are always nice.'

'He thinks I've given up.'

'He likes to tell you what is wrong with you.'

'And maybe he's right.'

'Do you love him?'

Before Dylan had been born, before she had known how far love could take her, Sophie had loved Adam. Over the years, that love seemed to have been usurped by need. Needing Adam, as she did now, felt like the nasty cousin of true love. It was an impoverished form of love, leaving her vulnerable and unequal.

She *needed* him to tell her she was more beautiful than any other woman; she needed him to pay the bills. She needed him to quell her paranoia; she needed him to share the school run. She needed him to satiate her in bed; she needed him to fix the shower curtain. She needed him, and she resented that need.

Perhaps this need of hers was where it had gone wrong between them. Perhaps this was why he had fallen for another woman, who wanted him more than Sophie did.

'I don't cook for him any more.'

'You cook the best *piroshki* I ever tasted! Better than Baba. Shhh, but don't tell her I said it.' He put his hands together in prayer and looked to his small gold triptych of Jesus on the narrow inglenook mantel. He looked back at Sophie. 'Do you love him?' he repeated.

'I'm not surprised he doesn't love me any more. Look at me.'

'Golden sunlight,' he said, reaching to stroke his fingers through her straggles, which reached her waist. He pinched her chin. 'But you're skin and bone, just like Suzanne.'

Sophie picked at her nail varnish. 'I don't want to be like her.'

'You're stubborn like her, Sophia. Don't be stubborn. If you love Adam, you have to fight for him.'

'I wish I was more like Naomi,' she sulked. 'If I was more like her, this would never be happening to me.'

He clicked his tongue and grabbed both her knees, squeezing them, his soft face close to hers. 'If only she knew what you'd done for her...'

The shot glass paused at her lips. She looked hard into her grandfather's eyes.

'She can never know,' she replied firmly. She did not like to feel angry with her grandfather.

He sat back. 'Do you want to be alone, like me?'

'Naomi will always be there for me.'

'Okay, Sophia. But I remind you of one thing, for your own good. If you tell her, the bond will be like this,' he said, interlocking his fingers and tugging at them to show its strength.

Sophie stood and kissed his hands. 'I love you. But I know what's best. I'll leave you to read now.'

'Don't forget to check on the car.'

'Tonight?'

'Yes. Tonight. It's important.'

'Okay, Deda,' she sighed.

Outside, the stars had come out and the trees were frozen solid like sculptures. Her nerves were frayed. She was shaken by her grandfather's advice. It spread through her mind like a crack in ice as she made her way out to the garage, which was a purpose-built, single-storey brick outbuilding a foot away from the cottage. In the absence of outdoor lighting, she had to feel her way along the bumped stucco frontage of the cottage, past the low, peeling windowsills, careful not to trip on overgrown weeds as she crossed the path that separated the two buildings. She would then trail her fingers along the red corrugated garage door, to the huge rhododendron bush that hugged its outer side wall, around which she would step cautiously, missing old bricks and debris, to reach the far side door, which was locked and heavy. It made an almighty noise as she opened it.

The reek of petrol and damp clogged her lungs. The button of her coat sleeve caught on a hook, where her grandfather's leather tool belt hung. It wasn't this that stopped her in her tracks. It was the car, whose lines and shine sent a tingle of fear down her spine.

This beauty, this feat of design, this blue Alfa Romeo Giulia 1967 1300 ti had provided the happiest and the saddest days of her life, and friendship with Naomi. Her grandfather had insisted she see it tonight to reinforce his point, to remind her of what she had hidden from Naomi. In this dark garage, the secrets of that one night, of a terrible accident many years ago, loomed large.

She reached in through the wound-down window to touch the elegant Bakelite steering wheel and brush her hand over the black wind-pressed vinyl seats.

The gap between the walls and the car was narrow, through which she edged to the workbench at the back to click on the metal lamp and find a cloth.

The smell of the chamois leather brought her right back to that night. She blinked and coughed the memories away.

Focusing her mind on the task at hand, she began rubbing at the top left of the windscreen, her fingers slipping across where the dent had been, shivering as though she had touched an old scar. Round and round in circles she moved over the same spot, wiping away the dirt, wiping away the worst of its history, moving systematically around its panels and across its small triangle sticker logo. The ritual made her tearful.

As a young girl, years before her grandfather had given it to her, she had dreamt of owning the car. She had admired his knowledge of its inner workings as he tinkered with it; his alone time, man and machine. When she asked him if she could learn, he had thrown an oily cloth at her and said, 'Mechanics is a dirty business, Sophia,' and he had ordered her to polish the bodywork. 'You make it look pretty,' he had said. But he should have taken the time to show her how to fix its broken parts. If he had, she would never have been forced to involve him in that night.

The workbench remained as organised as it had been when she was younger, crowded with pots of useless gadgets, tools and paraphernalia: old AA batteries, snags of rope, masking tape and junk. One of the pots was crammed with used toothbrushes. She took one, returned to the car and began rubbing at the crevices and hard-to-reach places, wanting to make sure it was spotless.

Lingering forever was the worry that a tiny remnant of its paint had been found at the accident scene; that there had been a witness who had spotted the car; that the investigation had been extended; that a search for an Alfa Romeo had been carried out; that an officer from the Devon and Cornwall police had logged a number plate or description into a system late one night in the summer of 1999. That one day, the Automatic Number Plate Recognition system would pick up on its registration and the police would haul Sophie and Naomi in for questioning. All scenarios were possible, though many years had passed, and all of them she still feared.

To clean the back bumper, she needed the torch. She popped open the boot, where she kept it, and gasped when she saw what was inside. There was a neat line of cuddly toys under a blanket, where Dylan had left them. Her son's innocent play was out of place in this dark space, and she scooped up the panda and giraffe and teddy bear and hugged them to her. They provided comfort. She slammed the boot down, leaving the torch inside, finished with her cleaning for today.

The car was her past. It was dormant. It gathered no new memories behind the garage door, which had been stuck closed for many years. She could never drive it. She could never get rid of it. She could never sell it. It was a secret that she would continue to keep well hidden. She would shine up the paintwork, turn the engine over regularly, keep it alive, prevent the rust; wipe the slate clean, over and over again. She was accustomed to the sense of loneliness that came with the job. Dragging Naomi into this, as she had been forced to do with Deda, would be a problem doubled rather than halved. To hold Naomi close, she did not need Deda's tactics. Protecting her was more important. It was Sophie's way of being the best friend Naomi could ever wish for.

CHAPTER THREE

A text pinged through from Sophie:

Running a bit late. Dylan's being a nightmare. He won't go to sleep. What time are the others arriving? Sx

I typed back:

Not until 8.30. We'll be okay. See you in a bit. Nx

I groaned and took my coat off, already regretting my invite to Sophie. The pads of my fingers hit the table, tapping, unsettled, the beat of an unknown tune. Harley jumped up onto my lap and stared right at me, making me smile. He seemed to have picked up on my frustration with Sophie. I had put a huge amount of effort into the organisation of this wine-tasting event and I did not want her to ruin it. There seemed to be more at stake when the attendees were friends, rather than clients.

After a reassuring scratch behind Harley's ear and a kiss into his soft black curls, he jumped down.

'What's up?' Charlie asked, as though talking for Harley.

'Sophie's going to be late.'

'I'm sure the pub has taken care of everything.'

'I hope so.'

Charlie chopped a lime in half on the big wooden chopping board. Behind his tortoiseshell glasses, his eyes were not sparkly or bright like the lime, but certain and focused like a calm British sea. And his distinguished grey hair, which had been prematurely grey ever since I had known him, gave the impression he could be the grown-up for both of us. How I wished I could stay at home with him tonight, curled up on the sofa with Harley at my feet.

'She might bail entirely if Dylan's playing up,' I sighed, remembering the countless times she had done this before.

'She's probably singing "Moonlight" to him in full costume while he plays Nintendo under the covers,' he teased, dumping the ice cubes into the gin and splashing in a dash of Angostura bitters.

'Stop it, Charlie,' I chided, putting my hands in my pockets to cease the tapping. 'Be kind. She's going through so much right now because of that prat. I really don't know what his problem is.'

'Being married to Sophie?' he mumbled, rattling the ice cubes in his drink.

'That's not fair,' I said defensively.

When I had first met Sophie, she had been dragging a large, old-fashioned suitcase down the hall.

The latch broke and a whole jumble sale of clothes and random objects exploded out onto the floor. I rushed to the girl's aid, gathering up some of her clothes, including three oversized plastic sunflowers, a wind-up radio and a dog-eared copy of Lolita.

She laughed when I handed her the plastic flowers. I felt parochial and intimidated by her. And desperately self-conscious of my chubby cheeks and unruly frizz of hair.

'I've brought these flowers, but I've probably forgotten my toothbrush!'

Everything about Sophie was just how I had imagined the perfect university friend should be. Interesting and eccentric – a little odd, perhaps – so different to the friends I had left behind in Dedham, who had been well brought-up and rather safe, like me.

'They're pretty.'

Then I picked up the Nabokov and gave it back to her.

'Have you read it?' she asked me.

'No,' I replied, feeling ignorant.

'You must. It's just such a headfuck. I'm obsessed. I've read it dozens of times. Read it. Let me know what you think.'

'Oh, no, it's yours, I couldn't…' I stuttered, but I kept hold of it, while staring in awe at her bright red lips and pale eyes, at the two ethereal curtains of white-blonde hair.

'What room are you in?'

I pointed to the room behind us. '149.'

'I'm just down there. 154. Drop it back whenever.'

Her long pale legs dragged her clumpy cowboy boots along the floor like a child in her mother's too-big heels. At her door, she turned round and waved, coquettishly, perhaps knowing her appeal, perhaps guessing I would continue to watch her.

As soon as I closed the door to my room, I lay on my bed and started reading Lolita. *An hour later, I felt sticky and sickened, and couldn't read on about Humbert Humbert's craven desires, and I wondered what it was about this book that Sophie was obsessed by. I feared that she might, at some point in her past, have been a little Lolita, which made me want to help her. It seemed to balance us out somehow.*

'Maybe we can take advantage of her lateness,' Charlie grinned, pinging one of my curls.

'She'll be here any minute,' I said. Harley trotted from me to Charlie and back again, and barked at me. I smiled down at his upturned nose and watery eyes, and stroked him. *It's okay. I'm okay. You crazy dog.*

'Go on. Let's have a quickie,' Charlie cajoled.

'There's not time.' I prized Charlie's glass out of his hand and took a sip.

The doorbell rang and Harley barked at me. Before he scrambled for the door, I pulled him up onto my lap, one last time, and cuddled him goodbye.

'See, Harley? No harm done. She's barely even late.'

I pecked Charlie on the cheek and went outside to Sophie's car, an ancient Saab hatchback. She didn't drive her grandfather's Alfa Giulia any more. At university, she had driven me everywhere in that car, to the beach or the pub or to the cliffs. It was a completely different experience to driving a modern car. I had loved it. I had loved those days. Until it had gone wrong.

'Hi! You made good time.'

I moved two empty smoothie bottles from the passenger seat and sat in.

'Adam said he'd take over, for once, while I got ready.'

She looked beautiful in a bohemian dashiki-print kaftan, which she had probably picked up in a charity shop or from a market stall for two pounds. Her make-up was a perfect balance of pale eyes and dark lips, and her white-blonde hair was tousled, celestial, falling from a centre parting either side of her face. I hoped Adam had appreciated her tonight, but I doubted it.

'You look gorgeous,' I said.

'You look nice, too,' Sophie said, glancing me up and down stiffly, appraising my crispy curls, overdone eyeliner and boring black dress. 'But then you *always* do,' she added, sounding sour. Sophie had the knack of making a compliment sound like an insult, but I had got used to her tone over the years. She meant kindness, she just didn't know how to convey it properly.

'I love this,' I said, plucking her sleeve.

'I feel quite hideous in it.'

'That's ridiculous.'

I couldn't tell her she looked beautiful again. It would sound insincere. She wouldn't believe me anyway, so I left it and wound the window down a crack. The smell of stale crisps and wet rug and old incense made me want to keep it open, even though it was zero degrees outside. Patches of snow left over from last week dotted the roadside as we drove.

'What sparkling did you bring?'

'I didn't know we had to bring wine.'

'I said in the email. Everyone is bringing a bottle, and I assigned you a sparkling. I've paid corkage.'

'Sorry.'

'No problem, I'll buy you one at the pub.'

'This will be fun,' Sophie said. Her hands were planted at ten to two on the steering wheel and her head remained stiff on her shoulders, facing forward. I imagined she was a ball of tension inside the shell of this dreamy, floaty vision.

'Don't be nervous.'

'I never go to these things usually.'

'These things?'

'School mum things. If they're anything like the mums at Dylan's school, I'm sure they'll hate me.'

'Of course they won't! They're really nice, I promise.'

'That's why I'm driving. So I don't drink too much and make a fool of myself.'

'You won't. Wine-tasting isn't about getting pissed. Or it shouldn't be, anyway. It'll be fun.'

'Adam was in a mood about me leaving.'

'Has he found anywhere to live yet?'

'He says it's hard finding an affordable two-bedroom in London. He might look for somewhere more local.'

'That would be better for Dylan.'

'We haven't told Dylan yet.'

'No?'

'I want to wait.'

'Until?'

'Until it's final.'

'Is Adam giving you the impression he's not serious about leaving?'

If he was in any way keeping the hope alive for Sophie, he was only prolonging the agony for her. He had told Charlie, categorically, that he was desperately unhappy and could barely stand being around her. Her denial worried me.

'Maybe,' she said, cryptically.

She was quiet for the rest of the journey, which suggested she might have been cross with me for questioning her about it. Sometimes I couldn't tell what she was thinking.

When we parked up, she reapplied her lipstick and offered some to me.

'Your lips are looking a bit pale, my love. Best brighten yourself up a bit,' she had said, smiling.

*

'Okay, now you've had a sniff, take a sip and swill it around in your mouth, and see if you can take in a little bit of air at the same time, like this,' I suggested to the group, pursing my lips, leaving a little hole.

Sophie laughed the loudest and tried to make a face like a fish. Wine dribbled out of the corners of her mouth and down her chin, like Dracula.

'You're supposed to spit it out, not dribble it out!' I laughed, looking around me at the group of fellow mothers from school – Jo, Megan, Cynthia, Kathy and Emma – whose smiles were wide and whose cheeks were bright. They swilled the wine, laughed and gossiped. So far, the evening had been a success. The worry was Sophie. Her eyelids were drooping and her conversation had turned into a slurry monologue about Dylan's eczema.

Knowing how Sophie could behave when she drank too much, I sped up proceedings, handing out a sheet of notepaper and a branded pencil to each friend.

'This red was an Old World Pinot Noir. Thank you for bringing this, Jo. It's really useful to write down what you like and dislike, so you can keep the list in your bag for next time you're in Tesco, baffled by the bank of bottles.'

A rare moment of silence fell on the room as we sipped the wine and wrote down our thoughts.

'This is what I think of that one, I'm afraid!' Sophie boomed, snorting, showing Jo her drawing of a cartoon cock and balls.

Jo's smile was more of a grimace. She was the kind of woman who held exclusive book clubs at her house, where they dissected 1970s trash literature with intellectual wit and irony. A cock and balls wasn't going to cut it.

'The next red we're tasting is Meg's,' I said, moving on quickly, pouring small amounts into the line-up of clean glasses. 'An Australian Shiraz from Aldi.'

'Meg! How did you cope with *Aldi*?' Sophie sneered, swirling her wine until it sloshed over the rim.

'What do you mean?' Meg asked innocently.

'I imagine you'd come out in a rash in any supermarket other than Waitrose,' Sophie sniggered rudely.

'I shop anywhere where there's booze,' Meg quipped, tugging at her short crop of hair, winking at Sophie, who guffawed at her, plainly unconvinced. The fingers on my right hand pounded my left palm under the table. I imagined that the patients Meg treated on the NHS cardiothoracic ward where she worked as a surgeon wouldn't have cared where she shopped.

To distract everyone, I kept up the momentum of the tasting.

But Sophie was no longer pretending to spit it out, and during the gargling and assessing of the remaining bottles – the Médoc, a cheap champagne and two rosés, one from New Zealand and the other from Provence – she managed to insult everyone at the event with her petty prejudices and chippy jibes.

'Would it be okay if I took some photographs for my blog?' I asked them, to end the evening with some kind of cohesion.

Everyone agreed, gathering together, linking arms, relaxing into it.

As soon as I brought the phone up to my face, Sophie began an infuriating campaign of photobombing, pulling silly faces or finger-swearing over their heads, stumbling around, prodding people in the ribs. The tension of Sophie's antics showed in all of their photo smiles.

'Are we allowed to vet these before they're posted?' Meg asked, once I had finished.

'I promise to be kind. No double chins or cross eyes. Let's take just one more in front of the fire with our wine glasses,' I said.

Sophie pushed Meg out of the way, and Meg almost fell back into the fire.

'That was a close one!' Meg said, holding her hands up at Sophie.

'Sorreee, Miss Waitrose,' Sophie mumbled.

Mortified, I apologised to Meg and faced up to the fact that the evening had been a disaster. Feeling a flush of exasperation and embarrassment, I took myself off to the toilets to calm down and call a taxi. Every single cab firm in the local area was fully booked or off-duty.

'Anyone got any space in their car?' I asked, returning to the table.

'We ordered a people carrier between us,' Emma replied. 'There'll be one space, though.'

'You take it, Sophie,' I offered.

'No way. I'm staying right by your side, Mrs Wilson,' she said, making an army salute and clicking her heels together.

I cringed, feeling deeply uncomfortable.

'We'll walk,' I suggested. 'I'm in flats and Sophie's got boots in the back of her car.'

The other women protested. 'You can't walk! It's miles away! No way! Why don't you call Charlie?'

'I'm fine to drive,' Sophie slurred.

Ignoring her, I said to the others, 'It'll take us forty minutes, tops, to walk. You guys get home. We're fine.'

'Are you sure?'

'Are you going to be okay?'

'We might need a bit of fresh air,' I said, raising an eyebrow at Sophie. 'We'll be fine, won't we, Soph?'

Out of nowhere, Sophie's mood turned on me. She rolled her eyes and drawled, 'Oh, yes, of course we'll be *fine*. Perfect Naomi is always *fine*, isn't she? *Perfect*, pretty Naomi with her *perfect* little life.'

'Sophie,' I chided, reddening.

'But I do love you,' she cried, hugging me around the neck, throttling me. 'You're my forever friend in all the world! We're friends forever, did you know? Known each other since we were eighteen years old. Twenty-three years!'

Seething inside, I heard Charlie's criticisms about Sophie ringing in my ears. The other five women stared at us, with tight smiles, probably wondering how we had stayed friends for that long. As was I.

'Come on, Soph, let's get going.'

Her arm fell over my shoulders, unsteadying me as we walked to the car, waving goodbye to the others as they climbed into the taxi.

I rummaged in her car boot for two matching wellies.

'Let go,' I said, removing her arm, shoving the boots at her, but she refused to take them.

'What's wrong now?'

'I don't want to walk on the road.'

'We don't have much choice.'

'Can't you drive my car?'

'No, Sophie. I'm not insured. We know from experience that it's not worth the risk.'

Sophie eyed her. 'Do we?'

I glared at her, loath to say it out loud.

'Okay then,' she sulked, pulling on the boots.

We set off, hugging the bank, trudging in silence.

I was cold to the bone, exhausted, and I raged internally at Sophie, whom I walked behind, to keep an eye on her.

As usual, I was rallying around her, editing my life to suit hers. She was a bottomless pit of emotional need. The more I gave, the more she needed. We were hopelessly entangled. Every single positive step I made in life had its reverse effect on her. At university, if I achieved an A for an essay, it undermined Sophie's B. If I made a new friend, she thought I liked her less. If a boy fancied me, it meant the boy didn't fancy Sophie. And it had worked in reverse, too. Whenever my life had taken a turn for the worse, Sophie's mood would improve: if I failed an exam, we could commiserate together. If I was dumped by a boy, I was more available to her. If I was let down by a friend, she could say I told you so.

It had been all about Sophie. It was still all about Sophie.

Left and right she wove on the road, mumbling pitifully to herself. A sorry sight. My sympathy began to fight its way through my anger. If Charlie had slept with another woman, I might be in a similar state. None of the other women tonight would have understood that.

The branches of the wintery trees were lit up by approaching headlights. The noise of an engine grew louder. Without warning, Sophie darted into the centre of the lane and stood with her arms wide. Her bright, patterned sleeves were like flags, as she howled over the noise of the oncoming vehicle. From around the bend, the car appeared, shooting towards us, the glare bigger and brighter with every second. My heart thundered as I ran out in front of the car and grabbed her, pulling her into the bank. We both fell onto icy snow and wet grass, yelping as the car roared past.

Sophie began to laugh.

'What the hell are you laughing at?' I screamed, brushing the clumps of cold mud from my trembling legs.

She laughed so hard, she could hardly speak. Her light hair was splayed across the bank, almost as white as the snow. 'It almost hit me!' she gasped.

'Get up! Come on! Please,' I begged, a desperate edge to my voice. She pulled herself up to sitting and grabbed her handbag.

'Are you crying?'

'No, I'm not crying,' I snapped, walking on ahead.

'I've made you cry,' she said, suddenly beside me. 'What are you crying about?'

'I'm not crying.'

I walked on ahead, tightening my jaw, spitting my words out. 'You scared me,' I fumed.

'Sorry,' she whimpered.

'Let's just get home,' I grumbled. She slipped her arm into mine and I left it there as we walked side by side.

'I was so rude to those mums,' she sniffed, hanging her head.

'Why *were* you so rude?'

'I don't know. I'm not good with big groups of women. I hate the small talk.'

'They're nice women.'

'Did you see the size of Meg's ring? It was like a paperweight on her finger. The NHS *can't* have paid for that.'

I chuckled, in spite of my crossness. 'Her husband's a hedge fund manager.'

'And what's with Jo's sense of humour failure?'

'That cock and balls picture wasn't that funny, Soph.'

'They were all so *grown-up.*'

I guffawed. 'Is that so bad?'

'Don't you find them dull, though, Naomi?' she said, bringing out a corked half-finished bottle of wine from her bag and taking a swig.

'Did you nick that?' I cried.

She offered me a sip. 'It was going to go to waste anyway.'

I took the bottle and knocked some back. 'They're not dull. They're just a bit straight.'

'Isn't that the same thing?'

'No!' I remonstrated, handing the bottle back.

We traipsed along in the dark for a few more minutes before Sophie broke the silence.

'I don't know what I'd do without you, you know.'

'You won't ever have to find out, you old lush,' I sighed.

'I'm going to try to be less of a lush for a bit. I'm not sure divorce and alcohol abuse are a good mix.'

I laughed. 'Careful, you sounded a bit like a grown-up then,' I teased.

'Never!' she shouted, laughing, and her voice echoed through the trees. *Never, never, never!*

I added to the echo, screeching as loud as I could, 'Never! *NEVER!*'

She tugged me along, and I began running along at her side, sprinting, exhilarated, shouting into the trees. Sophie suggested a game of dare. Throwing my good sense aside, swigging some more wine, I ran into the road to touch the catseyes, giggling uncontrollably, and then tightrope-walked along the white lines. When I heard a car, I hurtled to the bank, panting and gasping, heart racing, liberated, embracing fatalism.

Willingly, just for tonight, I fell back into the mess and the mischief with Sophie, unburdened by adult responsibilities and the tyranny of consequences. Tonight, Sophie brought me back to myself, allowed me to let go, go wild in the moment. Even though the moment was thoroughly naughty and entirely pointless.

At home, Charlie waited. A stickler for the rules. The game of dare would be anathema to him. He did not like risk. This safe life of his, the one we led together, was good for me. But right now, I didn't care what was good for me or what Charlie would think or what those mums tonight thought of Sophie's behaviour. Right now, I was willing to die in the name of fun.

CHAPTER FOUR

'Morning,' Adam said, shifting over to Sophie on her side of the bed.

Sophie's head was banging. Flashes of Naomi came back to her: of her collapsed over in fits of giggles, of her cheeky dimple, of their dangerous games, of their regression to adolescence. The innocence in Naomi's face had been captivating. Her round cheeks, like a baby, unmarked by guilt or shame, had beamed bright and rosy from the centre of her buzz of ringlet curls, her guileless blue eyes pure and trustful.

Sophie sat up and reached for her phone on the bedside table. 'Where's Dylan?'

'We put him in the pull-out bed, remember?'

'Oh.' She clicked straight onto Naomi's blog page to see the photographs from last night, but before the pages appeared, Adam snatched the phone and threw it onto the floor.

'How's your head?'

'Give that back!' she cried, straddling him across the duvet.

Adam laughed and pulled her arm up and away from the floor. 'Forget the phone.'

His black hair was mussed up and his full lips were parted with a smile. There was still an edge of the tan left over from his trip to Portugal. She pictured the girl-woman stylist in her bikini, unbuttoning his shirt in an air-conditioned hotel room, and she had an urge to bite his cheek until it bled.

'Want a rerun of last night?' she asked.

Last night, high and dazed from the antics with Naomi, Sophie's long thighs had gripped Adam either side of his hips, controlled his enjoyment, worked hard to deliver his orgasm, calculated her own display of passion, faking her orgasm, reminding him of what he would be missing when he left her.

'Yes, please,' he murmured hungrily. His gaze swept down to where her cotton vest gaped, exposing her breast.

She bent down to kiss him.

'Why don't we do this more often?' he panted, rolling on top of her.

The answer to his question was too blindingly obvious and irritating to answer. It had been easy to be loving towards him while she was drunk. This morning, with a pounding head, her ability to be affectionate and forgiving was more difficult.

She pushed him off, changing her mind about sex. 'I want to see if Naomi's posted photos from last night.'

'What? Seriously?' he collapsed onto his back.

'Phone, please.'

He pressed the phone into her hand and sat up, pausing for a moment on the edge of the bed. His ribcage expanded to almost double its size. A large breath. She examined the moles on his back, and his muscles, and she mapped them, storing them in her mind, possessing them. She wanted to scrape her fingernails down his back, punish him for breaking them apart. Sighing heavily, he left the room.

Puffing up her pillows behind her, she sat up and waited for the buffering on her phone to stop. She was curious about what Naomi might have uploaded. The evening was hazy. She wanted some gaps filled in. Her phone bars indicated there was no signal. The Wi-Fi reception would be better in the kitchen.

'I'd love a coffee,' she said, padding in to join Adam.

Instead of wearing her towelling dressing gown, she wore a soft, oversized cardigan, leaving her legs and décolletage bare.

She sat at the kitchen island, cradling her coffee and her phone, desperate to look online.

Adam leant across the kitchen island on his elbows, close to her. 'Did you sleep well?'

'Like a baby,' she smiled, raising her shoulders, vulnerable and childlike, locking eyes. His eyes were not to be trusted. They were frauds. She had to be wary. His feelings and needs were newly formed, heavily cloaked and difficult to predict.

'You?'

Dylan's iPad game bleeped from upstairs in the galley room. Abandoning her phone, she reached for her iPad, whose cover was dotted in shiny Batman stickers. Idly, impatiently, she picked at the sharp corner of a Batman mask, waiting for the appropriate moment to flip the cover open.

'Not great. You know, I haven't managed to find anywhere to rent yet,' he said.

Biting her lip, she replied, 'I think it would be weird if I helped you to do that.'

'Ha. No. Sorry. I didn't mean... But I don't know whether the properties are unsuitable or whether I'm dragging my feet because I don't want to do this.'

Her heart leapt, but she shrugged. 'Don't stay here out of sympathy.'

Before his announcement on Dylan's birthday, it had been easy to imagine chucking out a cheating husband while it remained a theoretical idea. Now it was really happening to her, she felt needy and desperate. Her instinct was to brush his misdemeanour away at the mere hint of hope, as though his betrayal held no weight.

'If I'm honest, Natalie is putting pressure on me.'

And then the sound of that name sent a bolt of fury through her. 'Fuck her,' she said, under her breath, feeling the chill of the room run over her skin. 'And fuck you,' she hissed, keeping her tone low so that Dylan didn't hear.

He flinched, and stood straight.

Sophie knew that she had undone all of her good work. It was too late to put the words back. Her brain clattered against her skull and tears pushed behind her eyes.

'I need some fresh air,' she said, dropping her phone into her baggy pocket.

'Don't you dare go over to your grandad's!' he shouted.

'You can't tell me what to do!'

He stood there, gaping at her, shaking his head. 'Go on, then. Why should I even care any more?'

Violence charged through her and she threw a fist into his upper arm.

He pulled her, aggressively, tightly, into him. 'Stop it, Sophie. Please. Stop it.'

She let her limbs fall limp, and she stayed there in his arms.

'Are you two fighting?' Dylan asked, coming down the steps.

'No. Come here, Dylan,' Adam said.

Dylan nestled between them, and Sophie wanted to stay there forever, just the three of them. A wind whipped through the house, the opened door banging. She thought of Deda across the drive hearing their fight.

Dylan wriggled free and kicked the front door closed with a karate chop.

She said to Adam, under her breath, 'Sorry. For being so horrible.'

Adam smoothed his hand down her arm. 'Don't be. I've caused this.'

She shrugged. 'I'll make pancakes for you boys.'

As she mixed the batter, she told them about her night out.

'We tasted eight different wines, and some of the cheaper bottles were the nicest. I've got my notes somewhere.'

The sheet of notepaper that Naomi had handed out was inside her bag. It was crumpled and she had to flatten it out to read it. When she saw her drawing of a cock and balls, heat crossed her cheeks.

'Let's see,' Adam said.

'Sorry, this isn't it actually. I must have left it at the pub.'

A vague memory of showing it to Jo came back to her in a hot flash.

'Who was there, Mumma?' Dylan asked.

'I'll show you,' she said, pulling back the cover to her iPad. 'Naomi will have posted some pictures on her blog. She always does it first thing. Let's have a look, shall we?'

She clicked onto Naomi's blog page, Wine O'Clock, slightly nervous of how she would appear in the photographs, hoping they would be flattering, for Adam. She scrolled through to the Events tab. A flicker of shame flared briefly, somewhere deep inside her, but she could not work out where it had come from. The evening was blurred at the edges, and maybe in the middle, too.

'Look, here are some,' she said, propping it up, clicking on the first photograph of Cynthia and Jo, who were holding up their glasses to the light to check the colour; to the second photograph of Cynthia, Jo, Meg and Emma gargling; to the third, of Meg and Naomi laughing together, with olives on cocktails sticks, heads close; and on she clicked through to the sixth photograph of the group shot in front of the fire. Sophie could make out her hand, but Naomi had deliberately cut her out of the line-up. None of the photographs included her. It was as though she had been airbrushed out of the evening, as though she had never been there at all.

She read through the article that Naomi had written, which was titled, 'How to Host Your Own Wine-tasting', but it did not mention any names.

'Where are you, Mummy?'

'She hasn't included any of me!' Sophie cried indignantly. 'Can you believe it?'

'She can't have done it on purpose.'

'Adam, it's not like we were at some massive party. There were only seven of us.'

'Maybe she thought you wouldn't like being put on social media.'

'But this isn't social media. This is her blog,' she said, checking Naomi's Instagram page, noting the enormity of her ever-growing following of 5,324, noting her smiley profile picture, noting the absence of Sophie in her post about last night, noting the 356 likes it had received, within the hour.

'The photos might have been crap of you. Double chins and red-eye,' he teased.

She thought about this, and decided that this was the most likely explanation. 'Yes. The other women were rather glamorous. In that rich, polished way. Maybe I didn't fit the image she wanted.'

'That is not what I meant. You looked stunning last night.'

Momentarily sidetracked by his compliment, she forgot her gripe and smiled. 'Thanks.'

'That lady isn't glamorous,' Dylan said wickedly, pointing at Jo, who had not worn make-up and had dressed in a plaid shirt.

'Don't be mean, Dylan,' she scolded. 'I'm going to check Facebook.'

With a churning stomach, she logged on to Naomi's page. Again, there were a series of photographs that did not include Sophie.

'Unbelievable.'

'Don't read too much into it.'

'It's a strange thing to do.'

'Very unlike her, I agree.'

Sophie tried to recall details from last night. She remembered the walk home: the brightness of the headlights that had dazzled her. Now she saw them again, right in front of her, and she shivered, screwing her eyes tightly shut. In the winding darkness, anything could have happened. It brought back thoughts and impulses that had come to her in fleeting moments last night. Her inebriation had heightened them, dangerous and powerful. She hadn't had the guts to play them out. *Thank god*, she thought, *thank god*.

Thoughts like that had not come to her for many years. Not since she had met Adam.

With a sting of panic, Sophie darted around to where Adam sat on the sofa and climbed onto his lap. She bent into his face, whispering, 'Sorry for snapping. I'm so sorry. Do you forgive me?'

You can't leave me. Please don't leave me.

The mere possibility of being on her own again destabilised her, poked at her coping strategies, was changing her back. Bad feelings were resurfacing, resentment was coming in pulses through her, fear was building again. None of it was manageable. *Please don't leave me.*

'I can't see the telly,' he said, pressing the remote and looking round her shoulder.

Her blood ran cold. She was in quicksand. Sinking. Suffocating.

She hissed into his ear, 'Go on. Leave me then, and watch what happens.'

She pushed her bare feet into her boots and pulled her cardigan tightly around her, grabbing her phone, running out into the cold morning and across to her grandfather's.

'Are you awake, Deda?'

'In here, child,' he called from the sitting room.

'I'll get our drinks.'

When she opened the fridge, she realised she had forgotten to make him more of her mince pasties. She cursed herself, furious that she had been too wrapped up in her own selfishness to forget him.

She brought the vodka and the glasses through, shivering.

Dedushka placed his book on the arm of his chair and took the vodka. 'You're distressed this morning, Sophia?'

With one sip, she felt a little calmer. She glanced at the mantelpiece. Jesus in the triptych seemed that much sadder today.

She took her phone out of her pocket. 'Why is everyone being so mean to me, Deda?'

'Adam the Pig, again?'

'And Naomi.'

'The wine-guzzler?'

Sophie picked at the frayed hem of her cardigan. 'That's the one.'

'What has she done?' he scowled.

'She thinks I'm too ugly and unsophisticated to be her friend.'

'Then drop her like a hot pasty,' he chuckled.

'But I can't do that.'

'Tell her how you feel, then. Do you *know* how you feel?'

She thought back to a conversation with Naomi's mother, Marjorie, years ago, at Naomi and Charlie's wedding. Marjorie had described, through dainty mouthfuls of cake, how bonny Naomi had been as a baby. She'd told Sophie about Naomi's fat thighs and ringlets, and how she had smiled – with that same dimple in her right cheek – weeks before the doctors thought it humanly possible. Eager for more insight, Sophie had grilled Marjorie for details of Naomi's childhood. Marjorie had answered in a prattling way, but Sophie had sucked up her silly stories like a baby on her mother's breast; going so far as to pretend that Marjorie was her own mother, basking in the praise and blushing at the embarrassments. It had fascinated Sophie to feel, almost first-hand, how much she loved her daughter. Traits that were formed in Marjorie's womb had defined Naomi's life from the moment she had drawn breath. As Marjorie had talked that day, her chubby hands had repeatedly snapped open her handbag to take out a hanky for Naomi's father, who was old and never spoke, who had needed his eyes mopped every time Naomi swished past in her silk dress. The day's floaty, flyaway mood – the marquee's tent pegs popping out with every gust of wind, the paper napkins floating into the water, the billowing train of Naomi's veil flying into a tree – held both their loss of Naomi and their happiness for her. This loss had stayed with Sophie. The loss that went with love.

But Sophie's own mother, Suzanne, had not lamented the loss of Sophie. She had not shown up to Sophie and Adam's wedding to cry and fuss and twitter on about Sophie as a child. She had not shown up at all. And if she had, she might have enjoyed telling their guests that Sophie had cried non-stop with colic as a baby. She might have laughed about how ugly she had been, with no hair and covered in eczema. And it would be no surprise to Suzanne that Adam was leaving Sophie now, had she known. Sophie's mistakes were the inevitable culmination of her imperfections: that bad-baby blood, those DNA failures, that fate.

'How do you feel?' Deda asked again.

Tears sprang into Sophie's eyes. 'I feel rejected,' she replied finally.

Certainly, Naomi had never been rejected and abandoned. Naomi had been born with a brighter spirit, an extrovert, who liked people, who adapted to her environment better.

'She'd never let you go if she knew what you did for her.'

'It's been too long now. She won't thank me.'

His milky eyes flicked in the direction of the garage. 'You think she won't thank you for giving her a life?'

'How would I even begin to tell her?'

'Do you have the cuttings still?'

'Upstairs,' she said.

'Get them.'

She climbed the stairs. There were remnants of Blu-Tack on the front of her door, where she had pinned her 'Keep Out' signs as a teenager. Her single bed was in the same place, with that same red and grey zigzag-patterned duvet set she had used at university.

She sat down on the bed, and traced her fingers under the sheet to the opening she had torn, enjoying the softness of its insides.

Her heartbeat sped ferociously when she pulled out the stack of brittle cuttings. The wooden frame of the bed dug into her thighs.

The face in the photograph stared at her from the fading poster. She knew the words that were written under the photograph off by heart:

MISSING PERSON

JASON PARKER
Missing from: Exeter
Date missing: July 19th, 1999
Age: 22 years old
Sex: Male
Height: 6' 2"
Build: Thin
Eyes: Blue
Hair: Wavy, blond
Race: Caucasian

Clothing: On the night Jason disappeared, he was carrying a black umbrella and wearing a black denim jacket, black t-shirt, dark blue jeans and white sneakers.

Circumstances: Unknown. On Saturday 19th July, Jason Parker was seen at an Exeter University student party at the Stoke Cannon Inn on Stoke Road, Exeter. He told a fellow student that he was leaving early in a taxi.

If you have any information about Jason Parker, or remember seeing him that night, please call the Devon and Cornwall Police on 222 444.

She crossed her legs and slumped over the photograph, staring at Jason Parker's face as though he were a lost love. She shuffled through the five newspaper cuttings, feeling the rough paper under her fingertips as she brushed over his face. The same photograph was used in three of the articles, in different sizes, black and white or colour, but always the same sullen expression, in a blue t-shirt with his greasy hair flopping either side of his long face. The local journalists had not cared enough about this young man to seek out more interesting or revealing shots of him from his family. His story had not been interesting enough to hit the headlines of the national newspapers.

Clutching them to her chest, she returned downstairs to her grandfather.

'You really think I should show Naomi these?'

'Yes, Sophie, I think so.'

'What if she does something stupid?'

'You think she wants to go to prison?'

'No.'

'You're safe, you see?'

'I understand.'

And she did understand, sort of. But she wanted to give Naomi another chance.

She kissed her grandfather goodbye and typed a text to Naomi on her way out.

Outside in the cold, damp night, she became aware of the Alfa Giulia sitting nearby in the garage, as though its engine breathed. She toyed with the idea of paying it a visit, like it might be alive and in need of attention. The pathway from Deda's doorstep cut through the narrow strip of lawn and pointed directly at the shack, whose windows glowed, but she detoured, trailing her fingers along the stucco frontage of the cottage, across the weedy path, along the groove in the rusted corrugated garage door. The bloom of red rhododendron bushes left droplets of rain across her left shoulder, and she shot sharply away. Suddenly, she did not want to see the car.

Back inside the shack, while she waited for Naomi's reply, it became stifling in the small space. And too quiet. The muffled, tinny sounds emanating from Adam's earphones upstairs in his galley room reminded her of how much distance there was between them. When she thought of him leaving, physically, her mind teetered on the edge of a precipice. She felt invisible, powerless, desperate. She was that baby again, the baby that Suzanne had not loved. She was the eight-year-old girl, with white eyelashes and long legs, whom Suzanne had walked out on.

She typed another text to Naomi.

The wood burner glowed hot and angry. Her hangover was worsening by the minute, until she felt quite panicky indoors with nobody but Dylan to talk to.

She sent another text, and another.

With every passing minute that Naomi didn't respond, her need to see her, to tell her everything, to hold her close, increased. She couldn't bear the wait. She would have to find her.

CHAPTER FIVE

*Hi Naomi – fun night. Thanks for the invite. But I was
hurt there weren't any pictures of me on your blog post. It
was a bit of a slap in the face, if I'm honest. And humiliating
if I meet those women again. Could you post one of me? I
know you took loads. Sx*

A hot flush crossed my cheeks, regretful and incredulous. I was
astounded that she was not acknowledging her behaviour, that
she had not taken responsibility for her goofing around. But I
regretted my decision to post my article before talking to her.

Earlier this morning, while everyone slept, I had crept down
to the kitchen, let Harley out of the laundry room, made myself
a strong coffee and sat down at my laptop. At the weekends, I
enjoyed writing my blog in this peaceful slot, before the girls'
demands crowded my thoughts. My article, titled 'How to Host
Your Own Wine-tasting', was aimed at the kind of woman who
had come last night: interested in drinking good, affordable wine,
but clueless about how to choose it. Thanks to five years working
as a wine buyer, I was not clueless. But when choosing the photographs to accompany the article, I *had* felt utterly clueless. Clueless
about what to do about Sophie's sabotage. Without exception, she
was sneering or pulling a face or being rude behind someone's back
in every single shot. Editing them down to six, I had accepted
that none of the images would feature her. Hoping that she would
be grateful that I had saved her from total mortification, risking

that she might be offended about being excluded, I had posted my piece with a nervous click.

On the way up the stairs to tell Charlie, probably to wake him, another text from Sophie came through:

Want to meet today? Quite like to talk about last night. Sx

'Charlie. Are you awake?'

'I am now,' he groaned.

'I think I've screwed up. Big time.'

I pulled the curtains open and he sat up in bed, rubbing his eyes.

'What have you done?'

I climbed back into the warm bed next to him, and pulled up the photographs of Sophie behaving badly.

'Look at these. I didn't add any of them on my blog post because they're…'

'Bloody awful?' Charlie said, finishing my sentence.

'But now she's sent me a text saying how upset she is.'

'Why not just post some now then?'

'Which one, though?' I said, sticking the phone closer to his face.

He put on his glasses and flicked through them. 'Oh dear. Bloody hell. Crikey. She looks totally smashed in every single one. It looks like she's taking the piss out of the event.'

'She was.'

'I hope you got a cab home.'

'There weren't any. We had to walk.'

Charlie choked. 'You walked?'

'It was fine,' I said, remembering our high jinks on the road with a smear of guilt. 'Seriously, though, I couldn't have posted any of those photos of her on my blog, could I?'

'Absolutely not.'

'Oh my god, she's texted me again!'

Naomi – could you text me back? I'm not sure you're getting these. Sx

'Read this,' I said, handing the phone to Charlie.

He read for longer than it should have taken, and then handed the phone back to me.

'Don't reply.'

'Don't reply at all?'

'It's not worth it.'

'I think I should take the whole post down. You know what she can be like.'

'Don't you even think about it! Sophie needs to understand that it's nothing personal. It's just work. If you post pissheads on your blog, it undermines the whole concept of drinking well.'

Both on my blog and in my weekly column in *Sky* magazine, I rammed the idea of moderate drinking down my readers' and followers' throats as often as I did the wines. I wrote about how drinking well could connect people. How it unlocked tears and laughter; how it broke down barriers and bonded us; how we celebrated with it and commiserated with it. The blog posts and articles were not about getting obliterated, offending your friends and playing chicken in front of oncoming cars.

'God. She was so embarrassing last night.' I sat forward. The pads of my fingers pressed those of the other hand in rhythmic succession, like a pianist's scale practice.

Charlie grabbed my hands and held them still. 'Stop,' he said gently.

Another text came through:

Why are you ignoring me? It's so cruel. Is it because you know you're in the wrong? : (

In a flash of anger, I ruffled my curls, getting my fingers caught in the knots, and blurted out, 'Maybe I *will* send those bloody photos to her and ask her to try and pick one herself.'

'It won't do her any harm.'

'I am going to send them right now,' I stated angrily. I did not show Charlie her latest text. As I selected an image to attach into a text, I stopped. 'I can't do it. It feels too mean. She only got that pissed because of Adam. If *you* were having an affair, I'd have probably got that pissed, too.'

'How do you know I'm not?'

I chuckled. 'Are you?'

'No. As it happens. But thanks for asking.'

We laughed, and he kissed me on the lips. '*There's* that dimple I fell in love with,' he said, kissing my cheek. But I could smell mint on his breath and I recoiled. 'You've brushed your teeth.'

He mock-slammed his palm into his forehead. 'I'm such an idiot. Can't we break the rule, just once?'

There was a nasty tug deep in my abdomen. I brushed his hand off my thigh. 'Inviting Sophie last night was a bad idea.'

He sighed. 'It is not your fault she got drunk.'

'I just feel it's all backfired. I wanted to make her feel good about herself, and now I've actually managed to make her feel worse.'

Charlie jumped out of bed, abruptly.

'Where are you going?'

'Downstairs, for a coffee.'

'But what am I going to do?'

As he walked towards the door in his rumpled pyjamas, he rubbed his hands underneath his glasses. 'Do I really have a say in it?'

'Of course!'

'Then tell her to grow up.'

I flipped the phone between my hands, knowing that I would not be telling her that, knowing that Charlie had a say in most things in my life, but rarely about Sophie.

When he had gone, another text from her came through:

I'm such a dick. I'm so sorry. We've been through a lot together ;) Don't give up on me. Sx

'Oh, Sophie!' I cried to myself, exasperated.

I flopped onto my back and undid my blog post, taking down the article, regretting the wasted work, wanting to weep over it. A whole event wasted.

I texted her back:

Hi Sophie – stop being mad! I've taken the post down. Sorry for being insensitive. See you soon. Naomi xxxx

Trying not to dwell on my worries about Sophie, I got dressed and went downstairs to rally the girls for a walk.

'Who's coming for a walk with Harley and me?'

It was a rhetorical question. The girls were going to come on a walk with Harley and me whether they liked it or not. My stewing thoughts would be dispelled in the fresh air.

'Nooo, Mummy, not now!' Diana moaned. Cornflour puffed up into Izzy's face as she poured it into the metal bowl.

'What are you two doing?'

'Making something.'

'Please, no more slime, darlings.'

'It's not slime, it's putty.'

'Put it away and let's take Harley out.'

Harley barked in agreement.

*

The stones underfoot were loose as we wove down into the bowl of the purple valley. A layer of frost shone from the heather and a low fog hugged the fir trees, muting the sunlight, pale and pretty.

'Aren't we going to the Devil's Lunchbox, Mum?' Izzy asked, noticing we had turned left instead of right out of our garden gate onto the heathland.

'Devil's *Punchbowl*, you ding-dong,' Diana giggled.

'No, darling. We're not going today.'

Harley ran off to the left. I whistled to him, and he scampered back and disappeared through the fern.

'Why?'

'I don't want to bump into anyone at the café.'

On Saturday mornings, Sophie and Dylan went to the Devil's Punchbowl café to drink marshmallow-and-cream hot chocolates after their ten-minute stroll. The last person on earth I wanted to bump into was Sophie and her reproach. The awkwardness about the photographs would be fresh between us. A few days for it to settle would be better. I did not want to see the accusation in her eyes, nor did I want her to see it in mine.

I inhaled heavily, sucking in the damp, earthy aromas, luxuriating in the emptiness of our trail. The girls ran off ahead, chasing Harley. Outdoors, I could breathe. I would try to stop worrying about Sophie.

After ten minutes of tramping along the sandy pathways, I heard loud barking from Harley. Diana appeared in front of me, out of breath and bright-eyed, holding a long stick.

'Dylan's here!'

For a second, I didn't click. It was slowness borne of denial. I wished it weren't true. It was miles out of Sophie's way, an hour on foot from the Devil's Punchbowl car park. Butterflies battled in my stomach.

'Is he with Sophie? Or Adam?' I asked Diana, taking hold of her hand, hoping my ten-year-old might protect me from Sophie's rebukes.

'He's with Sophie.'

As she answered, I noticed a pink fleck of a sticky substance on her cheek.

'Have you been eating sweeties?'

Her little face turned up to mine. 'No.'

I laughed, wiping it away. 'Don't fib, you little minx.'

So, sweeties had coaxed Dylan so far away from his hot chocolate. Bracing myself, I turned the corner, putting huge effort into the brightest smile I could muster, expecting three different responses from Sophie: either she would avoid eye contact or come out with a catty remark or enforce the silent treatment.

When I saw her, she was bent down to Harley, whose tail was wagging as she kissed his head. Her tortoiseshell bangles rattled as she ruffled his fur. He jumped up onto her legs as she stood. A smile formed on her pale lips. She looked like a nervous child lost in the woods, blue eyes darting around, a long wisp of hair twisted into her fingers.

'Hi!' I called out, with much enthusiasm.

'How strange,' Sophie said quietly, as though it really were a mystery.

'Have you come all the way from the car park?' I asked.

She ignored me. 'They ran on ahead.'

'Let's follow them,' I suggested. An offer of a walk, an olive branch.

We fell into step with one another.

'This fresh air will help my hangover.'

I glanced at her and smiled, a little sheepishly. 'Right. Yes.'

'I looked awful in all the pictures, didn't I?'

'Nooo.'

'Come on. You can tell me.'

'Just a bit tipsy, that's all.'

'Can I see?'

'No.'

'Please,' she begged.

Reluctantly, I gave her my phone.

She was quiet for a long time. The rustle of the undergrowth and the distant echo of the children were the only sounds. Then she handed it back, biting her lip. She said, 'No wonder you couldn't post them.'

'I didn't think you'd thank me if I did. I've taken the article down now, anyway.'

'I'm such a bitch.'

'No, you're not.'

'I shouldn't have sent you that text. I'm so sorry.'

Sophie's apology prompted mine.

'No. I was totally in the wrong to have posted those photos of the others without explaining first.'

For a few steps, we walked in companionable silence, until Sophie said, 'I wanted to talk to you about something…'

'Yes?' But I noticed that Harley was sniffing at the stagnant pond. 'No! Harley! No!' I shouted. Harley darted away, sniffing the ground. 'Sorry about that. What did you want to talk to me about?'

She held my gaze and tightened her hold on me.

'What is it, Sophie?' I asked, unsettled by the fear in her eyes.

Then she blinked it away. 'It's so weird between Adam and I. One minute we're fighting and the next we're having sex.'

Relieved, a little ruffled, I recalibrated my thoughts. 'You're still having sex? But I thought—'

She started walking again. 'We did last night. It's like splitting up has been an aphrodisiac. But then he said, in front of Dylan, "I don't know why I care any more", and then he kept going on about the properties he was looking at for him and Natalie.'

'Talk about mixed messages,' I replied.

'It's hard facing up to the fact that he is going to leave me. I don't think I wanted to confront it. That's why I drank so much last night.'

'Poor you. Honestly, I totally understand. I don't know how you're coping,' I said, sensing the ease between us returning.

Harley charged at our ankles and across the path in front of us, tripping us up.

'Silly mutt,' I laughed.

'Do you want me to take him out on my run any day next week?'

I hesitated, mentally clicking through the days I had meetings or tastings in London the following week, knowing that turning her offer down would be like rejecting her apology.

'Sally's not doing Tuesday… I have to be in London that day.'

'Great. I'll take him.'

'Thanks, Soph. That's amazing.'

'I like taking him.'

I nudged her. 'As I always say, you should get one yourself.'

'I will have to, just to shut you and Adam up about it,' she snorted.

'You love Harley.'

'He makes me feel safer on the trails.'

'Right, yeah. Harley would really terrify all those murderers lurking in the trees,' I laughed.

'You think the pepper spray is a better bet?'

'Er, yeah?' I laughed.

We chatted until we came to the junction, where the four main trails converged. 4 MILES DEVIL'S PUNCH BOWL was carved into the wooden arrow, which would take her back to the car park.

'I hope there are no tears on the way back,' I said, hugging her goodbye.

'Why would there be?' Her voice was always so gentle, even when she was defensive. I realised she thought I meant *her* tears, rather than Dylan's.

I explained. 'You've got another hour of walking, and Dylan's never keen.'

'Oh, right. Yes,' she said, puffing her cheeks. 'I'll have to bribe him with two hot chocolates at the café.'

She took Dylan's hand and they walked off into the mist.

Back at home, muscle-tired and refreshed, I told Charlie about bumping into Sophie.

'That figures,' he said, closing the newspaper he had been reading.

'Why?'

'When I went to get the papers, I saw her Saab parked down the lane in that little lay-by next to Hexagon House.'

'No. She came from the café car park.'

'Swear it was hers.'

'Can't have been.'

'AX14 RUT?'

'Can't have been,' I repeated, grabbing the magazine supplement from the kitchen table, tapping the words rather than reading them.

Charlie looked baffled. 'Why not?'

'You really know what her number plate is?' I guffawed, hiding how unnerved I was, sitting on one hand to stop its movement, flicking through the magazine with the other.

'Of course I do.'

Of course he did. Charlie was like that.

'It doesn't really matter.'

'What doesn't matter?' he asked.

'Where she parked. It doesn't matter.'

'No. Why would it?'

'Forget about it,' I said, closing the magazine and heading into the sitting room next door.

'Make the fire up, will you?' Charlie called through.

I was glad he had dropped it. I did not want to explain Sophie's lie to him.

I recalled hugging her goodbye on the heathland at the wooden sign, 4 MILES DEVIL'S PUNCH BOWL, which pointed in the direction that Sophie and Dylan had walked, and ¾ MILES POLECAT, which pointed in the opposite direction towards my house, and where I now know that Sophie's car was parked.

The only reason to lie would be to hide the fact that she purposefully went on the walk to find me.

I felt like I had been stalked. The heathland shrank in my mind, as though the hundreds of miles of National Trust land was not big enough for the both of us.

CHAPTER SIX

The road up to Naomi and Charlie's house was loosely gravelled and potholed, which added to the run-down charm of their modest Edwardian house. Every time Sophie undid the five-bar gate and secured it onto its hook, she would look up at the Wilson home with a sting of envy. It had been a miracle to find such an affordable property in this exclusive, leafy lane, within walking distance of the train station. The estates either side of them had pools and double garages and tall gates.

Harley barked from inside.

When she opened their front door with her spare key, he scuttled over the carpet, wagging his tail and yapping at her. He bounced up onto her thighs and snagged her running tights.

'Stop that,' she said, smacking his nose. He squealed and cowered.

She knew how to control dogs when she had to.

Before setting off with him, she ambled through the rooms. It was hushed, like a library. The muted colours of greys and faded corals and the worn oak of the furniture were offset by bright corners of books and photographs, filled with smiles. Sophie imagined she was Naomi as she sauntered into the kitchen, the heart of the house, where the units were Shaker, stripped oak with shiny black knobs. An oversized bunch of pussy willow stems arched from a glass vase on the central island. She rearranged them, humming to herself. The table, which stretched the length of the modern bifold windows, was worn and paint-splattered by the girls' art and craft projects. There was a woven multicoloured rag rug under the mismatched chairs to pull it all together and keep their cute toes warm. Their good life was ingrained in every piece of furniture, embedded into each nook and cranny.

In her head, Sophie painted a picture of eating warm croissants and jam with Adam and Dylan in this light, airy room, with its views across the Downs and its own garden gate onto the heathland. The space, the comfort, the style all formed the backdrop to a happier life. It would be impossible to be miserable here. She longed for this house, this kitchen, this family unit, and felt a tug of envy so strong she snatched a ceramic trinket dish from next to the kettle and slipped it into her handbag, as though having something of Naomi's would redress the balance somehow. She began scouring the room for something else to take.

Harley yapped at her feet. 'Okay, I'll take *you*, then,' she snorted, feeling powerful as he trotted at her heel to the bifold windows, through which they would leave.

As she opened the latch, she paused to look at the black-and-white framed photograph on the opposite wall. It was one of Adam's portraits. A Wilson family portrait. A present for Charlie's fortieth.

Naomi's eyes stared right out of the photograph at her, coming to life almost. What were they saying to her? At the time, they had been looking straight into Adam's lens. What had she been saying to him? She looked playful, a hint of mischief. Her blonde hair and rosy cheeks drew the eye like a burst of wild roses. Next to her, Charlie and his grey short back and sides was like a concrete pillar. The safe but dreary accountant from Surbiton had pruned and tamed Naomi's wild tendencies. He had brought her back home from where they had met in Sydney, during her Antipodean travels, and he had planted her deep into British soil again.

It had been the other way around for Sophie and Adam. Sophie had been the one to pin Adam down, luring him into the woods and making him a baby. And look how he was thanking her! The sixteenth of April was the day he had chosen to move out. Three short weeks away.

Sophie picked up a heavy stone tea light candleholder and chucked it at the frame. It fell from the wall and a spiderweb crack appeared across their faces.

Harley barked and began scratching at the back door, eager to get out. She clipped his lead on and slid open the window.

He strained at the collar, pulling Sophie along, his breath blooming in the cold air.

'Heel! *Heel!*' Sophie yanked him by her side.

Once they were through the gate, Sophie let Harley off the lead and began to run along the sandy trails through the fern. Every so often, the dog would weave across the path ahead, trot by her side for a moment, sniffing the ground frantically, before dashing off again. If she hadn't seen him for more than five minutes, she would call him and he would race back.

As Sophie's limbs warmed up inside, her skin remained chilled to the point of numbness. Her lungs were stretched and dried by the cold air. Towards the top of a steep hill, she was surprised to feel an oncoming sob push up from her chest. She slowed, to breathe the unwanted tears away.

As the path fell away beneath her trainers, she began to feel weightless, ethereal, disconnected from her moving body. Somehow, one foot after the other hit the ground with a momentum she had no control over, but she knew she was running on emptiness. She felt weak-kneed, spineless, ailing, as though her skeleton were shattering into a million pieces under her flesh.

Harley came up beside her, prompting her to run faster. Her pace faltered. The dog was refusing to budge. She sprinted as fast as she could, but still he followed.

'Stop it!' she cried, failing to understand why Naomi loved this stupid, needy little dog, who was more cocker spaniel than poodle. If she and Adam had *their* life, she would buy a collie dog for Adam, or an Alsatian, who were obedient and loyal and watchful.

Zigzagging in front of her, he tripped her up and her ankle turned over. 'Jesus!'

She limped a little, wondering if it was twisted, furious with the dog as the prickle of tears returned. 'Look what you've done!'

She managed to keep running, her ankle recovering; but as the dog yapped and circled, unpredictable and clinging, her mind became unsettled. It twisted with visions of Adam on top of Natalie, pounding angrily into her. The images were weakening Sophie, as though he was inside her, too, hating her, ruining her. She would not be able to tell Dylan that she had failed as a wife, that his father was leaving him because he couldn't bear to live with her any more. He would blame her, and he might love her less. The thought could have split her brain in two.

The dog whined. Why was he whining? She couldn't take it any more. She yanked his collar and clicked on his lead and ran faster and faster, but he began yelping behind her. She wanted rid of him. When they came to a gate to a field, she opened the latch and pushed him through. The sheep in the field mewed and Harley barked, running at them, forgetting about Sophie, probably thrilled to be let loose in a field that he was usually forbidden from entering.

As she jogged off, his bark died away. Her rhythm returned; her tears were sucked back.

But as soon as she felt the distance between them, she regretted how rash she had been. She looped back on herself, listening out for his bark.

His black form was nowhere to be seen. The sheep had returned to their quiet grazing.

She called out for him, running down to the bottom of the field.

Back and forth on the path, in and out of the heather, on and on Sophie searched and called out.

After an hour of looking outside, her flesh trembling and her voice hoarse, she ran back to the house to look inside, in case he had returned somehow, through an open window or the old cat flap. Then she thought of the garage, which was accessible through a hidden door that they rarely used but could have left open. There, she searched behind the boxes containing power tools and under the lawnmower and even inside their huge spare freezer. Her attempts to find him were beginning to seem token and pointless.

Giving up, she climbed into her car and sped home to Adam.

When she burst into the shack and told Adam what had happened, he closed his laptop and redid his hair tie. 'He'll turn up.'

'I'm not so sure.'

He took a sip from his coffee, and then another sip.

'Have you called her?'

'I've left messages. She'll never forgive me for losing him.'

'He'll turn up,' he repeated. 'He knows the way home.'

'What if he ran onto a farmer's land?'

'Then BOOM!' Adam mocked, pulling the trigger of a pretend shotgun.

'Don't joke about this!'

'Stop worrying. He'll be fine. Someone will find him and bring him home.'

'Yes,' Sophie agreed, wondering who Harley would come across in that closed field.

Adam opened up his laptop again. 'I took some great shots of the misty trees this morning. Look at these.'

'Creepy.'

'Atmospheric, you mean,' he teased.

Hiding her smile, she moved away from him over to the cacti on the windowsill. Staring out at the cottage, she said, 'At Naomi's today, I realised what a difference it makes to have space.'

'Uh-huh,' he said absently.

'I thought it might be time to rent this place out and think of moving into Grandad's.'

'Really?' She could hear the surprise in his voice. She swivelled round.

'Dylan could have his own room,' she said.

'He would love that.'

'And we could move Grandad downstairs, and we could have his room.'

A stripe of discomfort crossed his face. A twitch in his brow and lips. 'Right,' he said.

'I thought that's what you always wanted?'

'I do. I did.'

She turned away again and gripped the largest cactus. Her eyes watered.

'I'd better get back to Naomi's,' she said.

The snap of his wristwatch, the tap of the keyboard.

'I have to work abroad next week,' he yawned, pretending the conversation had not just happened.

'Okay.'

'And then I move into the Kingston flat the following week.'

'Fine,' she replied, her mouth dry.

She pulled Naomi's trinket dish out of her handbag and placed it in the centre of the kitchen island. The green and gold pattern swirled into a spiral, the plate spinning through her mind.

When he spoke next, she jumped. 'Are you okay?'

What a stupid question.

'Will you be here when I get back from Naomi's?' she asked.

'I'm going to spend the next few days at Natalie's.'

She took off her wedding band and engagement ring and placed them in the dish.

'What shall I tell Dylan?'

They both stared at the rings. She waited for him to protest about her removing them.

'Tell him I'm working away,' he said.

On autopilot, Sophie drove back to Naomi's, chilly in her damp running gear, feeling her naked ring finger against the steering wheel. The school run was edging closer. She would buy Dylan a special treat, before she told him that his father was a cheating scumbag who didn't care about them any more.

After parking up in Naomi's drive, she called Naomi on her mobile. When she heard the panic in her voice, she felt a curl of satisfaction roll up her spine.

Sophie hoped that they would not find Harley.

CHAPTER SEVEN

'Excuse me, sorry,' I whispered, shuffling through the crowd to the entrance, my phone buzzing in my hand.

Outside in the stuffy lobby of the hotel, I answered Sophie's third call in as many minutes, trying not to worry that something had happened to the children. I hoped it was about Adam, which was a mean thought, but preferable to any harm coming to Diana and Izzy.

'Harley's missing,' Sophie blurted out.

My head spun. The brown swirls of the carpet moved and distorted into a ghoulish pattern as I listened to her explanation.

Before she had finished speaking, I was running out of the revolving doors towards my car.

I drove recklessly. Speeding, overtaking, honking my horn. Every traffic jam was an obstacle to finding Harley. Horror stories ran through my head. A neighbour, a few houses away, had owned a terrier, whom they had put down after he was hit by a car. He had lain in the ditch for hours before he was found. The posters for Pebble, a lost Labrador, were still pinned to gateposts and trees, fading and mouldering, their owners losing hope. Daisy, the Staffordshire bull terrier, whom Sally had walked for years, had died of Lyme disease after an infected tick bite.

Refusing to believe that Harley could be added to that list, I conjured up his loyal, loving, black face, with his head cocked to one side, and I willed him to be safe with every fibre of my being.

When I had first seen a photograph of him, and the litter he had been born into, I had been lingering in the girls' school reception area, waiting to be seen by the head teacher. With swollen eyes, I had waited on the scratchy chair, preparing a speech to inform the school of how deeply my mother's death, followed shortly by my father's, had affected the girls. I had wanted to explain – without crying – that Diana's recent spate of misbehaviour was directly linked to her grief. If the staff had not understood this, I had planned to take them both out of the school before the end of Diana's Year Two.

I might not have gone that far, but I had never been tested, thanks to an angel from above in the form of a local breeder and fellow parent, who had been pinning an advertisement for the puppies on the school noticeboard. We had struck up a conversation about our children and the litter. There and then I had agreed to drive in convoy to her farm in Milford to meet the puppies. The school receptionist had rung to ask me where I was. I had explained to her that I had been called away somewhere urgently, which had not felt like a lie.

Harley's tiny body had curled in my hand and I had fallen in love.

When Harley came into our lives, Diana's behaviour settled and we had all found a way to carry our sorrow without falling apart completely.

If Harley was hurt, or worse, I did not know how I would ever forgive Sophie.

Sophie and I charged down the lane to my neighbour's house.

Sophie was in tears, falling apart already. 'I don't know what happened. Honestly, I just don't know.'

I was trying to keep it together. 'Let's hope Rosemary's seen him.'

'I'm so sorry. My god. I'm so sorry.'

Angrily, I wondered how often she could say sorry to me before I stopped trusting her completely. I was sick of hearing her idle apologies. Her thoughtlessness was nothing new to me, and I couldn't help questioning how careless she might have been with Harley; how involved in her own self-centred, self-pitying thoughts she had been at the time, and whether there was more to her story than she was letting on.

'Let's just focus on finding Harley, okay? He was wearing his collar, wasn't he?'

'Of course.'

We walked straight onto Rosemary's property. Behind the tall gate sat her sprawling, flat-roofed bungalow and empty swimming pool. The rooms looked dark behind the windows, but her car was there. As we approached, I could hear a radio playing from inside the door. I knocked.

'Hello, Naomi!' Rosemary said, leaning on her aluminium walking stick. A quick smile flickered and disappeared. I imagined it was too much effort for her to hold it for long through the constant pain of her rheumatoid arthritis, which had already twisted two of her fingers the wrong way.

'Hello, Rosemary,' I replied, concerned that her knuckles looked particularly swollen, wanting to ask her how she was, knowing I didn't have time, this afternoon, to focus on what she needed.

'Oh, the Tupperware!' she said, turning away from us. My heart slipped down my chest, disappointed that Harley was not here.

'Please don't worry about that. I'll pick it up when I pop round next. Actually, we're here about Harley. He's gone missing and I wondered if you'd seen him.'

The soft skin around her eyes drooped lower at the edges. 'No. I haven't. I'm so sorry.'

'Don't worry,' I said, 'I'm sure he'll turn up or someone will call us any minute. You're the first door we've tried.'

'I would come and help if I could.'

I smiled and touched the back of her hand. 'I know you would. I'll let you know when he's back.'

As we turned away, she added, 'Have you tried any of the Twitter forums? Haslemere Rants is a good one. When my friend's cat went missing, they posted it online and she turned up at someone's house.'

'Brilliant idea. I hadn't thought of that.'

Before we were at the next house, I had posted a message on Haslemere Rants about a missing black cockapoo.

Throughout our visits to the remaining neighbours' houses, I checked the forum feed every few minutes.

Sophie became quieter and quieter as the day progressed.

'It's almost pick-up time,' Sophie said.

'And it'll be dark after that,' I added, trying not to betray the quiver of fury in my voice.

'Adam can pick up Dylan. If you want me to pick up your girls while you keep looking, I can do that.'

'No, it's okay. I'd prefer to explain the situation to them myself.'

'Then again, Adam probably won't answer the phone if he sees it's me calling.'

I couldn't believe she was bringing her problems into the situation.

'Don't worry, you go home, Sophie. You've got a lot on your plate. We've done all we can for now. I'll go out later with the torch. I'm sure he'll turn up,' I repeated, for fiftieth time that day. The phrase had a hollow ring to it.

'I don't want to leave you, not until he's back.'

'Honestly, please. I'll call you as soon as I hear anything.'

The corners of her lips turned down. 'I know why you don't want me here.'

'It's not that I don't *want* you here, Sophie…' I began, amazed that she could turn this around, 'I just… it's just not helping anything, that's all.'

'I'm sorry I'm no help.'

Her morose expression, her simpering voice was sending off small firecrackers of irritation in my head.

'Sophie. That's not what…' I stopped. I would be a fool to expend one more second trying to make her feel better. 'I'll call you as soon as he turns up.'

She offered a weak hug. 'I understand.'

When I closed the door behind her, I screamed at the closed door and stuck two fingers up at it, at her. 'It's not always about you, you nutter!' I hollered, my voice ringing through the empty house.

I had half an hour before I had to leave for the school run. I would have one last look on the heath.

Wrapped up warm, I was about to step out into the garden again, when I noticed that the wall was bare where Adam's family portrait of us had been. Glass from the frame was sprayed underneath the kitchen table and the photograph itself was damaged. I spotted a tea light candleholder in the mess. Perhaps the girls had been fooling around or fighting before school. Charlie hadn't mentioned it. Neither Charlie nor I had ever liked this photograph. We had hung it for Sophie's sake. I decided to sweep it up later and I charged out, my mind immediately refocused on Harley.

On the way down to the gate, I rang Charlie to tell him what had happened.

'Do you want me to come home now?'

'No. Don't worry. Maybe when you get back you could go out to look for him while I put the girls to bed tonight.'

'Of course. Don't worry. He's probably found a warm hearth and some dog biscuits and he'll be home soon.'

'Love you,' I said, hanging up.

Charlie's words kept me motivated as I called out into the distance. 'Harley! Harley, come home to us, Harley! Please come home!'

The heathland did not offer him up, nor did any of the lanes around our house.

As I opened our garden gate to return home, I received a call from an unknown number.

'Hello, is this Mrs Wilson?' The man had a nasal, instantly unlikeable voice.

'Yes.'

'This is Gordon Lott, from Wesley Farm. I have in my possession a small black dog with a name tag stating your contact name and number on it.'

'Oh my god,' I gasped, clinging to the gate to steady myself, resting my forehead on the damp wood. 'Thank god.'

'Well, you won't be thanking our good Lord for long. You are, of course, at liberty to come and collect your dog, but I'm afraid it is within my rights to make a complaint about your animal to the local authorities, who could take measures to put him down for attacking my livestock in a closed field.'

My stomach rolled. 'No! They wouldn't do that! You can't do that!'

'I'm afraid I can, Mrs Wilson.' He sounded officious, like he was parodying a police officer in a crime drama.

'But he would never have attacked a sheep! He's as soft as anything!'

'I have an eye witness saying that he was chasing my livestock in a closed field.'

'I can't understand why that happened,' I replied, more quietly, biting my lip. 'I want to come and collect him right now. Are you at the farm?'

'I am.'

'I'll be there in ten minutes.'

The stench of manure came in waves, carried on the wind from across the fields and in through the window of the farmer's kitchen. A menagerie of animals covered the surfaces and moved around my feet, from fish to hamsters to rabbits, but there was no sign of Harley.

Tap, tap, tapping on the kitchen table as I waited for Gordon's wife – who was surprisingly neat and blonde – to fetch him from somewhere else in the house, I saw an incoming call from Sophie, who would have received my text informing her that Harley was safe.

I did not pick up.

Gordon appeared. He was a wiry, willowy man, who had to duck his head when he stepped in through the low kitchen door.

'I'm so, so sorry about this,' I said, holding out my hand.

I was prepared to grovel on my knees in the manure to beg him not to report Harley to the authorities.

Jangling a large bulge of keys in his pocket with one hand, he shook my hand slowly with the other. In spite of my judgement of him over the phone, I noticed that he had kind eyes. I wondered if he was the sort of man you could appeal to.

'I'll take you to him,' he said, before leading me into a courtyard through a rusty cattle gate. All the while, he preached to me about the dangers of untrained dogs. I agreed obsequiously as I navigated my way through the various clods of mud and hay in my clean trainers.

'And it was a closed field with clear signage about livestock,' he continued on accusingly.

'Might the gate have been left open by someone, by mistake?' I asked, pretending not to be accusing him back.

'From what I've found out, I understand that the gate was opened by a woman with blonde hair in running clothes, and that the dog was left to run loose. Luckily for me, my electrician was fixing the live fencing at the bottom of the field and apprehended your dog, preventing further harm, but it was within my rights to take a shotgun.'

Shocked, I asked him to repeat what he had said, which he did, word for word. Still unable to believe it, I said, 'You're saying the electrician saw Soph… saw the blonde woman actually opening the gate?' My foot swerved away from a large brown pat.

'Yes, I'm afraid so,' he said patiently, leading me into a large barn. I heard a bark that I recognised instantly. There, secured in a pigpen, was Harley.

When he saw me he leapt so high he almost cleared the gate to get to me. If dogs could smile, he was smiling from ear to ear, in line with mine.

As Gordon opened the gate, Harley charged at me, hitting his nose into my shins and wagging his tail so fast it looked like it might come off. I picked him up and let him mess me up with stinking manure and hay, and I kissed his face again and again.

'He's not such a bad little dog,' Gordon said gruffly.

But I caught a smile on his lips, and my heart lifted.

'Have you called the council already?' I asked, unable to look him in the eye. I clipped Harley's lead on, holding my breath for his answer.

'Look. If you promise to keep him on a lead around my sheep, I won't take any further action. But you know I had every right to shoot him on the spot.'

Losing all sense of decorum, I hugged Gordon the farmer, who stood stiffly in response to the inappropriate gesture.

'Thank you for keeping him safe!' I cried, and then more soberly, 'Thank you.'

Gordon nodded and simply walked away, which I assumed was his standard goodbye.

On the way home, Sophie called again.

As it rang out, I turned to Harley, who was sitting on the front seat with his nose poking out of the window. 'Let's give Sophie a wide berth from now on. Don't you think?'

He turned to me and I imagined him nodding. It seemed he knew more than all of us put together.

I laughed at him, overjoyed that he had been returned to me.

At some point, I might be ready to hear Sophie's excuses about why she let Harley through a gate into a field of sheep, but I was not ready yet, and wondered if I ever would be.

CHAPTER EIGHT

Sophie scanned all the faces of the post-school-run mothers supping on their flat whites and nibbling on date energy balls or chickpea rye toast. Most Fridays, Naomi's bright blonde curls would be added to the mix. The noise of their babbling beat at her eardrums as she turned to leave.

'Sophie?'

For a second, she wondered if she could pretend she had not heard the voice, and she reached for the door handle. A hand tapped her shoulder. Swinging round, Sophie took a minute to recognise the woman.

'Oh, hi Meg,' Sophie said warily.

'The wine-tasting last week was fun,' Meg said.

'Naomi told me off for being rude.'

'Nooo,' Meg laughed, ruffling her fingers through her pixie haircut.

Without make-up, she looked even younger and prettier, with her shiny skin and long neck. It was hard to believe that she was a surgeon. Poised to be rude again, Sophie decided it would be more constructive to plunder her for information about Naomi's whereabouts.

'You're just being polite. I'm mortified about my behaviour. But I'm going through a bit of a rough time, if I'm honest.'

Meg cocked her head to the side. 'I'm sorry to hear that.'

'That's okay,' Sophie said, unravelling a tight twist of hair from her finger, adding, 'Actually, I was looking for Naomi. Have you seen her?'

'Funnily enough, that's exactly why I stopped you. She wasn't at Pilates yesterday and I was worried she was unwell.'

A flutter of relief lightened Sophie's mood. Perhaps Naomi was ill. Perhaps that was why her house was quiet and her car was in the drive. Perhaps that was why she hadn't responded to her texts.

'I've been trying to get hold of her, too.'

'Well, I'm embarrassed now. I haven't actually called her to find out, but when I saw you here, it reminded me that I hadn't seen her about.'

'Oh.' A small crease formed between Sophie's invisible eyebrows.

'Now I've worried you! I'm sure she's fine. But she never misses Pilates.'

'I was thinking of joining that class. You and Naomi take the class on Thursdays at... what time, again?'

'Yes, Thursdays. Seven o'clock. Sign up! It's great fun.'

'Seven in the morning?'

Meg grinned. 'I know. Horribly early, but it's the only class I can catch before work.'

Sophie hit back at what she perceived was Meg's smugness. 'That slot's difficult for single mums.'

Meg fumbled around for the right response. 'Are you... Sorry, I didn't realise that you had... Is that recent?'

'I'd better go. Good to see you, Meg,' Sophie said, and she left the café.

Rattled by Meg, Sophie charged away, feeling even more determined to find Naomi but desperate to avoid bumping into anyone else.

On the way home, she stopped off at the less salubrious café on the other side of town, just in case Naomi was there. Then she checked the two lay-bys where she might have parked her car for a dog walk; then stormed up and down the aisles at Tesco and Waitrose, where she took the opportunity to buy some Stolichnaya for Deda; then she drove by Naomi's house again, stopping in the lane to run in and ring the doorbell. If she was ill, she might need some soup or some company. The door did not open.

Each disappointment added to Sophie's increasingly fraught mood. The palm of her right hand began to itch. Was Meg right to be worried? Had something more serious happened? Were Diana and Izzy okay?

At home, safely parked up in her driveway, Sophie stared out of the car window at her small shack in the woods: at the mishmash of wellies, at the log pile, at the row of cacti inside the window. To her left, she looked at Deda's cottage. Ivy roots were eating away at the stucco frontage, leaving cracks and holes. The waxy leaves crowded the window panes. If Deda was reading, he would be straining his eyes. She nipped over to check on him.

There was a dank and dusty smell inside.

'Deda? Are you here?'

'In here,' he said, as though he could be anywhere else.

'I've bought more Stolichnaya.'

In the kitchen, she wiped down the surfaces, poured the glasses and arranged the tray, remembering that she had made a batch of ten meat pasties, which she took out of the fridge and put on a plate.

She kissed his forehead and sat down.

'Hello, child,' he said.

'*Za vashe zdarovje,*' Sophie said, knocking back a finger of vodka.

'To your health,' he repeated in English.

When he refused to toast her in Russian, it usually meant he was in poor spirits. She saw that his nose was purplish and his cheeks grey. She felt his cheek. It was cold. 'You feeling okay?'

He replaced his book on the arm of his chair and bent his arms back and forth at her. 'You know, my joints ache.'

'Do you want me to call the doctor?'

'If I feel pain, it means I'm alive. This is good,' he replied, shrugging.

Sophie did up his middle button, where he had missed it.

'You must take care of yourself.'

'Stop worrying about me. You worry about yourself. I see your cheeks are a little flushed.'

'I've been searching all morning for Naomi. I've looked everywhere but I can't find her.'

The loose skin of his eyelids lifted and tremored. 'Is the Giulia clean?'

'Yes.' She confirmed this, but she had not checked on it.

'Have you telephoned her?'

'I have. Many times. And I've knocked on her door.'

'Now, you mustn't fuss over her. She'll only get awkward.'

'I'm worried she's ill. The house looks empty, but her car is in the drive.'

'Let her come to you.'

Sophie moved closer to her grandfather and spoke in a low whisper. 'What if she's hiding from me?'

'Why would she do that?'

'Because she's sick of me. Because she hates me.'

'Why would she hate you?'

'I had a dream last night that I was a giant monkey flicking the little humans away like flies on my skin. I felt good about it. I loved how I felt.'

'But now?'

'I feel very hateful, like one of the little humans in my dream.' She slumped and knelt at his feet, resting her head on his lap. He smelt decrepit and comforting.

'What will make you feel better?'

Sophie poured two more fingers of vodka. 'This?' she laughed.

'That will help.'

'Can she really be angry still about that stupid dog?'

'Some people love their dogs more than humans.'

'She seems to love Harley more than she loves me.'

'You know what my advice is?' he said, raising his thick eyebrows at her. 'A problem shared is a problem halved.'

'I was going to tell her, and then things got back to normal between us and so I thought, why stir things up?'

Sophie found the hole in the ribbed velvet arm and poked her finger deep into the stuffing, pulling out a wisp of synthetic fibre. She couldn't believe there was any left after all these years. As a child, she used to suck her thumb and pull the fibre out and rub it under her nose while she listened to her grandfather read storybooks.

She stroked it over her top lip and was consoled by the sensory memory.

'You tell her and all your angst will go,' he soothed.

As Sophie retreated to her old bedroom, her grandfather called out after her, 'Remember, Sophia, hold her close! I won't be here forever!'

With his words ringing in her ears, Sophie sat on her bed and pulled out the cuttings, sifting through them to read one particular article.

When she had first read it, she had been standing in the newsagents on the high street in Exeter. Her focus on the content of that article had been so intense, she could have been the only person alive on the planet.

THE EXETER LOCAL

5th August 1999

YOUNG MAN KILLED IN HIT-AND-RUN

A 22-year-old student, Jason Parker, has died in an alleged hit-and-run crash in Exeter.

Parker was reported missing two weeks prior to the discovery of his body, which was found in the undergrowth close to Stoke Road.

In a statement, Devon and Cornwall Police said: 'The investigation into the young man's death is in the early stages, but it is believed his injuries are consistent with being involved in a road traffic collision.'

The area was thoroughly searched, police added, but a vehicle has not been found.

A post-mortem is due to be carried out and officers continue to make local enquiries.

Strangely, Sophie recalled feeling sad that Jason Parker had warranted only a small article in the local newspaper, an impersonal yellow police sign and a small bunch of flowers pinned to a tree near to where his body was found. Her sadness had quickly passed: if Naomi had read about this man's death, it might have turned out very differently for both of them. But she had been thousands of miles away, jumping off waterfalls on islands in the Pacific and partying under full moons, blissfully ignorant of what she had caused.

Sophie tucked the article away and felt the rising of bile, which tasted bitter, like resentment.

*

It was the middle of the night, but Sophie was lying wide awake. She was fighting the urge to call Adam in Portugal, where he was working. If Adam had been there, next to her, she would have asked him if she should go ahead with her plan to surprise Naomi at her Pilates class tomorrow morning.

Hold her close, Deda had said.

Over the weekend, she had driven to Naomi's house, lying to Adam about where she had been going: to get milk, to clear her head, to pick up the newspapers. He had no inkling of her revolving worry about Naomi, whom she now believed might be terminally ill.

I won't be here forever, Deda had said.

By the time the piercing noise of her alarm clock burst into the darkness at 6 a.m. on Thursday morning, Sophie had decided. She would go to Pilates.

Any form of communication with Naomi would be preferable to her silence, even if it involved a shouting match.

She pulled on a pair of black leggings and a t-shirt and shook the dried mud off her trainers.

It felt painful to crease her hand to tie her laces. Water eczema on her right palm had flared up. It had been ten years since the last bout. The blisters prickled and itched. Thoughts of Naomi swirled.

Dylan had not yet stirred, and she wondered if she could leave him to sleep. Knowing how distressed he would be if he woke up and found her gone, she decided to wake him and dress him and take him over to her grandfather's.

'Why do I have to go?' he whined as she dragged him by the arm to the cottage.

'I don't want you to be on your own,' Sophie cried crossly, worried that she was going to be late for the class.

'But it smells in there!' he wailed.

She grabbed him by the shoulders and snapped at him. 'Stop being so ungrateful, you little brat.'

It was unlike Sophie to shout at him, and he stopped whining abruptly.

She led him into the house and through to the sitting room.

'You must be as quiet as a mouse. Deda's asleep upstairs.'

Before she left, she warmed Dylan a meat pasty and sat him down on the footstool with a stack of her old comics. 'I won't be long.'

Tears slipped down his cheeks.

'Don't cry,' she said. 'You're safe here. It's the safest place in the world,' she reassured him, kissing him goodbye, tasting the salty tears.

The emotional cord between them was snapped as she drove off towards the high street where the fitness studio was located.

The car park was empty, except for two estate cars and Naomi's black Volvo 4x4. Her guts churned. Furtively, she walked across the dark car park to the beacon of the lit-up frosted glass entrance.

Having paid at the reception desk, she peered into the studio space. Both Naomi and Meg were already sitting at the far right-hand corner on their rolled-out mats, cross-legged, chatting.

Sophie walked across the polished pine floor, her chest thundering.

When Naomi caught Sophie's approach, her features froze.

'Sophie! You made it!' Meg said with a friendly smile. 'Put your mat next to ours. We can be the naughty ones at the back.'

'Is that okay?' Sophie asked, hovering, looking to Naomi for an answer, wishing that there was a space next to Naomi. Meg's mat was a wedge between them.

'Sure,' Naomi said, flashing a painfully polite smile. In her lap, her fingers fidgeted.

The cool edge to her greeting sent a shot of fear through Sophie. She hesitated before laying down her mat.

'Did you find someone to watch your little boy this morning?' Meg asked Sophie.

Before Sophie had a chance to answer, the bony Pilates instructor entered the room and clapped her hands, introducing herself in a shrill voice as Louise. Sophie quickly rolled out her mat, noticing that the studio had filled up with seven other women.

The class began.

The small repetitive movements were mind-numbing. The exercise bands pressed into the rash on her hand. She glanced over at Naomi, who resolutely refused to catch her eye. Her face was set with steely concentration. Every minute that Sophie spent with Naomi, while being unable to talk to her, was torment.

As they came to the warm-down, Sophie saw that Naomi was already rolling up her mat, explaining to Meg that she had to leave early. Sophie did the same.

'Your muscles need to warm down, ladies!' Louise trilled as they left.

A white mist had spread over the car park.

'Naomi!' Sophie called out, jogging after her.

By the time Sophie had reached her car, Naomi was already shut inside.

Sophie stood in front of the bonnet, refusing to let Naomi get away.

The car horn blared, making Sophie jump, but she did not move.

Naomi's car door flew open.

'What the hell are you doing here?' she yelled, uninhibited by the other women who were now filtering out of the fitness centre.

Tears prickled Sophie's eyes. 'I wanted to see you. I want to know why you're not talking to me,' she pleaded.

Naomi looked flabbergasted. 'Are you serious? You really don't know why I'm angry?'

'No. I don't understand. I didn't lose Harley on purpose. He ran off.'

'Did you know that farmer could have shot Harley? *Did* you?'

'What farmer?'

Sophie felt new panic rise. The rash on her palm itched ferociously.

'The farmer who found Harley attacking his livestock!'

Sophie laughed. 'Harley wouldn't attack a fly.'

'It is irrelevant whether he did or not, the fact is you let him through the gate. Someone saw you do it.'

'That's a lie!' Sophie cried, shocked that she had been seen.

Naomi's mouth opened to say something, but she faltered, 'But… the farmer said…'

Interrupting, Sophie insisted, 'No. The farmer is lying. The gate must have been open already! I swear it, Naomi. Harley must have slipped through. When I was looking for him later, I noticed that the gate was pushed to, but it wasn't clicked onto the latch.'

'But why would the farmer lie?'

'I have no idea. I really don't. But, I mean, come on Naomi, why would I put Harley into that field with all those sheep on purpose? There's no logic to it.'

There was a pause. Then, as though she was thinking out loud, Naomi said, 'Unless the guy who saw you didn't want to admit to Gordon that he'd left the gate open himself.'

'What guy? Who's Gordon?'

'Gordon's the farmer. He sent an electrician down to the field to fix the live fencing.'

Sophie relaxed, knowing she had created doubt in Naomi's mind, just enough for her to wriggle out of this scrape. 'That sounds more likely.'

'But you still lost him!'

'I'm sorry. I am. I haven't slept a wink since it happened. But Naomi, you have to admit, Harley has gone walkabout a few times before…' Sophie reminded her cautiously.

Naomi rested both hands on top of the open car door. Her fingertips drummed the metal.

'I know. I know.'

'I love him, too, you know. I would never have put him in danger.'

'Of course,' she sighed, her hands finally calm.

'I wish you'd called me to talk about this,' Sophie said.

'I should have,' Naomi admitted.

'Fancy grabbing a quick coffee before the school run?' Sophie asked, a little shyly.

'Erm, I'm not sure. Charlie leaves for the train at eight thirty.'

'Go on. We've got twenty minutes. Just a quick one.'

There was a pause. She looked over her shoulder, then at her watch and sighed, 'We'll get them to go.'

It wasn't until Sophie had ordered her cappuccino that she remembered Dylan.

She made her excuses and ran from the café, put her foot down and took the shortcut through the lanes back home.

'Dylan?' she whispered.

In front of the hearth, Dylan was lying on his tummy, propped up on his elbows with an old *Beano* annual in front of him. The electric fire was on.

'Hello, my darling boy!' she cooed, lying next to him on her tummy. 'It's cosy here, isn't it?'

He scratched his elbows. 'I turned the fire on.'

'It would have been best to wait for Deda to do that when he woke up,' she said, pulling him onto her lap to inspect the eczema on his elbows and under his armpits and behind his ears. There were telltale blotchy red signs of a fresh flare-up.

'Daddy says that Deda won't ever wake up,' he said.

Sophie pushed him off her lap. 'Daddy is a mean, mean man for saying that,' she hissed.

Dylan climbed back onto her lap and stroked his hand down her hair. 'It's okay, Mumma.'

She kissed his lips. 'Come on, let's get some cream on you and get you to school before we disturb Deda. He needs his sleep.'

'Did you bring me a treat?' he said as they walked over to the shack.

'I promised I would, didn't I?'

She rummaged in her bag for the chocolate bar, which he gobbled on the way to school.

After pushing the last piece of chocolate into his mouth, Dylan said, 'I want to call Daddy.'

'When you get home from school, you can.'

'No. Now.'

'He'll be working too hard on his shoot to speak now.'

'You always say he never works hard. You say he plays with swans on the beach.'

She laughed. '*Swans around* on the beach. It's an expression for...' she stopped, refusing to get sidetracked. 'He'll be too busy to talk to you right now.'

'No! I want to talk to him, NOW!' he screeched.

Trying to stay calm, she clicked the indicator into School Road. 'No, Dylan. We are not calling Daddy.'

He began to rummage in her bag at his feet. 'Well, I am!'

Sophie pulled into a parking space.

'Give that to me now.'

'No. I know your code.'

She grabbed it from him. He caterwauled, 'I want Daddeee! I'm not going to school. I want Daddeee!'

'Okay, okay, come on. Calm down. Shhh,' she soothed, seeing a mother and her two children walk past the car. 'We'll call him. But you mustn't mention anything about staying with Deda this morning, okay?'

His tears were sucked back into his eyes and he blinked up at her. 'Okay, Mumma.'

Sophie clicked on Adam's name and handed the phone straight to Dylan. There was no answer. She texted him:

Dylan is refusing to go to school until he talks to you.

Seconds later, her phone flashed up with Adam's name.

'Here you go,' she said, passing over the handset.

'Hello, Daddy,' he sniffed. 'Mumma's fine... I don't know... Okay... I read three *Beano*s at Deda's today...'

Sophie's heart stopped. 'Dylan,' she whispered, holding her finger to her lips, *shush*.

He shot her a defiant scowl. 'I stayed there all on my own,' he said to his father.

Sophie inhaled sharply and then tried to take the phone from him, but Dylan clambered out of the car. The mobile was pressed to his cheek as he headed in the direction of the school playground.

There were streams of parents and their children on the narrow pavement now. Sophie wove through them towards Dylan.

As soon as she caught up with him, he hung up.

'Here you go,' he said innocently, giving it back to her and yanking his school bag out of her other hand.

'What did you tell Daddy?'

'Nothing.'

'Dylan… Tell me the truth now.'

'Bye,' he called from over his shoulder as he ran through the gates to line up for the bell.

Her phone began ringing as soon as she turned on the ignition. Of course, it was Adam. To shout at her. She did not pick up.

All the way home, it rang from her bag. She began to enjoy the power of ignoring it. It seemed she had Adam's attention, at last. She wondered if this was how Naomi felt in the face of all her calls. Perhaps Naomi had enjoyed feeling powerful too.

At home, she made a coffee and settled on the sofa before calling him back. Her stomach flip-flopped as she listened to the European dialling tone. She couldn't wait to hear his voice.

'Hi, Adam.'

There was a rustle. He spoke in a hiss. 'What was Dylan doing on his own in that house?'

'It was only for an hour.'

'Only an *hour*? Have you gone mad?'

'The cottage is more secure than this bloody shack. Our door doesn't lock properly, and the window to our bedroom doesn't even *have* a lock. Anyone could have walked straight in. I thought he'd be safer over there.'

Adam let out a strangled laugh, or gasp – Sophie couldn't tell which – before shouting, 'He shouldn't be left alone *anywhere, ever*!'

'He wasn't alone. Deda was looking after him.'

'Oh, Jesus! Oh, Christ!' he cried out, but it was muffled, distant, as though he had dropped the phone away from his mouth. Then his voice came back loudly, too loudly. 'SOPHIE, HOW CAN A DEAD MAN LOOK AFTER AN EIGHT-YEAR-OLD BOY? SOPHIE, HE'S *DEAD*. HE'S DEAD, FOR CHRIST'S SAKE!'

A sharp light shot across Sophie's vision. She was stunned.

'How can you be so hurtful, Adam?'

He dropped his voice to a strained, urgent whisper. 'You need to confront it.'

A lump formed in her throat. Speaking became difficult. 'He's still there in that house. If you came over, you'd see him, too.'

'Okay, Sophie,' he said, gently, softly, as if he was speaking to a child. 'That's fine. You believe that he inhabits that house, in some form. Fair enough. I can't seem to ever make you see it any different. But you need to promise me that you will never leave Dylan there ever again, not even for five minutes. The wiring is fucked and that heater is a bloody deathtrap. OKAY?'

She wanted to reassure him that her Dedushka was like an angel looking out for them, more effectively than any living person could, but she felt it might make him angrier.

'OKAY?' he shouted again.

'Okay. Okay.' She looked at her hand and saw that the blisters had split. Her palm bled.

'I'll be back tomorrow morning,' he stated, and then he hung up on her.

She threw the phone onto the coffee table and lurched to standing, looking around her for a window to open. There was no air.

She stumbled and tripped outside, out of their cabin, across the drive towards Deda's house, the gravel shooting up and hitting her shins, digging into her knees as she fell, sticking into her flesh as she ran on. The key in her hand wouldn't fit into the lock. Again and again she tried, banging on the door, 'Deda! Deda!' she screamed. The key finally slotted in, as though he had heard her cries for help.

'Deda!'

The house was quiet, like death.

'No! Nooo! Deda,' she sobbed, crashing into the front room, seeing the dead fire, the dead chair, the dead stool. It was not just empty, it was a void. A void, empty of all the love she had felt earlier that morning, when she and Dylan had lain cosy in the orange glow, sensing Deda's love all around them, knowing he had one eye from the heavens on them both. But Adam's words had flushed Deda out, drowned out his spirit, angered him in the next world.

'I'm still here, Deda!' she whispered, taking the black urn from the shelf next to the triptych, cradling his ashes in her arms; sitting in Deda's favourite chair, holding him close. 'I'm still here. Please talk to me.'

The room remained silent.

A thorny vine scratched at the window pane. A wood pigeon flapped in the chimney. The mice scuffled above her, where they ate at the mattress and lived in the wardrobe inside his old leather shoes.

Unable to bear the silence, she sought out the vodka from the cupboard in the kitchen and returned to her usual place on the stool. Trying to find a focus in the chair where his face would be, she conjured him with all her might. She blinked away the blur of tears, trembling as she sipped at the fiery drink, staring at his untouched glass.

The fire that his coffin had rolled into last year flared into her mind. She had wanted to lie on it and burn with him. The metal bars of the heater in the hearth seemed to sizzle. Absently, she wondered whether her clothes were flammable.

'I made up with Naomi…' she said to him, beginning weakly, shaking the macabre thoughts away, trying desperately to bring him back, to slip into their routine.

Her grandfather's words of comfort did not come. He was gone.

She ran upstairs, pulled out the clippings from their hiding place and then threw them across the room angrily. 'I can't do this alone, Deda! Not without you!' she cried, breaking down into sobs.

After a long cry, sitting in the middle of the scattered paper, she pulled herself together and pushed the cuttings back inside the mattress. But as she was closing the bedroom door, feeling a little lighter, she had an idea.

Kneeling at the bed again, she unhooked the corner of the sheet and partially pulled the cuttings out of the slashed opening, leaving their edges poking through. Might this be a way of revealing the truth to Naomi, without making a hash of telling her? It would be like leaving an email open on a laptop or a letter lying on top of a packed bag.

As Sophie remade the bed and smoothed the duvet flat, she imagined Naomi's curious fingers stumbling on the articles. If the truth slipped out, Naomi couldn't blame Sophie for that. Naomi was certain to think it noble of Sophie to have attempted, at the very least, to keep their secret forever, to have tried to protect Naomi from it.

CHAPTER NINE

I rustled inside the supermarket bag and lifted out a selection of cleaning fluids, cloths and bin bags, having agreed to help Sophie clear out her grandfather's cottage. Deep down, I was feeling resentful. Her pleas of innocence about Harley's disappearance had been convincing, but I still harboured a pinch of scepticism. I had known her to lie before.

'Start in my old bedroom,' Sophie said.

'I was going to do the bathroom first.'

'You do the bedroom. It'll be like memory lane.'

'Okay,' I shrugged, happy to escape toilet-cleaning. 'If you're sure.' I snapped on my rubber gloves. 'Here goes,' I said, grabbing the bathroom cleaner and the furniture polish and sticking two bin bags into my back pocket.

'Let me know if you find anything interesting.'

'Ha. Yes. Should I be scared?'

She closed her eyes and breathed in. 'This is going to be hard for me.'

I touched her shoulder and said, 'Yes, I know. Let me know if you want to stop. I can take over any time you like.'

Popping her pastel eyes open, she said, 'Deda will not want strangers in his house.'

Indignantly I replied, 'I'm not a stranger.'

'Not you. The people who'll be renting it.'

'They'll solve all your financial problems, Soph.'

'I know. But Deda will make his presence known, believe me.'

I checked her expression to see if she was serious. In the harsh stream of sunlight, her delicate lips had turned a purplish hue and her hair was blanched.

'Have you seen him?' I whispered, feeling my heartbeat speed up.

She pointed the nozzle of the kitchen cleaner at me and pulled it, spraying me. 'I was kidding. He's dead, you nincompoop. Next you'll be looking under his bed for creepy clowns.'

I ducked from the burst of liquid that disintegrated into the air. I laughed. 'Oh, shut up. See you in an hour for a cuppa.'

'Or something stronger,' she winked. 'And don't forget to strip the bed,' she added.

Upstairs, I peeked round the door to the bathroom and then the two bedrooms, stopping at Sophie's old room, where she had insisted I begin. I opened the door. It was exactly the same as it had been back then. Blu-Tack had not been left on the walls, nor were there yellowing strips of sticky tape. Unlike every other teenager I knew, there had never been any posters on Sophie's bedroom walls.

I walked in and over to the desk by the window, which looked out on to the back garden. A spotty-patterned ring binder folder was lying open on the desk. I leafed through pages of her unintelligible essays and caught words and doodles in my own handwriting. Aimlessly, I looked inside the drawers. The study cards and pen cartridges and old rubbers were as familiar to me from our university days as my own possessions might be. For twenty years, they had not been touched. It seemed that she had clung to these old things, these old memories. In her reluctance to clear out this cottage, she had held onto her grandfather for a while longer. It seemed she had clutched to her heart every single detail of both her past and his, and, strangely, as I felt it now, my past, too.

The pine bed was the same. The duvet cover and pillow set was the same red and grey zigzag pattern she had covered her bed

with at university. I had slept under it once. My stomach turned
and I backed out, closing the door firmly.

Instead, I would start in her grandfather's bedroom.

As I entered, I tried to pretend I was not scared of seeing her
grandfather's ghost.

To busy my fidgety fingers, I began by stacking the photographs
on his dresser, noting that they were dust-free. He could have died
yesterday, rather than last year.

Many of the photographs were of Sophie when she was
younger. How beautiful she had been. There was a blurred snap
of both of us as nineteen-year-olds standing on a beach in the
Highlands of Scotland, where her grandfather had taken us on
holiday one summer. It had been a happy week of ice-cold swimming, gritty sandwiches and toasted teacakes; innocent, childish
exploits after a year of heavy drinking and partying at university.
The bad living showed on me, but not on Sophie. I looked blobby
and frizzy next to her. Sophie's blonde strands whipped across
her blue eyes, and her long, skinny legs were crossed at the ankle.
Physically untouched by our hedonism, her willowy elegance had
been enviable. She could have floated down a catwalk in Paris and
the world would have been transfixed. When I thought of her,
downstairs, I realised that there was a listless, sucked-out quality
to her now that hadn't been there when we were young.

I scooped out her grandfather's vests and pants and shirts,
which were folded neatly in the drawers, and filled the first bin
bag. The bags were like black holes, swallowing his existence. It
seemed impersonal and undignified.

There were traces of mouse droppings in the wardrobe near his
polished brogues, but otherwise his woollen jackets and trousers
were hanging, clean and ironed, ready to be worn today. A collection of shirts was under plastic with the dry-cleaning label pinned
onto one sleeve. At first I thought it sad that he had dry-cleaned
them and never had the chance to wear them, but when I checked

the date on the pink ticket, I noticed that collection was for January this year. I couldn't understand why Sophie had wanted to dry-clean them eight months after his death.

The wire hangers clanged as I brought down his last jacket. A pair of gloves dropped out of the pocket. They were the old-fashioned ivory crochet and leather driving gloves that Sophie had often worn at the wheel of his blue Alfa Giulia. She had said she felt like Grace Kelly when she drove in them. Automatically, I put them on.

I thought of the Giulia in the garage, hugged by that overlarge red rhododendron bush, and a thread of ice ran up my spine. If I pushed my final memory of that car aside, a flood of fonder memories of our long road trips to and from Exeter came to mind. I could smell its plastic seats and hear the music blaring, and taste the crisps and Coca-Cola we would consume in large quantities, arriving at this cottage – my home-from-home – too full to eat her grandfather's strange Russian food.

My own parents had been too far away in North Essex to visit during term time. And if we had ventured there, we would have been fussed over too much. Endless orange segments would have been cut up onto plates by Mum – as though university might produce scurvy – and our knickers would have been picked up the second they were dropped. She had never recognised my adulthood, and I would have been embarrassed about her fretting in front of Sophie.

I buttoned up the gloves at the wrist, remembering the few times Sophie had allowed me to drive the Giulia: how loose the key was in the ignition, how stiff the handbrake was, how noisy the engine. Driving it fast had been the antidote to my mother's caution and control; a rebellion against her mollycoddling, a determination to break out, to find my own footing in the world. Shooting back and forth along the South Coast, with the window rolled down and the wind in our hair, Sophie and I had been free and independent. We had been a tight unit of two, scrabbling through our experiences together, bumping into trouble, crawling out of it, self-sufficient and sexually powerful.

'Naomi?' Sophie called up. 'Come down for some sustenance! And bring the bed sheets!'

I tugged the gloves off, stuffed them in my back pocket and ripped off her grandfather's bed sheets.

Laden with laundry, I went downstairs and into the sitting room. My heart sank when I saw the two shot glasses and a bottle of vodka that sat on a plastic tray on the floor.

'Is my bed linen in that pile?' she asked.

'I haven't done your bed yet.'

'No problem. After a drink then,' she said, waving her hand in the air.

I pointed at the shot glasses. 'Vodka at ten in the morning? Seriously, Sophie?'

'Babe, my grandfather was a true Russian. I want to say goodbye to this house and all my memories of him in style. He would have wanted it that way.'

She poured two shots. Out of respect for her grandfather, and out of sympathy for Sophie, I decided I could not refuse. I dropped the sheets in the corner, laid the gloves on top of my phone, took the shot glass from her. We sat opposite each other, cross-legged in front of the five-bar heater.

Holding her vodka up and nodding at the gloves, she said, 'Deda was the one who fixed the car.'

In my imagination, the ashes in the urn on the mantel re-formed into his person. He was standing behind me, over me, around me.

I placed my drink on the floor and rasped, 'But he was so ill.' The fear of that night I could taste even now, but very few facts came to me.

Sophie lowered her glass. 'We didn't have the money to take it into a garage.'

'Did he blame me?' I whispered.

Sophie looked away, almost in disgust, which I accepted, penetrated again by the sticky shame I had tried to slough off many years ago.

'He never judged.'

She closed her eyes before shouting, '*Za vashe zdarovje!*' and knocking her drink back.

I braced myself. 'Cheers,' I winced, sucking back the silky, thick liquid, feeling the burn on my throat, rasping like a novice. The instant hit was like an adrenaline rush, shooting me backwards to the days when I would live for this feeling: instantaneous escape, seeking absolute oblivion.

There was a slide of vodka up my throat. I swallowed, saying, 'I'm so sorry you and Evgeni had to deal with all that without me.'

'It was a long time ago.'

'I feel so bad that you had to care for him on your own.'

She ran the tip of her finger across the rim of her glass. 'I quite enjoyed his chemo days,' she said.

My eyes widened.

'Not because he was suffering,' she clarified. 'But I'd sit with him while he was on the drip and we'd chat or I'd read to him. I had him all to myself. And nothing else mattered except him getting better.'

'I should have called more often,' I said, sheepishly, remembering the challenging logistics and expense of making payphone calls from Thai islands, and how the days rolled into one another, and how selfish and nomadic and thoughtless I had been.

'He survived it, and I got another twenty years out of him.' She was trying to sound upbeat.

'You must miss him so much.'

She hung her head. 'I do. Very much. I don't want to let go of him. Or any of his stuff. Not even this horrible chair.'

I stared at her picking the stuffing out of the moth-eaten, stained armchair and remembered how her grandfather had sat in it and inspected us before we went out for the evening, making sure our legs or tummies were not on show. Always, he would insist on having a drink with us before we left and would pour us half a shot of vodka, while he told us stories from his past. They had been fascinating tales of struggles far removed from our sheltered peacetime lives, of how he and his two sisters had escaped Soviet Russia, and how his beautiful older sister had worked as a secretary at British American Tobacco in Shanghai to pay for their food and rent.

'I loved your grandfather's stories.'

'He should have been embittered by all that sadness,' Sophie said, sounding bitter herself.

'He never seemed that way.'

'Did he ever tell you the story about how his father died?'

'I'm not sure.' I trawled my memory, unable to remember.

'He was an alcoholic who drank meths secretly in the shed at the bottom of the garden and one day there was a fire and he burnt to death.'

'That's horrible!'

'The rumour was that his wife – my great-grandmother – killed him by locking him in.'

I stared aghast at Sophie, whose face was turned to the hearth, orange from the ugly bar heater.

'She got away with it?' I asked, swallowing.

Sophie shrugged. 'I suppose so. She never went to prison.'

'Wow. You have a black widow in the family.'

'It's not like I ever knew her.'

'No, of course not.' I laughed. 'But that's quite dark, as family histories go.'

'Most people don't know their family history.'

I thought about my own dull ancestors. My father had come from a long line of insurance brokers and my mother from a wealthy Northern construction family whose funds had dwindled by the time she was born.

'My family was too boring to have any shocking stories.'

'Until you came along.'

I laughed to cover my alarm. 'What do you mean?'

'Nothing. You're as white as snow.'

Rattled by what she was implying, I poured two more shots. 'I am indeed.'

'Tell me what you found in my room!' she cried, slapping her thighs.

'Actually, I started in your grandad's room.'

She seemed disappointed, or angry, and she slammed her glass down. 'Another.'

'No way! We've got the school run later.'

'I've asked Adam to collect all the kids. He said he'd take them for hot chocolates and bring them back here later.'

'You never mentioned it,' I said, surprised and a little irritated.

'I have now.'

'But I need to tell the school.'

'Call them.'

The effects of the first shot were already seeping through me.

'I'd better email them instead. I think I'm already slurring,' I snorted, composing an email, shoving my guilt aside, just this once. 'All done.'

'We need some tomato juice and a stick of celery like the old days,' she said.

'Oh, I miss those old days,' I said, feeling nostalgic suddenly, enjoying the tingles of my altered state. 'I don't remember ever having hangovers, do you? Now, I just have to sniff wine and I have a hangover the next day.'

At university, Sophie had taken me to all the best parties, in sticky pubs or on chilly beaches, where we had drunk wine and danced with boys. She, with a cool detachment; I, with too much attachment. But she had always picked up the pieces for me when I was too drunk at the end of the night. There had been a strange cycle to our friendship. We were a bad influence on each other, and we looked out for each other. She pushed me out, where I wanted to go, and I pulled her back to me, where she wanted to be. My inability to cope with the dangers of the world, thanks to Mum, was both exacerbated and cured by Sophie's influence. Sophie's desire to be the leader, to be in control, was both facilitated and challenged by my naivety.

'I admire how you sorted your life out after uni,' she said, as though present in my head, pouring two more shots. 'Now you're so… you've got it all worked out.'

Before I took up the shot glass, I hesitated, unsure of how to take her so-called compliment.

'Cheers to moderation,' I said defiantly, knocking back the drink, questioning how I had turned it around, questioning myself.

I remembered back to the bold red-and-black arrow on a graph in the documentary that Charlie had forced me to watch, many years ago, before the children. The nasty arrow, arching across the plasma screen and burning itself onto my retinas, had illustrated how easy – natural, almost – the slide from heavy drinking to problem drinking to full-blown alcohol addiction could be. A guilty feeling had sloshed around along with the Merlot I had been drinking. Then Charlie had pointed at the screen, 'You're there,' he had said, tapping at the heavy-to-problem-drinking stage of the graph. I had told him to fuck off.

'To moderation,' Sophie grinned, taking a sip from her drink with her little finger sticking out as though it were a sherry glass.

I laughed and then she gulped the rest back in one go and held the bottle poised above my glass. I shot my hand out.

'But I've still got your bedroom to do. I need to be able to see straight.'

'We'll do it together, drunk as skunks,' she said, moving my hand away and pouring.

The back of my head was lolling from side to side on the hard floor. I focused on the cracks in the ceiling. Lying here, doing nothing, letting my limbs flop about and my thoughts mellow and my worries dissolve, I was more relaxed and amused than I had been for months. Like a hallucination, the ceiling began bulging out towards me, closer and closer to my face, like a giant rising sponge cake. I laughed, screwed up my face, turned my head and met with Sophie's face. She stared at me and stuck her gloved finger in my dimple.

'Sometimes when you smile, your dimple doesn't dimple. That's when I know you're faking.'

'I don't fake smiles!'

'Yes, you do. Everyone does.'

I giggled. 'It's annoying you know me so well.'

'Let's go and see the car,' she said, jazz-handing the gloves in my face and pulling me up to sitting.

'Nooo,' I cried. 'Nooo. I don't want to.'

The inebriation was a comforting place to be, away from bad thoughts. I had no desire to rake up the past. It would be like picking at scabs that weren't ready to come off.

'Come on. It's all fixed up. Come on,' she said, physically dragging me by the arm.

I stumbled behind her, complaining.

The hit of cold air from outside almost stopped my heart, reminding me for a lucid, depressing second that sobriety was around the corner, reinforcing my reluctance to see the car.

The heavy side door clanged and scraped open, like fingernails down a blackboard, and I put my hands to my ears and ground my teeth together.

Sophie clicked on the light switch. The gloominess of the garage was accentuated by the bulb's dim glow. Cobwebs broke on my face as we edged around the Alfa Giulia. Sophie stopped to touch the steering wheel and glanced back at me, looking embarrassed, as though she had been caught brushing her hand over someone's thigh.

Sandwiched in between the wall and the blue car – the car that had taken us on so many journeys together – I was struggling not to sway and trying hard to focus.

'Come on, get in,' she said.

'We can't drive it! We're too pissed!'

'We're not going to *drive* it,' she said.

She climbed into the driver's seat. I opened the passenger door to see that she had pushed the passenger seat forward. 'Get in the back.'

'No,' I said, pulling the seat upright.

She pushed it back again. 'Come on. For old time's sake.'

I climbed into the back seat and perched awkwardly in the middle, leaning forward as much as possible, feeling instantly claustrophobic.

Sophie elbowed me in the ribs. 'Sit back,' she said, turning on the ignition.

'Don't turn it on!'

'It's okay, I left the side door open!'

The exhaust fumes became thick in the car as she revved. My stomach rolled slowly over, the vodka sloshing. I swallowed, pushing down the shoot of liquid that rose up my throat. 'I need to get out. I'm going to be sick,' I said, gulping away the saliva pooling in my mouth.

Sophie reached over to press down the lock.

'Don't, Soph,' I groaned. I had to lie down across the back seat.

She switched on the radio. 'Deda said I should turn the engine over every now and again.'

A love ballad blared out from the car speakers. Sophie sang a couple of lines at the top of her lungs before changing the station. Loud grime pulsed through the seats. She began dancing, swaying her arms, hitting the roof.

The car rocked. My head was splitting. The plastic seats stuck to my cheek. I remembered falling off the back seat.

The rain. The music. The thud. The jolt.

My body rolled into the footwell. My nose was squashed onto the floor of the car behind the passenger seat.

'Ouch. What? That hurt,' I rasped, winded by the dividing hump between the two footwells.

'Shut UP!' Sophie yelled.

I twisted round, rubbing my face, feeling my hands damp with sick and sweat.

'Stay there,' she said.

My head pounded. I closed my eyes, wanting to sleep forever.

When she returned to the driver's seat, I mumbled, 'What happened?'

'We must have hit a deer,' she replied, pushing down the handbrake, pulling away.

'No!' I wailed, beginning to cry, noticing that the windscreen was cracked in the top left-hand corner.

'It's okay. He didn't suffer.'

'No, no, no. Let me get out! Please!' I cried. I began to cough, inhaling the fume-laden air in sickening gulps, closing my eyes. But my head swam. 'I get what you're trying to do! I was to blame, wasn't I? I was behaving like an idiot and I distracted you.'

She switched off the music and there was a sudden quiet. I opened my eyes. She was looking down at me.

'Yes, Naomi. That is exactly why that dumb animal died.'

I looked away. Tears trickled down the seat, just as they had that night after impact.

The car moved away. The carcass was left behind, dying a slow, lingering, tortured death. 'We have to go back,' I cried.

'Stop whining. Let me think.'

'We must go back to check.'

'No. We can't go back.'

I released a sob. 'We can't leave it there.'

She twisted round. 'D'you want to break his neck? Do you? Could you do that with your bare hands? Could you?'

I reeled from her fury, flopping back into the seat, drunken and useless, closing my eyes to the fractured glass, the backdrop to her silhouetted form. I felt a wave of remorse. Time would not turn back for me and I cried; cried for myself and for Sophie and for the thing that we had left to die by the road.

Then the engine cut out and Sophie's smell pervaded my head, her smoky fingers and her damp palm stroking my cheek.

'Shush, shush. It's okay. I'm going to sort this out for us,' she had whispered.

I stared down at the dividing hump between the two footwells and remembered the pain in my ribs and the bruising, and how my forehead had been cut by the window-winder. On the plane to Bangkok, a few days later, my body and mind had been broken.

'It was a horrible night,' I shivered.

She snorted. 'Don't feel bad. People hit deer all the time. It's no big deal.'

I sat up, wiping my eyes, suddenly alert to her change of tone.

'The near miss scared me shitless, Sophie!' I cried. 'We could've had a much worse accident that night. I risked your life and mine by being a complete idiot. By being so fucking drunk all the bloody time. We could've died!'

Speaking of it, of my culpability, was as if a cork had been unplugged from my chest, as though my heart was beating for real, for the first time in years. The two decades between now and then had a veneer over them, polished and beautiful but designed to cover over the cracks and flaws. That night had been a turning point in my life, a ground zero. My recklessness had shocked me. There had been no conscious desire to die; there had been no conscious desire to live. I had never wanted to feel that way again.

'We didn't die,' she said, switching off the engine, just as she had that night. She reached back to stroke my cheek, soothing me with her calm voice, her hair tickling my nose. She did not smell of smoke as she had done back then; she smelt of cleaning fluids and petrol. 'Did something else happen before? At the party, I mean?' she whispered, with that gentle voice that drew the truth out, and, as always, I fell under its spell.

'No.'

'Come on, you can tell me.'

I lay there, still, for a few woozy moments, until my confession came up from the depths of me.

'I let that loser – what was his name? You see, I can't even remember his name.'

'Jamie?'

'No. Not him. The one with the horrible teeth. He lived in Will's house, with Debbie. What was his name?'

'Matt?'

'That's the one. I shagged him in the loos.'

'He was *disgusting*.'

Letting that revolting boy fondle and touch me had been like taking a knife and cutting at my own skin to feel pain. Neither emotionally engaged nor numb, I had enjoyed the euphoria of sex, then the disgust and the shame. I had deserved it. Yes, I had deserved his snuffling mouth over my breast and his vile secretions dampening my knickers.

'Why did I do that?' I whispered, massaging my fingers, crushing them together, trying to bring them to life.

Sophie looked me straight in the eye and said, 'Because of what happened to you.'

My whole body stiffened. I had goaded her for an honest answer, but I loathed her for answering honestly.

'I don't ever want to talk about that,' I said. I did not want to be that girl any more.

I clambered out of the car, managing to reach the rhododendron bush before throwing up. My guts heaved and twisted as I expelled our conversation, expelled her answer. I hadn't been looking for a real answer.

As I wiped my mouth and stood up, I saw the metal of Adam's car flash through the trees and swing into the drive.

The girls! I remembered. *They can't see me like this!*

It was too late. They were jumping out and racing over to me.

'Are you okay, Mum?' Diana asked, looking down at the pool of slimy sick at my feet.

'Sorry, girls. I'm not feeling too well. I think I must have eaten something funny.'

Adam approached. The hotness inside me clashed with the chill across my skin.

'Hi Naomi,' he said, more as a question, as though I wasn't recognisable in my current state. He removed his sunglasses, squinting at me.

'Don't come any closer,' I insisted, putting my hands up, worried that he would smell the vodka and see the tremor that had broken out across my flesh. 'I might've come down with some grim vomiting bug.'

He smirked, clearly cottoning on. 'Where's Sophie?' he asked, glancing behind me at the house.

My brain rattled as it sought an answer.

'We were just... er... looking at the... at her grandad's car.'

The three children stood by Adam's side with puzzled expressions. Dylan's small, wet mouth had a crook at its edge, as though he knew more than the girls. He scratched at his elbows.

'Hi, kids!' Sophie cried, stalking out of the garage, wiping her hands on a chamois cloth, looking sober and bright. 'Just cleaning the car so we can sell it.'

I noticed a twitch in Adam's eyebrow. 'Oh, yes?'

'Want to stay for tea, girls?' Sophie asked, opening her arms for Dylan's embrace.

I thought of her bedroom, which still needed clearing out. I couldn't stomach it. I was about to remonstrate when Adam saved me. 'No. Sorry girls,' he said. 'We can't this evening. Another time, maybe.' He looked straight at me. 'Come on, I'll take you and the girls home. I imagine you might feel too... ill to drive?'

While dying of humiliation, I was humbled and grateful that he was here as a sober, sensible grown-up to scoop us up and take us home. 'Thanks, Adam,' I said.

Having started off today with the intention of helping Sophie, of sorting her out, I was ending the day as a snivelling, vomiting burden.

'I'll walk over at some point and collect the car,' I said.

'How will you get the girls to school tomorrow morning?' Adam asked me.

'Charlie's taking the train up to Manchester for a conference tomorrow. We can use his car.'

None of us spoke for the rest of the journey. It was unlike Adam and I to drop the show; the two of us were the chatty, personable contingent of the foursome. Strangely, the girls didn't talk either. In spite of my vomiting bug lie, they knew something wasn't right. *I* knew something wasn't right. This had not been a boozy lunch or a birthday breakfast drink. This had been sad drinking. Inappropriate drunkenness. A depressing regression.

I stared out of the window, thinking of Sophie and how she attracted trouble, how I was attracted to her trouble. I had only wanted to help her. Helping her was not good for me. She wasn't good for me. But in spite of the splitting headache and the regret, I felt the tug of separation. If she was the only person in the world who connected me to my past, and understood who I really was, how could I ever let her go?

She was my unsuitable friend. My Achilles heel. She was the drink you reach for when you know you've already had too much.

CHAPTER TEN

Sophie's eyes were falling closed as she drowsily fumbled for the newspaper clippings in the mattress. She didn't feel drunk – she had chucked most of her vodka shots over her shoulder without Naomi noticing – but she felt tired and she was yawning every few seconds.

When she couldn't initially see the articles sticking out, she thought, for a second, that Naomi had found them without telling her, but it seemed they had been pushed back inside by the pressure from the fitted sheet.

Originally Sophie had enjoyed the idea of toying with Naomi, to tempt fate, to position her close to the evidence: *warmer, warmer, cooler, freezing, warmer, warmer, HOT!* Part of Sophie had truly wished that Naomi's never-still hands had felt inside the torn opening of the mattress to find them. But Naomi had been genuinely – endearingly – upset and vulnerable in the Giulia, and Sophie had felt bad for getting her drunk, for goading her, for forcing her into that confessional mood. Her openness had scared Sophie a little, as though she might have had more to tell than Sophie could have handled hearing.

Now Sophie lay down on the bed, curled up, with her right palm sticking out and lying upwards, open, sore, itching. The articles were right by her face. The smell of old paper reminded her of her grandfather's books.

If she fell asleep, she would dream. Her dreams always allowed Naomi to find her secret stash, but when she did, the newspapers would be blank. In her dreams, Jason Parker's face always faded to nothing. In her dreams, the event had been erased from history.

Dozing, she saw Naomi sticking her hand inside the mattress, and saw Jason Parker's face in full colour.

Her eyes popped open. She had drifted off. The crispy black-and-white pages had remained there next to her, untouched by anyone but her. The photograph in the article lay across her rash-covered palm.

She read it again, for the hundredth time:

THE EXETER DAILY

12th August 1999

EXETER: MOTHER APPEALS FOR HIT-AND-RUN DRIVER TO COME FORWARD

The mother of a young man found dead near the road-side in a suspected hit-and-run incident appealed to the driver to examine their conscience and come forward.

Jason Parker, 22, a student from Exeter University, was walking back from a party at the Stoke Cannon Inn at around 11.30 p.m. on 19th July, along Stoke Road towards Exeter.

Mrs Parker, 44, from Exeter, said, 'The driver might not have known that Jason was dead, or what or whom they had hit, and I'm appealing to that person – who would have been driving in the dark in bad weather – to come forward. If you are reading this, I'm begging you, please call the police so that me and my husband, and his brother, can move on and grieve for our beautiful son and brother.'

Mrs Parker reported her son missing two weeks prior to his body being found in a wooded area by the side of Stoke Road. A fellow student had mistakenly thought that Jason had left the party early, after a small altercation, by taxi to head back to Streatham Campus, where he lived as a student, taking his Bachelor of Science in Chemistry at Exeter University. The police made progress in their investigation when they discovered that Jason had failed to find an available taxi firm, and had possibly decided instead to walk back along Stoke Road when the party was over.

'When the police called round to tell me they had found his body, my life ended, too. I would not wish that moment on my worst enemy,' Mrs Parker said.

If you have any information please call Devon and Cornwall Police on 01428 444 222.

Sophie had information, for sure. But she doubted they still wanted it. After twenty years, his mother and his family would have made peace with his death. He had been dead for almost as many years as he had been alive. If she confessed now, their pain would resurface and they would relive their grief all over again. This was what she told herself. This was how she overrode her guilt. This was how she lived with herself.

But each flashback of the night itself, as and when it came, was infuriatingly short. More and more, she craved context and detail. She wanted to go back, to be there where it happened, play it out again, find a way to trigger new information and clear the black fog that had descended on her memory over time. And she knew exactly how she could do that.

Quickly, she shuffled away the clippings and stuffed them back inside the mattress.

She was going to drive to Exeter now. Like visiting the grave of a loved one, she would revisit Stoke Road, connect with her fading memory of that night.

Dylan was asleep. Adam was at home. She had sobered up enough to drive. She could make it there and back by morning, just as she had managed to do that night, all those years ago, in reverse, from Exeter to Surrey, with a cracked windscreen.

She nipped back inside the house and grabbed the Saab car keys. The shack was dark and she guessed Adam had gone to bed.

As she drove, the radio DJ spoke in low tones, reflecting how spooked she was by her thoughts and by the hoot of owls and the snake of lonely roads.

The twists and turns of tarmac fell beneath Sophie's wheels and she began to feel drowsy. The radio was beginning to grate on her. She switched it off, deciding to replace it with her own cheerier playlist. With one arm, she rummaged in her bag to find her phone and realised, with a sting of regret, that she had left it at home. The sense of aloneness was magnified by its absence.

She stopped off to get some coffee, returning to her car reinvigorated by the hit of caffeine. Thoughts of what she would find at her destination buzzed through her mind as she retraced the route instinctively. But the drive was taking longer than she remembered. Or it *felt l*onger. Back in the day, the time had floated by without any urgency attached, taken up by gossip, junk food and dance music. If only she could go back to those carefree days.

Three whole hours of endless catseyes later, Sophie spotted the signs to Exeter. Faced with red lights, she was tempted to ride on through the ghost town junctions, just as she and Naomi had done in the 1990s, when there had been few surveillance cameras. Now, she sat waiting, being a good girl, but impatient for them to change, impatient to get there.

When she turned into Stoke Road, near to the Stoke Cannon Inn, her impatience flipped to fear. She slowed the car, crawling along at ten miles an hour, wondering if she should U-turn and head back the way she came. Before she could decide, she saw the pub up ahead on the right. She remembered the revellers that night, how bright and alive and busy it had been. As she drove past, she could see that it was boarded up. Rusted metal barriers had been bolted to the windows and the white walls had been scrawled with graffiti. There was a FOR SALE sign hanging lopsided from the low stone wall where they had often sat, waiting for cabs.

She drove on, leaving what had once been the Stoke Cannon Inn behind her. Its decrepit state was a bad omen. The fun was long forgotten. Her past had been boarded up, spoilt and left to ruin.

That pivotal night was blooming in her mind.

She retrieved snippets of how rubbed-raw and laden-down she had felt as she had driven along this very road, in the rain, at fifty miles per hour, all those years ago. Only a few weeks previously, Deda had been diagnosed with stage three pancreatic cancer. The possibility of his death had made her angry. She had wished that Suzanne could die instead. She had wished that Naomi would not fly to Bangkok. Both potential losses had raged through her that night. The prospect of being abandoned and alone had been pent-up inside, making her ill. If she had been sharper, less fixated on Deda's and Naomi's departures, perhaps the accident would never have happened.

Then she thought about Jason Parker's eyes, and of Naomi's drunkenness: singing and dancing, vomiting and kicking. Naomi's messy state of mind had cancelled out her own. Any driver would have struggled to remain focused.

A car's headlights flew by, bringing Sophie back to the present. The arch of trees above her formed a tunnel into hell. She recognised the bend to the left up ahead, roughly ten minutes along from the pub. The lay-by was approaching on the left. On the right was the

River Exe. The footpath that veered off from the road and down to the river was signposted. This was the marker she had been looking for. It was directly opposite where Jason Parker's body had landed.

She screeched to a stop, blasted by a vivid memory: the thud of his body, the smell of the wet road, the wail from Naomi.

Holding back a scream, she restarted the car and parked up in the lay-by. As she got out of her car, she clicked on her torch, holding it with two hands to steady the shake of her muscles. Its beam jittered across the uninviting surroundings.

The walk to the forked tree in the dip was fraught with brambles and tangled undergrowth. A broken branch tripped her up. As she recovered herself and brushed herself down, another car's headlights illuminated the tree that she was heading towards, highlighting a small flash of bright colour sticking out of the ivy that smothered its trunk.

She could hear her own shallow breaths as she clambered over to take a closer look.

Her stomach swelled when she saw what was pinned to the tree.

There was a handwritten note, brand new behind a clear plastic cover, nailed to the tree, with a fresh bunch of flowers tucked into a ribbon that was tied around the trunk.

She read the note:

March 22nd, 2019

In remembrance of my beloved son, Jason, I write this plea, on this day, twenty years after his death, to the person who killed him.

Today would have been his 42nd birthday. Instead of celebrating with him, I am in as much pain as I was on the day I found out he had been taken from us.

This letter is to you, the guilty one, who took my boy from me, to tell you that I am unable to rest, that I am unable to live on until I can see the regret and remorse in your eyes, to know that you will be punished for walking away and leaving my son to die by this roadside. You are living your life with no thought of us, with a future – possibly looking at your own children's future with hope – but you took that future away from Jason and you have taken hope away from our family.

See this photograph of him, look into his eyes, remember that he was loved and know that, every minute of every day, I wonder how you can live with yourself for leaving us in limbo for so long, for letting our grief fester with unfinished business. Your dishonesty continues to ruin more lives than you can imagine.

Please, if you have a heart, be brave enough to step forward, face the consequences of your actions and end our suffering.

Ilene Parker

Sophie's diaphragm jerked, forcing a dry retch. She pressed her hand to her closed mouth, swallowing repeatedly, but her insides fought to expel her horror.

The letter made Sophie confront the misery she had inflicted on Ilene Parker, whose grief had been sustained and heightened by her cowardice.

She scrambled back to her car, bent double with the cramping in her guts, tasting salt in her mouth from escaped tears.

As she started the car, she could barely see, and the irony of her decision to drive while distressed was not lost on her. But she had to get away. If Ilene Parker had been here so recently, if she still lived nearby, if she had seen a car parked up here, she might guess it was the perpetrator, that the car belonged to the 'guilty one'.

As she drove, the blisters on her right palm burst under the pressure of her grip. She edited the letter, in her mind, to include two guilty parties. There was Naomi, whose life was how Ilene Parker described, with a future and a clear conscience, and then there was Sophie's, whose future had not been depicted in the letter with any accuracy. In truth, Sophie's future had been snatched from her the moment Jason's body had hit her windscreen. She had not got away with it. All of her dreams for her future had been warped and curtailed, dwarfed further as time went on by the magnitude of her secret. The effects of keeping it hidden had been insidious, allowing the contrast between her life and Naomi's to grow more pronounced by the day.

By protecting Naomi from the truth, Sophie had settled for vicarious happiness while Naomi's dreams had been realised in full colour. Through Naomi, she had a view from the sidelines of how life might have been. But Sophie could not continue to bear the brunt of the blame any longer. Unconsciously, she had carried it like a burden for two decades, and it had finally made itself felt. And she was angry. Angry with Naomi in a way she had never been before. The accident had been Naomi's fault, but Sophie was the one whose life was in tatters. It wasn't fair. It just wasn't fair.

CHAPTER ELEVEN

Harley's wagging tail flicked my face as I poured his food into his bowl. I crouched down to his level and asked him, straight up, 'Can you take the girls to school for me today, Harley?'

I was trembling, dry and sick with a hangover, and I worried about being pulled over on the school run for an alcohol breath test. If Charlie had been here, he would have dropped the girls off and picked them up, as he did every Friday.

After a couple of headache pills and a strong coffee, I turned on Radio 4, took out the chopping board and laid out four pieces of bread for Diana and Izzy's packed lunch sandwiches. Before gathering the butter and ham and carrot batons from the fridge, I checked my phone, which I had left to charge overnight.

When I saw three missed calls from Adam, I instantly forgot about my hangover and the girls' packed lunches and called him back.

He answered before the first ring. 'Do you know where she is?'

I planted my bare feet squarely, feeling the need to ground myself.

'Sophie, you mean?' I asked inanely, my slow brain kicking into life. Harley looked up from his curled position on the rag rug under the breakfast table.

'She never came to bed last night, and she's taken the car and left her phone.'

My stance weakened and I rubbed my scratchy eyes.

'Where do you think she's gone?'

'Who the hell knows? That woman is a live wire. But I'm working in London today and I'm already late. Is there any chance I can drop Dylan with you now?'

'I'm here. I'll take him to school.'

He let out a long breath. 'Brilliant. You're a star. Thank you.'

'Do you want me to pick him up this afternoon, as well?'

'I'm bloody well hoping that Sophie decides to show up at some point,' he snapped, adding more gently, 'but yeah, thanks, can I put you on standby?'

'Sure.'

There was a pause while I waited for him to say goodbye.

'Is there any chance I could swing by for a quick chat this evening?'

'Charlie's in Manchester, remember?'

'I know. I wanted to talk to you about Sophie.'

'Yup. Okay.'

'See you then.'

I hung up and glugged down a tall glass of water. My reluctance to get involved in their marriage problems was overridden by Sophie's sudden disappearance and by the urgency of Adam's request. It was impossible to dismiss. As was she. As ever.

The picture of her dead by the roadside floated through my mind.

As the morning wore on, my worry became a spinning wheel that I couldn't slow down.

After the school run and Harley's walk, I allowed myself a half-hour nap. It was blissful respite. When I woke, I tackled an article for my column, but my heart wasn't in it. There were unopened cases of wine, delivered that morning, which needed tasting, but the thought of going anywhere near alcohol terrified me.

The fretting increased. I began checking my phone, thinking of places that Sophie might have disappeared to, returning again and again to the idea of Exeter as a destination.

She was eternally nostalgic about our years there, our friendship, our antics. I understood why. In those days, we had existed in an intense bubble, coming of age together, binding our souls, imagining that a life of such closeness could last forever.

A flash of being stuck in the Giulia came back to me. Recalling the fumes, I began coughing, and I abandoned my article, which involved too much thought. A selfie-shoot for Instagram would be a lightweight distraction.

I painted my nails burgundy and put on a burgundy jumper to match the Burgundy I was tasting. I framed it as a close-up of the glass – almost gagging at the smell – including only my lips, also Burgundy, and fingertips. The tight framing cut off my puffy eyes.

After I had messed around for an hour or so to get a decent photograph, Adam finally texted.

Hi Naomi – Sophie called. She's home. Won't tell me where she's been. No need to pick up Dylan. Thanks for being on standby. Adam

Flooded with relief, I hoped that Adam would now not want to drop round to talk about Sophie. I texted back, without mentioning it, keeping my fingers crossed.

Phew! What a relief. Thanks for letting me know. Nx

Is it still okay if I pop over tonight? Adam

What will you tell Sophie? Nx

Working late ;)

I felt shifty, and I hesitated before replying, wondering if I should insist he tell her. But I didn't.

See you then. Naomi x

Little would be gained by telling Sophie. It was a white lie that I could live with.

To Sophie, I texted:

Hi Sophie – where have you been? Call me. Nx

*

'Glass of something?' I asked Adam, shaking a bottle of Merlot at him, trying to be casual about the strange circumstances of our meeting. My hangover made his presence in my kitchen that much more surreal.

As I poured him a glass of wine and made myself a cup of herbal tea, the thought of his cheating set me on edge. Not because I worried he would make a pass at me, but because he was no longer in my camp as my best friend's loving husband. Overnight, he had become a free agent, or a man whose boundaries had shifted. I wasn't sure quite how to place him in the context of our friendship. Did I take a balanced view of their separation or a blinkered, moral stance on Sophie's behalf? Guessing how difficult she had been to live with, it was going to be a real challenge to do the latter, but that was how it had to be, whether Adam liked it or not. My loyalties to Sophie were unconditional, sisterly, as though we were bound as friends for life.

'Did you get it out of her?' he asked, taking a sip of wine, his eyes darting around the room as though Sophie might be lurking in the shadows.

'She hasn't called me back.'

He raised an eyebrow at me and batted his long eyelashes. 'Really?'

There was no doubt about it, Adam used his good looks to get what he wanted. He would guess that I desired him, as so many other women might. His guess was wrong. I could appreciate his olive skin and white smile, but his vanity spoilt both. He had the habit of tucking his hair behind his ears, or tying it into a bun, repeatedly and self-consciously; and I would have wicked thoughts of him brushing it like a schoolgirl in front of the mirror.

'Honestly, she hasn't.'

'That's a first.'

Sophie had not called me back, which I had been both relieved about and perturbed by. I assumed it was because she was embarrassed or ashamed, perhaps expecting me to scold her about her sudden disappearance, which I had no intention of doing. She judged herself harshly enough – she did not need me to add to the flagellation. But there was a question lurking still: where had she been, and why had she taken off in the middle of the night?

'She doesn't always call me straight back, Adam,' I said, dunking my teabag over and over, rooting through my mind for examples of when she hadn't and drawing a blank.

He scratched at his overlong sideburns. 'She's not herself, Naomi.'

'Do you blame her?'

Shifting uncomfortably in his seat, he lowered his long eyelashes. 'I'm really sorry about what's happened between us.'

'I'm not judging you.'

'You have no idea what it's been like. It's been so bad, especially since her grandad died.'

'She was bound to take it hard.'

'Go ahead, get it out, call me a cheating wanker.'

I shrugged. 'You're a cheating wanker.'

We smiled at each other.

'I'm worried about Dylan when I move out,' he said, more seriously.

'Oh, come on! There's nothing to worry about *there*.'

'That's what I used to think.'

I raised an eyebrow. 'Used to?'

'She left him on his own in the cottage last week.'

I opened my mouth to speak, prepared to defend her parenting, but I was flummoxed. 'For how long?'

'A couple of hours.'

'Why?'

'She wanted to go to a Pilates class before school.'

'Was it last Thursday?' I shot back.

'How'd you know?'

'I saw her there,' I said, but I was not going to elaborate.

'I wouldn't have given a toss if she'd popped out for five minutes for a pint of milk or something, but a Pilates class? For over an hour? The whole thing was plain wrong. Dylan was disturbed after.'

'Did she say why she left him at the cottage?'

'She said the security was better,' he scoffed.

'I suppose that might be true,' I said, knowing this was beside the point.

'Dylan told me she'd said "Grandad will look after you".'

I frowned. 'I'm sure she meant that he was looking *over* them still.'

He shook his head. 'No, it wasn't that. She told Dylan to be quiet so that he didn't wake him up.'

'Wake up her *grandfather?*'

He nodded, wincing. 'Dylan thought he'd come alive again. He was bloody terrified.'

I bit my lip, remembering the dry-cleaned suits and the dust-free frames in his room. 'Yes. I imagine he was.'

'And before you guys cleared out the cottage, she went round there every single bloody day, just like she did when he was alive. God knows what she got up to in there. She's gone sick in the head, I swear it.'

'His ashes are there. Maybe it was like visiting his grave.'

'She always smells of booze when she comes back.'

I blushed. 'I know all about that.'

He grinned. 'How are you feeling?'

'Not great. But I didn't want to say no to the idea of giving Evgeni a Russian-style send-off.' I sounded prim, which was laughable considering.

'Is that how Sophie justified it?' he snorted.

'The grieving process can last years. It's probably why she's drinking more. Especially if she hasn't fully come to terms with his death.'

Adam threw his head back. 'Naomi, babe, stop defending her! She's got a problem and you know it.'

I withdrew my hands from the table, where they had rested at the base of my mug.

He continued, 'Sorry, but come on, you're not helping her by sticking your head in the sand.'

'I'm just trying to see it from her point of view.'

'Think about it, she must have driven that car well over the limit last night. And where the hell did she go? She still hasn't told me.'

In my head I counted out the shots I had witnessed her downing and I wondered how she could have seen straight, let alone driven. Even hours later, the alcohol would have been coursing through her bloodstream.

'She hasn't told me either,' I said, tight-lipped, smarting from his outburst.

'Is she seeing someone?'

It was my turn to laugh. 'Another man?'

'To get back at me, I mean.'

'That's not her style.'

'So where was she, then?'

'Maybe she just needed to get away for a bit. Clearing out the house would have been seriously traumatic for her.'

'Yeah, right, clear her head and kill some poor innocent bugger on the road 'cos she can't see straight.'

My stomach flipped.

'It was bloody lucky she didn't,' I said, deciding to pour a tiny drop of wine into my drained tea mug.

'If she stopped with the booze, she'd be all right,' he said.

The wine seemed to solidify in my throat. 'Yes.'

He picked up his phone in response to a text alert. 'Speak of the devil. She wants to know what train I'm getting.'

'You should tell her where you are.'

He began texting her back. 'No way. I value my life.'

I laughed guiltily.

He stuck his phone in his back pocket. 'What if she's not okay, like, in a really serious way? Like she's…' he paused, then dropped his voice a notch, '*unstable*.'

'I think she's been under a lot of strain lately,' I said.

'When I think of Dylan on his own with her, it freaks the hell out of me.'

My fingers tapped my knees under the table. 'Dylan will be fine. She would never harm him. She dotes on him.'

'Naomi, you have to understand, I love the crazy cow, but I can't be with her a day longer, I can't do it. I've tried to reason with her about stuff, I've tried to help her. I've tried *everything*. But I can't do it any more.'

I felt for him. I understood. 'I understand.'

He looked up, with eyes rimmed red, and he slid his hand towards me across the table, reaching out. 'I need you to look out for my boy,' he pleaded. 'For me, Naomi. You're the only one I trust.'

A pang of genuine fear sliced through me and I placed my hand on his and squeezed it tightly. Understandably, Sophie could have viewed this as a disloyal act – my touch too intimate for the man who had scorned her – but I felt real affection for him, real sisterly affection.

'I promise I will. I really do promise.'

CHAPTER TWELVE

They had waited – she and Dylan – and they had waited, and Adam had not arrived. Dylan had sat in the front seat, panting like a dog at the car window, as the passengers filtered out from the most recent London train.

'Is this the one Daddy's on?' Dylan asked.

Sophie's sleep deprivation from her road trip to Exeter last night had given her an ache in the centre of her brain. The nap that she had taken in the car in a lay-by had only provided a few hours' sleep. Thoughts about her decision to confess to Naomi drilled their way through her mind, leaving gaping holes of self-doubt.

'I don't know, Dylan.'

'When will he be here?' he whined.

'I don't know.'

She had wanted to surprise Adam, make amends for disappearing last night. In his text he had said he was working late, that he would be home at ten or ten thirty. It took ten minutes to drive home from the station, which would mean he was either on the 21.02 train from Waterloo, arriving at 21.50, or the 21.16, arriving at 22.10.

Dylan banged the glass with his fist. 'I can't see him!'

Neither could Sophie. She checked her phone to make sure that she had not missed a text from him. If he had missed the train or decided to stay in London, he would have told them. He would never have let Dylan down.

Dylan unzipped his puffa jacket and shrugged it off to reveal his Spider-Man pyjamas. The smell of his hydrocortisone cream spread through the air.

'I'm hot!' Dylan cried, fiddling with the knobs on the car.

She pushed his hands away. 'Don't do that. I'll turn it down if you're hot.'

He returned to his spot at the window.

By a quarter to eleven, after an hour of waiting in the car, Sophie realised that Daddy was not coming.

She turned on the ignition. 'Come on. Let's go. Daddy lied.'

Sophie waited for the tears. Instead, Dylan began scratching his elbows, then strapped himself into the front seat again and said sulkily, 'I want to go to bed.'

Within minutes of leaving the station, her phone pinged with a text. Dylan read it out loud. 'It's from Daddy! It says, "I'm home! Where the hell are you?" Ooh, rude word, Daddy!'

'He's at home?'

'Can I text him back?'

'Tell him we'll be there in ten minutes.'

When she glanced over, she saw that Dylan was choosing angry emojis.

It didn't matter. It kept him busy for the drive so that she could think straight.

If Adam was at home, how had he got there? They had seen all the trains arrive at the station and his car was in the drive. Eager to find out, wondering if a driver from the job had taken him home, she sped through the lanes.

Dylan was asleep by the time she pulled into the drive.

The door to the shack opened. The silhouette of Adam was menacing against the warm glow from inside.

'It's almost eleven at night! Where the hell did you take him so late?' he shouted.

'Shush. He's asleep,' Sophie whispered angrily.

She heaved a floppy Dylan out of the car and carried him inside and into their bed. *Her* bed. It was technically Sophie's bed now.

Having tucked him in, she crept out of the room and closed the door, relieved that she would not have an arduous story time session ahead of her, grateful for the time she would now have with Adam to find out how he had made it home.

Before she went through to the kitchen, where she could hear the chink of bottles rattling from the fridge, she checked her reflection in the bathroom mirror. She pinched her cheeks to add some colour and ruffled her hair forward, satisfied that she looked passable, as scorned wives go.

She found Adam slumped forward on the sofa, scrolling through his phone with one hand, taking a gulp of wine with the other.

'You must be tired. I've prepared supper, if you want me to put it on,' she asked.

He snapped his head up and glared at her. His full attention startled her.

'Where have you been?' he hissed.

She poured her own glass of wine and curled up on the sofa next to him. Her toes kneaded his thighs, but he shuffled over, away from her. This tiny rejection enraged her.

She ground her back teeth together, grinding away the anger, before replying in her sweetest voice, 'We wanted to surprise you at the station. That's all.'

It had thrown him, she could tell. How could he be angry with her now?

'Sophie,' he said, leaning back, running his fingers through his beautiful black hair, 'It's not appropriate for kids Dylan's age to be out so late. You do understand this, don't you?'

'It was a one-off, Adam.'

He stole a glance over at her, and for a split second she could see the depth of his feelings for her. Whatever happened, she knew he would always love her more than he loved any other woman.

'Can you just promise me that you'll not go out with him that late again?'

'Sure.'

'And that you'll not leave him alone again?'

'Promise.' At this, she pulled her knees up to her chest and rested her wine glass on the top of one knee, balancing it there, seeing how long it would stay upright before she had to catch it. She yearned to retreat to her grandfather's house for something stronger, but she was resisting its pull, reminding herself of its emptiness.

'What happened to your hand?'

She looked at the bandage she had wrapped around the seeping rash. 'My eczema flared up.'

'Sorry,' he said, inexplicably. But it reminded her of what he was to blame for.

'What train were you on, again?' she asked.

'Why does that matter?' he said, reaching for his phone again.

'Tell me, I'm interested.'

'I caught the nine sixteen.'

'It's funny, we didn't see you.'

'Well, I was there.'

'I suppose it was dark,' she mused, humouring his lie, clearly remembering the ten or so passengers who had dribbled out of the station from the 21.16. 'And my eyesight isn't perfect.'

He stood up and stretched his arms in the air, feigning a yawn. 'I'm knackered. I'm going to bed.'

She watched his every move as he washed up his wine glass, left it on the draining board, plugged in his phone to charge and removed his slippers before climbing the ladder upstairs.

'Night,' she said, more to herself.

And she waited. And waited. Waited to hear the familiar noises of a sleeping man.

As soon as she heard his changed breathing, she checked his phone.

The photograph of Dylan shone from the screen. She typed in the code 197710, his birthday year and day. In the past, he had used this code. It didn't work. She tried Dylan's details, 201023. It didn't work. After three more attempts, she crept into her bedroom, where Dylan was sleeping, and sat on the edge of the bed.

She stroked his head, whispering, 'Dylan, sweetie, Dylan, wake up.'

His eyes flickered open, and then closed. Gently, she shook him. 'Wake up, poppet. Mummy needs you to do something really important.'

He mumbled, 'I'm too tired.'

Impatiently, she continued to harass him until he sat up and rubbed his eyes.

She shoved Adam's phone into his hands. 'Can you type in Daddy's code?'

'Why?' he said, too loudly.

'Keep your voice down.'

'Why?' he whispered.

'I want to surprise Daddy with something.'

'Surprises are stupid,' he said, flopping down and pulling his teddy into him.

'Come on. Wake up. Come on.' She prodded his ribs and he squirmed and whined, 'Go away, Mummy. I'm sleeping.'

Her exasperation got the better of her, and she yanked him by the wrist.

'Do as I say. Now,' she ordered.

'Ow,' he whimpered, rubbing his wrist. 'You hurt me.'

She was trembling with anticipation as she placed the phone into his hands. 'Do it. Or you won't get any pocket money for a whole month.'

'You hurt me, Mummy,' he repeated as he typed in Adam's code: 197715. It was her own birthday year and date.

'Thank you. Now you can go back to sleep,' she said, kissing him on the forehead.

He curled back under the duvet and she left him.

Her heart raced as she navigated her way through Adam's phone to his texts. She saw the name 'Nat' at the top of the list. She scrolled through their most recent exchange.

I hope it goes okay. Kisses. Can't wait to see you. More kisses xxxx

This shoot is never-ending. Wish you were the stylist. She's shit.

Miss you xxxxx

And on and on they texted each other. After reading three days' worth of inane interchanges, back and forth, back and forth, she gathered that Natalie was away on a shoot in South Africa this week, and that she was the more forthcoming between the two of them, in terms of feelings. She was always the one to start up the exchanges and always the one to end them with a 'miss you' or 'can't wait to see you', which were often met with radio silences from Adam. This heartened Sophie a little and set her mind whirring with hope, believing that Natalie might be expendable after all. As an amusing aside, she fantasised about a GIF depicting a man in Johannesburg approaching Natalie's car at the traffic lights, opening her car door, snatching her handbag and shooting her in the face. As it replayed over and over in her mind, Sophie smiled to herself.

The other text exchanges between friends and family were useless and tiresome. She moved on to WhatsApp.

The name 'Naomi' was at the top of the list of recent contact exchanges. Her brain scrambled. It must have been another Naomi. A friend or colleague of his. There was no photograph in the contact details. It read:

Is it still okay if I pop over tonight? Adam

What will you tell Sophie? Nx

Working late ;)

See you then. Naomi x

The mucus thickened in Sophie's mouth.

Images of Adam and Naomi flirting and laughing together hurtled through her mind. Until now, their connection, their friendship had enthralled her. She had been proud of having them both in her life; as though Adam endorsed her character in Naomi's eyes, as though Naomi affirmed her in Adam's eyes.

Considering everything she knew about Naomi's past, it may well have been naive to view them so simply. Naomi's drunken promiscuity at Exeter had been amoral, at best; indiscriminate certainly, disgusting often. By day, Naomi had been the goody-two-shoes who had sat at the front of the lecture halls listening earnestly. By night, she had slipped in and out of the shadows of the university party scene enticing men into her bed. Only Sophie had been privy to her dirty little secret: by witnessing the boys leaving, by seeing their clinches, by rescuing her from precarious situations, by hearing her guilty disclosures.

When Sophie tried to scroll further back into their text history, she found nothing. If she and Adam had met before in secret, there was nothing to prove it. If they had sent each other messages, they had been deleted. As she scoured Adam's phone for more evidence, she wondered whether Natalie had been the red herring, the plaything, while he and Naomi struggled with their consciences, secretly in love. Surely Naomi could not be capable of such treachery.

It was an unimaginable thought, initially, and she dismissed the whole idea, convincing herself it had come from a bent, sleep-deprived mind. Although she wanted to know why they had met in secret, wanted to hear their innocent explanation, the stress of finding out made her feel lethargic. She could not keep her eyes open.

She curled up on the sofa, pulled the rug over her and fell into a fitful sleep, to awake abruptly an hour later, after a series of nasty, disconnected dreams. Her paranoia began wheeling around and around her brain. As she struggled to sleep, as the night wore on, their secret meeting became a tryst, became an affair, became a certainty.

At three in the morning, she shot up from the sofa and searched the fridge for some wine, which she hoped would have a soporific effect on her. There wasn't a drop of alcohol anywhere in the house.

Overtired, overanxious, she grabbed Deda's keys and ran over to the cottage.

'Deda! Deda!' she cried, regretting her clear-out of the kitchen. He had been the voice of reason, and she needed to hear him now. But he was gone. The clear-out had killed him for the second time. There was a void, and the paranoid voices of old rushed in, gabbling and chattering and goading.

She flung open the kitchen cupboards, knowing she would find nothing, wishing she had not been so thorough, wishing that she had left just three items: the bottle and the two shot glasses. The tension tightened her muscles until she thought they might snap. She paced back and forth, not knowing where to take her mind, not knowing how to throw cold water on it.

She needed the milk-and-honey drip of Stolichnaya down her throat, or she feared the sparks of agitation would explode into panic. Her hands began to shake. Her heart rate sped.

'Deda?'

She squeezed her temples and paced, willing his voice. *Deda, please, come to me*, she thought.

'Deda? Deda? I've protected Naomi, and this is how she repays me? Is she that spoilt, that entitled? Can it be true?'

Hold her close, my Sophia.

'NO! I can't!' Sophie screamed.

He was gone again.

'Deda? Are you still there? I'm sorry. I'm so sorry! Please come back,' she whimpered.

She stumbled into the garage to get a sleeping bag and a futon that had been stored under the bench for years. There, she also found a secret stash of vodka, which was like stumbling on gold nuggets in a riverbed. All of it she carried into the cottage, and she rolled the damp bedding out onto the green carpet in the front room. She felt closer to Deda.

Shot by shot, she worked through the vodka and her confidence grew again. In fact, she felt greater than ever, greater than everyone else. Those dreams about flicking little humans away from her with her fingertips had come to her because she was fearless, all-powerful, misunderstood. Whatever setbacks she had experienced in life had been the fault of a world not ready for her, a backward-thinking culture of small-mindedness, taking their narrow paths of convention. She didn't fit in, which was a good thing. She didn't need anybody except Dylan. Children were survivors. They were strong. Unlike adults. Like Naomi and Adam, who were weak, working against her with their petty jealousies and inadequacies.

She wanted Naomi to feel hurt, just as Sophie was hurting, and she knew exactly how to get her just where it would hurt most.

She reached for her phone and opened up Facebook.

Although Sophie had her own account, she had not posted a personal photograph for a long time and had very few friends, but Naomi had thousands, and she knew that Naomi used the same password for all of her accounts: DianaIzzy0609.

It seemed an opportune moment to give Naomi's 'friends' a glimpse into the real Naomi, share the highlights, remind Naomi of their friendship, flood her with reminders of who they had once been.

In the corner of Sophie's old bedroom, which Naomi had failed to get around to clearing out, there was a wire drawer under the bed, which contained photograph albums and Kodak envelopes filled with old snaps from childhood and university. There was bound to be something interesting in there to post, some nostalgia to exploit.

It didn't take her long to find a photograph that perfectly highlighted their friendship.

It was taken outside a pub in the centre of Exeter, on a street corner. Sophie and Naomi were arm in arm. But not in that way that shows happy, twee closeness. The flash was cruel. Naomi's pale, fat thighs dimpled under her velvet hot pants, her t-shirt was covered in a wet patch across one breast; her spotty chin and forehead shone with sweat or spittle and her half-mast eyes were reddened, their focus gone. Beside her was Sophie, who smiled awkwardly at the camera as she held Naomi by the elbow. Aside from the red-eye, she was slim, well-dressed in low-slung, flared jeans, a tight T and large belt. Her white-blonde hair fell about her face in flattering wisps and her lips were newly painted pink.

She took a photograph of it with her phone. It came out blurred. Her hands weren't steady. Leaning her arms into the desk to hold them still, she managed to frame a clean shot.

For full impact, Sophie decided to create a new post for each photograph. The first of her jaunty captions read:

Throwback Saturday! When you're young and drink
too many Jack and Cokes... Sophie and I outside The
Swan in 1998! #exeteruniversity #bestdaysofourlives
#foreverfriends

The next post was of Naomi in a low-cut black minidress
with her arms looped around the shoulders of two young men in
tuxedos. She was laughing, looking beautiful with red lipstick and
diamanté earrings. The two young men had one hand clamped
to each boob. A little inkling of Naomi's floozy ways back then.

There were three others that she deemed suitable for posting.
One of Naomi sitting on the pavement, smoking, with her purple
knickers showing; one of Naomi on the dance floor of a nightclub
holding two shot glasses up to her eyes like spectacles; one of
Sophie and Naomi together, with Naomi sticking her middle
finger up and pulling an unpleasant face at the camera.

For each post she carefully worded her upbeat strapline. To
the casual onlooker, it would be an innocent nostalgia trip. Many
would relate to those hedonistic days of wild parties and too much
drinking. Less so for Naomi, whose wine blogging advocated
drinking in moderation; whose drinking problem had once led
to trauma.

The last post was of Naomi hugging Trey, the mild-mannered
Canadian boyfriend of Amelie, a friend of theirs. It had been an
innocent hug, but who knew?

Hugging Amelie's boyfriend! What was I thinking?!
#maneater #getaroom #handsoffmyman

Sophie's heart fluttered as she clicked the little blue button,
sending it from her private world, from the little bedroom
belonging to a nobody, into the public arena, where the whoring
of private moments is celebrated, where whole lives are seemingly

understood by a few cheap posts; where Naomi's past would become imprinted on her friends' minds. All of her previous close-ups of water droplets running down cold glasses of rosé, elbows on weathered picnic tables, postcard backdrops of harbours or cityscapes, would be effectively smeared with a greasy stain. These new posts would wipe dirt across her depiction of healthy drinking, would mar her airbrushed lifestyle.

When she saw her latest post pop up on her newsfeed, she reimagined the photograph with Adam in Trey's place, with Naomi's arms around Adam's neck, and her stomach heaved.

Watery sick lay in a puddle by her sleeping bag. She left it. All the energy had been sucked out of her, a sudden depressurisation, like a hole in an airlocked plane. She let her head fall back onto the cushion and passed out with her phone in her raw, weeping palm.

In the middle of the night, her brain had stirred her awake with nightmares in words, written across her eyeballs in blinking letters, snippets of Mrs Ilene Parker's letter:

See this photograph of him, look into his eyes... how you can live with yourself for leaving us in limbo for so long... Your dishonesty continues to ruin more lives than you can imagine... if you have a heart... face the consequences... end our suffering.

CHAPTER THIRTEEN

I had woken up feeling revived by a long, deep sleep and lie-in. Harley was a reassuring lump at the bottom of the bed, where I had let him sleep while Charlie was away. For a second, I wondered if Adam's unsettling visit had been a dream.

It had not been. And I lay there, thinking about Sophie. I wished I could talk it through with Charlie, who was due back home later today in time for our dinner party, which we had organised months ago.

Worries about last Thursday morning, when she had left Dylan alone, niggled at me. I was his godmother, I had a responsibility of care. And I loved him, in a way, despite how intense and awkward he could be. Sophie's smothering of him, and her babying, had ruined his naturally sweet nature. I believed that Adam's criticism of Sophie, his fears for Dylan, were real. As were the effects of Adam's own selfish actions on her state of mind. Deep down, he knew his affair had ripped their family apart and he could not face up to his own guilt. It was easier to label Sophie as the mad and unhinged wife than to accept that he was to blame for her distress, and, in turn, for Dylan's. Her heavy drinking was a normal reaction to the breakdown of a marriage, but it was not going to help her cause or Dylan's.

On the way downstairs, I could hear the girls' cartoons from the television room. I snuck past, allowing them more time to slouch around this morning, giving me more time to catch up on work and write the *Sky* article I had been unable to face yesterday.

Settled at the kitchen table with a strong coffee, I let out a heavy sigh, pleased that I had resisted another glass of wine after Adam had left last night, even though I had wanted it very badly.

No thanks to Sophie and her dramas, my head was clear, as was my conscience. I had not slipped backwards, regressing to the bad old days, when I would break my promises to Charlie, when one binge could lead to weeks of heavy drinking and vicious hangovers. I had not forgotten about that bold black-and-red arrow in the documentary, whose warnings I had refused to heed for so many years after viewing it. I had denied how often my boozy weekend lunches with Sophie had stretched into night-long binges; how the sneaky glass or three before the girls' bath time had eased the boredom of routine; how I had waited for Charlie to go to bed before opening the second bottle of weekday wine; how the Bloody Marys with my brunch on Sundays were not a choice but a need; how I had stood behind the fridge door and taken neat slugs from an open bottle for top-ups; how I had lied to my doctor to get a double-dose prescription of my PPI medication for my acid stomach; how all of my jeans had remained folded in the back of the drawer in favour of stretchy trousers. It had taken years before the message of the black-and-red arrow had hit home.

This morning, willpower intact, I watched the whirling cursor on my computer, wondering how I should address Sophie's drinking problem, which I had conveniently ignored for too long. As her closest friend, it was up to me to be the bearer of an uncomfortable truth, out of love, to save her from herself, just as Charlie had saved me from myself.

Before checking the newsfeed, I clicked into my Facebook notifications.

While the page loaded, I scrolled through the photographs on my mobile of the Burgundy wine selfies. I chose the best shot and turned back to my laptop, where I was amazed to see over fifty notifications waiting for me in response to one of my Facebook posts. My latest post had been three days ago, and I wondered why there was a flurry of responses now.

I was intrigued as I clicked into the earliest tagged notification.

A photograph sprang onto my screen and my insides lurched.

'Oh my god.' I clicked into the next one. 'Oh no, no, no.'

The ugly photograph was blurred by my tears as I clicked into the next post, and the next and the next. The images of my purple knickers and thick cellulite, my damp chin and nasty grimaces, my aggressive hand gestures and flirtatious antics made me sick to my stomach. I came to the last post of me hanging suggestively off the neck of Amelie's boyfriend – what was his name again? – which I had no recollection of. The hashtag suggested I was trying to steal him. I could not remember stealing this man from Amelie. But who could say? My memories of those three years at university were patchy, at best. It had been Sophie who had filled in the gaps, just as she was doing so effectively now.

The flesh on my face pulsed. Collectively, the photographs built an obnoxious bigger picture of me.

I began taking down each post, petrified that there were more to come.

I could not believe that Sophie had hacked into my account, that she could be so cruel. What had prompted her to do it? How much damage had she done already? It was ten in the morning, yet already there were so many comments. Some were friendly, others edgy. One comment, from an older man wearing a black roll neck, read: 'Any chance I could cop a feel of those too?' to which he had added a devil emoji. Another comment was from an Exeter student, whose name I vaguely recognised: 'Hello "Pint

O'Wine" Naomi!! Remember the lost hours in the park?!' She had included two winking emojis.

'Pint O'Wine' had been my nickname at university, derived from one night at a pub when I had used a friend's pint glass to drink wine from, to save me the bother of endlessly filling up the 'silly little glasses', as I had joked at the time. I had enjoyed the laughter from my new friends, the buzz of confidence, revelled in the new identity I had formed out of the shy, frizzy-haired, chubby girl in the frilly blouses. 'Dead boring from Dedham!' or 'Nerdy Naomi strikes again!' the class bully at my secondary school had sniggered every time I had achieved a decent grade. In my new guise, as I drank, the boy's words had faded. The alcohol had helped me to leave behind that squirming feeling, that sense of my pen sliding in my fingers as I had sweated, as others had tittered.

Laughing emojis seemed to swim on the screen before me, multiplying, cackling at me and my disgrace.

I wondered if there was an emoji that could express profound regret.

For some, it might have been funny to look back at a bygone era, but for me, it was utterly wretched, as Sophie would surely have known. When I thought of her, my mind flashed white with fury. And then bafflement. The motivation for posting these photographs in such a public arena was unfathomable. I thought of Adam's warnings about her: if Sophie had a drinking problem, it might explain her actions. Whatever her reasons, I had to find out.

I closed the kitchen door and called her.

There was a rustle before she spoke. 'What time is it?'

Her voice was gravelly.

'It's just gone ten.'

'What's up?'

Was she really going to play dumb?

'I've just looked on Facebook.'

There was a pause, and some more rustling.

'Did you like them?' she asked. 'I found a stack of them when I was clearing out the bedroom.'

'Are you joking?' The tightness in my throat betrayed my anger.

'The one with those guys' hands on your boobs was the best. I laughed out loud when I saw it.'

'It didn't make me laugh.'

'You sound upset.' She seemed surprised that I might be.

My ear burnt against the handset. 'How did you know my password?'

'You use the same one for all your accounts.'

'How dare you hack into my account!' I cried.

'You're so oversensitive. It was joke, a trip down memory lane.'

'You have no idea what you've done, do you?'

'You're worried about what your followers think of you?'

'Of course I am!'

'Don't worry so much. They would've enjoyed seeing "Fun Naomi" for a change.'

'Sophie, it undermines everything I post about.'

'Maybe you should think about being more authentic, then,' she retorted.

'The images I choose to project are my own business, not yours. Okay?'

'That depends on whether that squeaky-clean image has a crappy effect on others, doesn't it, really?'

'I don't think that's fair.'

'There'll be people out there who might feel depressed when they see how great your life is and how shit theirs is by comparison.'

'Is that how *you* feel?'

She snorted, 'That's rather superior, Naomi.'

The kitchen door clicked open. Izzie wandered in. Her knotted curls fell down her bare back and her spotted knickers were on back to front. She reached up into the cupboard for the Rice

Krispies and then shoved two bowls and two spoons into the box. 'Will you bring the milk through to the telly room for me, Mummy?' she asked, standing in front of the fridge.

I shook my head and mouthed 'no', pointing to the phone in my hand. Izzy glared at me and stormed out, slamming the door. Her reaction seemed to echo the negative energy coming down the phone from Sophie, and I had the melodramatic, self-pitying feeling that the effort to care for those I loved had been futile, that their love for me was conditional, that it could wilt and die as quickly as picked bluebells.

'I always thought I'd been kind to you,' I said to Sophie.

'Like it's an effort? Please, don't put yourself out.'

Silence fell between us. I considered hanging up then and there.

'Why are you so angry with me?' I asked her, pained by my own curiosity.

There was a long silence, and I checked my phone screen to make sure we were still connected.

'I know about you and Adam.'

I laughed. 'My god! *What?*

'You met in secret.'

'Are you serious? Is that what this is all about?'

'What do you expect me to think?'

I snorted. 'Are you seriously suggesting that we're having it off?'

'Last night… I thought… it did seem unlikely. This morning, I mean, it seemed… less possible.'

'You can say that again!' I cried.

She began to whine, 'But why did he come over to your place while Charlie's away? And why did he lie to me and say he was working late?'

Incredulous, I shouted back at her, 'Because he wanted to talk about YOU! That's why!'

A beat, a cough, a low reply, 'Why?'

I pressed my forehead onto the bifold windows and stared down at my toes, my fingers rapping the glass. 'He's worried about your drinking, Soph.'

Behind me, I heard the door open again and I swivelled round. Izzy had returned to get the milk from the fridge. She dazzled me with one of her endearing, crooked-tooth grins and said, 'Sorry for slamming the door.'

'Who's that?' Sophie snapped.

'Izzy. She's getting the milk. All by herself,' I said, winking at her. Izzy beamed.

'Is she in the room? I'd better go,' Sophie said.

I, too, wanted to end this miserable call, but seeing Izzy's rangy little body – the innocence of it, the vulnerability of her – I thought of Dylan. If he wasn't safe, I could not turn my back on him.

'Sophie. Adam worried me. Do you think it might be worth looking at how much you're drink—'

She interrupted me. 'Sounds to me like you're projecting something.'

'This is not about me.'

'It used to be.'

'Okay! Yes! Back then, I drank too much. Yes, I partied hard. Yes, I slept with too many boys. Get over it!'

'Get over it?'

'What difference does it make now?'

'All the difference in the world.'

'Why, Sophie? *Why?*' I pleaded.

There was another long pause.

'I got a third because of you.'

I had not expected her to say that. A sharp cramp tightened in my abdomen at the memory of that hot, sunny week in June. Her hand had been in mine all week, whenever I had needed it. She had been evasive about her own exam schedule, self-sacrificing, and I had been unquestioning, utterly grateful. Now, I clutched my belly and squeezed my eyes closed. Behind a tall, wide sheet of glass, another me stood, a younger me, dispossessed, banging, asking to be let out, asking to be heard. That young woman would stay there, trapped forever. I had locked her away and I would not let Sophie smash through the glass.

'I've said sorry about that,' I said.

'I had big plans for my life.'

Quietly, with little conviction, I said, 'You can't blame me for everything that went wrong.'

'Can't I?'

Without thinking, I hung up on her. I couldn't hear any more.

My phone rang as soon as I had placed it on the kitchen table.

When I saw Sophie's name, ringing and ringing, hounding me, I pressed my hands to my ears. '*GO AWAY!*' I wanted to yell.

I dragged open the window and stepped outside, gulping in the wet air, thirsty for its life force, welcoming its space. If I slid down the wet lawn and into the trees, I could run through the woods, keep running and running, and never return. It would be my choice. My life. Charlie and the girls would find a way to get on without me. Nobody was irreplaceable.

Gathering myself, I stepped back inside. I would never leave my family. The young woman behind the glass might do that. Not me. I pulled the window closed and decided to open the case of Burgundy. To taste, of course. Not to drink.

If it was a good wine, I would share it with my friends this evening at our dinner party, with Meg and Josh, Cynthia and Nathan. Neither Meg nor Cynthia was neurotic or needy or insecure. I did not have to self-deprecate or duck from their envious blows. They had their fair share of problems, but they would not offer them to me with upturned palms, like Sophie, on their knees, expectant and damning, appealing to my inbuilt guilt, blaming me for my different choices. I did not have to nursemaid them, as I had always done with Sophie, who had suggested that she resented the life I promoted on my blog. In truth, it was worse than that: she resented my real life.

A speech unspooled in my thoughts, possibly written in my head a long time ago: *I'm so sorry, Sophie, I can't help you if you won't help yourself. I'm so sorry, I'm going to have to step away. And I know you'll never understand why, that you will always blame me, that you will forever be the victim, that you will never look at yourself and your own actions, and I will try to make peace with that. I have to, to move on. I can't allow you to drag me down with you. You will never feel the love I give. I am truly sorry for giving up.*

I wanted to say these words out loud to Sophie. They were heartfelt, they were harsh, they were my truth.

When she called for the tenth time, an hour later, I sent her a text:

> *Hi Sophie. You've really crossed a line. Worse than that, you don't seem to understand why it would upset me to post those pictures online. You need help. Until you have your drinking under control, I think it is best that we give each other some space for a while. Naomi*

Maybe one day she would understand.

CHAPTER FOURTEEN

Sophie parked the Saab in the lay-by down the road from Naomi's house.

The walk up the hill in the dark was hampered by potholes, and she twisted her weak ankle on a crumbled fragment of tarmac.

She didn't want to use the torch in case she was seen. Her right palm itched and throbbed.

Originally, she had not planned on sneaking around. She had intended to park up in the drive, openly, and apologise to Naomi face-to-face, like a grown-up.

After Naomi's phone call, Sophie had confronted how despicable her Facebook attack had been: concocted too late at night, in the throes of an attack of jealousy, too tired to see sense. The hurt in Naomi's voice had cut right through her. She had wanted the ground to swallow up her shame, but, stupidly, she had tried to defend herself, to wriggle out of it, by deflecting the blame.

After receiving Naomi's text, Sophie had pulled up the Alcoholics Anonymous website and read the section 'Is AA for you?', which had included a questionnaire, a test she had been nervous about attempting. If she answered four or more questions with a 'yes', the blurb warned, she would need help. She had answered 'yes' to only two of the questions. Then she had answered them as if she were Naomi. Naomi could have answered 'yes' to six of them.

It seemed to Sophie that Naomi's accusations were a projection of her own struggles with the bottle.

On the drive to Naomi's, she had rehearsed what she would say to her, how she would persuade her to hear her out, just for five minutes, which she had anticipated would unfold into a lengthier heart to heart: *I need help*, Sophie would say, making clear her good intentions to stop drinking, fairly sure that Naomi would forgive her if she went along with the AA smokescreen.

They had been good intentions, yes. They truly had been.

For all that, it was the number of cars parked up in Naomi's drive that had sent her focus and purpose veering off course. It seemed Naomi was having a party, which suggested she was moving on rather more quickly than Sophie had expected.

There was something brazen about having a party with other friends – no doubt Meg and some other bores – on this day, the day she had fallen out with the person she viewed almost like a sister. And something sly in it, having failed to mention it on the phone this morning.

Sophie edged past a large black Mercedes and hugged the low wall of the flower bed, where the gravel was sparse, to ensure her footsteps to the house were as quiet as possible. She could hear music from inside, and Harley barking, as though he had sniffed her out already.

Along the side of the house, she made her way to one small window that looked into the laundry room, from which she would have a view of the kitchen table, where the guests would be sat.

If the door to the laundry room was open, she would be able to see what was going on. If someone had been standing at the window on the other side, she would have been discovered instantly. The light reflections on the inside, and the darkness that enveloped her, would work in her favour. As she leant her back to the wall, summoning her courage, her heartbeat seemed to sit inside her head rather than inside her chest.

Slowly she slid her cheek along the scratchy brickwork and edged around to look in.

The sight of the smiling faces of Meg and Cynthia, huddled at one end with Naomi, sent the noise of their laughter crashing into her eardrums: a racket of happiness, a blast of rejection. Whether she imagined their laughter or heard it in reality, her breath was taken away by a sudden sense of loss. Not loss, exactly; loneliness, or perhaps both, like the onset of a condition, sped up inside her, hollowing her out in a matter of seconds.

When she allowed the air to rush back into her lungs, she gulped noisily and then froze, remembering that there was only one wall between them and her compromised position.

Harley began barking again. She detected his scratching at the bifold windows.

She had to get away. If they let him out, she would be discovered.

As she crept back along the wall, she heard the unmistakable slide of the bifold doors, and before she could escape, Harley was yapping at her heels.

A strong smell of cigarette smoke engulfed the fresh air.

'Who's there?' a nervous but forceful female voice said.

Sophie slowly turned to face her.

A haze of smoky orange light shone around Meg's cropped head of hair.

'Sophie? Is that you?'

Gathering herself, knowing there was nothing she could do but front this out, Sophie replied, 'Oh, hi Meg. I was knocking on the front door for ages and nobody heard. I was going to come round the back. But don't worry, I didn't realise she was entertaining. I'll come back another time.'

Of course, Naomi had a doorbell, and it would have been obvious that she had been entertaining by the number of cars.

But what else could Sophie say to explain why she was lurking in the shadows?

With an unsure sort of laugh, Meg said, 'Don't skulk off. I'll tell Naomi you're here. Come in and say hello. We wondered why Harley was barking.'

The talk at the table stopped when she followed Meg in.

Naomi's jaw visibly loosened.

'Look who I found on the doorstep!' Meg said diplomatically.

Charlie, barely missing a beat, stood to welcome her. 'Sophie! What a lovely surprise. I'll get you a glass. Come and join us.'

She glanced at Naomi, checking to see whether the invite was sanctioned. The hate shot from Naomi's glare, dart-like, rendering Sophie speechless. She picked at the bandage on her hand.

Sophie wanted to say, 'No. I mustn't. I must go now. I'm not really welcome.' But the words did not come out.

An extra chair was found and squeezed in between Naomi and Meg, on the corner. A glass of wine was poured. She wiped her hands on her sweatpants before reaching for it. It was a Burgundy. A dry red wine, but it thickened in her throat like syrup. Syrupy, like the atmosphere her presence had created: sticky and sweet, fake smiles and awkwardness.

'We were just talking about sexual turn-offs!' Meg announced.

Everyone laughed.

'It seems Meg doesn't like clean men,' Cynthia chuckled.

'It's not that,' Meg protested, 'but a shower takes all the spontaneity out of it, don't you think?'

Josh roared with laughter. 'Next time I'm back from a game of squash then, darling…' he winked.

'Too much information!' Naomi cried.

It was Charlie's turn to share. 'Naomi hates me brushing my teeth before we… you know…'

'Charlie!' Naomi spluttered, rolling her eyes, faking prudishness.

There were chortles and jokey outcries about Naomi's peculiar aversion to toothpaste before sex, but Sophie did not laugh. She locked her attention on to Naomi to track her reaction. Naomi performed well, laughing it off. Sophie knew she would be reeling inside.

Cynthia held both hands up and put on a mock-serious face. 'I think we should stop ribbing poor Naomi and return to the chat we were having about balls,' she chuckled.

'That doesn't sound much safer,' Sophie said.

'Not the hairy kind. We were complaining about how many we're all holding up in the air and how regularly they seem to come crashing down on us,' Meg said.

Sophie smiled, suddenly uncertain of her place there.

The men resumed their conversation at the other end of the table, withdrawing to the proverbial card table like Victorian husbands.

'Sophie doesn't work,' Naomi stated baldly, immediately separating her.

'I would have loved a career,' Sophie replied. 'But Adam's work is erratic and the childcare was too expensive to make it worthwhile.'

'Out of interest, what career would you have chosen?' Naomi asked.

After a couple of slow sips of wine, Sophie offered up her sad story. 'Something happened during my finals,' she said, looking into her lap, pausing for dramatic effect, noticing how Naomi shifted in her seat. 'I came out with a third, and I lost my confidence. I temped in London for a while – I'd always dreamt of working in publishing, like Bridget Jones! – but my grandad got ill, and then I met Adam, and, you know…'

Cynthia nodded sympathetically. 'Life gets in the way. When my son was diagnosed, I backed out of going for Partner, knowing it couldn't possibly work.'

Sophie glanced over at Naomi, who gulped at her wine and refused to look at her.

As the conversation deepened into a confessional about the clash of ambition versus childcare, Sophie's ear tuned into the conversation at the other end of the table. Charlie and Josh were talking about redundancies, she gleaned.

'When HR comes in, I dive under the bloody desk,' Josh joked, laughing heartily.

'Jobs for life are more like jobs till fifty, these days,' Charlie said, standing abruptly, pouring wine at the women's end of the table, trying to fill up Sophie's glass for the second time. Sophie had put her hand over the rim. 'No thanks, I'm driving.'

This had prompted Naomi to look directly at Sophie for the first time. Sophie had answered her with a tiny nod and a shy smile, confirming that it was true, that she had listened, that she was going to turn her life around. She hoped it was enough. There might have been a spark of uncertainty in those eyes, Sophie thought.

'We should have been born Norwegian,' Meg sighed.

'Real men, real equality,' Cynthia laughed.

Sophie glanced at her watch, remembering that she had promised Adam she'd be back within the hour.

'Real men? Bloody hell. Imagine that,' Sophie grinned. 'Look, I'd better go. I'm sorry for gatecrashing.'

As she stood up to leave, Sophie believed that she had accomplished more than she had set out to do, more than she could have hoped for. In spite of the inauspicious start, Naomi had, at the very least, allowed her to stay, which indicated there was room for forgiveness. Moreover, she had made a better impression on Meg and Cynthia than she had at the wine-tasting evening. It was clear neither of them knew about the Facebook episode. For a pleasant moment, Sophie felt she hadn't stepped too far over the line to be able to step back again into the comfort of Naomi's friendship.

But then, when she bent down to Naomi to kiss her goodbye, she saw Naomi's fingers pressed deep into her thighs.

Sophie dared to peck her on the cheek and Naomi flinched.

A blast of words followed. 'What *were* you actually doing here tonight?'

The man-talk at the other end of the table turned to a murmur.

Sophie thought quickly. Honesty would be the best policy. 'I wanted to apologise to you, Naomi.'

Naomi's stare remained directly ahead of her. Her forefinger on her right hand tapped a funereal drumbeat on the table.

Charlie's chair scraped on the floor. He cleared his throat. 'I'll walk you to the car, Sophie.'

'There's no need,' Sophie replied, and fumbled at the latch of the bifold window, realising how severely she had underestimated Naomi's wrath. Tears pricked her eyes.

'No,' Naomi said, 'I'll come out with you.'

Once again, hope bloomed in Sophie's chest as she stepped aside to let Naomi undo the latch. Perhaps Naomi was going to offer her a final chance.

Sophie followed her down the side passage, waiting for her to speak.

At the cars, Naomi stopped. 'I didn't want to embarrass you in front of the others, but I don't really appreciate you turning up on my doorstep like this, Sophie. I made it pretty clear in my text that I wanted some space.'

'I wanted to make it right,' Sophie said, her hopes dashed. This would be the time to offer up her pre-prepared speech about her intentions to change, but Naomi's refusal to soften, even for a second, brought old resentment roiling up from the depths of her.

'By spying on me?'

'I wasn't spying.'

'You might be able to fool Meg and the others, but I know exactly what you were doing and it is totally fucking weird.'

Like those powerful waves of nausea before you vomit, Sophie tried to swallow down the disagreeable feeling. But there was only one way to feel better. It had to come up and out.

'Too weird for your fancy dinner parties now, am I?'

Naomi pointed to the bar gate. 'Please leave.'

Here ended Sophie's grovelling apologies. Here ended Naomi's smugness.

'I used to think you were just playing dumb,' Sophie began. 'Thinking that you couldn't admit it to yourself. But if you'd known, if you'd kept it inside, like I have, it would've slowly destroyed you, like it has me. Unless you're a total psychopath.'

Naomi stumbled back, then righted herself. 'I don't know what you're talking about.'

'Yes, you do.'

'I'm going back inside.' But she didn't move a muscle.

'Ha! The luxury of your ignorance.'

'I am going to go back inside now,' she repeated. This time, she began walking away, but Sophie yanked her arm.

'See no evil, hear no evil, eh?'

'You're hurting me.'

'That night bound us together, whether you like it or not. You think you can walk away, but you can't. Ever.'

She twisted her arm out of Sophie's grip and rubbed at it. 'I can do whatever I like.'

'Not if I go to the police.'

Naomi laughed. 'What the hell would you go to the police about?'

'To make a confession.'

'About a deer?' Her voice was hoarse with fear.

'It wasn't a deer, though, was it?'

Naomi's lips dropped at the corners, dead weights pulling at them. 'Yes, it was.'

'You wanted it to be. We both wanted it to be a deer.'

Her head shook from side to side. 'That night,' Naomi said, 'I begged you to go back.'

Sophie ran her eyes across Naomi's house. There was a purple glow from Izzy's bedroom nightlight and a flowery border edging Diana's blinds. Both girls were cosy and safe inside as they slumbered. The chatter from the kitchen table, where Naomi had sat at its head, would have resumed between her friends and her husband, who loved her so much. Naomi belonged inside with them. But here she was, standing in the cold, on the outside with Sophie. It saddened Sophie to watch how Naomi had tried to form various friendships over the years, with women like Meg, who would become her new best friend and then fall by the wayside. It had been tough shielding her, preventing her from slipping up in a moment of intimacy, of false intimacy. Every detail shared, however naively, had been a potential threat to them both. Each new friend of hers had made Sophie feel anxious, and jealous. The affection had come easily to Naomi. Because she hadn't been knowingly hiding anything.

'All of this is built on sand,' Sophie said, sweeping her arm across the setting of domestic bliss.

Naomi's face marbled, swirls of leaf shadows whirling through her pallor. It seemed she had turned to stone: a statue depicting her terror, erected for posterity.

Barely audible, she wheezed, 'What would I have seen if you'd let me go back, Sophie?'

'Are you sure you're ready to find out?'

Then Naomi came to life in a bright flash of noise and movement. She ran at Sophie, pushing her in the chest, screaming in her face. 'NO! YOU'RE FUCKING WITH MY HEAD, JUST TO SPITE ME! Get the *hell* off my property! Adam was right. you've gone fucking *crazy!*'

Sophie let her push her again, and again, further and further out of the drive, until she was in the lane, shoved out – for the time being.

But not for long.

CHAPTER FIFTEEN

I ran round the back, tears flying off my cheeks.

Charlie and Meg leapt from their chairs, 'Naomi! Darling! We heard screaming. What was that all about?'

My muscles were trembling, working too hard to hold up my skeleton.

Meg said, 'Are you okay? What's happened? Oh my god, you're shaking all over.'

They flanked me, bringing me inside, as though I were a lost stranger found wandering alone in the dark. They led me into the warmth of home. My home. My home built on sand.

With one look at me, Cynthia said, 'I'll make a pot of tea.'

My sobs took me over. The tears were not of injury or distress, as those huddled around me might have suspected: they were tears of fright.

'What did she say?' Meg asked, leaving her arm around my shoulder, her head bent into mine, close also to Charlie, whose hand was heavy on top of my fingers, repressing their frenzied dance.

'Did she hurt you?' Charlie added urgently. 'Why was she even here?'

I feared what I might say in that untethered moment.

Had she hurt me? She had done worse.

In the silence I left behind, Charlie's brow furrowed and he looked to Meg, who looked straight at me again. A chain of confusion that I had the power to break. Each time I considered talking, telling them what Sophie had revealed, my chest would expand and my shoulders would shake and the tears would come.

Rewind, replay, rewind, replay, rewind, replay: looking back into that slice of time, that second in time, that jolt in time, when I heard the thump, when the bulk had hit the windscreen, when the car's abrupt stop had thrown me into the footwell, there was nothing new. There was no fresh evidence embedded or hidden in that glimmer of the past. Nothing came back to me to prove that the heavy mass was anything other than a deer. Still, the memory was an unchanged, unchangeable imprint on my experience. And I knew of no other way to retrieve more. If there had been more, it had been erased, either by time or by trauma. Had I blanked it out? Had I known? Had there been anything I was not willing to remember?

I certainly remembered how angry and snappy she had been that night, in the aftermath of the accident, when she had driven me back to campus.

The cut on my forehead was bleeding, my ribs were bruised, yet she dragged me out of the car, almost by my hair and shoved me in my back a few times, telling me to hurry up, shouting at me for being clumsy when I had tripped up the steps to my floor. I wasn't surprised or hurt. I was tearful and ashamed.

The next day, Sophie did not knock on my door, call or leave a note. I looked for her in the usual places on campus: in the café, in the supermarket, in the park, saying goodbye to the odd acquaintance. In the end, I packed up my small room and left for Dedham without saying goodbye.

On the spiral notepad at home, I found a message in my father's elegant handwriting: 'Sophie called. No point calling her back. She'll call again when she's at her grandad's'.

'Why didn't she want me to call back?' I asked my father, later that day, after he had poured his first gin and tonic. His routine had remained the same during my years away: 18.42 train from Liverpool

Street to Colchester, cycle ride home, key in the door at five past eight, ten-minute shower, first gin and tonic.

'Oh, something about staying with a boyfriend,' Dad said.

'With Will?'

'Was it Will? Possibly.'

Will was Sophie's on-off kind of boyfriend, whose telephone number I didn't have.

'Did she sound okay?'

'She was in very jolly spirits. She said she'd catch you before you left. I think she was planning to stay in Exeter for a few days with this Will chap.'

'I'm surprised she's staying. She's been so worried about her grandad.'

'Poor thing, having to cancel her trip.'

'She can come and join me when he's better,' I said, knowing this was a distant possibility.

Mum – who was cooking my father his meat and two veg dinner, and checking his glass for a refill – cut in.

'Thought we'd head into Covent Garden tomorrow, darling, and get this backpack from the YHA. Apparently it's the best place to get a good one.'

I happily allowed her to move the conversation on.

Internally, I was battling with my feelings about my friendship with Sophie. I was worn out by her expectations of me. I wanted a break from the guilt, from the second-guessing: had I been suitably attentive, suitably kind, suitably loyal?

Nevertheless, I knew I had been in the wrong, and I went to sleep that night churning with regrets about my selfish behaviour and how this had impacted upon Sophie. I considered returning to Exeter to see her before I left, to go out of my way to prove to her that I was a good person, a good friend: I would never drink again, I would pay to fix the car windscreen, I would set up a direct debit to a wildlife conservation charity. I would call her every day to check on her grandfather's recovery.

Much to my relief, Sophie's silent treatment did not last. Rarely had I known her to hold a grudge. We spoke a few days later before my flight, and we repeated 'I'll miss you so much!' about a hundred times in the space of a forty-five-minute conversation.

As the plane roared into the sky, I unwound like twine, twirling freely, free of the bind of Sophie's neediness. By the time the plane touched down onto the shimmering tarmac of Bangkok Airport, my three years at Exeter with Sophie was like a dream, as though I had lived through them decades ago. Everything was geared towards what was to come. Nothing was about what had gone before.

Now, everything was about what had gone before. For the past twenty years I had been on death row, unknowingly, in a holding pattern before the guillotine struck the back of my neck.

A cold shock of fear stopped my heart. I was catatonic at the thought of what we had done.

'Naomi, are you okay? Please tell us what happened,' I heard Charlie say. To Meg, he said, 'I've never seen her like this.'

When I finally gathered myself, I spoke to Charlie, and to Meg and Cynthia and their husbands, and I apologised for scaring them and took them through the Facebook page betrayal, like an impostor who had been programmed to be Mrs Naomi Wilson. I explained how our row had escalated. It was like telling children a sanitised version of a terror attack by removing the dead bodies.

There was no horror in my version, no substance.

I lay in bed, flat and still on my back, sweating into the sheets. Like a spectre hovering above my grave, I was separated from my body, floating away from my solid existence.

Finally, Charlie's breathing grew heavy. I slipped out of bed and crept down to my computer in the kitchen.

The blueish tinge of my screen illuminated the space around me, heightening the sense of unreality. It might as well have been a dream. My thoughts were fractured, my limbs light, my sense of logic had disappeared. Logic would have told me that this could not possibly be real.

A lie from Sophie's lips was real. The catastrophic possibility that we had killed someone that night was a cruel joke, sick-making, literally beyond my wildest nightmares.

So why was I typing 'hit-and-run deaths, July 1999, Exeter' into my search engine? Why was I following up on Sophie's insane claim? Why was I wondering whether this unknown mass, which had hit Sophie's windscreen that night, had had an identity? A gender. A family. A life. Had they been an old woman? A young girl? A drunk man? Why was I doing this? When, at the same time, I couldn't allow it to be true?

The search results popped up in blue type. There were a series of official websites, showing statistical reports and recent newspaper articles about the thousands of hit-and-run accidents that were recorded across the UK every year. Paranoid that my searches could be logged in some algorithm and stored up under my name, I tentatively followed some likely avenues, read some heartbreaking stories, saw some horrendous footage of bodies being flung into the air, and came up against many dead ends.

After an hour of delving into the ether, through endless newspaper archives, clicking and clicking further into the black hole of information, I gave up. Without a name, I could not find an online record of a hit-and-run death in Exeter at that time, unless I registered with the research data service or digital newspaper archive, which involved giving out my name and my reason for the request. Seemingly, it was going to be impossible to locate detailed information in the middle of the night, on my computer, anonymously.

There was a part of me that wanted to believe that my thwarted attempt to find evidence of this supposed accident proved that it hadn't happened, but I couldn't help the brooding in the back of my mind. My failure to find answers here and now left me hanging in a vast limbo land of possibilities.

The thought of seeing Sophie again was ghastly, but I would have to confront her, in a calmer state, to find out more, to glean the truth.

My mouth was dry. I needed a drink. I rinsed one of the dirty glasses that had been left on the side from the dinner party and filled it with the last of the Burgundy.

As I sipped it, I thought of other options beyond public records. Was there anyone I could call from my university days? Someone might have heard about a hit-and-run incident, if it had indeed occurred. Those who had stuck around after the end of term might have seen it reported in the local papers or driven past a police sign at the scene. Although few of the students I had known had lingered after the end of term, and the halls had been half-empty when I had packed up my room to leave for Dedham – it had been a popular day to leave, following the last of the final exams the day before – there was still the possibility that they had found out about the accident afterwards.

Sophie had not made it easy for me to make other friends during that era, and I had not kept in touch with anyone after I left. The handful of ex-students who followed me on Facebook would be surprised to hear from me randomly, and I risked raising suspicions about my motives for asking. Nobody should know I was looking into an incident back then. Not another soul.

Sophie was the only one with all the facts. Earlier, I had shut her down, unable to hear it, but I needed to know the truth.

The digital clock on the range cooker read 02:34.

I waited until six o'clock to text her.

Meet me at the Devil's Punch Bowl at 7 a.m.

CHAPTER SIXTEEN

Across the empty car park, Sophie could see Naomi cradling a blue Thermos mug. The dead light and the fine rain seemed to flatten her sweet features. She looked grey and haunted.

As Sophie walked towards her friend, the caw of birds was louder than any other noise. When Sophie thought of the world waking up around them, she thought of car engines and bulldozers and drills, like invaders; the noise of evolution thundering forward. She wanted humankind to halt progress from this moment on, suspend them in the peacefulness of birdsong, right now, forever. Maybe if the world beyond the two of them found peace, if it wrapped itself around them both like a blanket, her beleaguered brain would rest. Over the years, the temptation to tell Naomi had lurked as a dreamlike possibility. Now it seemed that a landmine waited for them on their walk through the wet terrain of the heathland, and it was poised to blow them apart. She thought of the Gandhi quote in black lettering on the back of the postcard that Naomi had given her for her birthday a few years back: 'The road to peace. Peace is the road'. She silently challenged Gandhi to help them find peace for their road. Bombs or Armageddon or a plague or some other world-ending nightmare seemed preferable to the admission she was about to make to Naomi.

With the cuttings close to her chest, she was flying, scudding over the ground, delirious with the sense of impending change. If the articles had been lost or damaged in the seconds it would take her to walk across the car park, there would be no replacements for them, or so she felt. Of course, records of Jason Parker's life could be found in libraries, or online, but these yellowed, brittle papers of that life-changing night belonged to Sophie, and they were as defining to Sophie as her own birth certificate.

With that sense of ownership burning inside her, she wasn't entirely sure of how much she was ready to reveal to Naomi. Her moral compass was whizzing round like helicopter blades.

Some of the details of that night would have to remain a secret forever, but how many could be shared? She was nervous about Naomi's reaction, regretting agreeing to this remote location so early in the morning. Last night, Naomi had pushed her, hurting her, and Sophie hoped she would be safe.

Automatically, Sophie leant in to kiss Naomi on the cheek, but Naomi reeled back and began to walk on ahead. Sophie jogged after her as she strode along the path, along the rim of the bowl valley, until they were out of the woods. They arrived at the Celtic Cross on the top of Gibbet Hill. They stopped there to look out across the panorama, which on a clear day showed green fields stretching all the way to London. Today, they could barely see to the bottom of the hill. As Sophie gathered her breath, she thought about the Unknown Sailor, who had been brutally murdered here hundreds of years ago by three villainous highwaymen. The murderers' bodies had been hung on this hill, near to where they had slain their victim, as a warning to other criminals.

The atmosphere of those four dead men seemed to cling to this beauty spot, like the mist to the heather, white and solid, tacky almost.

Not a soul had walked through it before them that morning. Or so it seemed.

And if they had, Sophie felt sorry for them. Only unhappiness and troubled thoughts would bring them into this damp, empty countryside this early. The contented were snoozing under their duvets.

'We'll go this way,' Naomi said.

They dropped down into the heathland, Naomi up ahead, charging along.

The gorse spiked Sophie's legs through her jeans.

Her hands were cold, and her body burning hot. Zipped, still, into the inside pocket of her down jacket nestled the papers that would change everything.

Sophie waited for Naomi to engage, to ask her the relevant questions. She braced herself, mentally preparing. She would not gabble the events. She wanted to hone her answers, as though she were explaining it to a judge and jury.

After fifteen minutes of tramping through the narrow pathways of mud and stone, the path widened and Naomi dropped back to walk by her side.

She spoke quietly, hardly audible over the brush of fern at their calves. 'Had you seen anyone on the road before the accident?' she whispered. A puff of her cold breath shot out in the small space between them.

'No, the weather was bad, remember?' Sophie replied.

That first sight of Jason Parker's slanted eyes under his black umbrella came to Sophie in a rush.

'How did you hit him?'

'You distracted me. Shouting and singing and turning the lights on and off. I couldn't concentrate.'

'But had you actually *seen* what hit the windscreen?' Naomi asked.

Lit up inside her, Sophie remembered the instant recognition and the hate she had felt for Jason Parker. She dug her fingernails into her palms, imagining the steering wheel pressing there. The night was coming back to her, so clearly into her mind: how, one minute, she had felt that strong surge of emotion, and the next, the unidentified thing had bounced onto her windscreen. What concerned her, now, was the in-between bit, the space that had been filled with an action, with her desire.

'No. It was dark. It happened too quickly.'

'So how do you know it was a person?'

The thud had been like an alien dropping onto the car. It had borne no connection to the man walking beside the road. It had no form, no approach, no clear journey or landing.

She swallowed hard. 'I went back after I dropped you off.'

Naomi's footsteps faltered. 'You actually saw it?'

'Him. Yes. I saw his body.'

Naomi had stopped and put her face into her hands. 'Oh my god.'

Sophie's chest expanded wide to encompass the return of that heart-stopping terror, and she recalled how the indent of his flung form had been like a black cardboard cutout in the green foliage. As she had approached, the fear had loaded itself inside her like a series of bullets in a barrel. The brambles had torn at her shins. She had pushed through the deep undergrowth to reach the body. Stunned and revolted, she had lifted his arm. Before the limb had had time to flop back, Sophie had felt its deadness, its dead weight, in her heart, and she had bolted back to the car. Born to run. Born to run away.

'What did you do then? Why didn't you call the police?'

'I drove to Deda's.'

'You drove all the way back to your grandad's that night?'

'It was a reflex. I didn't know what else to do. I just drove and drove. I was in shock.'

Naomi began to walk again.

'And your grandad knew it was a man? All this time?'

'I never told him.'

'But you think he knew?'

'He was very ill, pumped full of chemicals, but he fixed up that windscreen as though he knew.'

'He *knew* you'd killed someone, but you never actually *said*? Is that what's happening here? I'm supposed to just *know* it's true? How do I *know* that?'

Sophie let Naomi's insult slide, understanding that Naomi would not want to accept what she was telling her. A wry amusement pooled in Sophie's chest. The evidence was in her jacket, but she was stalling for a moment or two, enjoying Naomi's discomfited, childish denial.

'But I am telling you, it happened.'

'Do you even know who it was?' Naomi asked, almost shouting now.

'He was lying on his front. It was dark,' Sophie said, unzipping her jacket, realising how welcome the cold air was on her chest as she pulled out the folded piece of newspaper.

'What's that?' Naomi's head jerked back.

'Have a look.'

But Naomi simply stared at it.

'Please,' Sophie begged.

As Naomi put her hand out to take it, the diamond of her engagement ring fell to the left, her flesh shrunken by the cold, perhaps, or by terror.

'He wasn't found for a few weeks,' Sophie said, watching as Naomi slid out the short article outlining the discovery of the body. Sophie wondered and waited to see if Naomi would recognise the name, almost certain she would not. Purposefully, she had brought her the article without a photograph. Sophie was like a doctor, drip-feeding their terminally ill patient with information on a need-to-know basis, to soften the blow. Perhaps Naomi never need know his true identity. Perhaps the archived newspapers on a library's microfiche, or scanned into an online database, would be damaged and the photographs too faded for her to ever recognise him. Perhaps.

THE EXETER LOCAL

5th August 1999

YOUNG MAN KILLED IN HIT-AND-RUN

A 22-year-old student, Jason Parker, died in an alleged hit-and-run crash in Exeter.

Parker was reported missing by his mother, Ilene Parker, two weeks prior to the discovery of his body, which was found in the undergrowth close to Stoke Road.

In a statement, Devon and Cornwall Police said: 'The investigation into the young man's death is in the early stages, but it is believed his injuries are consistent with being involved in a road traffic collision.'

The area was thoroughly searched, police added, but the vehicle has not been found.

A post-mortem is due to be carried out today and officers continue to make local enquiries.

A gargled breath rattled from Naomi as she read. 'He was a student at Exeter?'

The piece of paper fluttered to their feet, out of place in the natural landscape.

Naomi's blue eyes fixed on Sophie, as bright and brilliant as pieces of sea glass.

'Yes, he was a student,' Sophie exhaled the words.

Sophie picked up the article and zipped it away in her pocket.

'We could have walked past him in the halls. We could have stood in line with him at the canteen,' Naomi said.

'Not necessarily. Exeter has over twenty thousand students.'

'But what if he was at that party at the pub?'

'He might have been, I suppose. If he was walking along Stoke Road.'

Sophie knew that he had been at the party. She knew that Naomi had not seen him. She had made sure of it.

'We could have been next to him at the bar. Met him, even,' Naomi whispered.

Sophie felt her heart slash open with love and regret.

'Perhaps.'

'But you saw his face, didn't you? Did you recognise him at all?'

Sophie would have recognised Jason Parker's face anywhere.

'No. I'd never seen him before in my life,' Sophie said, shivering at the thought of his death pallor, of his frightened, narrow eyes and bloody mouth.

But Naomi's face was the horror story in front of her now. Bloodless, as though Sophie had pulled her veins out of her flesh. Through Naomi, in one harrowing flash, Sophie felt that night again, felt it more than saw it. What she had done, what they had done, became ghastlier than it had been back then. Through Naomi, she was reliving it. Naomi's ashen face was a reflection of Sophie's guilt. All of it. Before now, she had never dared look.

CHAPTER SEVENTEEN

19 July, 1999

Naomi had looked perfect at the beginning of the evening. Now, her tights were torn and her make-up was rubbed from her face; her cheeks were raw and pink, her hair tangled, like a dirty doll on a rubbish dump.

I held her hand, steadying her as we walked down the wet steps from the pub to the car park, feeling her nails dig into my palm.

'I'm going to miss you when you're gone,' she slurred.

'You're the one going away, not me,' I reminded her.

'Oh yeah,' she giggled. 'I'm gonna be…'

Her body was thrown over her legs with the force of her vomit. Chunks of chicken from the party food splattered over my boots. I stroked her back, where the slow, heavy fall of raindrops left dark stains on her denim jacket.

She spluttered, wiping sick and tears away with the back of her hand.

'I'm so sorry,' she sobbed, stumbling over as she bent to rub my shoes clean. 'I'm so, so sorry.'

Huddled under umbrellas, fellow students poured past us, either laughing at her, drunk themselves, or casting sympathetic glances. A couple of friends asked if we needed a lift or whether we wanted to walk with them through the woods back to campus.

'I'm fine,' I said, holding her weight as we continued towards the car, which was parked further down the lane.

It was dark and wet. Her feet slipped and tripped over themselves; her breath was sour.

When I opened the passenger door, she did not sit inside. Instead, she opened the back door and stretched out along the seat.

'I need to sleep.'

I heaved her up to secure her into her belt.

Her face was close to mine, her eyes stretched wide, 'I'm not going to miss my flight, am I?'

'No, you're fine. It's a couple of days away, don't worry.'

Her lids drooped, and I smoothed a wet strand of hair away from her forehead.

I climbed into the vinyl front seat, relieved to be dry and safe, and smoothed my hand over the old Bakelite steering wheel.

The winding lane out of the village towards the B-road seemed treacherous as the rain battered my old car. The headlights dazzled the dark countryside, highlighting the dashes of rain on the windscreen, flashing across the hedgerows and woodland. In better weather, I enjoyed these night drives. Nobody else on the roads; obscure music on the radio.

I increased the pace of the windscreen wipers, whose rubber screamed with age.

'I love this song,' Naomi piped up from behind me, reaching forward to turn the dial, flopping over the handbrake, groaning and laughing as she clambered back.

Her knees punched into the back of my seat. In the rear-view mirror, I could see she was dancing, waving her arms about to the beat, singing off-key.

'I LOVE THIS SONG!' she wailed out of the window, hanging her head out.

'Stop it! Get inside!' I turned back, and swerved a little into the middle of the road.

A speeding car came out of nowhere towards us and hurtled past.

She screamed, elated, and then I heard the quiet moan and the dry retching as she threw up again. The odour was magnified by the car heating, turning my own stomach. I tightened my grip on the wheel, pushing my face close to the windscreen, slowing a little as the wipers slashed the glass, left and right.

Up ahead, through the thick weather, I noticed someone walking alone under a black umbrella, a straggler from the party, perhaps.

'I feel better now! Why don't you ghost-drive?' she hollered into my ear.

Her hands were on my shoulders, pressing down.

'What's ghost-driving?'

'Here.' She reached forward to the wheel, her elbow in my ear, and shut off the lights.

The darkness enveloped us. The rain was hard on the roof. My heart leapt into my throat. I clicked them back on, clenching my jaw, and reorientated myself, looking for the figure I had seen, anticipating how I would overtake before the bend. The cackling and caterwauling from the back was distracting. I wanted to open the door and roll her out.

As we got closer to the night-walker, he looked back over his shoulder. Our eyes met. With a jolt, I recognised him. Those eyes. I'd know those eyes anywhere.

Then I felt Naomi's hot, clammy fingers covering my face. I couldn't see. The world was gone. I yelled. Her knees dug harder into my back through the seat and her laugh rose, loud and high, calling out like a banshee. I bit her little finger. She yelped and fell back. As she flopped back, whimpering, I saw the man again, parallel to the car.

Those eyes. They triggered me. Compelled by a force too strong for pre-planning, too hateful for good sense, I jerked the car to the left and heard the *clomp*. The noise reverberated through me, through the car's metal bonnet and into my bones, where that dark instinctive power to hurt that man had come from: spontaneously, unpremeditated. A spiderweb of glass had appeared; a splintered, bloody hash in the top corner of the windscreen, no bigger than a fist. Somehow, my foot pushed the brake to stop the car. In the silence, the radio grew loud, my breathing louder.

'Ouch. What? That hurt,' she whined from the back.

'Shut UP!' I yelled, stricken.

Turning back, I saw her wedged lengthways into the footwell, rubbing her sick-encrusted face, head lolling, eyes closing.

'Stay there,' I added, grabbing my phone. My hands shivered. I opened the car door.

Nipped by a gust of cold rain, I walked around the bonnet, sickening for a terrible sight. I resisted the urge to twist away, knowing I had to search for what I couldn't even contemplate discovering: for the night-walker's body to be crumpled in front of my car.

There was nothing. Nobody. The road was slick, polished by rain, and I wondered if I had experienced an apparition of the man with an umbrella. It could have been a deer. Could it? There was a small indentation in the roof, and blood smeared onto the distorted windscreen. The bonnet was undamaged. But then I saw the tangle of an umbrella by the front wheel. My stomach heaved as I picked it up. I lurched back into the car and shoved the evidence under the seat.

'What happened?' she mumbled.

'We must have hit a deer,' I replied, pushing down the handbrake, pulling away. The windscreen was unbroken on the driver's side.

'No!' she wailed, beginning to cry.

'It's okay. He didn't suffer.'

She sniffled and murmured, 'No, no, no...'

CHAPTER EIGHTEEN

I was not certain how I had arrived home yesterday. The car had ended up in the drive and I had walked inside the house, but I did not have a clear recollection of how I'd made it. Nor did I understand how I moved through the day with the girls, figuring out maths homework, playing Monopoly, roasting a chicken, calling my older brothers in Sydney, drying two loads of laundry for sports kits and uniform.

This morning, after kissing goodbye to Charlie at the train station and dropping the girls at school, as I would on any given Monday, I was on the point of collapse.

With every blink, whole sections of time seemed to pass me by. If I had told a friend, they would have been making me cups of sugary tea and telling me that I was in shock.

That was not how this kind of shock would play out. There would be nobody to hold my hand through this.

I floated through the kitchen, through the hallway, into the sitting room, around the furniture. I wanted to settle; to think, finally.

The coral and grey interior of my home, coordinated with such care and attention to detail, had lost its calming, comfortable appeal, and I saw these material possessions of mine with a dispassionate separateness, as though they had never belonged to me.

I sat in the coral armchair that faced the slate hearth, ashy and cold, and opened my laptop.

Armed with new information, with an actual name, I typed 'Jason Parker' and 'Exeter' and 'hit-and-run' and '1999' into my search engine. Familiar lists of websites and articles rolled down my screen, disappointingly similar to the last time I had searched. There were hundreds of reported cases of hit-and-run accidents, including heartfelt appeals from family members of injured or deceased victims written up on local newspaper websites, pleading for the perpetrators to come forward and confess. As I devoured article after article, I found nothing about historic cases, but I found countless stories of dangerous drivers who had been convicted and imprisoned for their hit-and-run crimes.

I looked away from the screen and out through our bay windows. Puffs of white cloud moved lazily across the sky, revealing the sun, allowing it to be glorious against its blue backdrop. Silvery bursts shot from the reflective surfaces in the room, from photo frames, from chrome table corners, from the bottles of spirits that sat on the drinks cabinet. Soon, a large cloud eclipsed the sun and the room fell grey. But the bottles still shone. The alcohol inside offered a break, a way to smother the mayhem in my head. I did not move towards the cabinet. I had sought out oblivion in a bottle before. If I resorted to those bottles, I would be lost, lost to Charlie, to Izzy and Diana. To repeat that pattern would be a catastrophe.

A catastrophe was brewing anyway. My happy family life, as it stood now, had ended.

I had never previously wanted to go back into the past to change anything, but now I wanted to rip into the space-time continuum and storm headlong into that pub on Stoke Road to take back our errors. Armed with this luxurious hindsight, I would tell Sophie that I did not want a lift in her blue Giulia. Or I could go back further, to earlier in the evening, and decide against that third Jack and Coke. Yes, that would be the place to start.

In one respect, I should have been grateful to Sophie for giving me twenty years of a good life. I had enjoyed twenty years of freedom. If she had forced me to see that dead body, any semblance of a good life would have ended there and then. Just as it had for Sophie. But Sophie had given me all the facts, and now it was over. It was over because I would have to go to the police.

The time had come for full disclosure. If I was honest, if I came clean, I could try to make amends for the twenty years that this young man's family had suffered; a perverse contrast to my own relative lack of suffering. I had to tell the police what we had done: I would be reporting a crime, an accidental death, a terrible tragedy.

I closed my laptop. I would drive there now, without delay. If I thought about it for too long, I would never do the right thing. The temptation to hold back, to save myself, would be too strong, so I buttoned up my coat and wound my scarf around my neck, slowly, as though this were the last time I would have such a freedom.

The drive to Guildford took twenty-two minutes up the A3. I imagined a karmic force swerving the car off the road, rolling it into the undergrowth, killing me: the ultimate retribution.

By the time I arrived at the busy police precinct, I was shaking violently, and I was cold and clammy.

The car park was busy. I drove round and round, just as I had walked round and round my house, trying to find a place to stop, to park, knowing that when I did, I would have to go ahead with my plan. Was it a plan? There had been no planning; it had been instinct, a reaction, and now that I was here, I felt terror. Perhaps this needed more planning. If I planned, I might not have to tell, I might save myself and leave the young man's mother to die without knowing who had been responsible for her son's death.

A parking space opened up. I drove the car into the tight slot and then sat at the wheel, staring at the officers swarming in and out of the grey institutional building, where there was regularity and order and justice, where a confession led to prosecution, where a prosecution led to punishment. Black and white. Good and bad. The contrasting chaos inside me escaped in bursts of irregular, short breaths, until I was light-headed, until I could feel the blood inside my veins bubbling with too much oxygen. My coping mechanisms were breaking down. The right move now would release this tension, heal me.

I opened the door, swung my legs out, gathered myself. I had to push my body to standing, through this fear. I told myself that I was an honest person, a good person, and I resolved to be the person I had been brought up to be. And here I stood, at the open car door, staring at the police station. I tried to take a step forward. My phone pinged with a text. I slid it out of my pocket. The text was a delivery notice about a case of wine arriving today – irrelevant – but when I saw the screen saver photograph of Izzy and Diana's faces, as they stood laughing and hugging, I was overwhelmed by regret and I weakened, fatally. There was no way I could walk in.

Charlie should know first. I would tell him tonight over supper. Together, we could come here on another day, a better day, with a lawyer and more information. I had arrived here in shock, on a whim, without working it through. What had I been thinking? I couldn't simply walk into a police station and confess to killing a man twenty years ago.

I secured the seat belt, making sure my body was pinned to the seat, imprisoning it, so that I was not able to make the biggest mistake of my life.

As I drove off and away from the police station at speed, there was a moment of release and then the dread seeped back. This first escape had been only a temporary stay of execution.

*

With a superhuman effort, I survived the school run in the afternoon, fooling myself that nothing had changed, acting with a normality that was a million miles away from how I felt inside.

At home, safe in one sense, I boiled salty water for the girls' spaghetti while they did their homework.

I thought back to the playground, to my bright smiles and jolly chat, and it shocked me that I had been capable of such a deceit. *Deceit.* I couldn't call it by any other name. I had presented a most hideous lie, a concealment of my identity. While we had the right to hide anxieties and secrets behind a public persona – we could not emote and overshare all the time – this new truth about myself changed who I was. And perhaps those good people around me had a right to know, like an employer had a right to know about a thief's criminal record, or a mother had a right to know that a paedophile lived on their street. They had a right to know that I had killed someone. My heart stopped every time I revisited this fact. But it wouldn't sink in. I learnt it afresh each time I thought of it. And the shock never lessened.

As I reached up to the top shelf for the tomato pasta sauce, that night, twenty years ago, rushed at me, unsteadying me, and I wobbled, almost dropping the jar.

I slammed the lid onto the pan, too loudly, and the girls both looked up from their workbooks.

'Sorry!' I trilled.

I tried to listen to the girls' chatter behind me, tried to deal with their whining, respond to their random anecdotes, cook them their tea, but I was preoccupied by the past and already weary with it.

I needed the memories to go away.

I clock-watched. At exactly 6 p.m., I finally allowed myself to reach into the fridge for a glass of wine.

The fuzzy feeling layered itself on top of my troubled memories, over my angst about my plan to tell Charlie like a light protective gauze, helping me along with the girls' bedtime and bath-time routine.

I could do this. I could tell him. Yes, I could!

After three glasses of supermarket white wine on an empty stomach, I began to question this crazy idea I'd had of a confession. Was it so urgent? Did I have to tell him tonight? Was it not better to let it sink in first?

When Charlie arrived home, rumpled and tired, I tried not to slur my words.

'Cottage pie?'

'Great,' he said, taking a lime from the fruit bowl and the Angostura bitters from the cupboard. Everything was still normal in his world, and I wondered if he noticed that every single molecule of my body was vibrating with change.

'Can I have one of those tonight?'

'Are you sure?' he asked me.

Had I asked him if I should jump off a cliff?

'I fancy one tonight, for some reason,' I said lightly.

Would now be a good time to tell him?

'Okay,' he replied slowly, turning away to get another glass out of the cupboard.

If I do tell him, I'll wait until we've eaten.

By the time I had boiled the peas, prepared the salad and laid the table, I was sucking down the last few drops of my gin and tonic. I put two wine glasses on the table and brought the cottage pie out of the oven, burning my finger on the edge.

'I saw Alistair on the platform at Waterloo,' Charlie said, scooping up a huge spoonful of mince.

'Who?' I poured two glasses of wine and took a few gulps before I placed it back on the table.

'Alistair.'

'Alistair?' My mind wasn't engaging.

Charlie finished serving up. 'Tamara's dad,' he replied, and his eyes flicked down to my glass and away again. That disapproving little glance was enough to remind me of how sober he was. It convinced me to back away from a confession. If he had a problem with me drinking a couple of glasses of wine on a weekday – whoopdie-do! – what the hell was he going to think if I opened up to him completely?

'Oh. *That* Alistair,' I laughed. 'How did you avoid him this time?'

'I ran to the last carriage and hid behind my *Evening Standard*.'

'Lucky escape,' I said.

I looked at my husband's grey hair and muddy green eyes, whose mood was hard to pin down behind the reflection of his glasses, and I shivered at the thought of telling him.

Dutifully, I asked him about his day.

'There were more redundancies today,' he said.

'You're not worried, are you?'

'No. Not at all,' he replied, vigorously shaking his head. 'Last in, first out.'

Reassured, my mind drifted back; far, far back again.

'Earth to Naomi.' Charlie's hand was waving in front of my face, pinging one of my curls. 'Are you okay?'

I looked down at my plate, as though this might have the answers. It was empty. Had I eaten it?

'Sorry. Yes. Just a bit tired. I might go to bed early and read for a bit.'

And I walked out of the kitchen, leaving Charlie to clear up, which was unusual, possibly unheard of. But I could not have lifted one fork or one plate, let alone coordinated the clearing of a whole table.

I climbed into bed, took my watch off, placed it on my bedside table, reached for my book, stared at the pages, closed my eyes and felt my whole body seize up. Another memory came to me. It strobed through my mind in nasty bursts. It was not the night of the accident, it was before that, two months before.

I opened my eyes to stop the atrocity from playing out in my mind, disorientated, surprised I was still in bed with my book in my hands.

A violent rage thundered through me and I ran to the bathroom to be sick, just as I had been sick outside the pub that night.

CHAPTER NINETEEN

'What are you going to do now you know?' Sophie asked Naomi down the phone line as she continued her run through the woods.

'I went to the police station.'

A lag of recognition, as she paused to catch her breath, as she thought about what this meant for them.

'When?'

'Yesterday.'

Sophie's heart thundered. She started jogging slowly.

'Did you go in?'

'No. I'm going to tell Charlie first. Get a lawyer.'

She sounded bold and sure of herself.

'Do you know what will happen to us?'

'Yes.' There was a crack in her voice.

'You know, then, that it's an indictable offence. Death by dangerous driving. Fourteen years' imprisonment.'

'But it was an accident. They won't send us to prison.'

Sophie laughed at Naomi's naivety. 'They *might* not rely on our memory alone after all this time. They'd certainly need evidence to convict.'

'What evidence would they use? It's been twenty years.'

Sophie stopped in her tracks to explain.

'What if they decide to use our taped interviews for evidence? What if they already have more evidence from the crime scene than we think? What if someone saw the car? What if they found remnants of the car paint on his body? What if someone in the house-to-house investigations told an officer something they didn't follow up on at the time? What if they are waiting for one more piece to the puzzle, which you would provide if you walked in to report the crime?'

'Still…' she said, trailing off.

'Why do it now, Naomi? What's the point?'

'You really have to ask? Can you even imagine what his mother is going through?'

'But you're a mother, too, now. What about the girls?'

There was another break in the flow of their conversation. Then Sophie heard Naomi's soft crying. Sophie had to bite the inside of her cheek to stop the wry burst of laughter. It hadn't taken much to break Naomi's tough talk, to weaken her moral stance, but as she listened to her cry, Sophie felt a spasm of guilt: the emotion she had buried so successfully. Naomi's anguish was digging out her own. Her sympathy for Jason Parker's mother brought Sophie's to the surface. Before now, the event had been clear-cut, a cardboard cutout experience. The rest of it, the bulk of it, the panoramic emotional view of it had been pushed down so deep into her psyche that she had not been able to dredge out one iota of her empathetic self. The mess of it had been streamlined for survival. If she kept the secret, they would escape prison. If she kept the secret, they would have a life. The moral maze had seemed a luxury. Until now.

'I hate myself,' Naomi hissed down the phone.

'You know you wouldn't survive prison, Naomi,' Sophie said, poised to tell her the full story if necessary – the need-to-know moment – braced for impact, in full survival mode, which had served her well enough so far. She would not let Naomi bring her down.

Naomi sobbed. 'I'm not brave enough.'

And then Sophie knew they were safe. The tingles of angst dispersed. She was relieved that Naomi was not a brave person. Naomi was a charmed person, who had been blown through life, like a dandelion seed, by others' love for her: relying on her mother to steer her through childhood, then Sophie at university and then Charlie in adulthood. It was too late to become the self-sacrificing heroine. People didn't change. Neither would Naomi. She would continue to float on the breath of others: two breaths, two o'clock; five breaths, five o'clock; twelve breaths, midnight, until the stamen was bald, until time had run out, until death took her under its own aegis.

Sophie unravelled the greying bandage on her hand to see that the skin across her palm had healed.

*

Sophie held two linen swatches over the showroom sofa.

'What do you think? The grey or the coral?' Sophie called over to Dylan.

Dylan didn't answer, and continued grabbing handfuls of swatches from the cubbyholes.

'I think that might be enough now, sweetie,' Sophie said, rolling her eyes at the sales assistant, who offered a fake smile in return.

Dylan emptied three cubbyholes completely and returned to the sofa with the squares of velvets and linens bunched into his fist. Kneeling at the sofa, he began to lay them out over the seat cushions like a mosaic.

'Beautiful, darling,' Sophie said, returning to her own two linens. 'I think the coral,' she said to herself. 'I've decided,' she said to the sales assistant. 'Can I order it now, please?'

It took half an hour to work out the added extras, insurance and delivery options before she handed over her credit card to pay for it. She could afford the monthly repayments now that they had found new tenants for the cottage. A Mr and Mrs Etherington would be moving in on 1 May, in a month's time.

She walked out of the shopping centre, high on the money she had spent and thrilled by the prospect of this coral linen sofa, which was going to be delivered to Deda's front room in two weeks' time. She had not wasted a moment before setting out on the transformation of the cottage, spending all week painting the front room a fashionable light grey.

Adam had warned her that there was no point choosing good paint and furniture for a rental property, but Sophie had ignored him. Having pinned various photographs on a mood board on her phone, she had a dream of how it would look when she was finished. Creating it from scratch had given her a new lease of life.

In the future, when she had the money, when she had found herself a job, she planned to live in the cottage with Dylan, as she had once promised Adam they would. Naomi would approve of this plan. She and Naomi could repair their friendship in this new setting. They would sit curled up next to each other on the coral sofa, sipping weak tea with lemon out of delicate china – just as Deda had liked it – putting the world to rights. Dylan and the girls would play outside with the chickens or on a tree-swing or with a new puppy. Rare-breed chickens and puppies and tree-swings! Fresh paint and new floors and forever friends! That was all she wanted.

When she unwrapped the fresh, new life she was preparing, she wondered if Adam would be able to resist coming back home. Once upon a time, they had shared the same outlook and aspirations for their future: quite simple, low-key, happy. Somehow, along the way, Sophie had lost sight of this, by staying in the past, holing up in the mess of the shack like a chick burrowing into the twigs of her nest, waiting to be fed, beak open; waiting for Adam or Naomi or Deda to help her, unable to process her resentment towards Naomi, unable to accept that Deda wasn't coming back, dying of starvation before helping herself to what she needed.

Everything was different now. Her friendship with Naomi had been solidified. The secret was shared. The vodka bottles were in the bin. The shot glasses were packed away. The house was being renovated, with a new boiler and damp-proofing and fresh paint. The hovering fear of losing Naomi was gone, as though an aircraft laden with bombs had zoomed off, leaving her free to twirl under a crisp blue sky.

Sophie was sweeping the dust from the newly sanded parquet floor in Deda's sitting room. She wanted it to look perfect for Naomi.

The window was open to let the paint fumes out. Sharp, cold swirls of wind blew the windows, *bang*, back and forth. *Bang. Bang. Bang.* They did not have latches. As Sophie closed them, she glanced out and saw that Dylan was dragging the axe that was bigger and heavier than he was towards the small pile of logs in the middle of the front garden. 'Put that thing down, Dylan!' Sophie yelled out of the window.

'I can do it, you know! I'm the man of the house now.'

Sophie's insides melted with pride and sadness.

'As the man of the house, I need you to come and help me clean up in here.'

'Don't want to,' Dylan whined, lifting the axe, letting it wobble precariously in his skinny, scabbed arms, raising it higher and higher above his head.

The broom clattered to the floor as Sophie ran outside.

Just at the point when she was wrestling the axe out of Dylan's hands, Naomi's car swung round the corner. Behind the reflection of the shiny car windows, Sophie could see Izzy and Diana's mouths open, agog. Sophie yanked the tool forcefully from Dylan, feeling immediately judged by the Wilson girls.

Sophie expected them to slide off their cream leather seats, perfectly turned out, with neat jeans and brushed hair, as per usual.

She expected to see Naomi's beautiful corkscrew curls tamed and shined, her lips glossed, her plumped-up cheeks rosy.

And here Sophie was wrestling with Dylan over an axe.

The girls' car doors opened first. A crisp packet fell out and swirled in the wind at Izzy's feet, which were covered only by flip-flops on this cold April afternoon. She had a smear of milk across her top lip and her hair consisted of two clumps in pigtails. Diana was no less dishevelled. It looked like she might be in her pyjamas under her down jacket. Sophie was alarmed by this change in them.

Worse still was the state of Naomi. Her curls were greased into a tight, low, centre-parted ponytail. Her eyes were as puffy as marshmallows and her skin was mottled pink and white underneath smears of badly applied foundation.

Her greeting, *hello*, was loud and high and enthusiastic in Sophie's ear as she kissed her on one cheek, but there was no smile attached.

When she bent back into the car to bring a supermarket bag-for-life out of the front seat, she grunted as though the effort was too much.

Having felt rankled by the prospect of their smugness a moment before, having spent her life resenting it, she now wished they were back to their normal selves.

'I brought you something to celebrate with,' Naomi said, handing her the bag. The light in her eyes had returned for a second, and Sophie wondered if she had read too much into their outward appearances.

Sophie peered into the bag.

'Two rather posh sparkling wines. I was sent them yesterday with a complimentary box of chocs,' Naomi said, rubbing her hands together. And in a whisper, 'Thought we could sample some this afternoon!'

Sophie's optimism began to dissipate. 'I'm not really drinking at the moment, remember,' Sophie said, reminding Naomi of the sobriety that Naomi herself had insisted upon.

'A little glass of good-quality bubbly won't hurt. We're celebrating your new rental business, aren't we?'

'I can eat the chocolates, thank you,' Sophie replied stiffly. 'Come in and see. Come on girls, come and see what I've done.'

She chucked open the door to the sitting room. '*Et voilà!*'

'Wow! Lovely!' Izzy and Diana cried.

'Look at this!' Dylan said, surfing the shiny floorboards in his socks.

Sophie was endeared by his showing off, but she was the only one to laugh.

Naomi brushed one hand across the paint. 'We have the same colour in our sitting room.'

'I saw it on Pinterest,' Sophie replied defensively. Naomi wasn't the only person in the world to have light grey walls, she thought.

'It looks so stylish in here,' Naomi said, wandering over to the inglenook fireplace. Her fingers drummed the stone mantel.

'Mummy! Look!' Izzy cried. 'We have this table!'

'Do you?' Sophie said. Sophie had not consciously chosen the same chrome coffee table.

'Ours is slightly smaller,' Naomi said.

'Don't you think it's transformed in here?'

'Very nice,' Naomi said, and then patted the five-bar heater as though it were a dog. 'What are you going to put here? Wood burner or open fireplace?'

'We're keeping it, actually. Even with the fixed central heating, it gets cold in this room for some reason, and we wanted to keep the costs down.'

'I saw one of those pretty iron fireguards in that bric-a-brac shop on the high street. I'll get it for you as a house-warming present.'

Sophie flushed. She hadn't thought about its poor aesthetic. She had grown so used to the fireplace over the decades. 'The tenants didn't seem to mind.'

'They want the place furnished, I see,' she said, sitting down on the new coral sofa, which had been delivered yesterday.

'They're an older couple. Just retired. They've sold their house in London, and most of their furniture, downsizing or something, so they can afford to travel. They said they'll be off on cruises a lot, which suits me.'

'Well done for turning it around,' Naomi said, winking.

'Can we go outside?' Izzy asked.

'Of course,' Sophie replied. 'Off you go. Dylan can show you his new camp in the woods.'

The three children charged out, while Sophie and Naomi sauntered to the door.

'I've got a lot more to do, but I'm excited.'

Now the children were gone, it was like a cord had been pulled on Naomi's expression. All the muscles that had held up her features slackened. She rubbed at her upper arms.

'It's freezing in here,' she snapped.

'The fire's on in the shack,' Sophie said.

'Let's go and have a drink.'

The gravel under their feet was loud as they walked in silence across to the shack, which was hot and stuffy inside.

Before Naomi took her coat off, she put one bottle of sparkling wine in the fridge and popped the cork on the other.

Sophie noticed how her hands shook slightly as she tipped each flute to pour.

'Cheers to you,' Naomi said in a flat tone, handing Sophie her glass, barely waiting for her to clink their rims before she took a large gulp.

Sophie brought the drink up to her mouth, wrestling with an inner voice. The bubbles tickled her nose. She pretended to take a sip. The alcohol wet her lips and she licked it off, swooning at the taste.

'I'll open these chocolates,' Sophie suggested, craving distraction, placing her glass down to unwrap the cellophane.

Naomi's eyes were on her.

Then, in a shallow, breathy voice that Sophie didn't recognise or like, Naomi hissed, 'How do you do this *sober*?'

Sophie continued to open the chocolates. The waft of sweetness filled her head.

'I haven't, mostly,' she said, and she stared baldly at Naomi, waiting for her to recognise her memory lapse.

Naomi expelled an unhappy, dimple-free laugh. 'No. I suppose not.'

'But I'm telling you, from experience, it isn't going to make it any easier,' Sophie said.

'I haven't been overdoing it, you know,' she frowned, redoing her greasy ponytail. 'Just a few here and there to take the edge off.'

'Has Charlie said anything?'

'Why would he? I've just told you I haven't been overdoing it.'

'Fine.'

'It's a Saturday afternoon and we're celebrating.'

'Yes. Sorry.'

Naomi poured herself another drink.

'Do you want me to drive you home?' Sophie asked.

'This is only my second. I'm allowed two.'

But as the afternoon wore on into evening, as they talked about anything and everything other than the night that bloomed in a nasty cloud between them, Naomi had finished the bottle and opened the next. After the children had finished their pizzas, Sophie again suggested she drive them home.

'Might be a good idea!' Naomi chuckled, tickling Diana in the ribs and kissing her until she wriggled away.

She moved on to smother Izzy, who said, 'Yuck! You smell of wine!'

They piled into the car.

'It's dark, Mummy, and we're not in bed yet!' Diana cried.

'It's shockingly late, you girls. Straight into bed when you get home!'

'It's only eight thirty. Our bedtime is ten o'clock,' Izzy said.

Naomi twisted round to the three of them in the back. 'Don't fib, Izzy. Your bedtime is eight o'clock every night.'

'It said ten o'clock when you told me to turn my iPad off last night.'

'iPads in bed? You know I never allow that,' Naomi tutted, sounding angry now.

'But you did!' Izzy insisted.

'Sometimes it's okay,' Sophie said, trying to defuse Naomi's embarrassment.

There was a lull in the chatter.

'I've had a tough few weeks, that's all,' Naomi muttered, staring out into the black night.

And Sophie lamented the disappearance of her friend's kind, spirited disposition. It scared her that she wasn't the same.

'Bye, girls,' Sophie said as the girls, and Dylan, clambered out of the car.

Naomi didn't immediately follow her daughters. Her shoulders rounded and her head fell into her hands. 'What are we going to do?' she moaned.

'It's going to be okay,' Sophie whispered, stroking her back.

She could feel Naomi's ribs heaving with quiet sobs. 'I can't live with this inside me, I can't do it. I don't know how to live with it, Sophie,' she repeated over and over as Sophie continued soothing her, but Sophie was feeling increasingly unnerved.

'It'll get easier,' she lied, remembering this had been what others had said to her after Deda had died. Cold air ran up her spine. It wasn't true. It didn't get easier, it just changed into a feeling that was lower-level, that was just about bearable, that you could just about live through. There was nothing easy about it. Naomi would have to adjust, to toughen up.

'Dylan, honey! Back in the car please,' Sophie called out of her window, and Naomi's ribs jumped under her hand. 'You'd better get them to bed and try to act as normal as possible.'

'I want to tell Charlie,' she whimpered.

'You can't.'

'I keep thinking of that mother. I went to the library to see if there was any more information about the family, but I was too paranoid to do the research in case someone was watching me.' She looked around her furtively. 'I had to leave.'

'Nobody's watching you, Naomi,' Sophie said.

'Do you think the mum's still alive?'

'Who knows?'

'*Who knows?*'

'We can't bring him back for her, Naomi.'

'Have there been any more appeals in the papers?'

'None. And if you keep quiet, and if they don't find any new evidence, we'll be safe,' Sophie reminded her.

'I want to find out if his mother is okay. What if I went to see her?'

'Are you fucking serious?' Sophie hissed.

'I could pretend to be someone else.'

'No! No way, Naomi. That's insane. There'd be no point.'

'But I want to feel better,' she cried, groaning.

'Have you forgotten that you could end up in prison for fourteen years?'

A strangled noise came from deep within Naomi, and she opened the door as if she was going to be sick into the driveway. The girls distracted her.

'Are you okay, Mummy?'

Naomi rallied herself for long enough to get out of the car. 'Of course I am! Come on, then. Say thank you to Sophie and let's get you into bed.'

But Sophie knew that trouble was brewing. Naomi was unstable, which left them both vulnerable. Deep inside Sophie there was a disturbance, a rumbling of unease that Naomi's hysteria poked at. Sophie began to regret telling Naomi. Sharing it might have brought them closer, as Deda had predicted, but Sophie hadn't thought through Naomi's reaction. She had assumed that Naomi would be rational and sensible, self-preserving. The hope that it could remain as their dirty little secret – shared and halved, harbouring it together, hurting together – had been optimistic. Thrown, Sophie would have to think again, and find a way to stamp out Naomi's attack of conscience.

It had been a mistake to hold back the rest of the newspaper cuttings. It was time for her to read them. Once Naomi knew who he was, she would quit her brooding. She might even be pleased.

CHAPTER TWENTY

Hidden behind sunglasses, which shielded my eyes, bloodshot and bone-dry, I walked out of the car park and through the quiet residential streets of Exeter.

My mobile was directing me, with its blue line and its nine-minute prediction, to Ilene Parker's address, which had been so simple to find in the UK phone directory online.

I had not set foot in this town since the day I had packed up my room, stripped my bed and vowed never to come back.

Yet here I was, walking over a zebra crossing that had not existed when I had lived here. Nothing had existed, perhaps. We had been practising at life. We had fumbled through three years, hurtling towards a cataclysmic denouement; experiencing an ending to our youth, to our naivety, while covering our hands over our faces, peering through our fingers, too scared to view it properly.

On the eighth Google Maps minute, I arrived at the long, wide, speed-bumped avenue where she lived, thinking about how easy it had been to walk here, how easy it had been to find the address, how easy it had been to lie to Charlie. He believed that I was at a private wine-tasting function in Devon, and that I would be staying overnight. I had spun the same lie to Sophie, who had called me to suggest I meet her at her grandfather's cottage later. She had sounded cryptic, implying she had something to show me.

As I walked along the pavement, clocking the numbers on the doors of four bungalows in a row, I came within sight of the fifth bungalow, No. 9. It had a white door. All the bungalows had white doors. Her neighbour's house, to the left, had a front garden that was stuffed with roses of every colour imaginable. To the right, her other neighbours had squished a caravan onto their drive and covered it with a white tent. On the opposite side of the road there was a row of pretty flint terraced houses.

It was strange to see such normality, such a prosaic setting for such a monstrous situation.

I removed my sunglasses and approached her red-brick home and pressed the white doorbell.

In a strangely detached moment, I thought of a friend's account of her excruciating experience as a researcher, doorstepping potential contributors for a Channel 4 documentary she had been working on about the elderly victims of a Nigerian telephone fraud gang. Considering the nature of the crime, the only way of gaining the victims' trust had been to knock on their doors and approach them directly, with a young, innocent smile and an official badge. Her friend had described how grubby she had felt, almost as grubby as the Nigerian gang, by exploiting these frail, vulnerable people once again.

Trying to imagine myself in my friend's shoes, as a professional with a job to do,

I went over what I had prepared to say. It would be another lie. A lie to cover a bigger lie.

I wiped my sticky hands down my trousers and straightened the pendant around my neck. It shocked me that I was really here, that I was going to do this without Sophie's knowledge. I would play a part, method-act my way out of my head and into her home, and I might survive it without breaking down, without giving myself away.

There were no guarantees she would be in, nor could I assume that she would talk to me for more than two minutes before closing the door in my face.

Blowing out puffs of air to allow my voice to hold steady, I pressed her doorbell. A long tune, like a pop song verse, rang out from behind the door. There was no response. I pressed it again.

There were potted hyacinths sitting either side of the doorstep, and three macramé hanging pots filled with wild strawberry leaves. A pair of large black trainers was positioned neatly in front of one plant pot. The size suggested they might belong to a man, but I had found no record of a husband in the directory. Through the frosted glass panel I could see a heart-shaped ornament hanging there. Already it was clear that the occupant of this house was neat and house-proud.

I would ring the doorbell once more.

But before my fingertip touched the white button, the locks were being rattled from the inside. The unlocking took a while, suggesting she was extremely concerned about unwanted visitors, and I realised that I was one of them. My stomach crunched with nerves.

Seconds before she was revealed, I almost ran, but once I caught a glimpse of her face, I was transfixed.

She had a ratty grey-blonde fringe, long over her narrow forehead, and her skin was orange and deeply creased into jagged tributaries that split in multiple directions across her facial bones, too many to identify any frown or laugh lines. And then there were her eyes, slits of milky blue, menacing and cold.

'Can I help you?' she asked, impolitely, flashing a quick, sharp smile.

She was a small, slight woman, but her voice, her face, her presence before me was larger and more vivid than anyone I had ever met. I couldn't believe I was standing in front of her. I paused, fearing, illogically, that she would recognise me. The power of my connection to her son was so great, it amazed me that she would not know who I was. I had the sense that I'd pulled a mask off my face.

A macabre fascination had drawn me to this woman's door. I should not be here, under false pretences, to meet this grieving mother, from whom I had already taken so much. I should not want to seek out evidence, to hear live testimony that she had loved her son as I loved Diana and Izzy, that she had felt his loss as keenly as I would, that she could not rest until her killer was brought to justice. I wasn't sure I was capable of bearing witness to that kind of pain while knowing I was responsible for it. But here I was. I knew I deserved to see it. I was magnetised by the idea of putting myself through it.

'Hello, sorry to disturb you, but I'm thinking of renting that house over there, and I just wanted to ask you about the area,' I said, pointing to the letting sign across the road.

With an irritated sigh, she said, 'It's a dump. Does that help?'

Taken aback, I stuttered, 'Oh, I'm sorry, really?'

Ilene Parker pressed her cheek into the door frame, glancing over my head as though someone might jump out at her. 'That bastard refuses to move his rotten old caravan and that cow the other side of me snips at those bloody roses all day when she knows they play havoc with my hay fever. There's no community spirit here, love.'

'That's a shame,' I said. 'I really value community.'

She cackled, but it turned into a chesty cough and her eyes wept. 'I'm sure you do,' she spluttered, looking me up and down with a sneer.

Her rude manner threw me. I found her repellent, as though she had crawled all over me, licking me with a foul tongue. I had expected to feel even sorrier than before for what had happened to her son, but I did not.

'You get the measure of your neighbours when something bad happens,' I continued, seeing an in, trying to fight my urge to run. While standing in her presence, I scrabbled to find sympathy, contemplating how her grief might have changed her, but I found nothing generous inside me.

Her lips puckered into a hard pout. She let go of the door frame and crossed her arms over her chest, but her voice softened. 'There was a time when this community bent over backwards for each other, but it's gone. All gone. It's the way of the world now.'

I wanted to cry. A fellow human being, in that world she talked so cynically about, had left her son to die by the roadside to be eaten by creatures and bloat and stiffen until he was found by the police. Twenty years later, they still hadn't confessed. *We* had not confessed. I could not blame her for being bitter.

'I'm sorry,' I said, before I could stop myself.

I wasn't sure I had been heard, but she laughed at me again. 'It's not your fault, love.'

Her words smothered me. Blobs of white formed across my eyeballs and my head lost its weight.

'I'm so sorry, but I'm feeling a little faint,' I said, hanging over my knees. The blood rushed into my face. I stood up, mortified.

She stared down at me and a fleeting frown passed across her features. I felt a rush of regret. I had made a terrible mistake in coming here.

'Would you like to come in for a glass of water?' she asked, with a stick-on smile.

'No, no, it's okay. I didn't mean to bother you,' I said.

'Come on, we're going to be neighbours, aren't we?'

I wasn't sure her kindness was sincere, but I had a decision to make in a split second. I had come all this way to know more about her, and I was being invited into her home. Fleeing, suddenly, might seem suspicious.

'That's very kind. Thank you.'

'Come on in.'

Her home smelt of stale biscuits and dirty bedclothes.

We walked through to the kitchen at the back of the house. On the way, she closed a door to a bedroom on the right. I thought I heard someone moving in the bed, and I thought of the black trainers on the doorstep.

'I'm so sorry about this,' I said, walking very slowly past the other open door, to the left, which revealed a small sitting room. The three walls that I could see were white and bare. The sills and coffee table were clear of frames or ornaments, except for a crystal glass fairy that sat on a corner table and refracted rainbows across the room. It was oddly pretty in such a soulless room. I shivered, imagining its glassy eyes watching me, all-seeing, all-knowing.

We had to walk through a bamboo curtain, painted with a sunset pattern, to get through to the kitchen. One of the beaded strands got caught on my bracelet and I felt caught like a fly in a web as I untangled it.

My eyes darted around the purple kitchen trying to find evidence of her late son's life. One of two magnets on the fridge door was in the shape of a flip-flop, pinning up a shopping list; the other was a clay disc depicting white stone houses on a hillside, holding up an NHS referral letter. Two crayon drawings were Blu-Tacked to one of the kitchen cabinets, both signed by a child called Molly in Year One. Still I could not find a photograph of Jason Parker.

The water made a loud splattering sound in the metal sink. 'What did you say your name was again?' she asked, handing me the filled glass.

'I didn't. But it's Gaby,' I replied, smiling, having thought of the false name this morning. I had planned this intrusion carefully. I had tied my dirty hair into a bun to hide its memorable curls. I had worn black, nondescript clothes. I had even taken off my wedding ring and swapped my expensive handbag for a cloth holdall. My car, with its identifying number plate, was parked anonymously in the car park a few streets away.

'I'm Ilene,' she said, jamming her fingers into her jeans pockets, spreading her elbows wide, making her thin frame bigger. 'What estate agent did you say you were using?'

'Bellows and Turner,' I replied. It was an online agency, with which I had registered my fake details. The pads of my fingers began rolling up and down the glass.

'Rip-off merchants,' she said.

'Bellows and Turner?'

'Estate agents, the lot of them.'

'That's why I wanted to ask around a bit.'

'What did you want to know?'

'A few things I was worried about. Like the traffic. Is it bad in rush hour? I've heard it can be a bit of a cut-through.'

Her eyes passed over me from head to toe. 'Not since the speed bumps.'

'And there haven't been any town planning notices for high-rise tower blocks or nuclear power stations at the end of the street?' I laughed, remembering that a prospective buyer of our flat in Richmond had asked us this.

Ilene did not laugh. She answered me earnestly, as though it had been a serious question, as though a catastrophe like that would not be a surprise to her. 'Not that I know of. You'll only be renting, is that right?'

'Yes. We won't be here long. I'm looking to buy in one of the villages.'

'Where do you live now?'

'London.'

Her eyes narrowed, barely open enough to see her iris. 'I thought I'd be here three years, tops, and I'm still here twenty-three years later.'

The mouthful of water lay like a lake sloshing over my tongue. Twenty-three years ago Jason Parker would have started his degree course.

'What brought you here?' I asked, gulping my water down, ploughing on.

She hesitated. 'Work,' she replied, picking at her earlobe, where four empty piercings gaped. She was lying.

'Do you get many noisy students crammed into these houses?'

Her hand fell from her ear and she glared at me. 'The students give the place some bloody life.'

'I have a thirteen-year-old son,' I said quickly. 'I'd quite like him to go to the university one day.'

A twitch of a smile came to her lips. I waited, quietly.

I wanted her to talk about Jason. I wanted her to tell me he had died, and how. I wanted her to tell me how she had coped when the police had discovered his body, two weeks after he had been reported missing. I wanted her to express her feelings about the hit-and-run driver. I wanted her to detail her experiences of waiting, day in, day out, for a witness to come forward after her appeals. I wanted to know how she remained sane in the face of never knowing.

But it had been more than curiosity and concern and self-flagellation that had brought me to her door: it had been my soul on its knees, forehead on floor, arms outstretched to her feet, begging her soul for mercy, desperate for her touch, for a blessing from her higher self. I had come here to lay the groundwork for my confession, to spot potential for forgiveness, to seek out an avenue for my own redemption. It had been wholly selfish and cowardly in spirit. It would be worth very little to her and very much to me.

Time was running out. She would not let me stand here drinking water all day.

Into the silence came the rattle of bamboo, and in slid a man of about thirty, wearing tracksuit bottoms and a vest. His muscles were pale and his shoulders rounded, like he had been scooped out from hips to chin. A line from the pillow worked its way down one of his cheeks like a scar.

He stared at me as he bowled across the room to stand by Ilene's side. 'Who's this, then?' he asked Ilene, kissing her, open-mouthed, while reaching for a box of teabags. I wanted to gasp in shock. It was like watching a grandson and his grandmother in a sexual tryst. This young man could not possibly have been Jason Parker's father.

'She's thinking of renting across the road,' she answered him, as though I was no longer there.

'We've got to be at Mike's at eleven.'

She put her hand out to take my empty glass. Her gaze was no longer searching. She had moved on from me to her young boyfriend's needs, and to Mike, whoever he was. I must have imagined her suspicion of me. Perhaps she was suspicious of everyone in equal measure.

'Thank you so much for this. I'm so sorry for disturbing you,' I said, handing her the tumbler.

'No harm done,' she said, and she followed me out of the kitchen.

No harm done, but nothing gained either. Why had I come here? It wasn't clear to me now. I had discovered very little that satisfied me, other than how much I disliked her, and, possibly, that she had moved here twenty-three years ago to be near to Jason when he had started at Exeter, which suggested they had been close. But why no photographs anywhere?

Our three souls would never meet here today. Ilene Parker's had been barricaded in by her anger, and I guessed she would never place a hand of forgiveness anywhere near my head. If Sophie and I confessed, I imagined she would want us to burn alive, let alone in hell. I loathed myself for coming here, for cheating her out of her right to the truth once again.

On the way out, I noticed that the door to the bedroom was now wide open.

And there, on the chest of drawers, I saw what had been missing from the rest of the house. There were multicoloured fairy lights draped around a cluster of photographs of a sandy-haired, narrow-eyed boy. Baby snaps and school photographs crowded for space around a burnt-down candle. Dozens of greetings cards were slotted in and around the frames as though he had died only yesterday.

Ilene must have noticed my staring.

'That's my son,' Ilene said softly. She ducked into the bedroom to pull a photograph of the same boy, as a teenager, from the chest of drawers, to show me.

As soon as I clapped eyes on his face, I became rigid. My bones fused under my flesh. Those eyes. I would remember those pale, thin eyes forever. And that grey skin that was pulled back across his features, tight and mean. Forever imprinted on my mind.

I was pinned to the spot by his ghostly presence, just as I had been pinned to the bed once, and I experienced a sucking sensation in my stomach. It was horror and shame, pulling out my insides. I reeled back from the photograph as though swerving away from his outstretched groping. But he was dead. I was safe.

I hurried out, glancing behind me one more time, to see that face in the largest colour photograph. It brought back a series of sickening flashes, over which I heard Ilene Parker's voice echo around my head. Most likely she was saying goodbye, and I responded as well as I could, somehow finding a way to walk with forward momentum, promising to knock on her door when I moved in across the road.

This last spineless lie, this final sidestepping, almost knocked me down. I would never knock on her door again. Not now I knew; not now I recognised who her son was.

CHAPTER TWENTY-ONE

Sophie watched Diana, Izzy and Dylan being told off by the lifeguard. Dylan had narrowly missed jumping on top of an old lady who was doing lengths with a shower cap on and plastic bags tied to her ankles. Naomi stood up from the viewing platform, where she and Sophie sat, and gesticulated at the three children, wagging her finger.

Sophie pulled her down to sitting. In the light of what Naomi had just told her, the children's antics were irrelevant. They spoke in whispers, although the distorted, amplified noises from the Saturday swimming pool crowds would have soaked up their voices even if they'd been shouting at one another.

'You did *what*?' Sophie hissed.

'I went to see her.'

Instantly, Sophie's right palm began to itch.

'Who picked up the kids?'

'Charlie. I told him I was working in Devon.'

'Are you *insane*? He could have checked.'

She brought her face close to Sophie's. 'It was *him*. It was *Jay*.'

'I know.'

Naomi's pretty eyes became hollow shadows. 'You *knew*?'

'Yes.' Sophie breathed deeply. 'Do you feel better about it now?'

'*Better*?' she spluttered.

'You're sure Ilene Parker believed your story?'

Naomi avoided answering. 'Was it a terrible coincidence, Sophie? Please tell me it was a coincidence.'

'You're sure she didn't suspect anything?' Sophie asked, also sidestepping.

'No! She didn't suspect a thing.'

'She didn't suspect a thing,' Sophie said, repeating Naomi's words, as though allowing them to settle.

'If she suspected anything, she would have asked me more questions. She wasn't interested in me.'

But Sophie could hear tears in her voice, and saw how fast her fingers tapped her knees.

'I told you not to go.'

'I wanted to know what she was like.'

'Did you find out?'

'She was horrible.'

'Good.'

'That doesn't matter any more.'

'I think it does,' Sophie said.

Naomi dug her fingers into Sophie's upper arm and whispered urgently at her, 'Sophie, please tell me you didn't see who it was before... before...'

'I told you what happened. I saw a man and you distracted me and the car swerved,' Sophie said, turning her eyes from the pool to Naomi.

'I didn't see him at the party...' she said, shaking her head.

'I did. I saw him when I was having a smoke outside and I told him to leave.'

Naomi was aghast. 'You saw him there and you never told me?'

'I didn't want to bring it all up for you again. I was protecting you, Naomi.'

Naomi's fingers clamped over her plump thighs like claws. 'Oh my god. Oh my god. I can't believe this is happening. I don't know what to do. I don't know what to think.'

'For starters, I think you need to leave that poor woman alone.'

Naomi shot out of her seat. 'Dylan! Stop that right now!' she screamed, and sat down again.

'Don't tell my son off like that,' Sophie snapped, the panic bursting out for a second.

'He was about to jump on that old lady again.'

Sophie exhaled, scratching at her head. 'He would never do that.'

Naomi laughed. Sophie resented that. Naomi's ups and downs were beginning to grate on her.

'Promise me you won't go and see her again.'

Naomi bit her lip. 'No. No. I can't. Not now.'

'We're in this together, remember.'

'Together?'

'Yes.'

'We are not together at all.'

Sophie was wounded. 'Why do you say that?'

Naomi shoved her hands under her thighs. 'If you'd seen that shrine for... for...' she began, but she didn't finish.

'Going to see her was the wrong thing to do,' she replied calmly. 'Now you'll never get her out of your head.'

Sophie's gaze ran over Naomi. She was swollen. Her flesh had reacted to the news like an allergy. The hourglass, full figure, usually dressed in cinched-in wrap dresses or elegant blouses, was hidden under a frumpy jumper, making her look plump. Sophie realised that Naomi had not wanted to confess for Ilene Parker's sake. She had wanted to confess for her own sake, like a man telling his wife about an affair he had years ago, to 'get it off his chest'.

'Think of how you hated him once, Naomi. Just think about that.'

'I can't think about that!' Naomi cried.

A child, who had been running along the poolside, looked up at them.

'Keep your voice down,' Sophie hissed. 'Don't you realise, you've had a *life* because of me. That man almost ruined yours but he's dead now, and you have everything you could ever dream of. Don't blow it all up now.'

Naomi's mouth opened and closed again. And then she repeated, 'I can't think about that.'

'Okay. Good. Don't ever think of it. Put it all away, just as I have done,' Sophie said, standing. 'We'd better get them out.'

Naomi stayed sitting.

Sophie bent down and whispered in her ear. 'I won't let you do anything stupid. Just think of life without those two girls.'

Naomi took her eyes off the children for long enough to show Sophie how frightened she was. 'Don't threaten me.'

Sophie laughed at her. 'I was talking about life in prison, without them.'

'Fuck off,' she snapped back.

*

Sophie spied Adam from the door as he put one black bin bag into the boot of his car. She hated Sunday evenings, when he would leave for Kingston.

'Is that all you're taking?' Sophie asked.

'That's the last of it.'

With a start, Sophie realised that he had been emptying the shack of his possessions over the previous weeks, gradually, stealthily. A bag of stuff last weekend, a lamp the other, two picture frames another. Until now, she hadn't noticed how much had gone. There was so much she hadn't noticed about him throughout their marriage. It made her feel angry with him.

'You've always been sneaky.'

He slammed the boot. Simultaneously, there was a loud rattling bang that came from the garage.

'Where's Dylan?' he asked.

Both of them ran to the source of the noise. The red corrugated door of the garage was clattering and squeaking.

Sophie's heart was in her mouth. If he had damaged the Giulia, she didn't know what she would do to him.

Adam and Sophie darted in through the garage side door and peered into the gloom.

'Dylan? What are you doing?' Adam shouted over the banging.

When Sophie's eyes adjusted to the dark, she saw that Dylan was wielding the axe and hitting at the rusted lock on the garage door.

Adam squeezed past the car, yelling at him to stop, and managed to wrestle the tool out of his hands. 'You must never play with this, understand me?' Adam shouted.

'I want the big door to open so that the car can come out!' Dylan screamed, thrashing about, reaching out for Sophie, squirming out of Adam's arms and into Sophie's. 'I want to drive in the blue car with you and Mummy! Just as you promised, Mummy!'

Sophie carried him outside and soothed him. 'It's okay. Calm down. Calm down,' she whispered in his ear, feeling his limbs flop. 'We'll get someone to open the lock and we'll have a drive with Daddy soon, okay?'

'But Daddy's going forever! He's leaving us!' he wailed, sobbing into Sophie's shoulder.

Sophie looked over at Adam reproachfully. *See?* She was saying with her eyes. *See what you've done?*

'How did you get into the garage, Dylan?' Adam asked, sounding angry, setting Dylan off crying again.

'Through the *door*?' he wailed sarcastically.

Sophie could feel the lump of the keys in his shorts pocket. They dug into her stomach. 'He must have taken the keys from the peg in the house. He likes playing in there sometimes,' Sophie explained.

'Promise me you won't go into the garage without asking Mummy first, yes?' Adam said, nuzzling into Dylan. Sophie could smell Adam's hair. It was fresh, like a barber shop. Unfamiliar. She wanted to take a chunk of it and rip it out of his head.

She began walking to Adam's car, clutching Dylan, who was getting too heavy. 'You had better get going.'

Adam stood at the open car door, looking at them both. She couldn't read his expression. He might as well have been looking at a painting of them on a wall. He then took a hairband from his wrist and tied his hair into a bun. Sophie thought of Deda's disparaging comment about men with long hair and she smiled. Adam smiled back, having misread her. His teeth looked whiter than ever against his olive skin.

'I'm coming to collect you on Friday, Dylan, that's only three days away! We can go out in the Giulia then, how about that?'

Sophie shook her head at Adam. 'I've got the Wilson girls that night.'

Her stomach fluttered at the thought of her plan for Friday night with Izzy and Diana, or, more accurately, her plans for Naomi. A surprise for all of them.

'Saturday morning, then,' Adam frowned.

'Can we go out zooming around in the blue car then, Daddy?' Dylan said, perking up.

'Yes, we'll take her for a spin then, we promise,' Adam said.

Sophie stroked the hair from Dylan's sweaty forehead. 'If you're late, you'll miss out. I can't hang around waiting.'

His white teeth disappeared. 'See you at ten next Saturday.'

She watched his car go and then looked over at the dent in the red garage door. She would fix that and they would go for a spin. It was time.

Before then, she had to fix Naomi.

*

Sophie knew that every Friday, ever since the two Wilson girls had started school, Charlie came home from work early to meet them at the gates, unless they had playdates or parties or special events.

This Friday was going to be one of those special events.

14.23, Friday 20th April
Charlie.Wilson@LLPA.co.uk
SUBJECT: pick-up this afternoon

Hi Charlie –

Naomi forgot to tell you I'm picking the girls up this afternoon and taking them to the cinema with Dylan. Lucky I texted her with a reminder! Could you email the school for me to tell them? Naomi would do it but she's stuck in this awards ceremony and asked me to ask you!

Sorry for short notice.

Sophie x

14.35, Friday 20th April
sophiesoaps@yahoo.co.uk
RE: pick-up this afternoon

Sounds fun. All done.

Are you dropping them back or do we need to pick them up from yours?

Charlie

14.37, Friday 20th April
Charlie.Wilson@LLPA.co.uk
RE: RE: pick-up this afternoon

I'll drop them back. See you then. Sx

'Hi, Diana!' Sophie called out across the playground, waving. 'Come on, Dylan. Hurry up.'

He was lagging behind her, but she wanted him by her side when she approached the teacher.

Diana beamed at her. 'Hi, Sophie. Where's Daddy?'

'Daddy forgot to tell you I'm taking you and Izzy out to the cinema with Dylan today.'

'Yeah!' Diana cried, giving Sophie a hug around her hips before saying hello to Dylan.

Sophie took Diana's rucksack.

'I'm so sorry, could you hold on a second, please?' the teacher said, holding Diana's shoulder proprietorially, scanning down a list of names on her clipboard with a hot-pink nail. She had the looks and manner of an air stewardess.

'I'm Sophie King. Charlie said he'd email, but he may have forgotten.' Sophie ruffled Diana's hair, but her teeth ground together. She was worried that Charlie had forgotten to email, or worse, that he and Naomi had spoken, that Naomi had refused permission. It had been one of the potential risks. Dylan clung to her leg and scratched at his elbows, as though he, too, knew how dicey her plan was.

'Mummy forgot to sign my permission slip for confederation sports yesterday,' Diana said.

'That's unlike your mummy, isn't it?' Sophie replied.

'This is my mummy's BFF, Mrs Figgis,' Diana told her teacher.

'I'm afraid I'll still have to check with the office before we can let you go, Diana. I'm so sorry.'

Mrs Figgis did not look sorry.

Sophie's heart pounded beneath her ribs, but she smiled, pretending to be unfazed, looking at her watch. 'I understand.'

While Mrs Figgis was in the office, Diana mooched at Sophie's side, sticking her head inside Sophie's billowy sleeves.

'Daddy's taking me in the blue car tomorrow,' Dylan declared.

'That will be fun,' Diana said earnestly. Sophie noted how smart she looked with her stripy tie and tartan kilt. Their school uniforms were classier than Dylan's. Overall, it was a better school, with its Ofsted Outstanding in every category, and a forest school. Sophie had tried to get Dylan into this school, but their address was half a mile out of catchment. It had been typical that Naomi had won the postcode lottery without even trying.

The teacher returned.

'All done, that's fine, Mrs King, the office hadn't seen the email. You can go, Diana.'

'Bye, Mrs Figgis,' Diana said, taking Sophie's hand, while Dylan trailed behind.

'Goodbye, Mrs Figgis,' Sophie said.

They did not have to go through the same rigmarole at the other corner of the playground with Izzy's teacher, who had been briefed by Mrs Figgis.

When the two girls and Dylan were strapped into her car, Sophie turned the ignition on. Triumphantly, she brought out the three chocolate bars from the glove compartment and handed them round. How ironic, that Naomi would fear more the stranger in the white van who might lure her girls away with sweeties.

As she turned left out of their school, rather than right towards Guildford, where they would usually go to the cinema, Sophie hoped that Diana would not notice. She might have been old enough to know the way, but in fact, none of the children noticed.

When they reached Billingshurst, Izzy complained of feeling sick.

'I get carsick on these windy roads,' Izzy said.

'You shouldn't have eaten your Crunchie bar so quickly,' Diana said smugly, sounding just like Naomi.

'Do you need me to stop?' Sophie asked.

'No. It's okay.'

'This is taking ages,' Dylan piped up.

'Mummy goes a much quicker way to Guildford,' Diana said.

Sophie decided it would be safe to tell them where they were going now.

'Well, actually, we're not going to boring old Guildford, we're off to the big Imax cinema in Brighton. They've got a special 3-D showing of *Mamma Mia 2*, but before that I thought you might like a doughnut on the pier and then supper at Bill's.'

There were yelps of delight and then a full rendition of all the ABBA songs, most of which Dylan knew off by heart. Even Sophie joined in for 'The Winner Takes It All'.

*

The wind was whipping off the sea and blowing up through the wooden slats of the pier. Sophie looked down, beyond her feet. The white froth below made her head spin.

The three children did not care about the tide beneath them; they were awed by the doughnuts being plopped into perfect rings behind the glass.

Sophie bought three.

Izzy and Diana's noses were pink from cold and covered in sugar.

She took a photograph of them against the railings. They were bright in their coats against the backdrop of the grey, squally sea. The girls' blonde ringlets were whipped straight by the wind.

Usually she would send photographs of the girls to Naomi straight away. Not this evening. She wanted her to sweat, to feel the girls' absence, to fear for their safety. She wanted Naomi to know how far she was prepared to go. This was a warning shot. This was a taster of how vulnerable her two beautiful girls were. What would become of them if Naomi dared tell?

Izzy dashed off to the coin-raking game and Diana ran straight to the shooting stall and Dylan ambled over to the queue for the ghost train. Sophie kept her eye on Dylan only. Gathering the three of them together, with scary warnings about creepy strangers, was what she might have done if Naomi were around. This afternoon, she didn't feel especially nervous for the girls' safety. Their fate was in the lap of the gods tonight. *Poseidon's, perhaps*, she thought, amusing herself, looking out to the choppy horizon.

She looked at her phone. Naomi would not be worried yet, she didn't think. An hour or so, she gave it.

'Can we go on the helter-skelter?' Diana asked.

They battled the wind to the end of the pier, where Sophie watched the three children whoosh around and down the helter-skelter, legs and arms flying over the edge.

At the point when Diana was pleading for another token, Sophie received her first call from Naomi. The circular photograph of her smiling face was central on the screen. It rang out. Sophie could not imagine that there would be a real smile on Naomi's face right now. She hoped there would not be, and she contemplated keeping the girls for longer, finding a hotel for a sleepover in Brighton, to fray Naomi's nerves further. If they left first thing the following morning, she and Dylan would have time to get back for their planned drive in the Giulia with Adam. It would depend on how frantic Naomi became. If the girls' absence failed to have the desired effect on Naomi, Sophie would prolong their Brighton excursion indefinitely. They were having so much fun, after all.

CHAPTER TWENTY-TWO

'Are the girls watching telly?' I said, scooping Harley into my arms, exhaling heavily and kissing Charlie on the lips.

Almost out of habit, I was pleased to be home. The good feeling did not linger. I found it impossible to sustain any positive feelings about anything of any importance. The awards ceremony had been debilitating, beyond tiring, surreal almost. I had managed my inebriation carefully, to function, to forget. It was a balancing act. One drink would not be enough to repress everything; one too many brought it rushing to the surface.

'They're with Sophie, remember?'

Harley scuffled at my feet when I put him down too quickly. 'No, they're not.'

Charlie laughed, innocent in his Friday-night casual crew neck, chopping the coriander with his double-handled herb knife. 'The cinema, remember?'

'No. I don't remember.'

Charlie stopped chopping. 'Sophie said you'd forgotten and that I should email the school with permission.'

'Are you telling me the girls are with Sophie right now?'

'Yes.'

'You mean, she tricked you into emailing the school for permission, and then she just turned up at the gates?'

'She didn't *trick* me.'

'Well, she and I never arranged it, Charlie.'

He frowned at me. 'You must have.'

'I did not, I swear it.'

Charlie swept the green leaves into his palm and sprinkled them over the dish bubbling on the stove. 'I don't mean to be funny, Naomi, but you have been a bit away with the fairies lately.'

The smell of the herbs lingered sweet and sharp in my head.

'Charlie, I am telling you, I did not arrange it.'

'It's just a case of crossed wires.'

'Why didn't you call me about this?' I said, pulling my phone out of my bag.

'You never have your phone on in those awards thingummy-jigs.'

'I did today.'

'Are you bothered about Sophie taking them out tonight?'

I ignored this question. How could I possibly answer him? *I won't let you do anything stupid. Just think of life without those two girls*, Sophie had said.

'What time did she say she'd drop them back?' I asked.

'She didn't specify.'

The officious use of the word 'specify' grated on me. He would speak to me like this when he was cross or disapproving.

'It's six already,' I said.

'That's not late. If they went to a film, it won't be finished yet.'

I searched the film showing times on my Odeon app.

'*Lego 3* is the only kids' film at the Guildford Odeon and it starts at 3.45 p.m. and finishes at six.'

'It's only just gone six now.'

I checked my watch again. It was true. I was panicking unnecessarily. 'True,' I admitted.

I put my phone down, beginning to think I was being paranoid.

Sophie's behaviour could be unconventional, imprudent even, but she was not capable of taking my children as a threat. She

would never want to scare me or the girls. She loved them almost
as much as she loved Dylan. I might have forgotten a conversation
about this cinema plan of hers, maybe.

'I guess they'll be eating out afterwards, too,' Charlie said.

'I'll try her now, to find out. Just so we know.' I pressed her
number and waited. Her voicemail message announcement came
into my ear and panic bubbled up inside me again. 'It's her voicemail.'

'She'd have it on silent in the cinema. Naomi, really, I don't…'

I put my finger to my lips to shush him and I left a message.
'Hi, Sophie. It's Naomi. Just wondering when to expect you back.
I'd completely forgotten about this plan! Sorry. Hope you're having
fun! Give me a bell. Bye.'

I had hoped to sound light and casual. I imagined I had not
pulled that off.

'I wish you'd called me,' I said, reaching for the bottle of wine
in the fridge.

'I didn't think it mattered so much.'

I took a sip from the glass before I had even put the bottle back.

'It doesn't. It shouldn't. Sorry. I've had a stressful day,' I sighed,
glancing at the wall clock, working out timings of the girls' evening
as I could best imagine Sophie had planned it. I couldn't help
myself, I couldn't stop the low-level churn of worry.

If the film finished at six, they would, most likely, be walking
over to Franca Manca or Jamie's Kitchen by now, which would
take no more than fifteen minutes, even if I factored in a loo
stop. If they ate starters and puddings, they would be leaving
the restaurant by seven thirty latest. The journey from Guildford
would take roughly half an hour, which meant they should be
home between 8 p.m. and 8.30 p.m. Latest, 9 p.m.

Until nine, I would not think about them, and I would try to
enjoy some rare time alone with Charlie.

*

But, of course, I did think about it, continually, barely allowing Charlie's voice to penetrate my thoughts long enough to engage in a conversation, more and more certain that Sophie had never once mentioned this cinema plan. With every second that passed after 8.30 p.m., my worry grew.

By 9.33 p.m., I called Sophie again, unable to hide the frantic edge to my voice when asking her to call me back.

'She must have left her phone somewhere,' Charlie said, coming in again with his sensible explanations.

'Yes, I'm sure,' I replied, rechecking my texts between Sophie and me. I could not find a thread of text chat about a cinema trip.

To calm myself down, I began to think out loud.

'They could be stuck in traffic, I suppose,' I said.

'Exactly,' he said, placing two plates of curry on the table.

'Or had a flat tyre or something, and her phone battery has run out.'

'Let's hope they haven't had a flat.'

'Charlie. What do you think has happened?' I asked, taking the wine out of the fridge.

'I think Sophie's chaos happened. When has she ever arrived on time for anything?'

'Good point.'

Nevertheless, throughout the meal I continued to hazard guesses, concocting various plotlines: she had lost her car key and had to retrace her steps; she had run out of petrol and they had to walk to the petrol station; one of the children was sick in the car and she was by the roadside cleaning it up.

My theories sounded bland to my own ear, babyish even, never coming close to what I really thought.

I could not share what I feared most.

While we were clearing up our meal, I added more scenarios to the list. Charlie cut me dead, irritable. 'Stop with the conjecture. They'll be home any minute.'

'You're not worried one bit?' I asked him, once again taking the bottle of Pinot Grigio out of the fridge to top up my glass, my fourth glass.

He did not answer me. Instead, he took the bottle out of my hand and placed it back into the fridge door. 'How about a decaf espresso?'

I gaped at him and took the bottle out again, pouring my glass right up to the rim. He turned away to wipe the hob down.

'You can be so *cold*, sometimes, did you know that?' I said, mean and hard.

I regretted it as soon as it had come out of my mouth. He would be hurt, but he remained composed.

'Sophie's been taking the girls out since they were babies and she's never once brought them back on time,' he said quietly, calmly, wiping, wiping, wiping around in circles, cleaning what was already clean.

'Adam's really worried about her.'

'He said something?'

'He dropped round to talk to me about her.'

'Adam dropped round? Here?'

During the mania of organising the dinner party, I had failed to mention it. Afterwards, after the bombshell of Jason Parker, it had seemed irrelevant.

'It was the night before the dinner party,' I began, having to draw extra breath into my lungs at the memory of that dinner party. 'You were in Manchester. He was really worried about her state of mind.'

'He's leaving her. It's obvious why he'd want to justify it.'

'It's not that, honestly. That's what I thought at first, but he was more concerned about Dylan than about himself.'

'He's finally noticed that he can't compete for Sophie's love?' Charlie grinned. He was trying for a change of mood. It was my cue to change course, salvage the evening.

'This isn't funny. Something happened… it's… well…' I stammered, rubbing my face, trying to organise my brain through the wine to remember the story properly. 'She left him on his own in the cottage… to go to Pilates, to see me, and Dylan was really upset.'

My pronunciation was baggy, my tongue too loose to sound convincing.

'I'm still not sure why her strange parenting of Dylan has any bearing on tonight.'

'You don't understand,' I cried, exasperated.

'You're right. I don't understand your turnaround. Yesterday, she's your best friend in all the world. Today she's… what, kidnapped the girls?' he laughed. 'There's no logic to it, Naomi.'

I wanted to throttle him. 'Logic? Why can't you just trust me for once?'

He placed the cloth into the sink and turned to face me. 'Because I think you're drunk.'

I felt a surge of humiliation.

'Ah, right. We've got to the bottom of it now,' I sneered. 'That's why you're behaving as though you've got a rod up your arse, is it? Oh, I'm so, *so* sorry I'm a little bit tipsy after a long day. Woohoo, wow, god forbid we might have a few too many on a Friday night and actually enjoy ourselves. What a bloody shocker.' I threw my arms about, sloshing wine on the floor, taking up the room with my panic.

Charlie tugged the bottom of his sweater down and pushed his glasses up on his nose. He looked like a schoolboy and I wondered how I could be so unpleasant to him.

'I'll be in my study,' he said, squeezing past me, head down, uncomfortable to pass by me so close.

At his back, I threw up my two fingers, mouthing expletives. He thought I was drunk, unreasonable, but I was armed with more facts than he was. I knew what Sophie was capable of. If he knew the truth, he would be frantic, too.

But he didn't know. That was the point. A key piece of evidence had not been given to him. A vital slice of my past was missing from his knowledge, with its potentially dire consequences for our shared future and I was blaming him for it, as though he should be able to mine my mind for information at his own convenience, like he might flick through a document at work.

My unjustified, wrongly directed anger at Charlie brought a rush of tears to my eyes.

When I imagined the girls' innocent little faces smiling at Sophie, with her underhand motives, I wanted to unleash a scream so loud it would break the windows of our house and send its soundwaves rattling through Sophie's bones.

I sat forward on the sofa as I watched television. The volume was low. My phone was clutched in my palm. I had stopped drinking, to clear my head, but I craved another. When this was all over, when everyone was safely tucked up in bed, I would be able to open the bottle of Malbec.

Every quarter of an hour, I called Sophie. Her mechanical message rang in my ear, repetitive like a line in a film that is echoed to evoke fear, to signpost upcoming danger.

Occasionally I leapt up and checked outside, listening out for the sound of an engine on our quiet lane, looking for the flash of headlights across the tangle of trees.

A rota of those reassuring scenarios continued to run through my head: she had lost her phone, they had broken down, they had seen a later film, they had got lost, they had gone home to Sophie's where they would call, and so on. There were a million and one different sequences of events that could lead to their late return and her failure to call.

The palatable alternatives drowned out what I feared most, and I enjoyed imagining how I would laugh with the girls about my neuroses when they came through the door any minute now.

At eleven, they had still not come through that door.

I knew I had to do something.

I burst into Charlie's study.

'I think we should call someone.' I meant the police.

Braced for a fight, I mentally prepared to blurt out the whole truth, to give him the full measure of Sophie and the volatility of the situation, if I had to.

Then I noticed that there was a window open on his laptop showing the screen times for the Chichester Odeon. This was the other cinema that Sophie might have considered travelling a little further to.

'You're worried too!'

He turned to me. There were smears on his glasses.

'It's very late now,' he conceded.

I wanted to collapse. 'It is. Yes. Shall I call the police?'

'I've just called Adam and left a message, so let's wait and see whether he knows anything.'

'Really?' I asked. The delay would be excruciating.

'Adam might know where they are. She might have mentioned something to him.'

'Why don't we call the police while we wait to hear from him?'

'The police won't do anything for us anyway unless we've exhausted all avenues.'

'Okay.' My breathing became shallow. I understood why we had to be methodical, but I was not sure I could wait a second longer without combusting.

I sat on the arm of his low leather armchair. We remained silent for a moment, staring at his phone, waiting for it to ring with news. Doing nothing made time go slowly.

'Is it true we have to wait twenty-four hours to ring the police if you think someone is missing? Or is it different when it's about children?'

'I've looked it up. You can ring any time.'

My heart bulged. He had looked it up. 'You've looked it up already?'

He handed me his phone. On the screen were clear instructions about how to call the police when you suspected a missing person.

As I read it, the phone rang in my hand. I almost dropped it in shock.

'It's Adam,' I said, shoving it at Charlie.

Our eyes met as he answered it. I looked deep into his soul, seeing my own love for the girls reflected back at me.

'Hi, Adam. Sorry to call so late... We've been expecting Izzy and Diana back from a trip to the cinema with Sophie and Dylan, and it's getting rather late. Have you heard from her? Did you know of any cinema plans this evening?'

Charlie's tone sounded accusatory, which I knew he did not mean. It was concern rather than blame or suspicion. If Adam had seen his face, he would have seen that his brow was raised in boyish hope as he waited for Adam to deliver reassuring news.

Before I heard any words come from Charlie's mouth, I watched his brow fall into a frown. I watched how he rubbed at his forehead, as though soothing the ache of disappointment.

'Ah. I see. Right. Sorry for bothering you so late. Thanks for calling back... Yes... Let's hook up... Yes... Of course... Bye.'

His voice had been flat, almost unrecognisable.

'He doesn't know anything, does he?' I asked, wishing that I might have misread his frown.

Charlie stared straight at me.

'He does, actually. She's taken them to the cinema.'

'What? But... it's so late!'

'She's taken them to the Imax in Brighton. *Mamma Mia 2.*'

Confusion stopped me from fully taking it in. 'How does he know?'

'Because he's Dylan's dad?'

'But he's moved out. He wouldn't necessarily know.'

'He wanted to take Dylan this weekend, straight from school this afternoon, but Sophie suggested Saturday morning instead. Because of the cinema trip and because of some drive they're going on, or something. Apparently she's taken them to Bill's tonight, too.'

Those eyes that had connected with me minutes before were now black and deep in his sockets. He took off his glasses and cleaned them with the rim of his sweater, looking down, looking away from me.

'I swear to god she didn't tell me that, Charlie.'

He replaced his glasses. 'Strange that she would tell Adam, and email me, but not you.'

'You have to believe me. She's trying to mess with my head.'

Standing up, he said, 'But why?'

I pulled at his arm, trying to stop him from leaving the study. 'Charlie, you have to believe me, she and I have had a falling-out, she's...'

And then the doorbell rang.

I let out a small cry and ran to the door.

Standing there, with wide smiles and wild eyes, were Izzy and Diana. Sophie followed them up the terrace steps.

'Oh my god, darlings, oh my god, come here,' I said, rounding them into my arms, kissing their faces and squeezing the life out of them. Incense lingered in their hair. They smelt of her.

'We've had so much fun, haven't we, girls?' Sophie chirruped.

Slowly, I raised myself off my haunches and stared at Sophie. She looked so pale and pretty; too pretty to be guilty of stealing my children, some might think.

Charlie and I listened as the girls chattered about the helter-skelter and eating hamburgers and watching 3-D.

At the end, Charlie came in with his deepest parental voice, 'What do you say to Sophie, girls?'

They swivelled on their heels and grabbed Sophie around the middle. 'Thank you so much, Sophie. It was really, so, so fun.'

'Right. Off to bed, you little rascals,' Charlie said.

They giggled and ran past him, with their pink and white bags of sweets clamped to their chests.

'Dylan's asleep in the car. I'd better head off,' Sophie said, turning to leave, swinging her wide-hemmed, Indian-print skirt.

'Thanks so much, Sophie. What a treat for them,' Charlie said, standing wide in the doorway, as though barricading me in.

'It's nothing, I've had just as much fun as...'

I pushed past Charlie to stand in front of him, to confront Sophie.

'Why didn't you return my calls?'

'What calls?' she asked, twisting a strand of her white-blonde hair behind her ear, biting the bottom lip of her reddened mouth.

'Are you serious? *What calls?*' I cried.

Charlie interjected calmly, 'We didn't know when you were coming back. We were a little worried, that's all.'

'Oh, gosh, really? I'm so sorry,' she said, rummaging in her bag. 'I've had my phone on silent all evening... We've been so busy... Oh...' She took her phone out of her bag with her long fingers and laughed. 'Oh my god. I'm such an idiot. I had no idea you'd be checking in. I'm so sorry.' She showed us the screen. Fifteen missed calls from Naomi Wilson. 'I'm so sorry,' she said again.

Charlie shot a look at me, his eyes narrow with reproach. My skin prickled across my chest. I could not allow him to think this was my fault.

'Sophie, you know you didn't tell me about your plans for the girls this evening, so let's just stop pretending you did, okay,' I said.

Her white lashes flickered and she batted them towards Charlie and back to me. 'Naomi, we had a whole conversation about it at the pool, last week, while the kids were swimming.'

'No, we did not,' I insisted.

'I asked you to talk to Charlie about it.'

I let out a sharp laugh and turned to Charlie. 'She's lying!'

Sophie added, 'It was quite hectic in the pool, maybe you just didn't hear or something.'

'It was not hectic enough for me to forget a whole conversation, seriously, I really think you—'

Charlie cut in. 'Look, the girls are back, it doesn't matter who told whom, what, when. It's very late and I'm sure you want to get Dylan home, Sophie.'

Sophie smiled. 'Yes. Bye, guys. Bye, Naomi. Maybe get a good lie-in tomorrow morning. You look tired. The girls were great, by the way. Such a credit to you both.'

I was speechless.

'Thanks, Sophie,' Charlie said, moving to close the door. 'That's really kind. See you soon.'

'I'll give you a bell, Naomi!' she said over her shoulder, casually.

I could have run at her, pushed her, insisted she tell the truth, but I was clued-up enough to know that I would be the one to come out worst. Her barefaced, shameless lie was too expert to compete with.

With the door closed, I heard Charlie's voice telling me he was going to get the girls into bed, but I did not respond. I stood, fixed to the spot, dumbfounded, listening to Sophie's car pull out of the drive. The noise of the spitting gravel was like a 'fuck you'. I imagined her laughing as she drove off, knowing she had won.

I was sitting on the bottom stair when Charlie came down again. He stopped a few steps behind me.

'The girls are in bed,' he sighed. 'I'm going up myself now.'

I twisted round to look at him. 'All's well that ends well,' I said, unable to hide the sarcasm in my voice.

He shook his head at me, as though he were amazed at my stupidity. 'Do you have any idea what you have just put me through?'

I leapt up. 'I...' I began, but tears stopped me from saying anything coherent. 'I didn't *want* to put you through *anything*. It's Sophie... she's gone... She's up to something, I swear it.'

He sighed again, heavily, hooking one large hand across the back of his neck, letting his arm hang from there. 'What is she up to, exactly?'

'I can't put my finger on it, I can't say *exactly*. I mean, I'm not the only one, Charlie. I told you that Adam was worried too, didn't I? He actually said he thought she was unstable. He used that exact word.'

'When I spoke to Adam earlier he implied things were back on track between them. They're taking the old Giulia out tomorrow, as a family. He said she was on great form.'

My thoughts froze. 'She's doing what?'

'Taking the Giulia out for a drive.'

I couldn't believe what I was hearing. It couldn't possibly be true. The worry of tonight shrivelled to the back of my mind, dwarfed by the greater imminent danger.

'They can't!' I cried.

'Why ever not?'

I had a mouthful of why nots, twenty years of them, ready to blurt out, but I didn't have time, I had to get in contact with Sophie. 'It's an old car, that's all. I was worried it wasn't safe,' I blustered. 'Sorry.'

Charlie looked up at the ceiling and spoke, as though reading from an invisible script in the cornicing. 'I told you last time that I wouldn't go through all this again. I'm telling you, Naomi, I can't do it. All the histrionics, all the paranoia, all the lies... Especially not now.' His voice faltered and he dropped his arm, as though giving up.

'What do you mean, *not now*?' I asked, absent-mindedly.

Charlie's heavy, slow footstep trudged up the stairs. 'I'm going to bed. We can talk about it in the morning.'

'Sure,' I murmured, shaking my head, watching him go, preoccupied with thoughts about the Giulia. Sophie had clearly outlined the risks of taking it out for a drive. Her warnings flashed through my mind now.

Back in 1999, the number plate could have been seen – in its entirety or partially – by a witness and logged into the police system when the original investigation was carried out. If remnants of paint had been found on Jason Parker's body, or if there had been tyre marks left on the road, the investigating officers might have pinpointed the make of car, if not the model or year. They might have carried out a search for owners of Alfas in the local area, possibly spread their search nationwide. The fact that they had not yet located the car did not mean that they had not identified it at the time. Feasibly, if Sophie took the car out on the roads, the registration could be picked up by a modern ANPR system and she could be hauled in for questioning. It would mean the end for us. I had to stop her.

Having found my phone in the kitchen, I typed a text:

Sophie – call me urgently. Naomi

The cork – a proper cork – popped out of the neck of the smart bottle of Malbec and the aroma filled my head with reassurance, with its promise of calm, with its companionship.

I sat down at the kitchen table to wait for Sophie's call.

I would have felt lonely without this glass of Malbec, which I had been sent as a complimentary gift by Selfridges. The PR department were clearly hoping for a favourable review on the blog in return. I had been saving it for the right moment. The right moment would have been late summer, with friends around a firepit; sausages in buns, tartan blankets, stars above our heads, the wine poured into tin mugs. The photograph on my blog would have depicted glowing, tanned faces in a circle of contentment.

I had not imagined the downlighters above my head, spotlighting me, sending a flare of cold light across the surface of the wine as I took it to my lips. My needy, quivering lips, tinged with salty tears. I had not imagined I would have turned to it like a friend. My only friend.

The phone lay black next to me. It was clear Sophie was ignoring me, as she had done all evening. I decided to be more direct:

Sophie – you can't take it for a drive. It's dangerous. The risk isn't worth it. Please, reconsider. Call me. Let's talk about it. Naomi

As I waited, I drank, thirstily, just as one shouldn't with such good wine. The Selfridges PR woman would expect me to describe its velvet-smooth texture and its inky colour and its full-bodied, juicy flavours of plum and black cherry and blackberry. She would hope for an attractive accompanying photograph.

Three more texts and two phone calls later, there was still no reply. I drank more, knowing I would not review and post this wine. I did not care that I would fall out of favour with Selfridges PR. I did not care about its texture or its colour, I cared only about how it made me feel, how its silkiness let me slip and slide away from my fear about Sophie's drive tomorrow, how it allowed me to dive into its deep-purple pool of denial. Maybe the police had not managed to gather the physical evidence at the accident scene. Maybe the dent left in the roof had been too minor for chips of paint to lodge into Jason Parker's hair or clothes. Maybe the rain had wiped out the tyre marks. Maybe the drive would be fun. Maybe. Definitely maybe.

CHAPTER TWENTY-THREE

'The guy promised it would work now!' Sophie cried, infuriated as she rattled at the lock from inside the garage. Dylan and Adam waited behind her.

She was determined to go ahead with the drive, but her mind was crowded by Naomi's texts and calls advising her against it. It wasn't helpful to have Naomi's agitation inside her head today.

'Try it with the key, from the outside,' Adam suggested calmly.

Sophie grunted and then kicked the lock. 'It's totally broken.'

'Give me the key,' Adam said, exiting the garage from the side door.

A second later, she and Dylan heard the key turn and then she saw a chink of daylight turn into a gaping shaft of sunshine which flooded the gloomy garage, as though the car had burst into song.

'You did it! Hooray!' Sophie cheered, hugging Adam.

'I know, I'm your hero,' Adam winked, flirting with her.

Dylan chattered excitedly to Adam as the three of them climbed into the wind-pressed vinyl seats of the Giulia. The little blue car held power, strange power. It was able to pull people together, but it wasn't always a force for good. Overriding her unease, Sophie pushed it into gear and out of its space. The engine purred like new.

As she sped along the lanes, Dylan wound down his window and yelped with glee. Sophie flinched. The drive was a nerve-jangling thrill for Sophie. She understood why Naomi had reminded her of the risks, but Sophie had wanted the car's coming-out to mark a new chapter, to be symbolic of leaving the past behind. Her trip to Brighton yesterday with the Wilson girls had cut dead Naomi's shilly-shallying about confessions and Sophie wanted to celebrate, to throw Naomi's caution to the wind for once in her life. She was sick of living in fear. She was sick of Naomi, perhaps.

Naomi had spent years enjoying the fruits of Sophie's cover-up, for which everything in Sophie's life had been put on the line. Sophie had tidied away their shared mess, leaving her friend to live out the happiness that she herself had felt too unworthy to experience.

One twist of that steering wheel, one twist of fate did not have to lead to a lifetime of self-reproach. It did not have to. Who was writing the rules? Sophie could. From now on, Sophie would grab what was rightfully hers and claw back what she had given away to Naomi, what she had yearned for and felt undeserving of. It was time to kill off her child self; the child who had believed she wasn't worthy of anything good. It was time to take back the life she had been denied.

If the police had the car's registration plate on its system, today might be the day they were caught for Jason Parker's death. But if it wasn't, she would be freed, liberated from twenty years of angst. It was a risk worth taking.

But her eyes were hawkish, roaming the countryside for CCTV cameras, fearing the authorities' watchful eyes. As she powered through the lanes, she imagined throwing a black cloak over each camera she saw.

Then, stopping her heart, the worst happened. A police car appeared in her rear-view mirror. She bristled; her mouth dried. Her hands clawed at the slippery wheel. She became hypervigilant, keen to stay under 30mph, anxious about making a rookie driving mistake. She feared that Naomi's trepidation had been well grounded. How arrogant she had been. As she recalled her warnings, and those of her grandfather before her, and tried not to panic, Dylan suddenly leant forward and throttled her with a neck hug.

'Stop that!' she had screamed, losing her temper with him, quickly checking her rear-view mirror.

She couldn't believe her luck. The police car had turned left. Off and away from them. Disinterested.

Trembling all over, Sophie pulled up into a village parking space. The flood of adrenaline had almost killed her.

'Are you okay?' Adam asked.

'Can you drive us home?' she said, blowing out short, sharp breaths.

Disorientated by the whole experience, she tugged out the key, but failed to cut the engine or pull up the handbrake. The car rolled back as she got out.

Adam pulled up the brake and scooted over to sit at the wheel. 'The car's running without the key?'

'Oh, here,' she said, handing it to him through the window, still unsteady on her legs.

'Sorry, Mumma,' Dylan said, squishing his nose into the glass.

She managed a small laugh, but knew the ordeal wasn't over. They had to make it home safely before she could relax.

'Jump in then,' Adam said.

She had taken a few deep breaths before she felt she could return to the car.

'A worn ignition barrel, I guess,' Adam had said.

'What?'

'You were able to take the key out when the engine was still running.'

'So?'

'A Scooby-Doo phantom car,' Adam chuckled.

'What the hell are you *talking* about? Can we just go home?'

But he was right. It was a phantom car, filled with ghosts: Jason Parker's spirit took shape through the windscreen, and the ghost of Naomi and Sophie's youth, their innocence, jangled its chains across the locks of the doors.

Dylan broke into the *Scooby-Doo* theme song, remembering every word of the lyrics.

'A modern car wouldn't do that,' Adam mumbled sulkily, yanking the gearstick back and forth.

'Careful,' she insisted, through a clenched jaw.

After a bit, they recovered their moods, but the drive had been ruined for Sophie.

As Adam manoeuvred the Giulia back into the garage, Sophie was cross with Naomi. Her scaremongering texts had jinxed her, made her nervous when she hadn't needed to be. Like a bad omen, the drive had shaken Sophie, bone-deep.

*

It was a hot May day. The change in the weather seemed to mark more changes in Sophie's life, more disturbances at the cottage, where removals men were unloading Mr and Mrs Etherington's few possessions.

Sophie watched from the long, narrow window of her shack, peering beyond her cacti, to see the strangers cross her grandfather's threshold. Their tenancy reflected Sophie's new choices, her free will, unhindered by the ready-written fate she had once believed in. A few weeks ago, Sophie had gone so far as to burn the newspaper cuttings of Jason Parker and expose the torn mattress, ready for its new occupants' sheets. But since her excursion in the Giulia, Sophie had become wary of exposure and change and choice. Her dreams of affording a better life, of living independently of Adam, free of the secret she had harboured, seemed naive today. She wanted to put all her dreams back in a box and shut the lid, tidying away the colourful strips of hope that had fluttered in the breeze and offered up such a bright future. And she wanted to push Naomi back inside, too. Increasingly, the friendship served as a reminder of all that was bad.

The timer for the biscuits, which she and Dylan had baked together, pinged. She had already been to the farm shop to buy some other house-warming goodies for the Etheringtons. Despite her misgivings about their arrival, she ploughed on, reminding herself of the bigger, better picture, elbowing the doubt out of her mind. She remained committed to the dream, single-mindedly refusing to let anything derail her plans.

As soon as the removals men had driven away, she wrapped the cooled biscuits into a cellophane parcel with ribbon and nestled them into a gift basket next to the punnet of strawberries and bottle of Prosecco.

Armed with her gift, she went to find Dylan, who was messing around in the garage. Frequently, these days, Dylan played with his cuddly toys or games in the Giulia. Once, Sophie had discovered him there after his lights-out. Apparently, he had snuck past her while she had been watching television and had nipped out of the back door in his slippers. The magnetism of the Giulia was spilling down through the generations, which both delighted and worried Sophie in equal measure. But she had not discouraged him. If the car could not be driven and shared with the world, at least Dylan could enjoy it. His grandfather would approve of that, and she hoped the Etheringtons wouldn't mind. They had been warned that their silver Prius would not find a home in the garage.

'Dylan! Dylan! Come on, I want you to come with me to welcome the Etheringtons!' she called out into the garage.

She heard a noise from the back of the car. 'Dylan?'

The boot sprang open. 'Coming,' Dylan said, climbing out.

'How did you close the boot?'

'It wasn't closed.'

Intrigued, Sophie scooted round to see. He had twisted a piece of green string around the silver boot catch, levering it closed. Sophie was impressed by his ingenuity.

But she said, 'Don't do that, Dylan, that's dangerous.'

'I like it dark.'

'But imagine if you got stuck in there.'

'You'd get me out.'

'Fine,' Sophie laughed. 'Come on, then.'

Sophie, with Dylan by her side, knocked on the cottage door and waited for its new custodians to appear. The basket obscured Dylan's head.

Mrs Martha Etherington answered, smiling on the doorstep of her new home, blinking into the sunlight.

'Hello, Mrs Etherington, I just thought we'd drop this by to welcome you,' Sophie said.

Dylan shoved the basket at her as though throwing a basketball and then he darted off back home. She and Martha laughed.

'Oh, thank you! How lovely. You shouldn't have,' she said, admiring the gift before putting it down by her feet and shooting her hand out to shake Sophie's, crunching her bones slightly.

She was wearing a cotton tank top, showing a solid, muscular frame. Her face was just as bold and healthy, with a helmet of white hair, centrally parted and bluntly cut to the tips of each ear.

'Please, call me Martha.'

'If there's anything you need, just pop over to my little shack and knock on the door. Any time.'

Sophie was waiting to be asked in, keen to inspect the house and to check that they were being respectful of Deda's home, that they were worthy of it.

'That is very kind, Sophie. I will,' she said, wiping the back of her hand over her forehead. 'When we've done with this awful unpacking business, we might well realise we've forgotten the sugar or something.'

Poised to push past her, Sophie said, 'Do you need any help unpacking?'

'No, no. We're getting along nicely, thank you. Kenneth's busy doing upstairs.'

Sophie thought it rude that she was not being invited in, that Kenneth did not come downstairs to say hello to his new landlady.

'Oh, that reminds me,' Sophie said, concocting a cleverer way of getting in. 'I wanted to show you where the stopcock is, for the water.'

'Just tell me, I'm sure I'll be able to find it myself.'

'It's awkward to get at. I'd better show you.'

There was a little twitch of Martha's right cheek that did not turn into a smile.

'Come on in. Please excuse the chaos.'

'It's upstairs,' Sophie said, walking slowly across the threshold, holding her breath, wishing the walls were bare again, wishing to see Deda's chair in the front room.

Already, there was a series of three African masks, with slits as eyes, lined up on the left-hand wall. At the foot of the stairs sat a stuffed, rag-cloth elephant with mirrored circles stitched into its pink material. Deda would have thought it absurd.

Upstairs, cluttering the floor beside a large empty bookshelf were stacks of books, glossy photographic hardcovers on top of well-thumbed paperbacks, all of them about to topple. They had to inch around them to get into the bathroom.

'My books are the first to be unpacked, always,' Martha explained, and then she called out towards Deda's bedroom, 'Ken? *Ken!*'

There was no reply. Was he deaf?

Sophie knelt down on the tiles and pulled the panelling from the side of the bath to reveal the stopcock. 'You have to hook your fingers into that little gap, see?'

'Ah, thank you, yes, I wouldn't have been able to find that myself.'

'No problem,' Sophie said, eyeing the beard clippers on the edge of the sink and the grubby purple washbag next to it. Their creams and lotions along the small alcove windowsill were in reds and pinks, fruity and organic, and smelt wrong in there. Sophie's eyes stung with that acidic smell. Long gone was the old-fashioned woody tang of Deda's shaving-soap dish.

Before heading downstairs, Sophie stopped on the landing, looked at her old bedroom door, contemplated its emptiness, dragged her eyes away from it and said, 'One thing I forgot to mention: the window latch in the main bedroom is stiff. I'll show you how to close it properly. For security reasons.'

Without waiting for permission to go into Deda's bedroom – she owned the house, after all – she barged in. There, lying on the double bed, where her grandfather's body had been, was Kenneth, whose ears were covered in large red headphones. His eyes were closed, his feet were jiggling to the beat and his hands tapped an imaginary drum in the air.

Martha laughed, went over to him and pinged one headphone, 'Busy, are we?'

He sprang up, yanked his headphones off and reached down for his iPhone, which dangled at his knees, having fallen from the pocket of his corduroy trousers. 'How embarrassing,' he chortled, pressing at the screen, scratching at his thick white beard.

'This is Sophie. Our landlady, remember?' Martha grinned.

Composing himself, he said, 'Hello, Sophie, yes, we've met, my apologies, I was so hard at work I didn't hear you come in.'

Martha and Kenneth laughed. Sophie should have laughed with them. She could not. Her heart had stopped at the very moment she had seen him lying there, where Deda had once lain dead. It should have been Deda in this room. Alive. Not this impostor, casually listening to music and dancing in this sacred space. Were they going to have sex in here, too? The thought sickened her. She wanted to shove them both out and kick them back into their electric Prius.

When she had first met them, briefly, with the estate agent, they had been like ciphers, nondescript old people, meek and without personalities. She had not predicted the extent to which their presence here would feel wrong, violently wrong. Here, as they settled in, jamming the rooms with their lives, opening up boxes full of colour and exoticism, they seemed to be changing the vibration in the air left by Deda's memory. There was not enough space for him and them. These people came with an energy of their own that might silence Deda's voice in this house forever.

She could have said something, she could have told them to get out. She could have.

A wail from Dylan cut in, disturbing what could have been.

Sophie bolted from the room and charged downstairs.

Dylan was on the doorstep, always reluctant to come inside, bent over, pressing his hands down on his foot.

'It hurts, Mumma!'

'Oh my god! What happened?' Sophie cried.

'The axe fell on it, you *idiot*!' Dylan screamed back at her, but Sophie could see there was no blood.

As she carried him back to the shack, he wept on her shoulder and pounded at her back. Martha's voice was behind her, asking her if he was all right. Her heart beat fast. If she had turned around to reply, she would have told her it was her fault that Dylan was hurt. Instead, she ignored her.

On the sofa, inside, she made sure that Dylan could move his toe and rubbed arnica cream on the reddened patch. 'It's probably just a bruise,' she exhaled, relieved, wondering if she should make the trip to A&E anyway, as a caution. 'I'm putting that horrible thing away, okay, poppet?'

He nodded, licking a lolly she had given him, peering over her shoulder to watch a cartoon on the television. The path of a tear was still visible down his dusty skin, but it was clear there was no pain as she gently wiggled his toes.

'Can I play *Fortnite*, Mumma?'

'Of course,' she said, kissing him, leaving him to rest on the sofa, lighting some incense, returning to the window to look out at the cottage.

The door was closed. The windows were dark. There was a shadowy movement upstairs in the bedroom window. She brought her binoculars to her eyes and watched, waiting for the dusk to creep through the trees, to infiltrate their little enclave in the woods and shroud the cottage in darkness.

A missing toe, some sliced-off flesh, a deformed child. All of it had been possible. All because she had been distracted by those housebreakers. Another omen.

The lights were turned on. It seemed true to type that Martha would not close the curtains. She was the sort of woman to stroll around stark naked. Now, she was downstairs in the kitchen, fully dressed, filling the two small cupboards with food. Packets of brown rice and lentils; cans of chickpeas and chopped tomatoes. At one point the woman sneezed, and brought out a white cloth hanky from her pocket to blow her nose.

Sophie pointed her binoculars at the central window above the front door, where she could see that the books were slotted into the bookshelf already. Finally, she moved her binoculars downstairs, to see into the windows of the sitting room. Kenneth was lounging on the coral sofa that Sophie had placed by the bar heater; the sofa she dreamt of sitting in one day, with tea, with Naomi. A flicker from a television screen illuminated his face. He laughed at something and scratched his beard, then reached for a glass on the side table. Deda's side table. He sipped from the glass, which was most probably beer, and rested it on his belly.

How comfortable he looked, how entitled.

Deda would be rolling in his grave at the notion of this trespasser. Sophie had to get them out. She couldn't wait any longer to live there. Then she thought of the rent dropping into her account every month. She and Dylan needed an income. Adam had become unreliable as a provider. Only twelve days after moving out, he was whingeing about buying new trainers for Dylan, he was begrudgingly increasing her food shopping budget by a measly five pounds, he was late to pay the utility bills and refusing to pay for a private clinic appointment for Dylan's eczema.

She needed a job.

The only other single mother in Dylan's class at school had two jobs to make ends meet. She worked as a receptionist at a local graphic design firm in the daytime, and two nights a week she worked as a carer at an old people's home, relying on her mother to babysit for their three children. She looked permanently shattered and harassed. The married mothers talked of how much they admired her, but Sophie pitied her. She did not want that life.

A deep well of insecurity was stirred in her when she thought of finding herself a job. Before becoming a mother, her previous temping jobs had not paid well, nor had they lasted for long. After six months as a waitress in a chain brasserie, she had suffered regular panic attacks on the late drive home. At the bookshop, she had a bout of severe claustrophobia in the basement storeroom and quit. During her time at the boutique dress shop, under the aegis of a controlling manager, she had experienced low moods and rapid weight loss, which had worried Adam enough to ask her to hand in her notice. Soon, she had stopped pretending to look for a new job and Adam had accepted that he would support her.

The jobs that she was faced with now, squeezed within school hours, would be worse than the work she had hated so much back then.

After some time thinking, another idea took shape in her head.

Perhaps she still needed Naomi after all.
She texted her:

Hi Naomi – Trip out in the Giulia was great fun. Your worrying gets you nowhere! Just wondering if I could pop by for a cuppa? Have something to discuss. Big hug, Sophie xx

*

Through the narrow opening of the Wilsons' front door, Sophie could see only a slither of Naomi. Her arm was wrapped around the bulge of her stomach. A few drops of dried red-brown liquid were splattered on the hem of her nightie; blood, perhaps, but more likely to be red wine.

'What the hell are you doing here?' Naomi spat.

It was clear to Sophie that she was cross about Brighton, and the trip out in the Giulia.

'Didn't you get my text?'

'I got your text, and I do not want to discuss anything with you.'

'I brought you a frothy coffee.' Sophie pushed a steaming hot cup through the gap, under the security chain.

'I can't believe you're here,' she said, wide-eyed, and then looked down at the cup she had taken, as though she was surprised it was in her hand. She frowned, and shoved it back through.

Sophie let the coffee cup hang in the air between them.

'Can I come in?' Sophie twisted her hair down around her right shoulder, feeling bashful about what she had come to propose. She looked down at her feet, seeing that the frayed edges of her bell-bottom jeans covered the tips of her trainers, like a child's. She felt like a child who was about to ask for a biscuit they knew they weren't allowed.

'I told you, I have nothing to discuss with you.'

She sounded aggressive, brave, but Sophie thought she detected something else in her eyes. Wariness, perhaps. Or was it fear?

'We can't talk about it on the doorstep.'

'I don't want to talk about anything,' Naomi whispered hoarsely, looking over Sophie's shoulder shiftily. A second later, she slammed the front door in Sophie's face.

Sophie tightened the thin belt looped through her jeans waistband, just by a notch, enjoying the loss of breath. Then she pressed both palms, and her right ear, up to the glossy painted door panel, feeling the vibrations on her cheek of the locks being secured on the other side. Sophie spoke, loudly, hoping Naomi would hear. 'I don't think it would be wise if we shout about this through the door, do you? But I'll start telling you now, if you'd prefer.'

The door unlocked again. 'Keep your voice down!'

Storming away, she let the door fly wide open.

Sophie hesitated on the threshold, considering Naomi's tetchy mood, doubting, for a moment, whether this was the right time to broach such an important subject. Her right palm became itchy. Deciding that there might never be a good time, she entered the house.

The bifold doors in the kitchen were open. The coffee had been poured down the sink. There were three ready-rolled cigarettes lying on the counter. Charlie wouldn't like that.

Outside, on the two-seater bench, Naomi sat, round-shouldered, weighed down by a woollen peacoat that would be too warm for the May day. She was smoking, stroking Harley's head.

Harley left Naomi's side to scamper up to Sophie, yapping at her, wagging his tail.

'Hello, you,' Sophie cooed, grateful that he seemed pleased to see her even if Naomi was not.

Sophie sat down next to Naomi. Naomi stood up, but did not walk away. Harley began charging between them, sitting at Naomi's feet for a second, springing up again, back to Sophie, and so on.

'My new tenants moved in last Saturday.'

Silence.

'They seem nice.'

More silence. Small talk was a waste of time. She decided to get on with it.

'I have come to discuss a business idea,' Sophie began.

At this point, Harley ran off.

Naomi took a long drag from her roll-up. Sophie continued, 'I was thinking we could become partners.'

Naomi flicked her half-smoked cigarette onto the ground, laughing, stamping at the butt. 'Partners in *what*?'

'Your blog.'

'You really are fucking delusional,' she muttered, shaking her head.

Sophie ignored that. 'I know it doesn't make an awful lot of money, but I don't need to make much.'

'But you don't know anything about wine.'

'I know a bit, through you. I could be a silent partner with a fifty per cent stake. Perhaps add my name to your limited company. King and Wilson? It has a nice ring to it.'

'Were you planning to give me any money for the privilege?' she retorted sarcastically.

'I don't have any, you know that.'

'So, you have no money, you can't write and you know shit about wine. Why the hell would I sign half of my business over to you?'

'I could learn.'

'Not a chance in hell.'

'There's no need to be so unpleasant.'

'I think you're missing a cog in here,' Naomi said, pressing her forefinger to her own temple.

Sophie played with the amber beads of her necklace, retying the knot. 'Could you please think about it?'

'Why? *Why* would I think about it?'

Sophie let go of her necklace, stood up and stepped very close to her, so that Naomi would not miss a syllable of what she was about to say. 'Because I think you owe me that, don't you?'

The shock seemed to unscrew Naomi's jaw, letting it fall open, letting her pithy retorts roll unspoken off her tongue.

She rasped, 'You're *blackmailing* me?'

'Don't put it like that,' Sophie frowned, stepping away. 'We're great friends going into business together.'

'Do I have any choice in the matter?'

'Choice can be an illusion,' Sophie said, rather too grandly, having read the line somewhere. She elaborated, 'One decision, or another decision, it doesn't matter, it leads to the same conclusion.'

'What are you *talking* about?' Naomi scowled.

Sophie was losing her patience. 'Okay, no. No, Naomi, you don't have any choice.'

Naomi clawed her fingertips through her hair, wild blonde curls against the deep green of the fir trees behind her. 'I can't believe you're doing this to me.'

Sophie stood up, galled, biting back everything she wanted to remind Naomi of. She could feel the rippling of the rash inside her clenched fist.

Before now, Naomi had been the first one to stop and note the fleeting beauty of a sunset or pause to savour the sound of children's laughter. Well, maybe it worked the other way around, too. When the going got tough, why not believe that everything was just as it should be and live in that moment as powerfully as you might want to under a sky full of glittering stars? Naomi was trying to hit reverse on the earth's spin, but couldn't they simply enjoy the ride, and live as though it was all just *meant to be*? God might judge them, but would the universe care in a trillion years' time?

'You should be grateful for all you have,' Sophie said.

They both needed to stop wrestling with their regrets. It was pointless of Naomi to pretend that she was the better person for wanting to confess. The simplicity of good and bad did not need to exist; the moral and legal parameters could become irrelevant to them, if they so chose. For both their sakes, Sophie wanted Naomi to accept this, to accept their shared destiny. They could either let it destroy them, like Sophie had almost done, or they could work together and give it meaning, huddle into the closeness and comfort of friendship, look around them, see what they had within their grasp to feel grateful for.

'Fuck you,' Naomi replied.

Sophie sighed. 'I want my name added to the business by the end of next week. I'll send you my bank details, and any other info you might need.'

She walked away from Naomi, back through the house and out of the door, with a ball of excitement gathering speed in her chest. The thrill of her achievement propelled her into a run. She felt the wind in her hair and the air filling her lungs. She was alive, finally. The realisation of her dreams was closer than ever. Change felt great! What a wonderful day this was.

CHAPTER TWENTY-FOUR

Two hands were pinning my shoulders to the bed, pushing me down when I wanted to get up. I could smell incense. My eyes shot open but there was nobody there. I blinked, trying to find something to focus on in the dark. My rapid eye movement accentuated how motionless the rest of me was. If I had been able to breathe properly, I would have tried to inhale and exhale, to centre myself. I tried to move, but my chest seemed put upon, pressed upon, crushed by the air around it, which was leaden, heavy with my worry.

I had until Monday to decide whether to contact Mike, the accountant at Charlie's firm, about Sophie's request. He would be able to make the changes easily. It was a technicality that he was not in a position to question. Knowing Mike, he would. He was a good accountant. It would be easy to allay his fears. I would lie about Sophie's motivations, about her skills, about what she could offer the business. I could explain that I had been finding the juggling of work and childcare tiring, or that I missed the company of others, or that I wanted to build a business with someone who had fresh ideas. Any of the above would have been enough to persuade him that I was of sound mind. He knew that Charlie's income covered our overheads, just.

In the early years of the girls' lives, I had hated relying on Charlie for handouts. With my own money, I contributed to the family. In small ways, I enhanced our lives. While Charlie paid the mortgage and the utility bills, I bought the added extras, like holidays and the girls' after-school clubs and new clothes and the lease-purchase payments on a car that didn't break down every week. Not only that; my earnings allowed me small luxuries, like breakfast out at the organic café on Friday mornings, or a Pizza Express meal with the girls on a school night or theatre tickets in London.

If I gave half to Sophie, I would have to explain to Charlie why I needed to dip into our shared account again. If I told Charlie that Sophie was benefiting from half of my profits, he would not accept my reasoning in the way Mike would have to. He would be suspicious and obstructive.

The only other option was to say no to Sophie.

I considered this, and then tried to twist myself physically out of the progression of that thought. My skull was a bell and her threat a gong. It was loud and clear: she would harm my girls. Their trip to Brighton had been designed to deliver that exact message.

Panic exploded inside me. I opened my mouth to scream but nothing came out.

Sophie thought she deserved to take what was mine as recompense for the secret she had carried for us. In her mind, in her warped mind, she was only taking what she deserved.

She imagined that I had been an unwitting beneficiary of her sinister, wicked cover-up. The so-called favour – which I had not asked her for, which she failed to accept responsibility for – had been her own unilateral decision. Not mine. If she was capable of leaving a young man to die by the roadside, of letting his mother suffer in the dark for so long, she would be capable of anything.

I knew that I could not risk her wrath, that I could not risk derailing her. I knew I had to give her the money. For the girls' safety, it was a small price to pay.

Charlie and I would survive. We could take the financial hit, just about. I could make up some nonsense about the business that he would have to accept. If he suspected foul play, there was nothing he could do to prove it.

The decision loosened my limbs. I was able to sit up.

Quietly, I snuck out of the bedroom and headed down to the laundry room, where Harley slept and where I kept the wine boxes. I chose a cheap plonk, given to us by a couple who had come over for dinner. That sourness, that acid in my throat was fitting. It would send me off to sleep with indigestion, but it would fill me right up and push the nastiness up into my gullet, and possibly make me sick if I drank enough of it.

Hot breath was on my cheek.

'Mummy,' Izzy's face was inches from mine. 'Why are you in here?'

The room was brighter than the bedroom.

As I focused, I saw the television screen and the coral linen of the armchair and felt the lumps and bumps of the sofa underneath me.

Izzy did not wait for an answer; she climbed under the blanket and pressed the television on with the remote control.

I lay there with her snuggled into the curve of my body, and felt a throb in my head from the bad wine, from the excess of wine, and wished we could stay huddled here together all day. I tried to remember if we had anything planned today. I didn't think so, which was perfect for me. With this acid hangover, I wanted a too-much-telly-and-cereal day.

The sound of Izzy sucking her thumb was almost as comforting for me as it would have been for her. Normally I would tell her off, remind her of the dentist's threat to fix braces, but I could not rob her of a simple pleasure this morning. Under the cloud of Sophie's menace, none of the peripheral concerns of parenting registered as important to me. Izzy's life with me, Diana's life with me, safe in this house, was all that mattered.

Five minutes later, Diana came in, taller than Izzy, but just as wobbly and ruffled from sleep. She curled up at my feet. With her eyes on the screen, she asked, 'Did you sleep in here, Mum?'

Unlike Izzy, Diana would not let me get away without answering.

'Daddy was snoring,' I said, knowing they would instantly understand.

Last year, when camping together, both girls had been woken at first light by 'the scary noise coming from Daddy', which Diana said was so loud it rattled the tent poles. To be fair to Charlie, he only snored when he drank red wine, which was rare in itself.

'Poor you, Mummy,' Izzy said, very seriously.

They both began doing impressions of him, which sounded more like donkeys braying or bears roaring than his snoring. Their noises might have been what brought Charlie downstairs.

'What's all this racket?' he asked, bending over the back of the sofa to tickle Izzy and kiss Diana on the head. His pyjamas had twisted around and a patch of his hair was flattened in the wrong direction. I loved him dearly.

'It's your snoring!' the girls giggled.

He rubbed at his head. 'Was I snoring? Did you sleep in here?' he asked me.

'Yes,' I murmured, turning away from him to look at the television, uncomfortable to lie about this small thing, as though it symbolised all the other lies.

'What's this rubbish you're watching?' he asked.

'It's so good, Daddy. Come and watch it.'

I hoped he would settle into the armchair and pretend to enjoy this trashy sitcom with us. The girls loved it when he did. They would provide a running commentary throughout, explaining each and every character and plot twist in detail, fully expecting him to be as invested in the show as they were. If he tried to criticise any aspect of it, they would get cross and shout him down and tell him he was too old and boring to get it. He moved over to the armchair, and was about to sit down when there was a clink of glass. With a sinking feeling, I knew exactly what he had stumbled on. His brief, charged glance at me confirmed it.

Instead of sitting down, he picked up the empty wine bottle and glass, smeared with my handprints and lip marks, and left the room.

I heard the clattering of crockery from the kitchen and Harley yapping. I had forgotten to let him out.

Reluctantly, I crawled out from under the blanket and nipped upstairs to brush my teeth and hair, sort out the Burgundy stain on my lips, pop a Nurofen and climb into clean sweatpants.

Before I had a chance to return to the kitchen to make scrambled eggs and bacon for everyone – with a plan to eat a large pile of them, with ketchup, in front of the television, where I wanted to lie all day – Charlie came into the bedroom and closed the door.

'Harley left a puddle in the laundry room,' he said.

'Sorry. I forgot.'

'Are you going to be okay for this afternoon?'

'What's happening this afternoon?'

'The Festival Hall?'

I had a caving-in feeling. How had I forgotten? A few months ago, I had booked tickets for me, Charlie, Meg and Josh for a performance of Beethoven's 5th Piano Concerto at the Royal Festival Hall on the Southbank. It was a birthday treat for Meg, whose birthday was next week.

'Oh. Of course. Why wouldn't I be okay? I'm really looking forward to it.'

I tied my hair up and stared at my reflection in the dressing table mirror, seeing the dimpling of my chin as my muscles fought away the tears.

From downstairs, I heard Harley barking.

'I'll take Harley for a walk if you feed the girls some eggs,' I bargained.

If I returned to the sofa with the girls, I would never be able to rally myself out of the door with Charlie later.

A bracing walk with Harley would sort my head out.

*

The steep climb out of the valley and the aromas of damp, peaty soil had been an antidote to the bad wine. As had the strong cup of coffee.

I now stood in a hot shower, letting the steam cleanse me of my sins, detoxing me, preparing me for the glass of wine I would be able to drink in the interval. In fact, the wine would be a better cure for the hangover than scrambled eggs.

A rush of cold air broke my reverie.

Through the frosted shower door, I saw Charlie come in.

At first, I worried he wanted sex. It was the last thing I wanted.

'Can I talk to you about something?' he asked.

I shut the water off, grabbed the towel and hurried out of the shower. 'No. You cannot,' I snapped over my shoulder as I rushed back into the bedroom, knowing exactly what he wanted to talk to me about.

I struggled to pull a pair of black, slightly bobbly, tights over my damp skin, dreading his lecture about my 'problem drinking', as he would no doubt call it.

He emerged from the bathroom. There was silence. He stood with his hands twirling the cords of his pyjama trousers. There was a fleck of egg at the side of his mouth. He looked as tired as I felt.

'What then?'

His eyes – lost, crestfallen – were searching me for something I didn't have, and I wanted to shrivel away in shame.

'Go on,' I said, less aggressively, accepting he needed to get it off his chest. I was poised with promises of my reform.

Then, unexpectedly, he said, 'It doesn't matter,' and left the room.

For a minute, I wanted to run after him, and insist he tell me what was on his mind, wondering if perhaps it had been unrelated to my drinking. In the fug of my own despair, I had forgotten that Charlie had his own life and his own problems, separate to mine. But I could not think about Charlie's problems right now. I did not have the headspace. Moreover, if I didn't solve my own problems, they would become Charlie's, too.

I stepped into my black shift dress and undid my hair from the towel to dry it.

As the hairdryer blared into my ear, I gave myself a pep talk. All I had to do was get through this afternoon. Bed and sleep were waiting for me afterwards as a reward. If not, peace of mind. Sophie's business proposition hung in the air around my head like a swarm of bees. Tomorrow, sobriety and a clear head were waiting for me. As soon as today was over with, I could make a decision about what to do.

Ironically, I had been the one to book the tickets for the concert, before Sophie had unleashed the past on me. It was the kind of present I would never have been able to justify buying with Charlie's money. My wine blog had afforded us the luxury of treats like this, which Sophie was going to take away from me. There were worse fates. Charlie and I could go back to living as we had before. It had been tight, but we were fortunate enough to have his regular salary guaranteed every month. I was lucky. I didn't need extras. I could handle it, as long as I could handle Sophie's audacity, her nerve, her turncoating. She had been my friend, and now she was my enemy.

They say first impressions are everything, and that it is foolish to dismiss them. Back then, through naive eyes, I had seen Sophie as a true eccentric; an ethereal, bony, pale-haired beauty, who was brave enough to stand out in the crowd of freshers, enough to wear unfashionable cowboy boots and pack plastic flowers instead of toothbrushes and drive classic cars. She had hidden behind her kooky cool and her controversial literature. My own insecurities had been too great to see beyond her pretensions.

When I thought of yesterday, and how she had stood in my garden with her plans of stealing half my business from me, there had been a disconnect between her actions and my reaction, just as there had been for Humbert Humbert when it came to his desire for Lolita. With hindsight, when I thought of Sophie's fascination with that novel, I understood that Sophie was more likely to have been absorbed by the amorality of Humbert Humbert, whose intellectual sophistication and good looks and shyness obscured his dark nature, his paedophilia. His internal struggles were never quite convincing enough to allow the reader to believe he was remorseful or fully aware of how damaging and unnatural his crimes towards Lolita were.

It had been obvious, yesterday, that Sophie could not understand why I was upset about her business proposal, her blackmail. She had not been capable of empathising. She could only see it from her own point of view. Life had been unfair to her, and with self-pity at the heart of everything she did, she was redressing the balance. Through the prism of what she needed for herself, she justified her crimes. It was all about her. But I had refused to see it.

Now, I recognised the steel inside her. If I were to meet Sophie for the first time again, today, with my worldly, adult eyes, I would see a parasite who wanted to feed off me.

I sat down in front of the mirror of my dressing table and reached for some under-eye concealer. The liquid replaced my shadows with unpleasant semicircles of light beige. My mascara clumped. My eyeliner was too heavy. My lipstick bled into the fine lines around my lips. The make-up would not be absorbed, as if my skin was rejecting its falsehoods.

Underneath was me. The real me; a separate entity to Sophie. All about me. An alien concept. Could it ever be all about me? What could that possibly look like? What chasm would open up in me without Sophie?

*

The piano notes wrapped around our minds, silencing the auditorium, holding us in its magic. As I looked along the row of seats, I noticed that Meg's shoulders were pushed forward towards the orchestra. Her chin was resting on her hands and her cheek was brushed up against Josh's expensive suit sleeve. One of her satin high-heeled shoes danced to the music in between his splayed legs. Across the intricate beading of her structured dress, across the contours of her back, Josh's fingers fidgeted, up and down the long zip, from the nape of her neck right down to the base of her spine.

I looked away, back to the young conductor, who was flipping his hair as he thrust himself forward, bringing the second movement to a climax. Here I was. Just me, alone among all these people. It was all about me. My emotions were crashing and soaring like the music. The thrumming rhythm dredged up my darkest thoughts, thrusting a deeply buried memory into the front of my mind. A memory that felt like a silence. I saw it, I couldn't hear it. All I could hear was this music, its gentle cradling of me, how it enveloped me, almost holding me up. There was a giving way of something inside me. This chair, this auditorium, this setting wove itself into this startling act of remembering, imbuing everything around me with momentous significance.

My body was sunken into a softness that smelt wrong. There was pressure in my hips and a deep throbbing between my legs, as deep as any kind I had felt before, pressing up into my stomach. The space around me, with no walls or boundaries, moved in fractured shapes, disintegrating. Yellows and golds and bronze. At the centre of this collapsed reality was a tunnel, narrowing into a white light. It offered a release, it offered the discontinuation of everything, it offered death. Tacitly, I allowed the exchange. Death was a fair deal for a cessation of this ordeal. I yearned to say goodbye to Sophie and to my mother and my father. And I aimed for the light.

My mind had given up its searing truth and the revelation had hit me, the revelation that I had been raped. Yes. Raped. *Rape.* I tried the word out in my mind. I had not been drunk or careless, I had been drugged and attacked. I had been raped.

Had I always known this?

Had I?

Not really.

Yes, I had. Back then. Sophie had told me.

Had she?

I had let it burrow deep inside me.

And now this. Now this rapist of mine was back inside me, in a different way, yet the same, and he was dead.

Killed. It was a more accurate word.

Had I wished for it? Had I asked her for it?

His eyes, those eyes, with little puffs of swollen, sleepy flesh under each, stared down at me, a shot of minty breath unleashed with each jerk. I hadn't asked for this, but I was getting it anyway. Until it stopped; somehow, sometime, I woke up, with Sophie's face looming in place of his, saying something, covering me up, asking me the name of the nameless man whom she had seen leaving my room. Sophie was always there. Always there for me...

I went back even further, to the hours before that, to a bustling student union bar. There had been a loud DJ playing hip-hop that had vibrated inside my chest, just as the Beethoven did now.

A handful of male faces encircled me and Sophie, up close, jostling for attention, laughing, drinking. There was Will, his ratty arm dangling over Sophie's shoulders. There were three of Will's friends.

There was a face with narrow, pale eyes and sandy hair and clusters of angry spots on each cheek.

'Hey. It's my round. What are you drinking?' he said, into my ear. Close up, he smelt of TCP.

I looked over at Sophie and Will talking. They had full drinks. There were many full drinks. I doubted it was his round, but mine was empty.

'Sure. Great. Thanks. Jack and Coke. Double.'

I had not asked his name. I had not cared who he was. He was buying my drink. That's what I cared about. I had taken it from him. I had drunk it.

'What's your name?' he said, touching the rim of his beer glass with mine.

'Cheers,' I said.

'That's an odd name.'

'Naomi,' I laughed, looking over to Sophie and Will, who were kissing.

'I'm Jay,' he smiled.

And then the Jack and Coke made me woozy. The music was turned up. The lights turned down. The crowds swam and swirled, heads floating upwards. Time disappeared. He was in my room, unzipping his flies. Taking from me.

If I had refused that drink, my life would have been different. A good place to start the reworking of my life. That exact point. The knowledge that it was not possible to go back dug a hole in the pit of my stomach, filling it in with sorrow, like cement. I didn't know what to do with these brief, badly ordered images of my past; where to take them. I wasn't even sure they were mine to own. Perhaps I couldn't bring myself to absorb it. If they were mine, I wanted to see them again.

They flared up, again. Mine, all mine. I didn't want to see them and I wanted to; I wanted to reject them and I wanted to own them, greedily almost. Unbidden, they clicked into their rightful place inside me, slotting in, answering a distant question that I had never been courageous enough to ask.

In the corner of my eye, I caught Josh massaging the back of Meg's neck. She tilted her head, letting her hand fall onto Josh's upper thigh. While the music played on, while a rape played out in my mind, they were flirting with each other, dancing with each other in tiny, almost imperceptible movements, using the constrained environment of this closed auditorium as foreplay.

How I envied the ease with which they touched each other.

I could not touch or be touched like that. I had been raped. Thinking of it was a punch that I could not physically reel from.

Charlie and I sat tall and stiff. We could barely look at each other, let alone touch each other. I felt his reproachful sideways glance every time my plastic wine glass met my lips. He would not understand that my consumption of this warm, white wine was about survival rather than recklessness. I had been drinking when it had happened, and now I drank to forget it had.

I sensed the tension in Charlie's body underneath his starched white shirt. His hand gripped his water bottle, tighter and tighter, until I feared it would crack and disturb the pianist's flow. I imagined that my stress was a series of soundwaves diffracting from my brain across the audience to meet head-on with the roll of exquisite notes from the orchestra, the two conflicting, invisible waves coming up against each other, creating a wall, a blockage, a battle, one not letting the other through. My ugly flow of thoughts versus the sublime genius of Beethoven were in a clash of the bad and good.

I wanted to separate my head from my body. My breasts, my buttocks, between my thighs, all that he had touched, were hideous to me. I was disgusted by them.

I wanted to walk my mind away from my body, to enjoy the concert; I wanted to sink into the music as I might have done only weeks before. The simple pleasure of listening to live music had been spoilt. A note. A song. A symphony. Simple pleasures. A painting. A poem. A book. A sunset. A smile. A laugh. A hug. A hand in mine. Would they be permanently lost to me, my mind now crowded by ugliness? Might my smile become like Ilene Parker's? Tight and mean, embittered and broken?

The applause thrummed and pushed at my eardrums. Charlie, Meg and Josh rose in a standing ovation for this energetic Russian and his orchestra. Forty minutes had passed already, and I had been trapped inside my own head.

As a delayed reaction, I stood too, smiling and clapping along with everyone else.

After three standing ovations and an encore of the second movement, the audience's cheers turned to satisfied mutterings and mumblings.

We shuffled out. Bursts of praise could be heard all around us as we made our way out onto the Southbank. The lights of London gleamed across the surface of the Thames. I imagined what it might be like to fall in, and how cold the water would be, and how its slow churn would drag me down, swallowing me into its darkness.

'That was absolutely wonderful, thank you, Naomi,' Meg said, linking arms with me as we walked ahead of Charlie and Josh along the tree-lined bank. 'Did you enjoy it?'

'Of course! It was wonderful,' I replied.

Meg continued to rhapsodise, telling me how in awe she had been of the conductor's power and the orchestra's energy.

'Absolutely. That's just how I felt,' I agreed, trying to put some expression into my voice, trying to think of something intelligent to say about it.

We walked a few more paces before Meg said, 'Everything all right, hon?'

I squeezed her arm with mine. 'Sorry. I'm just a bit tired, I think.'

'Been busy?'

'Manic.'

'Josh said Charlie was having some problems at work, or something.'

'Did he?' I asked, taken aback.

'Nothing serious, I don't think,' she reassured me quickly.

'He clashes with his boss. It might have been that.'

'Yes. Possibly.' But I could hear the doubt in her voice. I did not ask her for more information. I was too embarrassed to admit that I might know less than Josh.

'He's very closed off with me sometimes,' I said, wanting to apportion blame, to deflect it from me.

'That's public schoolboys for you,' she tutted.

I laughed, enjoying the sensation in my chest, unfamiliar, like a muscle that hadn't been used.

'Seriously, I think Josh wishes he could have stayed at school all his life.'

'That's a bit sad.'

I wanted to turn back to look at both men, assess them again. On paper, Josh was a good fit for Charlie. They had both gone to good schools and good universities and now wore good suits as markers of both, proud of their status as family men, proud of their sacrifices. But I guessed that the conversation would be stilted and rather dull as they walked alongside each other. I thought of Sophie and Adam. Around Adam, Charlie was less tucked in. Around Sophie and Adam, we were both less tucked in. Or had been.

'Honestly, Naomi, Josh is never happy, ever. Which is *really* sad, don't you think? And it makes me feel a bit shit, quite frankly. Like he's disappointed by me, or something.'

I stopped walking to gape at her.

'No! How could he be disappointed by you? Look at you!' I cried. 'You're clever and beautiful and successful. He's lucky to have you.'

Meg laughed. 'Thanks. It's not true. But thanks.'

Meg had said it wasn't true, but I believed she understood her own worth, on some level, deep down. Whereas Sophie did not. Her self-deprecation was not throwaway; it was genuine gold-standard self-loathing. Over many conversations, I had tried to boost her self-esteem. My praise would be an injection of love and encouragement that would last only so long. Each time the effects would wear off, and she would need another booster shot. I had learnt that there was nothing you could say to Sophie to change the blueprint of her: her mother's rejection had been a needle inserted deep into her soul. Its inky poison had seeped in and spread throughout, wreaking its damage many years before I came along with a placebo cure.

And here was a friend, next to me now, who might have been good for me, better for me than Sophie had ever been, less insecure, less intense, less life-changing, but I could not be her friend now. I could not amble down the road, side by side, chatting with her lightly about our lives, complaining about our husbands, listening quietly without an agenda, offering advice that might sometimes grate and always come from the right place. It was too late for us. For every year that I had lived in denial, our crime had been further embedded into my life story.

There might have been a time when I could have held my hands up and accepted the part I played in a young man's death, dealt with the psychological fallout of our actions, within context, with perspective, in the moment: I had been twenty-one years old, drunk, disorderly, dangerous, but there had been no intent. I had not been a murderer.

Every day that I harboured the secret about Jason Parker's death, regardless of Sophie's threats, I became guiltier, almost as guilty as Sophie.

Josh and Charlie's presence was closer behind us. 'You'll have to stop talking about us now,' Josh said.

Had we been? Yes, of course we had been. And yet we had also walked in a comfortable silence with each other, as our respective thoughts had drifted to our separate troubles. This, too, was friendship. Allowing the other space. Why had I not understood how unhealthy it had been within the confines of my bond with Sophie? Our friendship had been like a long, stressful conversation that would never end, where I offered my opinions and she mistrusted them. Every time we left each other, I would replay our chat, mostly regretting what I had said or how I had said it; constantly second-guessing her mood changes, trying to discern whether her sadness or crossness was my fault.

I realised that Josh and Charlie were talking to me and Meg, reiterating their enjoyment of the concert, saying their goodbyes.

'You're not getting the train with us?' I said, surprised we were parting here, at the top of the tumble of steps towards the train station.

The three of them stared at me for a second. Meg said, 'We've booked a hotel,' she said, without a 'remember?' at the end of her sentence. It was kind of her. She had understood that I was preoccupied by concerns beyond tonight.

'Oh god, sorry. I'm so distracted these days.'

I noted Charlie's glance at Josh, and the flicker of Josh's eyebrow. Seemingly, they had been talking about me.

On the way back to the train station, Charlie and I walked in silence. It was different to the silence between me and Meg. It was charged, just as it had been in the bedroom this morning. We had left home but we had carried our problems with us through the throng of London life.

We spoke about the train times, staring at the big board for too long, speculating on which platform would be displayed, eleven or twelve.

It was twelve. He put his hand in the small of my back when I stepped into the carriage.

We found two seats next to each other on the packed last train. There was a group of noisy, drunk teenagers eating McDonald's and laughing at YouTube clips.

'I need to talk to you about something,' he said, echoing his statement this morning in the bathroom.

I sighed, resigned to the lecture. 'Sure,' I said.

'I've been made redundant,' he said.

Blood rushed the wrong way up my veins. I thought I might have misheard over the cackling from one of the teenagers.

'What?'

'I've lost my job, Naomi,' he said softly, turning his head at me. His face was as grey as his hair under the strip lighting.

This could not be true.

'No. Why? No.'

'Cutbacks.'

'*Cutbacks?*'

One of the girls turned to look at me, a French fry dangling at her plumped lips.

I scowled at her, wanting to gag at the smell of her greasy food. I hated her. She knew nothing of how tough life could get.

'I don't understand,' I said, dropping my voice. 'You work so hard. They're so lucky to have you.'

He tried to explain to me the structures in place at his firm and their legal justifications behind his redundancy, in terms of restructuring following the effects of economic uncertainty. He sounded so calm about it. He could have been siding with his boss.

'You'll find another job, won't you?'

He scratched his fingers up and down his trousers, taking too long to answer. 'Yes, of course. I've already put the feelers out.'

'How long have you known?'

'A couple of weeks.'

'And you've been trying to tell me, haven't you,' I said, pressing the back of my head into the seat, pressing away the headache that was forming. 'I'm so sorry.'

He took my hand and squeezed it. 'I've got a decent enough redundancy package.'

'Does it give you enough time to find another job?'

'My reference is a worry. I'm not Tina's employee of the month.'

'She's the arsehole, not you.'

'Nobody else will see it that way.'

'What about our savings?'

'That went on fixing the roof last year.'

'I thought we remortgaged for that?'

'They turned us down. Not enough equity.'

'What are we going to do?'

'If we live off your salary and the redundancy money combined, it'll give me a couple of months to look.' He had thought it through.

'It took Cynthia's husband at least a year to find another job, and they had to sell their house.'

'But Cynthia isn't a brilliant wine blogger,' he smiled.

My heart began racing with fear. I saw the blink of Sophie's white eyelashes. Her pale smile and thin limbs, frail but all-powerful. I pictured the FOR SALE sign in front of our home, and the girls' school shoes too small for them, and a repossessed car, and ketchup and rice for supper. Rice and ketchup had been the meal we had eaten when my father lost his job in the 1980s. I saw my father's depression and my mother's fretting. I saw half a life. And Sophie wanted to take half of that again. I wanted to bang my forehead on the front seat and howl.

Swallowing a few times, I geared up my voice box. 'Yes, we'll be fine,' I managed to utter.

And his hand stayed holding mine, in my lap, for the rest of the journey home.

I had always known that happiness was temporary, that you had to grab onto it the moment it came your way, but I had never believed it was possible that I would lose it forever, that it might never pass my way again.

CHAPTER TWENTY-FIVE

Kenneth and Martha Etherington had left Deda's cottage in their electric car at 7 a.m. to catch the 10 a.m. ferry from Dover to Calais, from where they planned to drive to the Dordogne to stay with their son and their grandchildren. Sophie knew this because Martha had knocked on the door to the shack a couple of days ago to tell her of their plans. They would be away for seven days, and she had asked Sophie to keep an eye on the cottage for them.

On the afternoon of their departure, when they were guaranteed to be in France, Sophie had taken up the axe from the woodpile and dragged it over the shingle drive into the cottage. The wood pressed into her sore palm, which had blown up and turned to scabs over the last few weeks.

She left the axe where one might leave an umbrella, and wandered through the rooms, inspecting the walls, rapping on them with her knuckles, deciding which wall would be best.

The fruit shampoo smell of the Etheringtons was ripe in the air.

Having moved through each room, Sophie stopped at the dividing stud partition between the sitting room and the hallway.

Carefully, she took the three African masks down and laid them next to the mirrored elephant at the foot of the stairs, and returned for her axe.

'*Prosti menya, Deda,*' she said, looking upwards, imagining him in the heavens looking down at her.

Then, squeezing her eyes tight shut, she swung the axe at the bare wall, just below the three nails. Bits of debris flew at her face, her shoulder jarred and the axe left one jagged hole in the plasterboard.

The next blow created a hole big enough to see through, right through into the grey sitting room. It was a shame to have wrecked the new paint job.

By the time the wall was a mess of rubble, Sophie was sweating and excited, wishing she could knock another wall down. The violence had been cathartic. Nobody was writing *that* advice in self-help books.

She made herself a cup of tea in an Ikat-patterned mug and took a few photographs of the destruction, satisfied that it was bad enough to show a solicitor, guessing it would be sufficient to justify a break in their six-month tenancy agreement.

After knocking back the last dregs of her tea, she scrolled through her contact list to find the solicitor's telephone number and gathered some tears into her throat. It would be so much more authentic if she cried.

'… when they first moved in,' she explained to Henry, the solicitor, 'they'd asked me if they could knock through to the kitchen, to make it open-plan, and I told them absolutely not. I just can't believe they've gone ahead and done it. They seemed so nice. I just can't believe it,' Sophie wept.

Henry was not emotional, but it was clear that he was sympathetic. He expressed shock when she emailed him the photograph, confirming that she would be able to keep their deposit and break the lease agreement on the grounds of damage to the property.

Sophie understood that there was a risk the Etheringtons would try to prove their innocence by fighting her in the small claims court. It would be hard for them to win, considering how highly improbable it was for a landlady to break apart her newly decorated house only weeks after agreeing to their tenancy. It would be their word against hers, and it would cost them more in legal fees than their lost deposit to have this confirmed in court. Sophie guessed they would accept that she had beaten them, cut their losses and leave her house in their woolly, mild-mannered way.

Sophie did feel bad about them. They seemed like good people. If she had needed tenants, they would have been ideal. But they were in the way.

Filling herself with tears again, she made another phone call.

'Adam...' she spluttered.

'Sophie? Are you okay? What's happened? Dylan's right here. Do you want to speak to him?' Adam asked frantically.

Sophie let the sobs subside a little. 'No, no. I don't want to upset him. It's just...' And she explained the whole story of how Martha and Kenneth had knocked the wall down.

'What a headfuck. They seemed so chilled.'

Sophie could hear the crash of crockery in the background. 'Is Natalie there?'

'No, Sophie,' Adam sighed. 'When Dylan's here, she stays at her mum's. You know that.'

This had been an arrangement that Adam had wanted, insisting he wasn't ready for Natalie to meet Dylan, which had pleased Sophie greatly.

'He doesn't need any more crap right now. Especially after the Etheringtons. He was getting to know them quite well. They're *physically* so close to us, and then they do something like this. It's really scary.'

'You have to get them out of there as soon as possible.'

'Yes. I've been on to my solicitor already. He'll be contacting them on Monday.'

'On their holiday?'

'You think I should wait?'

'No. Get them out.'

'What am I going to do about this wall?'

'Use the deposit to fix it, I suppose.'

'I need that to live off.'

There was a long pause. Sophie could hear Dylan's game bleeping near the phone.

'I'll drop by next week and take a look, see if there's anything I can do, okay?'

Sophie smiled to herself. 'Thanks.' She sniffed. 'I really appreciate it, Adam.'

'No problem. See you tomorrow. Do you want to say goodbye to Dylan?'

'No, no. Don't disturb him. I'll let you go.'

'Okay. Bye then.'

'Bye. Love you,' she said automatically, and then hung up, flushing. She had not meant to say that.

On Monday afternoon, she decided to read through Naomi's blog posts on Wine O'Clock. There was an article titled 'Too Much of a Good Thing' that offered tips on how to drink better-quality wine and less of it. For example, putting a hand over the glass if someone threatened to pour that third large one. Another post focused on Dry January and Sober September, and weekday summer 'Mocktails'. Last month, she invited a variety of contributors to discuss the risks of binge-drinking. In the past few weeks, she had written an article about her distaste for alcopops or any alcohol sold to look more like a soft drink. There was another article about how Europeans drank better than we did, called 'Je Ne Regrette Rien!' Sophie decided she was a secret agent for Alcoholics Anonymous, and began to jot down some ideas for ramping up the fun side of drinking.

Sadly, most of the advice Sophie had given Naomi so far, to boost business, had been ignored. After Sophie's needling, she had begrudgingly changed her profile photographs and blog opener, replacing Naomi in a vineyard in France with one of Sophie and Naomi together, clinking Prosecco in short dresses. The 'About Me' drop-down tag had been renamed 'About Us', and included the biographical paragraph Sophie had written up.

Her creative flow was interrupted when she received a call from a mobile, prefixed with a French dialling code. Her instinct was to let it ring out. She was busy with a new list: a weekly vlog, some collaborations with targeted retailers and some small changes to her Instagram feed, stolen from other social media influencers. With this knowledge, she would plan a meeting with Naomi.

Her phone rang off, making her decision for her. But then the same number rang back half an hour later. At some point she would have to face the Etheringtons. She picked up.

'Sophie speaking.'

'Sophie. I'm so glad you've taken my call. I think there's been a terrible mix-up,' Kenneth Etherington began.

Sophie interrupted him. 'It's best you speak directly to my solicitor about this.'

'But you have to believe us, we didn't knock that wall down, Sophie. We love living in your house. You've been so good to us. You must have had a break-in, or something.'

Sophie's throat constricted.

'There has been no break-in, Mr Etherington.'

'But I don't understand… I… We've been good tenants. I don't know what's going on, but…' his voice began to break, and he coughed, and then there was a rustle. A younger male voice came on the line. 'Hello, Mrs King? This is Tony Etherington speaking, Kenneth's son. We'll be engaging solicitors to deal with the legal side of things, but I'll be sending a removal van to pack up their stuff at the end of this week.'

Sophie was shocked that they were moving so fast, and she began to worry about Tony Etherington's legal intentions. 'The end of the month will be fine, honestly. Until they've found somewhere else.'

'Do you really think I'm going to let my parents go anywhere near your house again, after what you've done?'

'I'm not the one who has done anything wrong here.'

Sophie scrolled up and down Naomi's website, seeing the photographs of sunshine-filled glasses whizz past; of smiles and sips at picnics, on boats, beaches and balconies. Every shot of happiness came with an enticing wine. Sophie wanted a drink for the first time since she had given up, and she zoomed in and out of each photograph, enlarging the dewy droplets on a glass of rosé as though this might give her a vicarious hit.

'Dad is giving you the benefit of the doubt. He can't believe anyone could be so devious and dishonest, but I'm a young cynic, I'm afraid, and I know you're up to something. I don't know what that is, and, to be frank, I don't care, but I would like you to understand this: my father was gravely ill last year, and this move out of London was meant to be a fresh start, an easier life for them both. The stress you have put on him and Mum at this time in their lives is unforgivable. If we had the money, we'd fight you on this all the way to court.'

'I'm the victim here, you know,' Sophie replied weakly, trying to keep the wobble out of her voice.

'I honestly don't know how you sleep at night,' he said, and the phone line went dead.

Sophie threw her phone on the sofa and slammed her computer closed and then burst into real tears.

She had not wanted to cause any hurt or stress to Kenneth and Martha. If only she could explain that her circumstances had changed, that new opportunities had arisen. If they'd had the same chances for their own son, when he had been eight years old, wouldn't they have grabbed it, just as she was doing for Dylan? Wouldn't they have done anything they could to give him a better life, a better home? Maybe they had. Maybe they had made decisions for Tony that had been selfish, and maybe those decisions had affected other people in ways they had no idea about. It was easy for them to judge her, but Sophie wondered how hypocritical they were being. It was her choice for Dylan. She was a single mother and she wanted him to have a proper home to grow up in, with central heating and a bedroom of his own, and she had now found the money to make that happen. What good mother would deny their child this better life?

This was how she had talked herself down, but for the rest of the week she had moped about, vacillating between regret and defiance.

By Friday, when the removals men arrived to pack up the Etheringtons' possessions, it seemed a weight had been taken off her shoulders. Her days of being a landlady were over. It had not suited her. She couldn't work people out. People had needs and demands, they made noise and expected kindness. Isolation was what Sophie wanted; was why she would never want to move from this secluded woodland plot.

But when she burst into the empty cottage, wanting to hug its walls and say sorry for the damage, she felt a rush of coldness, as though there was a draught coming up from the floorboards. Suddenly, the house was too empty. A sense of aloneness ached in her bones. She wanted Adam to clutch onto. She wanted Dylan to hold. If she took one step further into the house, she worried she might fall into a black pit, unable to climb out. Before now, the cottage had only ever provided comfort. It didn't make sense. She had everything she wanted, now, but something fundamental was missing.

She sat down on the doorstep, half in and half out, and put her head between her legs to send the blood back to where it should be.

At first, she wondered if she should have another baby to fill this emptiness. The very thought scared her rigid. She couldn't share her love between two. And then she thought of paws scuttling around on the empty floors, barking and filling the space with energy and joy. Adam and Dylan had always wanted a dog. It would give her an excuse to go out for dog walks with Naomi. She would get a bigger, better dog than Harley.

As soon as the idea had entered her head, she was determined to make it happen. She pulled out her phone and clicked on to the Battersea Dogs Home website, where she could find a cheaper dog and skip the puppy phase. Within half an hour she had registered online for the rehoming process.

*

Adam was wide-legged, arms crossed, assessing the damage like a real builder, reverting to how his father – a real builder – used to stand when he had been alive.

'Wow! Those two old hippies did this?' Adam exclaimed, whistling.

'Did you see her muscles?'

He laughed and his eyes turned to hers.

'It'll cost ya,' he teased.

Looking at him, listening to his breathing so close to her again, Sophie felt the heat build between her legs. She cocked her head to the side. 'How much?' she flirted.

His expression rearranged itself back to sensible. 'I'll need money for materials.'

Sophie was reminded of the long game. She couldn't push him.

Through the gap in the wall, she stared through to the grey sitting room, whose three other walls were undamaged. Before Adam's arrival, she had hoovered the dust from the coral sofa, placed fresh roses from the garden on the windowsill and positioned brand-new scatter cushions and coffee table books decoratively.

'When you've fixed it, I'm going to live here with Dylan.'

'But you need new tenants for the rental money. I don't have enough to...'

'Don't worry. Things have changed.'

'You've got a job?'

'I have.'

His jaw dropped. 'Seriously?'

'Why is that such a surprise?'

He stammered. 'I... It's not... I'm happy for you.'

She moved over to the roses in the vase and breathed in their scent. 'This is the life we always dreamt of, Adam,' she whispered, playing with the strap of her dress. 'I wasn't ready before. But I am now.'

He shook his head, his lips parted. 'No.'

'I'm not drinking any more.'

His eyes glistened as he stared at her, as they locked onto her, mesmerised, recognising the change in her in this new space. The sun was beating down from the windows, forming the shape of the panes on the floorboards at her feet. She imagined him stepping across them towards her, and the spots of sunlight shattering like real glass under his feet.

'It's a lovely room now,' he rasped.

'I'm thinking of getting a dog. You always wanted one.'

His eyes lit up. 'A collie?'

'Maybe. I was thinking about a rescue dog.'

'Sure. As long as it's good with young kids, I think it's a great idea. Dylan will freak.'

'There'll be loads of collies to rescue.'

'Whatever. It's not up to me.'

'Why don't you stay for a couple of days?'

'Why would I do that?' he asked, but it was obvious he was considering it.

'While you're fixing up the stud wall, it would make sense.'

'No.'

'Because Natalie won't allow it?'

He tucked a piece of his hair behind his ear. 'She has got nothing to do with it.'

'Come upstairs,' she said.

'I've got to get going.'

'Please.'

'Quickly,' he sighed, looking at his watch.

As she led him upstairs, she brushed her hand across the back of her dress, pretending to hide her knickers.

They arrived at her old bedroom door, which she opened.

'Look. Dylan is going to have his own room at last.' She lay down on top of the duvet and tucked her hands behind her head and crossed her ankles. 'I'm going to paint it racing green and fit stripy blinds.'

Her dress had large black buttons all the way down the front. The split where the buttons stopped revealed a little too much thigh. She arched her back and exhaled. 'I still miss it.'

'What do you miss?' he asked, staring down at her greedily. She felt like a package, ready to be opened by him.

'I miss this room,' she said, rising, kneeling on the bed in front of him, looking up to him like a little girl at an altar. 'You could stay here when you're fixing the wall. It's comfy.'

'I know for a fact that it isn't.'

'It wasn't made for two,' she laughed, remembering how they had panted and giggled together in this bed once.

'I can't stay here. It'd be weird.'

'It's weird for a married couple to sleep under the same roof as their son?'

'A *separated* married couple.'

'Details,' she chuckled, shrugging her shoulders, reaching out to touch the top button of his shirt.

He pushed her hand away.

She tucked the tips of her fingers into the pocket of his jeans. Through the material, she could feel the blood pumping through his flesh.

'What's the job?' he asked, pulling her hand out.

She flopped back on the bed. 'I'm going into business with Naomi.'

'*What?*' he spluttered, jamming his hands into his pockets where hers had been.

'She wants input from a new partner, someone whom she can bandy ideas around with. She's sick of working alone.'

Adam's lips puckered up to one side as though twisting off his face. 'Right. Okay. Sure.'

The energy between them fizzled out. She had lost him.

Sophie shot up to standing. 'You don't think I can do it, do you?'

'It's not that, it's just, you don't have any experience. I'm surprised that Naomi…' He broke off. 'I'm surprised, that's all.'

'You're all the bloody same. I'll prove it to you. Just you watch me!' she cried, flouncing out.

Nobody had any faith in her. Nobody understood. But she would prove her worth to both Adam and Naomi. She would force them to drop their doubting, smug smiles.

CHAPTER TWENTY-SIX

'Please, turn it off,' I insisted, wincing at the vlog Sophie had shown me on her phone, cringing deep inside, disturbed by the woman in Utah who had revealed her breasts in a Jacuzzi while describing the acidity of the white wine she drank from.

'That's how *not* to do it,' I said, dropping a pinch of the tobacco on the grass, making a mess. More mess. It didn't matter. Sophie had insisted on this meeting about Wine O'Clock, not me. I was beyond fighting her. I was beyond anger. I was trying to position the filter on the cigarette paper.

'I dunno. She got twenty-three thousand hits,' Sophie said, tapping pause.

'You're not seriously suggesting we get our boobs out, are you?'

'No. Of course not. But there's no harm in a bit of sexiness. We're both attractive women. There's that Insta woman in California who always wears low-cut tops. In a classy way,' Sophie said.

'I draw the line at sexy tops, Sophie.'

'I think you should open your mind to it.'

I poured two more glasses of pink champagne and spilt a bit and wiped a bit, and replaced the bottle in the silver bucket and lit my cigarette. Harley scampered out of the trees and ran up to me with a pine cone in his mouth. He dropped it in front of me and wagged his tail, telling me he wanted me to throw it. It was his favourite game. After years of telling him off, he had learnt not to chew on them. The fetch game was our little compromise.

'Go on then, Harley-Barley,' I said, chucking it across the garden, watching him scrabble to get it, drop it and charge off, distracted by a bird or a rabbit.

The pleasures of the champagne and the nicotine ran through my blood. I had waited all day for this. Sophie had provided the excuse to indulge. It had become hard to hide from Charlie the amount of wine I wanted to consume most evenings. Usually I would wait for him to be asleep before relaxing into it. Tonight, I didn't have to hide it. He was out in London at his leaving party, and Sophie and I were celebrating our lucrative collaboration with a well-known champagne brand.

Hooray! Cheers! Bottoms up! Boobs out! Well done, Sophie!

This celebration would not have pleased Charlie, who did not yet know about my new business partner. Since the news of his redundancy, I had decided to withhold the information.

'How shall we style this bottle, then?' Sophie asked.

I took a large gulp of the champagne, letting the bubbles tickle my brain. This felt good. Just like the old days, I was smoking and drinking and laughing, with no good reason to stop. I enjoyed the tinge of self-loathing that went with it, the knowledge that my lungs were filling with death, that my arteries were clogging with toxicity. Less and less did I mind that Sophie had suggested we sell our bodies for more followers, that the girls were watching YouTube in bed, that Charlie was at his redundancy party in London. It was fine. It was summer half-term. We were fine. I was fine. Everything was fucking fine!

'Dunno,' I replied.

'Did you have any ideas?'

'Nope,' I said, taking in a long drag of my roll-up. Then adding, 'Do you know the grape?'

'For this one?'

I nodded, smiling wryly.

She hesitated, biting her lip, shooting her eyes to the sky to think. 'Pinot...'

I hoped she would get it wrong.

'Noir,' she finished, triumphantly.

I slow-clapped her. 'And?'

'Chardonnay!'

'You've done your homework.'

'I told you I would.'

This worked for me. Personally, I couldn't be bothered to think about wine or how to take a photograph of another bottle of alcohol. I had run out of ideas. I was dried up. If Sophie wanted this, she could have it. Perhaps that was me, done. I'll drink it, she can post it, breasts and all.

She sighed and leant forward, eyeballing me.

'The drive was fun,' she said, lowering her tone.

I burnt my lips on what was left on my roll-up. 'I still can't believe you took the risk,' I said, stubbing out the singed roach, beginning to roll another.

'A police car trailed us, you know.'

The open cigarette was poised at my lips where I had licked the paper. '*What?*'

'They weren't interested in us, but it freaked me out. Not helped by Adam, who kept going on about it being a ghost car. It was awful, I almost had a panic attack in the middle of East Dean.'

My heart lurched. 'A ghost car? What did he mean by that?'

'He was talking about the engine running without the key in it.'

'Oh, right. It's always done that,' I said, relaxing a little again. I flared the lighter up and burnt the twisted end of the cigarette, watching it brighten and curl, inhaling deeply.

Sophie rubbed her right palm.

'Then Dylan sang "Scooby-Doo" all the way home, over and over.'

'Sounds like a car ride from hell.' In the old days, I would have laughed with Sophie about this.

'I wished it had been us two in it, again. You know, to wipe the slate clean, reboot our mem—' she stopped. 'Oh, hi girls,' she said, placing her glass down.

Izzy and Diana were standing in the gap of the bifold doors in their nighties, stroking Harley, who had pottered up to them without me noticing. In a panic, I threw my cigarette onto the grass, hoping it landed far enough away.

'What are you doing, Mummy?'

My lips were numb. I puckered them up, mobilising them before I spoke. 'What are you doing out of bed? Off you go.'

'The iPad has run out of battery,' Diana said, stepping forward, staring at the burning cigarette a foot away from her. Its smoke trail wound into small white loops, showing off, rebellious in the face of my failed attempt to get rid of it.

Diana did not take her eyes from the cigarette. 'Were you *smoking*?'

Izzy stepped forward, also staring down at the evidence. 'You said people die if they smoke.'

'That's not mine! That's Sophie's,' I blurted out, wincing at Sophie.

Sophie put her finger to her lips. 'Shush. Just a couple of puffs once a year. Don't tell Dylan.'

Izzy gasped. 'That's horrible! You shouldn't smoke. It's really bad for you. It causes cancer.'

'I promise never to have another one again, poppet,' Sophie replied, very seriously.

The weight of the champagne came down on me, as though every single sip had been collected into a large bucket and dropped on top of my head.

Izzy scowled at us, picked Harley up and went back inside, but Diana had put away her outrage and her expression became inscrutable. 'Can we watch telly?'

'No. It's nine thirty. Time for bed now.'

'Please. Just one programme.'

'No. Come on. Off to bed.'

But I didn't move to take them to bed.

'Just one programme, Mum, please, and we'll go straight to bed.'

In the same way that I couldn't fight Sophie, I could no longer fight my daughters either. In fact, I had lost all fights before I attempted to win them.

'One more and then straight to bed, okay?'

She ran off before I could change my mind.

The early June light was almost gone. If Sophie had wanted to take a photograph of the bottle and glasses, our opportunity for sunshine had passed us by. Did I care? Not much. I didn't care for sunshine and smiles any more. Therein lay emptiness. A grimace and a middle finger would suit me better. Unfriendly; unfriendliness to provoke some unfriending, perhaps.

'I think it would be good if we posted both of us together drinking this,' Sophie suggested. 'We could get Adam to take some flattering ones for us, tomorrow maybe, in good light.'

Sophie still wanted sunshine and smiles.

'We could use our friendship,' she continued. 'Like that footballer's wife – ex-wife, now, I think – and that blonde stylist who set up that fashion blog. They look like great friends. Always smiling and laughing. It's a really warm, feel-good feed. Look,' she said, thrusting her phone in my face. 'We have to sell ourselves in our posts if we want to compete with other social media influencers,' she went on. 'Your posts up until now have been too modest. Modesty doesn't sell,' she explained. 'If we want to build a strong brand, we have to be braver.'

With indifference, I scrolled through the ex-wife of the footballer's Instagram page, stopping at one pink and gold post in swirly cursive script: 'Three things in human life are important.

The first is to be kind. The second is to be kind. The third is to be kind.' In the next post on, there was a photograph of the footballer's ex-wife lying in a cashmere tracksuit on a white sofa next to a bunch of peonies the size of a bush. Following on from that, there was a post of the footballer's ex-wife and her stylist friend sitting al fresco at an expensive London restaurant, heads together, cuffed and throttled by gold chains and bleached smiles. Showing off did not come under the umbrella of kindness.

Were Sophie and I going to post about kindness, too? If we did, we wouldn't mean it. We would post about kindness to get more followers, to make more money. The richer we were, the prettier we could be in our posts. A glass of wine sipped by a swimming pool looked better than it would by a paddling pool. A champagne flute looked better than a tin of beer. A tumbler of red wine cradled in front of a glowing firepit looked better than in the cupholder of a soggy canvas camping chair. The least sexy of the three scenarios was more representative of our lives, but it wouldn't sell a lifestyle. Apparently, Sophie wanted lifestyle. We were going to sell the tanned cleavage and the expensive backdrop. We were going to sell sex and money. We all loved sex and money, didn't we? Why the hell not?

I suggested another alternative. 'How about posting this, "A lie told often enough becomes the truth"?'

'Don't be so sour. It's just the way of the world now, Naomi,' she tutted, twisting a blonde straggle of hair, adding, 'The quicker we jump on the bandwagon the better.'

I heard Harley bark. A few minutes later, Charlie appeared.

'Hi,' he said, hovering behind me.

'You're home early,' I said, twisting round, almost falling off the bench.

Instead of feeling caught out, or embarrassed by my drunkenness, I felt bold and insubordinate. *For better or worse, Charlie, eh?* I thought. *Can you handle me now?*

'It finished earlier than I thought. It was a depressing affair.'

'No kidding,' I snorted. 'Come and join us. We were just talking about sex and money.'

I allowed the tight, bunched-up feeling in my brain to unclench. The hostile persona, that I had spent a lifetime concealing, was out and proud. This was authenticity: brashness and belligerence and self-destructiveness, from deep, deep down inside me, this felt right, bad, true. Truer than the well-behaved success story I projected outwards. Inwards, nasty grubs had been burrowing for years, rippling and swelling, and they seemed to be coming up for air, crawling out of my head, flopping out of my ears and nostrils and mouth. Unpleasant, faceless and unexplained. But part of me.

Charlie said, 'Sex and money? I'm afraid I've nothing to offer on either front.' He waved at Sophie vaguely. 'Hi, Sophie.'

'We were talking business, actually,' Sophie corrected.

My brain spun. 'She's giving me some ideas.'

'That's kind of you.'

'It's not kindness,' Sophie frowned. 'Didn't she tell you?'

'Tell me what?'

'I was going to tell you…' I began.

Sophie completed my sentence. 'We've gone into business together.'

It was too dark to tell how his features would have changed in reaction to this news, but I heard how his voice dropped an octave. 'When did this happen?'

'A few weeks ago,' Sophie said, standing up. 'Anyway, it's late. And it seems you two have some stuff to catch up on. I'll leave you to it.'

She would leave us to it. Leave us to another argument. There had been too many to count over the last few weeks. They kicked off at the smallest problem and often escalated into full-blown rows. Mostly about money. After one particularly unpleasant one about Harley's dog insurance – Charlie had wanted inferior cover for a cheaper monthly outgoing – I had apologised to Diana and Izzy for 'shouting at Daddy', as though it was a joke, as though this was just what mummies did, trying to diminish the implications of our fighting, explaining away the constant flow of bad feeling that shot out at each other on a regular basis.

Charlie and I were toing and froing from the garden to the dishwasher, clearing away the mess.

'Why were the girls still up when I got back?'

'I don't know,' I slurred.

'And they were on their iPads.'

'Sorry. I know. It's really bad.'

'You're drunk,' he said, which depressed me with its lack of originality. He didn't know what else to do with my lack of fight.

'I am. Very drunk.'

I dropped a mug, which seemed to prove the point, but it didn't break.

We both stared down at the blue mug that had missed the dishwasher. I didn't want to pick it up.

'When were you going to tell me about Sophie?'

I pushed at the mug with my toe. 'I didn't want to worry you.'

His salt-and-pepper hair and his tortoiseshell glasses were symbols of a distinguished man, older than his years, wiser perhaps. Possibly more distinguished than he felt. He wanted to be. He showed quiet strength. But if I looked beyond what he gave to me, right into those muddy green eyes, behind the good sense and even temper, I wondered if I had failed to see his deeper vulnerabilities. He had not offered them up to me before, insisting that his parents, whom we visited in Cornwall every year, were as functioning and happy as they seemed. I had never questioned this. There were the usual stresses at work and the frustrations of family life and endless worries about money, but he had never hinted at any deeper dissatisfactions, never mentioned anxiety or depression before. But maybe I had never looked properly. Why had I never looked properly?

'Well, I'm worried now, anyway,' he said.

'Sorry.' Again, I said sorry, but I wasn't sure that I felt any emotions of any sort strongly enough to be really sorry. I wanted to roll another cigarette.

'I never see that dimple these days,' he sighed.

I shrugged, 'Anything else?'

He frowned. 'What has got into you lately?'

I picked up the blue mug. 'Nothing's *got into* me.'

'I'm imagining it, am I?'

'You have been under a lot of strain at work,' I replied facetiously.

I closed the dishwasher, pressed the program and the start button and went into the laundry room, where there were piles of dirty clothes to sort. In the absence of a cigarette, which I could not smoke in front of Charlie, I had to find something to do with my hands. Harley scampered out of the small, stuffy room, and Charlie followed me in.

'I'm sorry, Naomi, but you can't put this on me.'

Three piles. One for the bright colours. One for the whites. One for the dark. A red t-shirt, a pink skirt, a turquoise blouse in one pile. A white towel, a white pillowcase, a white pair of pants in the other. Order.

'I don't know what to say to you,' I said.

'You can tell me what the fuck is going on.'

I flinched, throwing a single black sock onto the white pile. He never swore. 'Don't swear at me,' I said, moving the black sock into the darks.

'One minute you don't trust Sophie with the girls, and the next you're going into business with her. Forgive me if I'm finding this hard to get my head around.'

'She has some good ideas.'

'And that's enough, is it? What about the way she behaved at your wine-tasting evening? Have you forgotten what she was like?'

'She's stopped drinking.'

'For how long? A few weeks?'

I had not yet concocted the lies to justify the partnership with Sophie. I had to think on my feet.

'She's my best friend.'

'She wasn't when she took the girls to Brighton.'

'I was being paranoid. You were right.'

'I can't keep up. You need to back out of whatever it is you've decided on.'

'It's too late for that,' I said, getting the sleeves of an inside-out white shirt tangled as I tried to turn it back the right way.

'Please don't tell me it's already official.'

'Yes. It is.' The shirt missed the pile of whites when I balled it up and threw it too hard.

'What kind of deal did you give her?'

'Fifty-fifty, basically. It was just a case of registering a new partner for self-assessment and informing HMRC. Mike handled it.'

'Mike? Mike Klein?'

'Yes. Our accountant. Mike.'

'Wow. That is… I don't know what that is… that is total and utter madness.'

'Stop worrying. She's ambitious for us.'

'She's ambitious for her.'

'I wanted to do it for her.'

He screwed his eyes closed and opened them again, like he wanted to see something – or someone – new. 'It's *charity* now?'

'She deserves it. She's been an incredible friend.'

'Incredible enough to sign half your business away to? When she has nothing to offer?'

'Yes. Actually.'

'What is it that I'm missing? I've been hearing for years about what a brilliant friend she is to you, and I like her, too, clearly, but why do you give her so much leeway? From what I've seen, she's not the greatest friend, if I'm frank. Apart from when she took the girls to Brighton – which you had some strange aversion to, perversely – she hasn't done anything for you or the kids in all the years I've known you. Ever, to my knowledge… In fact, you spend your life rallying around—'

'You wouldn't understand,' I interrupted. He was talking too much in his slow, deep, good sense voice, with his asides and bracketed add-ons, and I felt the pressure building inside me as he went on and on. I needed him to stop.

'Try me,' he said.

'I can't explain it.'

Chaos. A pair of green pants. A pair of black boxers. A white vest. Order.

He let out an exasperated groan. 'We can't afford to give away half of what we have for no gain, not now, Naomi. You'll have to find a way of getting out of it. I'll talk to Mike.'

I spun around. 'No! Don't you dare!'

His eyebrows rose, but he spoke quietly, 'Why not?'

I turned back to my three piles. 'It's *my* business. I can do what I like with it.'

A black pair of leggings. A yellow sweatshirt. Two white hand towels.

'Even if me and the kids suffer?'

That's your fault for losing your job, I thought, but I didn't dare say something so cruel.

'With Sophie's input, and some paid content, we can make more money,' I said. 'We're just about to make nearly a grand by posting one bottle of champagne.'

'Naomi,' he said, quietly. 'What hold does she have on you?'

Before I could stop it, my foot careered into the coloured pile, white-hot rage burning my insides. 'You wouldn't understand. Nobody would bloody understand. Nobody!' I yelled, kicking at the laundry. The ordered piles were ruined. Blues, reds, pinks, whites, greys, yellows flew around the small room, colours magnified as though suspended inside the tears in my eyes.

'Naomi! Naomi! Stop it! What are you doing? Calm down,' he said, grabbing me around the waist, pinning my arms to my sides, holding me from behind. 'You have to tell me! Please, Naomi!' he pleaded.

I struggled out of his grip. 'Get the fuck off me!' I hissed.

He let go, shocked by my aggression. 'Sorry. I just wanted to...' he said.

'What? Save me from myself? Is that what you wanted?' I screamed.

'No. You're quite capable of looking after yourself.'

'I don't need anyone to take care of me!'

'I know that!'

'Do you? So why are you always telling me how to live my life? Do you really know what's best for me? *I* know what's best for me! I know *who's* best for me! And it's NOT *YOU!*'

He stepped back.

Under his breath, he said, 'And who is good for you? *Sophie?*'

'Yes, actually. She gets me. She is the only one who does.'

'Sophie only gets Sophie. She couldn't give a toss about anyone else.'

I banged my fist on the washing machine behind me and through my clenched jaw, I blurted out, 'She gave a shit when I was raped. Okay? She was there for me every minute of every day after that fucker attacked me. She missed her final exams to take care of me. It ruined her life.' My legs felt weak and I sat down right where I stood, in the middle of the strewn laundry.

Charlie's throat rattled, 'What?' He fell onto his haunches and pulled my hands from my lap and held them between us. 'You were *raped*?'

I felt the pads of his fingers press into my palm and I felt my bones throb but I did not pull away. 'Yes.' As I saw his dismay, I felt that same dismay for myself. The dismay I had dismissed and denied myself, the dismay that made it real.

'At Exeter?'

'Yes.'

'Can you tell me what happened?'

'I think it was Rohypnol,' I began. It was all I had for now. The rest was too much.

'You don't know for sure?'

'I was drunk. Very drunk,' I said, with a strange smile. *Nothing changes there.*

Charlie did not smile back. 'Who was he?'

'Some chemistry student. I met him in the student bar and I took him back to my room.'

Charlie swallowed. 'That's where it happened? In your room?'

He was doubting me. *He didn't believe you could be raped in your own room.*

'Sophie found me totally out of it, just after he left,' I explained, recalling how disorientated I had been.

Sophie arrived in my room a minute later. I was flat on my back. She covered me with a dressing gown and helped me to the chair. I slumped there, in a stupor, watching her change my sheets. She made tea and I crawled back into bed.

'I'm so sorry,' I repeated, for the hundredth time.

'What happened here? You're a mess.'

'Did you see him leave?'

The top I had worn that night was lying on the floor at the foot of the bed. Its mass of material could have fitted into the palm of my hand. The neck had been too low, the straps too flimsy.

'I did see him,' she answered, wrinkling her nose.

'Not my finest conquest,' I joked weakly.

'He wasn't very friendly.'

I was confused. 'No. Wasn't he? He bought me a drink.'

'Who the hell was he?'

'Wasn't he a friend of Will's?'

'No, we left with who we came with.'

'Oh.'

'What was he called?'

'I can't remember.'

'Do you remember anything?'

'He stank of TCP,' I shuddered. 'And toothpaste.'

'Try and think of his name.'

Squirming, I put my fingers into my eye sockets. 'I can't.'

'How many did you have last night?'

'I'm not sure,' I murmured, reaching for the lukewarm tea, sucking it to the back of my dry throat. 'Too many.'

'You were pretty drunk when I left.'

'I don't remember you leaving.'

'You were on the dance floor. We hugged and you said you were staying.'

I remembered colours and tilted floors and his bumpy, sweaty skin on my cheek.

'I don't remember... Until... I'm so sorry you had to see me like that.'

'Did he force you...?'

'No,' I said, beginning to cry, feeling the stinging between my legs and the bruises on my thighs.

'You have to go to the police.'

'No way.'

What would I tell the police? That I was revolted by the man I'd had sex with, that he had been rough with me, that I had made a bad decision after too many Jack and Cokes, that I had been too drunk to say stop?

'The sooner you let someone examine you, the better.'

'No,' I replied, folding my body under the duvet. Never again was I going to let anyone see or touch me. I turned onto my back, and I saw his narrow eyes above me. Sophie might have changed the sheets but he was there, still. I flipped onto my side, away from the ceiling and from Sophie, who asked me, 'Do you think he slipped something in your drink?'

'I drank too much, that's all,' I said into my pillow, feeling the tears form behind my eyes.

Even now, the very thought of my complicity, my flirtation, scraped up the deepest of the shame from within me. Looking back was like re-watching a horror film that I had seen in secret, behind my parents' backs, too young. And the distressing scenes stunned me. I saw how ill-equipped I had been to cope with such a gratuitous attack on my senses, on my psyche.

'Did you go to the police?' Charlie asked now.

'Nope.'

'Why not?'

I was fascinated by how appalled Charlie seemed. It was indeed incredible that I had not reported it. How could I not have? Because I had exaggerated it? Because he had not really raped me? Because I had been too drunk to say no?

'Sophie wanted me to. But I couldn't face it. I don't really know why I didn't. I was too shaken up, I think.'

Three weeks after his attack, Sophie had driven me to the police station.

'This is definitely not the supermarket,' I laughed, but I felt betrayed.

'It's been three weeks now. You have to go in and tell them,' she insisted, presuming that I felt like the victims we had read about or seen interviewed on the news. But I did not. I did not have their certainty. They knew they had been raped. They called it rape, openly. Victimhood was simple, wasn't it? The victim felt wronged and the

guilty were in the wrong. But my conscience was not clear enough to accuse that man of rape. How I longed for that simple view to make clean lines of my memories of that night.

'I've moved on,' I told Sophie.

'You think?'

'I'm fine.'

'Panic attacks? Nightmares? That weird tapping you do,' Sophie said.
I sat on my fingers. 'What tapping?'

I was embarrassed by my fear. The tap of fear. The fear that I would see him again, that he would be at my door – the man with thin eyes and that TCP stench – and around every corner I turned. I wasn't able to tell her that a coil of blood-red humiliation had twisted up from my guts when I thought of seeing him, that I was degraded by him forever, that I had been disgraced by my open legs, by how dirty my nakedness had become under his touch. Thinking about it, I sickened myself. Talking about it to anyone was unimaginable, but Sophie persisted. 'You can't walk around scared for the rest of your life. You have to do something.'

'I'm not scared!' I laughed.

'What about the other women he might do it to?'

My heart slowed right down. 'It wasn't his fault that I was totally out of it.'

'It really worries me that you say that.'

'Seriously, Sophie! Drop it! I picked up a total dickhead and had bad sex. End of,' I trilled, my voice high, too high.

'Isn't it worth talking to a police officer about it? Just in case someone else has come forward about him before? Or maybe you could see a counsellor?'

I brought out my best smile, trying not to lose it with her, and I spoke clearly and slowly. 'There is nothing to talk to the police or a counsellor about, Soph.'

And I got out of the car and walked to the supermarket, where I bought gin.

Later that same day, I filled up a hip flask and went out to a birthday party on the beach, without Sophie, to prove I wasn't scared: a swig from my flask, a wash of relief.

Around the fire that night, I noticed a handsome face flicker behind the flames. I moved closer, made eye contact. He asked me for a sip from my flask. We talked. He was a first year psychology student, whose name I forgot as soon as he had told me. I led him into the sand dunes and seduced him, playfully, naughtily. For the first time in weeks, I felt euphoric rather than traumatised. My enjoyment allowed me to forget. The spell was broken and I wanted more. I decided not to be a victim. I was Naomi. Happy-go-lucky, live-in-the-moment, dimple-smiled Naomi.

How faraway she seemed now, as I sat on piles of dirty clothes in the laundry room.

'Did you see him again?' Charlie asked, sounding angry, as though he was angry with me.

I spluttered, 'Are you serious? Oh, right, yeah, I really wanted to hang out with him.'

'I didn't mean that. Of course I didn't mean that. I meant, did you have to see him on campus?'

'No, I never saw him. There are over twenty thousand people at Exeter,' I said, regurgitating Sophie's fact.

'I can't believe you've never told me.'

'Sorry,' I stuttered. I was truly sorry about this.

'Don't be.'

A pool of acid saliva formed in my mouth and I nodded, unable to speak for a moment.

'Sophie was absolutely amazing when it happened,' I said to Charlie, automatically.

The drama had appealed to her, as had my vulnerability. My refusal to go into the police station had upset her. How she would later – only a few weeks later – take back control was then to become the defining incident of our friendship, the moment when we were joined in our guilt forever.

'Is she the only person who has known all this time?'

'Yes.'

'Do you ever think of going to the police now?'

'Absolutely not. Don't you even think about trying to persuade me. It's in the past. Please, Charlie. Please don't go on about doing the right thing. I'm telling you, nothing good would come of it.'

He put his palms up at me. 'Sure, sure. Don't worry, I won't. I promise you, I won't.'

I exhaled and he moved closer, saying, 'You know the toothpaste thing…'

'Yes. Yes, that's what he smelt like,' I said, beginning to cry.

Charlie pulled me into him and I laid my head in his lap and he pinged a curl of my hair and held me there for a long time. A ribbon of pain stretched and twisted right back, back to Jason Parker, its frayed tip fluttering at his heels, the pulled-down trousers around his ankles, wrapping itself around his leg and along his penis and inside me, where we had connected as one malformed, repulsive entity. Until this moment, we had been a secret pairing, a shared, astonishing experience that had risen up in my mind but had never been recounted. There had never been a right time to tell Charlie, or anyone else. It was the sort of oversharing that would stop the fun, that would flounder around in the middle of the room, nobody knowing how to catch it and kill it.

I wished, as I mourned the loss of my innocent self, that the rape had been the beginning and end of my pain, that it was the only story I had to tell.

Lying here, on the lumps and bumps of laundry, my head cradled in his warmth, I appreciated Charlie's love. Nevertheless, like an interrupted exhale, I knew there would be little long-term relief, and I wondered whether Charlie understood that the wickedness of that night had settled into my being, that its resurfacing, twenty years later, had made me feel dirty and unlovable all over again.

'I can't believe he got away with it,' he said.

Thanks to Sophie, he had not, I wanted to say. *We* had. But there was no joy in that. There was no joy.

Sophie and I were stuck together now. Perhaps we always had been. Always, when her pale eyes were hangdog and her long fingers scratched at her palm, my instinct was to go to her, to take care of her, with my simpleton's kindness. Now, she expected my gratitude for protecting me from Jason Parker; she expected my thanks for hiding our crime; she expected my guilty acquiescence in the face of her blackmail. She expected a tightened bond, a lifelong friendship, in response to her big reveal. And I wanted to die in the face of all of her impossible expectations.

'Charlie, help me,' I said, clutching his knees, pressing my face into his thigh.

Could Charlie help me get away from her? Could he become an ally, my co-conspirator? Together, would we be brave enough to go to the police?

'Of course, my love. You're safe now. I'll always be here for you,' he said, kissing into my hair.

But he wouldn't be. His love was conditional, as it was in every marriage. My drinking had almost broken us before, and he had warned me that it could break us again. He wanted me to be happy-go-lucky Naomi with the dimple; he wouldn't love me as much if he knew I had killed a man. If he suspected I had wanted Jason Parker dead, he wouldn't love me at all. And I wondered whether he would love me a little bit less, now, if I poured myself a little tipple before bed, for sleep to come easier, pleading distress after my outpouring. Under the circumstances, anyone would need a drink, wouldn't they?

CHAPTER TWENTY-SEVEN

Hi Naomi – Haven't heard from you for a while. Bring the girls over to meet the newest member of our family! He's called Bear. Look at his eyes! Sophie x

To accompany the text, Sophie had sent a photograph attachment, imagining that Naomi would call or text straight back, excited for them. While she waited for a response from her, Sophie arranged a vase of white gladioli in Deda's kitchen, *her* kitchen now.

As she snipped at the long stems, humming to herself, the sun warmed her back and she was heartened by the happy yelping sounds of Dylan and Bear getting to know each other outside in the garden.

Last week, through the metal bars of a kennel at Battersea Dogs Home, Sophie and Dylan had fallen in love with Bear, a husky-collie cross, who had jumped up at them, wagging his tail, choosing them with one high bark and some enthusiastic panting. He had the clearest blue eyes Sophie had ever seen and a silky coat of white and cappuccino. She had felt a keen desire to free him. And that same day, Blue Bear, or Bear for short, had met them properly in the dog meeting room, before being microchipped and sent home with them.

For the first two days, he had darted around the cottage with nervy, manic energy, keeping them awake at night with howls from his crate in the hallway. On the third night of this racket, Sophie had let him sleep with Dylan. The following morning, Dylan had explained to Sophie that he had cuddled Bear after his nightmare, and that his eczema had stopped itching as much. From then on, each time Sophie had peeked into his room at night, she would see Bear curled up at the bottom of his bed – in the same room that she had grown up in – and she would feel a deep stirring of love for them both.

Sophie checked her phone again, making sure it was not on silent. It had been three weeks since Sophie had seen Naomi, since their celebration of the champagne collaboration. She texted Naomi again, desperate to arrange a date for them to meet Bear:

Please call. Dying to see you. Sx

Having placed the gladioli on the windowsill of the kitchen, Sophie moved to the sitting room to light incense, to snuggle onto her coral linen sofa with a cup of Earl Grey tea and lemon. She logged on to Wine O'Clock to look for a new post from Naomi, hoping it might hint at her whereabouts. There was nothing, and there had been nothing for three weeks. It was very unlike Naomi to miss her weekly post, let alone leave it for so long. She texted her again:

Hi Naomi – You must be getting my texts. Why are you not responding? It's not fair to keep Dylan waiting like this. He is dying to introduce Bear to the girls. Sx

The last Wine O'Clock Instagram post had been Sophie's. A week ago, she had posted a snapshot of Blue Bear with his translucent, ice-blue eyes boring holes in the screen. It wasn't wine-related, but Sophie thought it was too beautiful to keep to herself. It had received 705 likes. In her first ever post, Sophie had worn a short, floaty dress and had sat on a log in the woods drinking a sparkling wine, which Naomi told her she had spelt wrong. In another, she held a glass of rosé, almost as clear as white, up close to her décolletage, brilliantly taken by Dylan, which had received 612 likes. After that, she had posted three other selfies with wine, which had received fewer than 60 likes each. This had humiliated her. The blog needed Naomi's attention just as much as Sophie needed it. She texted again:

URGENT. Call me back. Sx

After a few more texts and calls, Sophie decided to try another tack. She emailed Diana, who had an account linked to Naomi's, enclosing a photograph of Bear, asking her if she and Izzy would like to come over to meet him. Sophie hoped this would be a reminder to Naomi of how easy it was to get hold of her children. Diana immediately replied to say she would ask Mummy.

Mummy got back to Sophie within the day:

Sorry. Had my phone off. Diana is harassing me about coming to see your new dog. Does Saturday work? Will he be okay around Harley? Naomi

Sophie confirmed the arrangement straight away, reassuring Naomi that Bear would be fine around Harley. The rehoming team at Battersea Dogs Home had warned Sophie that he was 'particular about his doggie friends', and that they had to be careful about the 'high prey drive' of a collie-husky mix, but Sophie did not mention these details to Naomi, fearing it would give her the wrong impression of their friendly dog. In fact, Sophie laughed at the thought of little Harley cowering in the corner as Bear raced around barking. Bear barked a lot, but he wouldn't mean to scare him. He was only two, and he was lively. They'd get used to each other.

*

Sophie held Bear by the collar as Naomi, Izzy and Diana edged past him. His lip was curled. It was the first time Sophie had heard him growl.

'Stop that, Bear,' Dylan laughed, rubbing him under the chin and kissing his head.

'Don't worry, he's a bit wary around new people,' Sophie explained.

Once the door was closed, Sophie let go of him and he raced up to Izzy and Diana barking and growling. They waited behind Naomi cautiously.

'Will he bite?' Diana asked.

'He wouldn't hurt a flea. Just ignore the noise. Want some juice?'

'Look at his blue eyes. They look like glass,' Izzy said, backing off further.

Bear stayed in the hallway barking at them as Sophie fixed their drinks. 'Shush, Bear,' she scolded.

Dylan stroked him and soothed him and reassured him. Sophie admired them together. Both had light hair and clear eyes. Sophie couldn't stop taking photographs of them.

'Can I pat him?' Diana asked, crouching down, holding out her hand to let him smell her.

'Of course,' Dylan said proudly.

Bear licked Dylan's face and allowed Diana to stroke him, before dashing into the garden. All three children scrambled off after him.

'I've left Harley in the car,' Naomi said. Her eyes were wide as they scanned the kitchen, perhaps marvelling at the smart new stripped-oak Shaker units and black enamel knobs and large glass jar of gladioli on the sill.

'He'll be fine around him, Naomi.' Sophie switched on the kettle.

'Do you know his history?'

'He was badly abused at his last home. They told me he was starved and hit and holed up in a tiny London flat.'

'That's awful.' Naomi stared out of the window, with her back to the kitchen.

'He needs a lot of walking. That's why I wanted him to make friends with Harley, so we could go on dog walks together.'

Sophie read a lack of enthusiasm into the silence that followed. She understood why there might be a difficult period with Naomi, for a while. This would pass, like the other phases they had moved through in their long friendship.

'Do you want to get Harley out now?'

'I'll get him out in a bit.'

'I think now would be good.'

Naomi turned to face Sophie. Her brow was furrowed, her eyes pleading, almost. 'Sophie, you promise he'll be safe around him?'

Naomi's gloom was getting on Sophie's nerves. If it was possible to look drowned without being wet, Naomi had achieved it.

'Wow. You, of all people. Your attitude is exactly why a third of all dogs at the Battersea Dogs Home are put down – a *third* – because so few people believe in giving them a second chance. Bear was abused. He had no love from anybody, and he was never allowed to socialise with other dogs or go for runs outside, and now we've given him a chance at another life. Don't you think he deserves a bit of a chance?'

Cowed, Naomi looked to the floor. 'Sorry. I know. If Harley had been treated like that…'

Sophie put a hand on Naomi's shoulder. Naomi jerked away suddenly, as though Sophie had burnt her.

'Let's get him out of the car and introduce them,' Sophie said, leading the way to the front door and the car. 'They'll be lifelong friends.'

Before reaching her car, Naomi pointed at Sophie's new car. 'It's like a Volvo convention out here.'

'Do you like it?' Sophie asked, admiring the black sheen of the polished bodywork. She had bought it on lease-purchase last week. 'I wanted space for a dog cage in the back.'

Naomi opened the boot to her own black Volvo and Harley scrabbled out, almost falling over his little feet as he circled Sophie, barking hello.

'He thinks it's walk time,' Naomi said, swooping to clip his lead on.

'I've reinforced the fencing in the woods at the bottom of the garden. You can let him off if you like.'

'While they meet, I'll keep it on,' she said firmly.

With Harley trotting at Naomi's heels, they went through the house and out to the overgrown, stepped garden, where the three children were running around in the bright noon sunshine with Bear.

Instantly, both dogs began barking at each other, attracted to each other like magnets. Harley strained on the leash, his yap as fierce as Bear's throaty baying. They circled and sniffed, interested rather than hostile. Still, Naomi did not let Harley run free.

Izzy came panting up from the bottom of the garden. 'Mum! Can we go into the woods with Harley?'

'If you keep him on the lead.'

'Why?'

'Just do as I say.'

Izzy took the lead.

Sophie's lips straightened. 'I'll get the tea.'

She brought out a tray of Earl Grey tea and lemon wedges and shortbread, placed it on the garden table and sat down on one of the two chairs to pour. The brick patio was uneven and the tea spilt, but she did not care. In spite of Naomi's suspicion of Bear, the high jinks of the dogs and children, who ran in and out of the woodland and up and down the garden, made her smile. Up until now, there hadn't been many moments in Sophie's life when she could survey the scene around her and feel a pang of satisfaction and pride. But Naomi was ruining it, hovering, watching them with a frown and crossed arms.

'Shortbread?' Sophie asked, trying to distract her.

Naomi ate four shortbread biscuits and let her tea go cold. They talked about the blog. Or Sophie talked and Naomi listened, occasionally sanctioning an idea of Sophie's. When the children were out of sight, Naomi's fingers drummed her thighs, stopping intermittently when barking was heard, her neck stretching long.

Shortly, Dylan and Izzy and Diana raced out of the woods and past them, inside, bored of the dogs, dumping Harley's lead on the grass by Naomi's feet.

'Girls! Girls! Why is Harley off the lead?' she called after them, picking up the lead.

Bear appeared from the woods and trotted up the stepped garden to sit at Sophie's feet. His head was high and alert. When Sophie stroked him, his fur was soft and a little damp. Then Harley shot out of the woods but scampered around the lower terrace. His little black form ran back and forth, sniffing, rustling through the undergrowth, leaping up at the foxgloves, nose trained up a tree trunk or down a hole. His speed picked up suddenly, and he raced across the garden.

Bear barked, lurched forward and left Sophie's side.

'Harley!' Naomi called out through cupped hands, starting to run. 'Harley!'

'Stop being so jumpy!' Sophie shouted down to her. 'They've obviously just smelt a rabbit!'

Full pelt, Bear charged down the small verges like a racehorse, body low, hind and front legs splayed almost horizontal, head stretched forward, focused and determined. Watching the speed at which he moved gave Sophie a thrill.

Sophie laughed at Naomi stumbling down the garden, shouting at Bear, who had overtaken her. Bear's barks turned to growls, and Harley began squealing, high-pitched and continual. With a jolt, Sophie clocked the danger and sprinted down to them.

'Bear!' Sophie screamed, running closer. She stopped still in horror. Bear's jaws were around Harley's neck.

Sophie lunged at Bear and tried to pull him off, but Bear refused to let go. Sophie dragged at his collar, harder and harder, until he finally released Harley onto the grass, where the little dog fell limp and still.

Naomi scooped him up, wailing and crying. 'Bad dog! What have you done? Bad dog!' Sophie shouted breathlessly, in disbelief, her heart hammering at her ribs. He whimpered at her and skulked off into the woods behind them.

Naomi ran through the house, screaming at the girls to get into the car. The girls came thundering down the stairs and began crying when they saw Harley flopped in their mother's arms.

'Harley needs to go to the animal hospital, right now. Forget your shoes, just get in the car,' Naomi said.

'I want my shoes!' wailed Izzy.

'Just go! I'll look after the girls for you!' Sophie cried.

Naomi's face jerked into Sophie's, contorted and furious. 'Never,' she hissed, yanking at her shocked daughters with her one free arm, and pushing them out of the house and into the back seat of the car without their shoes.

'Diana. You're going to have to be very brave and hold Harley on the way to the hospital. Can you do that for me?' Naomi asked, straight and firm.

Diana nodded, tears falling down her face as she took Harley into her arms.

As Naomi careered out of the drive, Sophie heard Bear padding up to her. He nuzzled into her legs, whining, and she sank down to his level and kissed him on the head, letting him lick her. 'It

CHAPTER TWENTY-EIGHT

The space around my head spun like a hurricane as I drove. I have no idea how I operated a car. Somehow, I navigated my way to the vet hospital and allowed a nurse to take Harley from me. I couldn't process what she was saying as I followed her to a room where Harley was laid down in front of a vet with a bleach-blonde crop. As the vet examined him, I tried to relay what had happened. My account was back to front and upside down. He was rushed away to surgery.

In the reception area, where Diana and Izzy had stayed, Diana was crying about the blood on her t-shirt. She trembled as I changed her into a spare sweater, which I had found in the car. When I called Charlie, the sound of his panic cleared mine from my mind, as though he had scraped it all up for himself. Charlie's upset made it real. I wanted to withdraw from that. I became clear-cut and to the point.

My girls' hot bodies were in my arms as we waited; heavy on my lap or leaning into my side or wrapped around my waist, their wet, pale faces were buried in my neck, their grass-stained socks wrinkled around their toes.

The walls around me were cream and pine and aluminium. Everything was pale and tidy, while inside my head there was violence and chaos. My fingers drummed on the clean surfaces.

The vet with the bleach-blonde crop had returned to us in her blue scrubs too soon. Her face blurred as I watched her pink lips tell us that Harley had sustained fatal injuries in the attack, that he had died before they had administered the anaesthetic for surgery.

I clutched Izzy and Diana's hands, swallowing back a wail of pain that could have brought the world to a standstill.

The girls collapsed into me, their shoulders juddering as they sniffed and whimpered. Their hair was infused by that musty stench of Sophie's incense.

I don't know whether it was right to let Diana and Izzy, so young, see Harley's body under that red blanket on the operating table. I wanted them to have a chance to say goodbye, to bury their faces in his black, curly fur and to kiss that silky head of his one last time. But I don't think I had fully accepted that he was dead until I touched him, until he hadn't responded to us, to our stroking or kissing. Why hadn't he rolled over for a tummy scratch? Where was the thump of his tail? Where was that rough lick? It had been unbelievable, unbearable.

'I love you, Harley. I'm so sorry I couldn't protect you,' I whispered, shedding tears into his black fur. 'I hope you're in a better place. Full of pine cones,' I wept.

'Bye-bye, Harley. I love you forever and ever,' Izzy sobbed, laying her head on his body.

Diana's words were incomprehensible through her crying as she said goodbye. I had to gently prize her off him when the nurse told us it was time to go.

The girls were probably too young to experience the lifeless body of their pet, the dead body of the fifth member of our family, of their Harley. They were definitely too young.

By the time we were home, it was late. Izzy and Diana were as pale as ghosts. Charlie was waiting for us, red-eyed, with hugs and hot chocolates and a story for the girls before bed.

Back downstairs in the kitchen, Charlie and I exhaled in unison and we stared at each other, like strangers at first, and then the tears came. We hugged. I could not believe that Harley was not at our feet, that he would never circle and yap and jump up at us ever again.

Together we went to the car boot to fetch Harley's body. Charlie carried the black bag to the freezer in the garage. The buzz of its generator seemed louder than ever as I removed the tub of vanilla ice cream and some ancient rabbit pies, brought to us once by Charlie's mother. Charlie laid his body in the cheerless, unadorned container and I felt such a wrench, I wanted to bring him out again and warm him up.

'You're only here for one night, Harley-Barley,' I whispered to his body, closing the lid.

'Did you call the police?' Charlie asked, as we walked back to the house.

At first, I thought he was talking about Jason Parker. In my dazed state, I imagined that he knew, magically, and then I realised he was referring to Bear's attack.

'No.'

'You should. I've read up on it online. Under the Dangerous Dogs Act, that dog should have a control order put on him, at the very least. He could even be put down. For now, they can insist he wears a muzzle and a lead when he goes out.'

'I'll call tomorrow,' I sighed, weary of Charlie's pragmatic approach. I didn't want to be pragmatic. I wanted to be emotional and useless.

'Tell me everything,' he said gently, sensing my fragility, pinging a curl from my hair. Since I had told him about the rape, he had been very kind and very cautious around me. No longer was he scowling at the fourth glass of wine poured over supper, no longer was he making disparaging remarks about Sophie's involvement in the blog.

'Everything?' I said, more to myself than to Charlie.

I had been waiting for the right time to tell him everything. In fact, I had longed for one day in my life when I didn't feel dragged down by exhaustion, for one day when I didn't feel too beaten by the daily grind to open up such a monumental conversation. But Sophie's repeated texts about Bear had thrown me off and frightened me. When she had emailed Diana, I had thought of her threats, and their trip to Brighton, and I had capitulated. I had turned up at their house to meet Bear, and look what had happened, and now I was going to tell Charlie about the attack. He would not know that it was the first layer of many to peel back.

As I talked, I relived it, seeing again and again the appalling vision of Harley being mauled. Charlie listened quietly, pulling out a box of cereal and pouring us two big bowls of our favourite comfort food. Spooning the sugary treat into our mouths, we moved into the sitting room and onto the sofa, pulling a blanket over us. The chink of the spoons against the bowls punctuated our conversation.

'Did the girls say anything about feeling responsible, because they let him off the lead?'

Until now, I had not thought of that. I had blamed myself entirely and always would.

'I don't think so. I guess they'll blame Bear. I'm sure. I hope.'

Charlie threw his spoon into his bowl with a clatter. 'That stupid bloody woman.'

'I should've trusted my instincts.'

My instincts had been to stay away, emboldened by my confession to Charlie about Jason Parker. I had not. Worse than that, I had failed to stand up to her, had failed to protect Harley.

'Your instincts tend to side with her.'

I let his loaded comment slide. There was too much to say to be weighed down by a row. Anyway, he was right.

'You should see what she's done to the cottage.'

'What's she done?'

'It's creepy. She's decorated it exactly like this house. The sofas and the walls are the same colours as in here and she's even got the same enamel black knobs on her kitchen units. And she's bought a black Volvo.'

He grimaced, as though disgusted. 'Really? Did you say anything?'

'I was too embarrassed to say anything. I'm not even sure she realises what she's done.'

'Oh, come on! She must do.'

'Seriously, Charlie. I really don't.'

Charlie continued spooning the cereal into his mouth. He was brooding. I knew exactly what he was thinking. On this sad evening, on the day our dear Harley had died, he would be wondering why I had remained friends with Sophie for so many years. If I had ended our poisoned friendship earlier, if I'd stood up to her blackmail and her threats, Harley might still be alive. I had Harley's blood on my hands.

'The first day I met Sophie, she gave me *Lolita* to read,' I said.

'That's a strange icebreaker.'

'Especially as the only books I'd read up until then had been Jane Austens and Jilly Coopers, and a few thrillers my father would nick from holiday villas. I didn't really know how to take it.'

'She was trying to shock you?'

'I guess so. I was an obvious target. All keen and dorky. You've seen the pictures. I was plump, back then, and I had that awful bloody hairdo.'

'That's how *you* see yourself. But everyone else would've seen a gorgeous, smiley, happy person, and she would've been spitting with jealousy.'

He brushed his thumb over my right cheek, over where the dimple should have been.

'Not so smiley any more,' I said, luxuriating in his touch, but continuing before I lost my thread. 'But you're right, she was a jealous person.'

'Why did you put up with it?'

My feelings about Sophie began to unravel, as though unwrapped finally from some kind of protective film.

'Sophie's dad left her mum when she was pregnant with Sophie. To this day, she's never met him. He legged it to Canada, or somewhere, and then when Sophie was eight, her mother left her in the middle of the night without saying goodbye. And her grandfather was left to pick up the pieces, and he was basically a functioning alcoholic, but then…'

He interrupted. 'I know her bloody sob story, Naomi.'

I pushed on. 'But then she met me, and I'd come from this loving home with two sensible parents who had plodded along, and had always been there for me, and I think she resented it and made me feel bad about it.'

'And you felt sorry for her.'

'Not really. She was very cool back then. She was so guarded and aloof, and that intrigued me somehow, as though her life was more exciting and exotic than mine. But she was damaged, that was obvious, and I thought I could help her.'

'You were trying to save her, or something?' he asked, looking hopeful, as though he needed to believe that my part in the friendship had been less about being a wet blanket and more about being noble and impressive.

'I wasn't together enough at the time to save anyone. I just wanted her to feel as good about herself as I felt about her. I think I wanted her to know she could be loved, that's all. I really believed it would make a difference to her. To know that one person wasn't going to leave her like everyone else had.'

'Her grandfather didn't abandon her.'

'He was a lovely man, but honestly, he thought vodka was the cure for everything. He wasn't equipped to bring up a small girl. It was heartbreaking, really, what she had to cope with. From ten years old she was making her own supper and washing her own clothes. She basically brought herself up.'

'It sounds like you're making excuses for her again.'

'No! No way. I know I've always used her childhood as an excuse for her bad behaviour, but I'm over that now. I know people who've had some serious shit thrown at them and they still manage to be decent to other people. I'm trying to understand it myself, I think.'

'So that you can forgive her again?'

'After what happened today to Harley? That will never, *ever* happen,' I shook my head, gulping down my last mouthful of cereal. 'She'll *never* change. Never. I know that now.'

Goosebumps ran up my arms. Until I had said it out loud, to Charlie, just then, I had not accepted that Sophie was utterly incapable of overriding her insecurities, that her self-worth had not improved, even by an inch, since the beginning of our friendship. Even now, even after her confession about the hit-and-run, part of me had hoped that she would change. Once she was settled into the cottage, once she had made a bit of money, she would realise that material gain could not possibly compensate for what she had done, could not possibly wipe it out. I suppose I had still hoped that she might grow a conscience, learn something finally. But in spite of my best intentions, and in spite of her grandfather's love, she had not.

'Shall we have a cup of tea?' Charlie asked, clearly lost about what else to suggest.

Now that the cereal, the sugary comfort, was gone, I wanted a glass of wine. There was no way I would be able to tell him everything without one.

'I'll make them,' I said.

'Are you sure?'

I kissed him on the lips. 'Yes.'

In the kitchen, I put the kettle on and found a screw-top bottle of wine, knowing that it would not make a sound when I opened it. Quickly, into a mug, I poured the wine up to the top, planning to get as much down me as I could before the tea was made.

Just as I poured the boiled water onto the teabags, with the mug of wine at my lips, the liquid melting inside me, Charlie came into the kitchen.

He must have seen the guilt flash across my face.

'What's that?'

'I was thirsty,' I said, my heart pounding over my lie.

He walked straight over to me and took the mug out of my hand to smell it.

I stood there, arms flopped at my sides, head down, a child caught out. I couldn't look at him. My cheeks were flaming.

A long, deep exhale. 'I'm going to bed,' he muttered.

I could have followed him. I could have insisted he hear the rest of my sorry tale, the winding back of the clock, to the night Jason Parker died, when the timer had been set, the countdown on a bomb that would explode my life. I could have chosen tonight to tell him. For a moment, there, I was going to. I should have.

I preferred the taste of the wine in the mug.

Tomorrow, I would tell him, maybe. Or the day after that. Or next year. Or never.

Never, never, never.

I became drunk. So tired and so drunk.

I played loud, angry music from my mobile into my earphones. I danced in the kitchen, wild and unseen. The wine provoked bad thoughts, dredged up raw anger: Jay had deserved to die. Jason Parker, the rapist, had deserved to die.

I hated him with every fibre of my being. I did not care that he had let out his last breath alone, face down in a ditch. It was a blessing to the world, to lose such a predator, for whom only his mother felt the loss. His death on that road that terrible night had been timely; it had saved other women from being abused and violated. Nothing we did now would bring him back, and I was glad of it.

My life was not going to be ruined by Jason Parker a second time. A confession to the police would be like flipping a coin on my own life. Heads you win. Tails you lose. Why risk losing? I would not go through with it. Not a chance in hell.

Sophie had acted out what I had secretly desired, and I experienced a ghastly rush of love for her. *In vino veritas.*

*

Charlie was digging the grave, while Izzy and Diana had decorated a cardboard box with stars and moons and dogs and cats floating in a dark blue poster-painted sky. It was a messy, heartfelt work of art in honour of Harley.

The drunken, warped love that I had felt for Sophie, last night, was now a splitting headache, and my feelings had flipped comfortably back into the more permanent state of hatred for Sophie: pure, neat, justifiable hatred. Fuelled by that hatred, I was going to battle on, in defiance of how she had used me for her own gain. Nobody was going to use me any more. Nobody was going to push me around.

While the girls were upstairs getting ready, changing into black clothes – they insisted we all wore black – I had placed the small black bag inside the cardboard box, shuddering at the hard, cold form inside. I secured the lid with masking tape.

'We're ready, Mummy!' Izzy called through the closed kitchen door.

'It's okay now. Come in.'

The two of them walked in with a sombre air, a little overdramatic. Diana wore a black sweater of mine, belted at the waist, and had tied up her blonde ringlets with a red satin ribbon. Izzy wore black leggings and an inside-out black t-shirt with the yellow stitching of the logo for their theatre club showing through. They didn't own black clothes. The colour didn't suit them.

'Mummy. You can go and change now.'

I wished I did not have to change out of my pyjamas, which I had wanted to live in day in, day out, but I could not let the girls down. I was battling on. And they had conjured up a ceremony in their heads, possibly based on a scene in a film or a cartoon, and I could not disappoint them. Harley deserved it.

Wearing my black dress, holding the decorated box, we walked down to Charlie. His face was pale and sweaty from the exertion of digging a hole two feet into the hard ground.

The morning sun did not penetrate the canopy of the pine trees, whose cracked, thin trunks seemed to stretch into a dark infinity above our heads. The spongy carpet of pine needles under our feet released a damp, sweet aroma and spiked my knees as I lowered Harley into the hole.

Charlie wiped tears away from his face with the backs of his hands, leaving soil smears. For two days, Charlie and I had barely communicated, barely looked at each other, but he grabbed my hand as Diana read a poem called 'Unicorns in Space' and crushed my fingers when Izzy scattered glitter onto the box.

After a few words from each of us about what Harley meant to us, Charlie shovelled the soil on top of his makeshift coffin.

I thought of my parents' funerals, held in close succession. My grief came back to me as a twist of pain. I looked at the girls and thought of Ilene Parker burying her son. I could not imagine what she had gone through.

After Izzy and Diana had decorated the mound of earth with pine cones and rocks, they made a cross with two sticks and some string.

'Daddy, will you bash this in? I can't do it,' Izzy asked, struggling to push it into the ground.

The two girls held the cross still at its base and Charlie used his shovel to sink it deep into the soil.

The three of them – the reason for my existence – were grim and sad and focused in their task. Black figures in grief saying goodbye to a family member.

In my head, I, too, wondered if I was saying goodbye. Not just to Harley, but to this. To them, to this closeness I shared with them, to this family unit as it stood now and would never be again. With my eyeballs skinned of their rosy tint, I scoffed at my original plan to go to the police. I had believed it would release me from the lifelong burden of Sophie. Such naivety! A confession would achieve nothing. If I told my story, Sophie would tell hers, and she was likely to lie, exonerating herself completely, condemning me further. If the truth about the rape came out, they would inflate our charges from death by dangerous driving to murder, and enrage Ilene Parker. Whichever way I looked at it, nobody would gain. However much I tried to bring Sophie down, I would risk dragging myself and my family down with her. Unless Jason Parker was outed as a rapist, the whole truth would not prevail, rendering the honourable motivations for the confession null and void.

Effectively, Sophie had played with me, played with the secret, harnessing its power to take more and more and more away from me. And still she wanted more. She was insatiable, and I was the life force that she sucked from. Unless I stopped her, she would continue to take from me, until I was in my own coffin being covered in earth; too late to wonder why she had ruined my life, too late to stop her. I had no choice. I had to stop her. And as I stood there, dressed in black at Harley's grave, I said goodbye to my naivety and said hello to survival.

CHAPTER TWENTY-NINE

Dylan burst out of Adam's car and ran straight over to Bear, who bounded up to him, whining and barking. Adam turned off the engine to get out, which was a surprise to Sophie. Usually, when he dropped Dylan off on Sundays, he would stay in the car and speak to Sophie through the open window with the engine running.

This time, Adam approached Sophie and stood on the doorstep of the cottage, by her side. Together, they watched Dylan and Bear greet each other with kisses and cuddles.

'How's he been this weekend?' Sophie asked.

'A bit subdued.'

'How're his elbows?'

'Very itchy last night. I've put the hydrocortisone in his washbag,' he replied, handing her Dylan's rucksack. 'How are you?'

'Not great.'

He stroked her arm. 'I'm not surprised.'

His touch gave her goosebumps.

'Thanks for taking him when it wasn't your weekend. I needed the headspace.'

'Any time. You know that.'

All weekend, from the moment Adam had collected Dylan on Saturday evening, shortly after they had heard the news about Harley, Sophie had been in turmoil. She was sad about Bear, she was sad about Harley, but she was frantic about Naomi, about losing her, after everything they had been through. If Naomi wasn't on her side, Sophie would have nobody. Nobody.

In a state of wretched loneliness, she had spent hours outside, weeding the flower beds around the house, walking in circles, in tears, barely eating, struck down by the sudden knowledge that she had no friends or family to call. Not a soul in the world to ask advice from or to listen to her. Deda, Adam and Naomi – and, by proxy, Charlie, Izzy and Diana – had been her only true allies in the world.

The newly exploded rash on her palm had sweated into the glove; Bear had run up and down the garden terraces, more nervous than ever. In spite of his mood, he had been a gratifying companion. All her life she had wanted to make more friends, but the secret of Jason Parker forbade it. She could never have forged close bonds with anyone new while she harboured such horrors. The idea of relaxing or getting drunk or having intimate chats with someone who had not been part of that night was a fantasy. All human interactions were limited to superficialities, were dangerous even.

When she had met Adam, she had thought she'd found a way to be close without revealing herself fully, but even that was over now. He was here, next to her, but he wasn't truly here in the way she wanted him to be.

'Will Bear be… you know… be…' Adam stuttered.

She said it for him. 'Put down?'

He nodded.

'The police haven't been round yet, but I've read up about it. It's more likely they'll recommend a muzzle and a leather lead.'

'That's not so bad.'

'I feel awful for Naomi and the girls,' Sophie said, swallowing hard. 'She'll never talk to me again.'

'It wasn't your fault.'

'Naomi won't see it that way.'

Adam's worry fell into the creases across his brow. 'Call her. Talk to her about it.'

He did not know that their friendship was at a crisis point. All the same, she piggybacked on his hope, wanting to believe that she could find an opening in Naomi's heart, somehow.

'Want to come in for a beer before you head back?' she asked, taking the risk, cashing in on his sympathy.

'Yes, I'd like that.'

Glad of the company, she decided not to care why he had agreed to cross the threshold of the cottage.

After two beers, Adam had agreed to read Dylan a bedtime story.

After three, he had agreed to stay for supper.

After four, he was in her bed.

Sex had not felt like sympathy, but it had felt familiar and comforting, rather than shocking or forbidden. It seemed that their connection had not been lost in their separation.

The next morning, early, as the sun came through the curtain at six o'clock, he was still there. She couldn't believe her luck.

She watched him wake, and then she brought him coffee.

'I miss this,' he said, placing the cup on the side table.

'Natalie doesn't make you coffee?' she asked facetiously.

'I meant you, I miss *you*.'

'You say that, and then you'll go back to her.'

'She stayed at her mum's all of last week.'

Sophie's breathing stopped. 'Why?'

'We had a row.'

Trying to sound nonchalant, she asked, 'About what?'

'She folds my socks.'

Sophie guffawed. 'You mean, she rolls them?'

He had begun to laugh. 'No, properly in half, one on top of the other, and then lines each pair up next to the other in the drawer, and if I mess them up, she goes mental.'

'Who *does* that?'

'Natalie does!' he had chortled.

Sophie and Adam had descended into giggles. He had pulled her onto the bed again, knocking the coffee cup over, ignoring it, fumbling to get her nightie off.

'Shush, Dylan's still asleep,' Sophie had said, pressing her hand over his mouth as he groaned.

Afterwards, they lay there, in bed, in the white, bright bedroom of the cottage and they chatted about Dylan and Adam's latest jobs, and the awfulness of Bear's attack, over which she shed some more tears.

They fell back to sleep, until Dylan knocked on the door at seven thirty. Their little boy, whom they both loved so much, climbed under the covers in between them, just like old times.

'Will you take me to school, Daddy?' Dylan asked.

'You won't miss driving with Mummy in those hot new wheels of hers?' Adam grinned, winking at Sophie.

'It's a Volvo four-by-four. It's hardly hot,' Sophie scoffed.

'It's so cool, Daddy, it even has a television!' he cried. Then he added, 'But I love your car, too.'

'Come on then, if you get dressed into your uniform quickly, I'll make creamy porridge before we go.'

Before scurrying out of bed, Dylan snuggled into Adam's chest. 'I love you, Dadda.'

'Love you too, little man.'

Sophie wanted to spring out of bed and pump her fist in the air, sensing a sizeable shift in Adam, but she remained composed, inscrutable.

After a fun morning – the three of them working as a team again – Dylan hopped into Adam's car, with a belly full of his

Daddy's porridge, smarter than ever in the tie that his Daddy had knotted for him.

'Bye, then,' Adam said, kissing Sophie and squeezing her bottom playfully.

She squealed, then pressed her lips onto his, holding them there, sensing his reluctance to part from her. Dylan honked the horn and they jumped apart, laughing.

'What time do you want to pick him up next Saturday?'

'I've been meaning to say, I'm working next weekend. July the nineteenth,' he said, kicking up some gravel. 'But Soph, what if I stayed here again sometime? The following weekend?'

'What?' Sophie said, truly wondering if she had understood him correctly.

'Can I stay here again? Dylan doesn't like being away from Bear, and there's no way that dog can handle the Kingston flat.'

She grinned. 'I think Dylan and Bear would love it if you stayed here.'

'See you the week after next then,' he beamed, waving at them both as he drove off.

Sophie was left glowing, boosted with happiness.

But as soon as she stepped back inside the cottage, her joy shrivelled. Adam had been holding up a ceiling of unreality and it had just collapsed onto her head in tiny pieces. Thoughts of Naomi began pounding in her skull like an oncoming headache.

*

The ostensible reason for driving into town was to visit the pet shop to buy a muzzle and a leather lead for Bear. But in every car and with each person, Sophie searched for Naomi's plump, pretty face. The face that had always cheered her up.

The town was school-run busy. The radio warned of a three-day heatwave. She listened to the summery songs on the radio. Her brand-new Volvo smelt of pristine leather and the air-conditioning was on full blast, protecting her from the heat outside. Life should have felt as bright and beautiful as the pop songs and the weather. But her hand itched.

When she spotted a black Volvo turning left off the roundabout, she craned her neck to see its plate, and came close to bumping into the van in front of her. It was not Naomi's car. Her mind was scrabbling. She wanted to know what Naomi was doing, what she was thinking, what she was saying behind her back, what she planned to do next: about Bear, about Jason Parker. All of their intertwined troubles were scrambled together into one big mess in her head.

She would not be able to settle until she saw her.

Instead of parking up in the high street car park to go to the pet shop, she continued driving and swung the car left into Naomi's lane and wound up the hill.

The powerful engine purred as it came to a stop outside Naomi's driveway. She couldn't see through the windows in their house, but their car was there. She waited a few minutes.

Then the front door opened and Naomi came out in a t-shirt and Lycra leggings.

Sophie yanked up the handbrake and ran over to her, leaving her car in the middle of the lane.

'Naomi!' she cried, hearing the screech in her voice.

Naomi's eyes seemed to recede as she jogged over to her car and slammed herself in.

'Please, hear me out,' Sophie cried, pressing a palm at her window, but Naomi looked ahead as though Sophie wasn't there. The black locks flicked down and the car fired up and sped out of the drive, wheels spinning, swerving out of the way of Sophie's open car door.

Refusing to let go, Sophie followed behind her, all the way to the high street, where Naomi found a space in the main car park next to the fitness studio. Sophie waited in an available space in the same car park, and watched her greet Meg, who had emerged from a grey Golf. They hugged. Their heads were together as they walked towards the studio entrance. Sophie scrambled out and ran over to them, blocking them, feeling the sun's heat scorching her pale skin.

'Naomi,' she said, pleading, tears forming. 'Please, I just want to talk.'

'Please leave me alone,' Naomi replied, looking at the ground.

Meg added, 'I think it's best if you give her a bit of space, okay? For the time being.'

'Fuck off, Meg,' Sophie spat.

Meg's bright eyes flared. She did not look scared, like Naomi.

'I think you're the one who needs to fuck off, Sophie,' Meg said, with a politeness that riled Sophie further.

Sophie's palm bubbled as she watched Meg lead Naomi into the studio. A car beeped its horn and Sophie realised its bumper was at her shins.

Overheated and sweaty, she returned to her car and waited, scratching at her palm, encouraging the blisters to form. The hour was a lifetime. When Naomi and Meg came out, this time laughing, Sophie did not get out to join them. She let them get into their cars, let Meg drive away first, and then she followed Naomi.

It was soothing to know that she could. Everywhere Naomi went – into the petrol station, into the chemist on Barnes Hill, into the dry-cleaners in Godalming – Sophie was close behind, careful not to be too close, certain that Naomi had not seen her.

They continued in convoy into Guildford to the NCP on the hill, where Naomi parked on the fifth storey. Sophie parked on the fourth, waiting for her to take the lift down, watching to see where she went, jogging after her, following her as she walked to the organic café on the sunny side of the cobbled side street.

Through the café window, Sophie saw her sit with her back to Sophie, on the cushioned bench seat, and take out her laptop.

The waitress, who brought Naomi a cappuccino, caught Sophie's eye through the window.

Worried about looking suspicious, Sophie slipped off to the dingy greasy spoon across the road, where a group of red-faced men laughed at each other over their full English breakfasts. There was no sun brightening this café, just a sweltering, sticky heat inside. Sophie felt hot and agitated, like the man dressed in a Hawaiian shirt in the corner who was pouring a third sachet of sugar into his mug of tea. But the view of Naomi was bright and pretty. The street between them was cut into two by the buildings' shadow: light and shade.

Naomi was nearby. Sophie felt close to her, and she was comforted by her closeness. This would have to be enough for now.

The blisters on her palm had bloomed fully in the heat. It hurt to bend her hand. She used her left hand to lift her mug to her lips and sip her watery, bitter coffee.

While she watched Naomi slurp the froth on her drink and type furiously, Sophie hoped that Naomi was working on an article for Wine O'Clock.

Taking her eyes off Naomi's back for a minute, she checked their social media pages to see if there were any updates. As much as she didn't want to do the work herself, she had to make sure Naomi was keeping it up. Her livelihood depended on it.

There was a sweet photograph of Harley and an RIP message, posted yesterday, followed by a badly lit shot of a smeared glass of whisky at 2 a.m. this morning. Already there were 698 likes to the former, and only 109 to the latter. The discrepancy was not surprising. She would keep an eye on the likes on Harley's post to make sure there weren't more for Harley than there had been for Bear. She would take Harley's post down if there were. But this terrible thought made her want to run across the street to Naomi, to tell her that she was sorry about Harley, that she was here, that she would always be here for her, remind her that she would never again find such a loyal friend.

An hour and a half later, Naomi paid the bill and left the café.

The journey back home was hampered by traffic, which angered Sophie. Without thinking, she hit her horn, hoping that she had not drawn Naomi's attention. Anxious, Sophie pulled off at the next turning and took a different route home.

At first, she was relieved, free, but when she arrived home, the yearning came back, as did the frantic feeling.

After feeding Bear and letting him run around in the garden, it wasn't long before Sophie got back in her car again and drove over to Naomi's lane.

The waiting outside her house was like a vigil. Sophie felt she was sleepwalking through it. When Naomi didn't appear, she became lethargic. With her eyes drooping, she surveyed Naomi's house, which she had once desired. It seemed modest and uninteresting to her, as though the fabric of it had changed. There was something depressing about its peeling paintwork and its dirty brickwork. In the drive, their black Volvo sat dented, six years old, with a rattling exhaust pipe. All of this decrepitude reminded Sophie of Charlie's redundancy. The Wilsons would not be able to repaint the windows or buy a new car. When she pictured Izzy and Diana's faces, she imagined sadness in their eyes. Lately, they had looked neglected and depressed, as had Naomi. Her dimple had gone, and her springy blonde curls had fallen flat. Harley had once scampered around the drive, barking at squirrels, symbolic of the happy family he had belonged to. Now he was gone, and the whole family was broken. It was unpleasant to see them in this state. She had not predicted how it would feel to witness their downfall, nor had she fully understood how her gain would be to the detriment of Naomi's well-being. She had just wanted a better life. She had wanted it to be fair. *Life isn't fair, Sophia*, her grandfather had said. And it seemed that fairness for Naomi had finally run out, proving his point.

When Sophie compared their two separate lives, when she thought of her own pretty white cottage and garden, of Bear and Dylan running down the terraces, of her smart Volvo and new summer dresses, of the promise of a future with Adam, she realised she had gained everything and nothing. Her possessions morphed into holograms, unreal and hollow. All she had wanted was Naomi's friendship. That's all. But Naomi did not seem to want the same thing.

Then, Naomi emerged from the house, her make-up heavy like putty. Immediately Sophie perked up and checked the time. She had an hour before she would have to collect Dylan from his after-school club.

She followed Naomi along the familiar route to the girls' school.

When they arrived in School Lane, Sophie parked with a view of Naomi's Volvo. Izzy and Diana appeared from the gates, hand in hand with Naomi. They looked scruffy as they tramped along the pavement. Their hair was greasy and their white shirts and socks were grey and the pleats in their skirts were gone.

They climbed in and Naomi drove them home again. Trailing her to the school gates had been a pointless exercise. What had Sophie been expecting?

Sophie continued sitting outside in her car, in plain view, observing Naomi bundling Izzy and Diana into the house.

All day she had kept a watch on Naomi and Naomi had not acknowledged her. Whether she had noticed Sophie or not, Sophie felt isolated by Naomi's silent treatment, rejected. She wondered if it was time to go.

But minutes before Sophie had to leave to collect Dylan, Izzy skipped out of the house towards Sophie, stopping at the open gate to stare.

Sophie wound down her window, letting in the wall of heat. 'Hi, Izzy.'

'Hello,' Izzy said in a very small voice, checking behind her.

Then there were rapid footsteps across the gravel. Naomi was walking towards them.

Sophie's heart soared. It was finally time to talk.

'Get away from her! Get away!' Naomi screamed.

Sophie gaped at Naomi and then at Izzy, who stared at Sophie with wide, frightened eyes. 'I just wanted to say hello,' Izzy said.

Naomi grabbed hold of Izzy's arm. 'Get inside. I told you not to come out.'

'But it's only Sophie, look!' she cried, wriggling free and pointing at Sophie.

Naomi and Sophie locked gazes.

Sophie had never seen anything like it. The vitriol in Naomi's eyes cut right into Sophie's soul. A veil of falsehood had slipped from Naomi's face. She had taken off her good-natured mask to reveal a rawness, a coldness, that Sophie had never seen before. It stopped her heart. She felt a trickle of sweat wriggle down her temple.

In that one look, Sophie saw her friend's ghastly transformation, as though Naomi's face was the personification of Sophie's guilt.

Gasping for air, Sophie swung the car round, hyperventilating, pausing as the bumper faced the two retreating figures, mother and daughter, hand in hand. For one second she imagined driving into them, knocking them off their feet, mowing down what she had seen in Naomi's eyes, what had scared her witless. It threw her back to that night, when her hands on the steering wheel had reacted to a feeling. Jason Parker had hurt her best friend and she had acted out her rage instinctively. One split second and he was dead. The knee-jerk reaction had been born out of hatred for a man who had hurt Naomi, who had been changed, frightened, indelibly marked by this man. It had led to dire consequences: Jason Parker had died, and a mother, like herself, had lost her only son. It was not what she had wanted. She had wanted him to suffer somehow, yes, but not to die.

In her mouth, at the back of her throat, she could taste the acid she had suppressed for so long. Remorse was burning her gullet, pushing this grim, undeniable, delayed reaction up and out of her mouth, until she was spitting it into the footwell.

As she pulled up the handbrake for a three-point turn, keen to get away, her foot fell heavily onto the gas pedal, revving the engine by mistake. Naomi turned to look over her shoulder. At the sight of Sophie's car pointed towards them, she gasped, scooped Izzy up and ran at full pelt into the house.

Sophie placed her hand on the handbrake lever to make sure she had not acted without thinking first. The handbrake was up and the car remained safe in a stationary position, confirming her own self-control. It proved that her love for Naomi was as intuitive as her hatred for Jason Parker had been.

With the image of Naomi's petrified face looming in her mind, Sophie made her way through the lanes to Dylan's school. On autopilot, she picked him up and took him home.

She told Dylan to play outside with Bear while she tidied the house, plans spinning.

An organised house, an organised mind, her grandfather had said.

After hours of deliberation, it became clear to Sophie that there was only one way of earning Naomi's respect.

She called for Dylan in the garden, but he wasn't responding. She needed to talk to him about her plan. If he wasn't in the garden, she guessed he would be in the garage, and she was right. He was there with Bear, who was sitting in the boot of the Giulia, where the cuddly toys had once been lined up. The dog's eyes were ice blue and knowing.

'Come on, out of there, you two,' she said. 'I want to talk to you about something, Dylan.'

Dylan climbed out of the boot and followed her into the house.

In the kitchen, with Dylan standing on a low stool at her side, she whisked sugar and cream and milk and vanilla bean into a pan and brought it to the boil.

'My mother made this hot drink for me, once, before she left me and Deda to look after ourselves.'

'Where did she go?'

'She had grown very tired of me. I was very naughty.'

'Naughtier than me?'

'Very much so,' Sophie laughed, taking the pan off the heat, dolloping in the butter and chocolate.

She handed Dylan the whisk, remembering how her mother had kissed her temple, how she had held her hand over Sophie's as they stirred. She recalled how the hot liquid had splashed up onto their faces. Her mother had said, 'Careful, my darling', and she had kissed the inside of Sophie's right palm. Those words of hers had been the last Sophie remembered. She could hear her voice in her head now, soft and caring. Her right palm – broken and bloody – throbbed with the sense of her mother's lips pressed there. There must have been more words from her afterwards; a 'goodnight' or a 'brush your teeth' or a bedtime story, perhaps, but Sophie could not recall them. All she could remember was 'Careful, my darling', and then her mind flashed forward to the next morning: waking up, padding into her mother's room and discovering that she was gone.

Sophie placed her hands over Dylan's hot little hands and inhaled the smell of him, just as her mother had back then. Her heart was swollen with love. She wondered if this was how her mother had felt. Sophie was hit by the certain knowledge that this was true. It became as plain as any truth could be. On the evening that they had stirred butter and chocolate, Sophie had felt her mother's love through her hands, deeply, right to her bones.

'Was she my grandmother?' Dylan asked.

'She's still your grandmother. She's called Suzanne. You met her once when you were a very little baby. She brought you a snow globe all the way from America where she lives.'

'I want to go to America.'

'One day, maybe.'

'Do you miss her?'

'I've always been too angry with her to miss her.'

'Why?'

The noise of the metal whisk on the bottom of the pan was like a scraping in Sophie's head. Her tears fought through the lump in her throat.

'Because she didn't say goodbye.'

'That's mean,' Dylan said simply.

'Dylan, if *I* had to go away somewhere, I want you to remember that it would never be your fault or because of how naughty you've been. It would be because I loved you, not because I didn't. Do you understand?'

Dylan stopped whisking and stared at his mother. 'You're not going away,' he said.

She grabbed his hand. 'If I do, you mustn't be a baby about it. Promise? You have to be a really good boy, especially when you stay with Daddy and Natalie.'

'I hate Natalie!' he screamed, throwing the whisk across the room. 'I don't want you to go away.'

She grabbed his chin, squashing his cheeks, wiping both their faces of their tears, looking straight into his eyes.

'There is something I have to fix, something Mummy did a long time ago that I have to make right, and it might mean I have to go somewhere for a while.'

'How long?' he whimpered. The rims of his big blue eyes were drooping with the weight of his tears.

'Not long,' she lied, kissing his head and pulling him into a hug. 'Not long. And one day, you'll be proud of Mummy for taking responsibility for the bad thing she did. One day.'

She did not want to be like her mother. She could not run from what was hard, what was right. Not a day longer could be spent pretending that it was anyone else's fault, that the world was not on her side, that she was the only person suffering. Everyone suffered in some shape or form, everyone found life taxing, often punishing. Even for those whose lives looked Instagram-perfect on the outside, like Naomi's, their struggles were going on inside, just as Naomi's were now.

Naomi's spirit had once been a magnet for happiness. What she put out there, she got back. Her true spirit had once embodied happiness and naivety. Fidelity and selflessness. Sophie might have wanted Naomi's life, but she had not gained it with that same honesty and kindness. She had sought out the material trappings, expecting them to make the difference.

The night of Jason Parker's death had lain inside her like a deep dream, a scary thing to fight against, like a shadow in the dark, and she had not opened her eyes, she had not turned the light on to look the intruder in the eye. She had not confronted what she had done. The true consequences had finally dawned on her and come into the light. For the first time in her life, Sophie felt the full impact of her actions. Not in terms of facts, but in terms of feelings. Through Naomi's suffering, through her guilt, Sophie had learnt how to imagine someone else's pain, to feel it, and in doing so, she had dredged up her own.

The love that Naomi had shown Sophie had penetrated, at last. Naomi had been a role model and finally Sophie was learning. Perversely, with this realisation, Sophie would now have to step away from Naomi, and away from all of those people she had hurt most and loved most, to heal them, to save them.

Naomi did not deserve to suffer any more. And Dylan deserved better than a mother like Suzanne.

CHAPTER THIRTY

Through the open kitchen window, I could hear Charlie trudge across the gravel. I stood behind the fridge door, taking a few surreptitious swigs. A little top-up to help me on my way. I was itching to leave, to get it done.

As I reached for my handbag at the front door, I caught a glimpse of myself in the hall mirror. My reflection shocked me. Grey corkscrew curls had grown out at the roots and my eyes were smaller, bloodshot from a permanent hangover. Deep lines seemed to pull my mouth down at each corner. I looked haggard, worn by life, damaged.

'Did you get my text?' I asked Charlie as he came in, before he had a chance to tell me how badly the interview had gone. He hadn't needed to tell me. It was heavy in his movements, as though he were carrying weights under his clothes.

'I did. Are you sure it's a good idea?'

'Yes,' I said, but something caught in my throat. I began to cough. I had a dry mouth and a smoker's chest. It seemed that my breathing had not regulated since the day I had run with Izzy into the house for safety, the gleam of Sophie's headlights burning into our backs. Days had passed but the shock had not diminished.

'Are the girls in bed?' Charlie asked, looking straight at me, straight through me, lids at half-mast. His glasses were wide and large on his face. It seemed he had lost weight without me noticing.

'Fast asleep,' I replied.

Throughout the girls' bedtime routine, I had been efficient, verging on tyrannical.

'It's so bloody hot out there,' he sighed.

I grimaced at him, intolerant of his moping. 'Did you get the job?' I asked, with a cruel directness.

'No.' I watched him dump his briefcase on the shoe bench, and watched it fall from the shoe bench, watched him pick it up and reposition it, watched it fall again as he walked away. He must have heard it clunk onto the wood flooring. If he did, he ignored it. I stared at the brown, worn leather on the floor, baggy where once it had been stuffed full. It was lying there as redundant as Charlie.

'That's not good.'

'It would have been a demotion anyway,' he said.

'It would have been a job,' I said, stuffing my swollen feet into my shoes.

I made the mistake of looking up, seeing how he looked at me. His eyes roamed my face. He was looking for something in me that wasn't there any more. Some kindness, perhaps.

'I won't be long,' I said, my heart lurching up my throat.

'Careful of that dog,' he said. His parting words were protective. He was aware of so little.

'It's the weekend. Dylan will have taken him to Adam's,' I replied.

Even so, the dog would not have scared me. I had feared my own inaction more. The risks I had taken by allowing Sophie near my family made my stomach seize up. After Sophie's little excursion to Brighton with the girls, Charlie had accused me of being drunk and paranoid; with hindsight, I had been at my most alert, acutely aware of the danger. I had heeded her first warning shot, responded to her blackmail. If Charlie knew what I planned now, he would think I had lost my mind. In one way, I have. In another, I'm stepping up to the challenge, fighting back, responding to the level of her threat. Standing up for myself. Surviving.

My body pumped with adrenaline as I drove away from home, feeling clear and determined, heroic even. I reached for the packet of cigarettes in the glove compartment, swerving in the middle of the road, correcting the car's path, lighting up.

In my rear-view mirror, I looked for Sophie's car. If she was following me again, she would be confused that I was heading straight to her house.

Last week, I had felt her eyes in my back, seen her figure through the reflections in windows; spotted her car in my rear-view mirror; heard her footsteps behind me.

She had thought I hadn't seen her, but I had. I had thought she would get bored. She had not. I had refused to acknowledge her, to show her I was unnerved, refused to give her the attention she so craved. My strategy had been to rise above it, but terror and despair had raged through me. A sort of vibrating madness had buzzed continually in my head. She was a swarm of wasps crawling over my body; I had to keep still to get rid of them but my instinct was to run and scream, to shake my head back and forth, crashing my brain into my skull until I couldn't see her any more.

When she had dared to rev her engine at Izzy in the driveway, I had momentarily lost my head, startled by her threat, enraged by how far she was prepared to go to control me.

To protect my family, to outwit her, I had to be cool-headed and cunning. I had to adopt her thought processes, become selfish and wily and ruthless to gain what I wanted. And I wanted her gone.

I parked up next to her Volvo, which was the same make and model and colour as mine. They say that imitation is a form of flattery. I was not flattered, I was violated. She had stolen my whole life; reached into my heart for my happiness and pocketed it for herself.

Shifting from one foot to the other, I knocked on her door.

'Hi, Sophie.'

'Naomi?' she cried, falling a few steps back. There was that familiar waft of incense that spilt out from the open door. Her white-blonde hair was tied into a high bun, pulled off her face for a change, opening her up, showing her face as she might have been as a young girl. Her right hand was bandaged, suggesting her eczema had flared up. I experienced a split second of doubt, and then I thought of Bear's jaws on Harley's neck and her car pointed at Izzy, poised for another attack.

I wiped my sweating palms down my thighs.

For too long I had lived in fear of Sophie's moods, sucked up her manipulations, swallowed her jealousies and her insanities; apologised for them, talked her through her problems, shown her unconditional love like a sister. *Poor Sophie, so neglected as a child*, I had thought. *Poor Sophie, abandoned by her father and her mother.*

Boohoo. There were no more excuses left. My sympathy had dried up, along with my fear. Her neuroses had ruled my adult life. My fear of her reactions had overridden my own sense of self, my own needs. Almost before I thought of myself, I had thought of how Sophie might react. I had spent so much time kowtowing to her, and then worrying about what she might do to the girls, that I had forgotten I was in charge of my own life.

'It's July the nineteenth and I want to take a drive in the Giulia,' I said to her, too bluntly.

My heart was large in my chest, beating into my eardrums.

Her mouth fell open. 'What?' She stepped outside and pulled the door to, but not completely.

'It's the anniversary of Jason Parker's death, twenty years on. Let's take a drive to mark it. As a remembrance,' I continued, trying to be softer. 'I want to find our way back to where we were. In here,' I said, pressing my fingers into my chest bone. 'I want to feel that freedom and joy again. We were a team, remember? Us against the world.'

She was blinking wildly at me, biting one side of her lip. Then I heard a loud bark from Bear. Sophie glanced up to the window above the door.

'I thought it was Adam's weekend?'

'Umm. It is,' Sophie said, holding the brass handle of the door. I wasn't sure whether she was going to go back inside or close it completely to come outside to the garage with me.

'But he left Bear,' I said.

'Bear can't be cooped up in the Kingston flat. He's too sensitive...' she stopped. 'I'm so sorry, that was really rubbish of me, after... Since Harley... He's muzzled, and we've got a better lead for him. I'm so sorry, Naomi. I wasn't thinking...'

'Please,' I said, trying to loosen the tightness in my jaw. 'It wasn't your fault.'

'Oh my god, Naomi. I can't tell you how much... I really thought... I don't know what to say,' she stuttered, flustered and eager.

'Come on then. You can leave Bear here, can't you?'

'I'm not sure...' she said, almost in a whisper, again looking up to the window.

I hadn't been expecting such hesitancy from her. I had expected her submission. For a long time, she had wanted us to drive together in the car again, wanted us to return to the way we were, wanted to wipe out the secret between us as though it had never been. She wanted these things more than she wanted anything else in the world. It gave me power that I had never before misused.

'You've left him alone before, haven't you?'

'Once.'

'We'll be gone fifteen minutes. Half an hour tops. He won't even know.'

'He's shut in Dylan's bedroom.'

I looked at the empty dog cage in the hall and wondered why Sophie had put him upstairs, but I couldn't digress. I needed her to do as I asked. To speak again, I had to lubricate my dry mouth. 'I need this, Sophie. *Please*. For me. Just as you said the other evening, in the garden. If we took a drive in it again, together, tonight, on July the nineteenth, it might reboot our memories of that night and replace it with something happier. I don't want to be haunted by it any more, I want to move on. *Please*.'

Before I had uttered the final 'please', she was reaching for both the green leather key ring, which held the two garage keys, and the Giulia car key from the hooks on the wall.

'Let's go,' she said, and I followed her across the gravel to the garage.

She unlocked the red corrugated iron door first. 'It won't open from the inside any more.'

I knew this already. 'Dylan's axe attack?' I laughed. It released some tension inside me.

'I've bred a psycho child,' she replied, pressing her bandaged hand onto the closed boot, smiling to herself about something that I had no interest in any more, twirling green string in her fingers. Her mysterious thoughts were irrelevant now.

We felt our way into the garage to reach the light switch by the side door, which was open by a crack.

'Dylan left the side door open, too,' she tutted, pulling it closed and locking it up. 'He plays in here sometimes and I keep telling him to lock it up. He's in big trouble this time,' Sophie harrumphed, slamming the garage door keys on the workbench.

'Chuck me the car key,' I said, holding my hands in a cup shape.

The light bulb cast a nasty, bland light across her face, almost wiping her out completely. I couldn't read her expression.

'You want to drive?' she asked.

'Yeah, why not?'

'You remember how awkward the gear lever is?'

'Of course I do.'

'Okay then.' She shrugged, throwing the key to me.

As long as she acquiesced, it didn't matter that she questioned my behaviour. It wouldn't be long before it would be too late to question it.

As she slammed the passenger door closed, I scooped up the garage door keys. My fingers quivered as I dropped them into my pocket.

I climbed into the seat next to her, positioning myself in front of the shiny Bakelite steering wheel, running my hands up and down in semicircles, feeling my stomach turn inside out as I placed the key into the worn ignition. Instantly, the fumes from the exhaust hit the back of my throat. My eyes watered so much I couldn't see, as though rain was streaming in a sheet across my vision.

My body rolled from the back seat into the footwell. I was winded.

'Ouch. What? That hurt,' I said.

'Shut UP!' Sophie yelled.

I collapsed back, rubbing my face, feeling my hands damp with sick and sweat.

'Stay there,' she said.

I closed my eyes. My head was thumping. I wanted to sleep forever.

A few seconds later, roused by a gush of cool air from the open driver's seat door, I pulled myself up. There was steam on the window, which I wiped clear. Through the arch of cleaned glass, I peered out and saw Sophie bend down, pick up a mangled black umbrella and climb back into her seat. I ducked down and lay where she had seen me last. Through the crack between the seat and the door, I saw her hide the umbrella.

'What happened?' I rasped, terror rolling over me.

'We must have hit a deer,' she replied, clicking her seat belt closed. I knew she was lying and I cried out. A feeble remonstration.

'It's okay. He didn't suffer.'

'No, no, no…' I whimpered, suddenly so sober and afraid.

The car started. We moved off.

I lay in the dark discomfort of the car floor, feeling the road rushing at speed, too close to my ear. I stayed very still, my breathing heavy, my eyes closed, trying to shut out the memory of that umbrella. My thoughts were so loud and savage, I was surprised the noise wasn't rattling out from my skull.

Stunned into inaction, tongue-tied by my own shock, managing unprecedented spikes of terror, dizzied by the stark choices we faced, I waited for Sophie to speak, to take charge.

I waited to hear the truth. She did not utter that truth. She continued to pretend we had hit a deer.

We could both pretend. If we never talked about it, it did not have to be real.

I turned the radio on and pulled the key out from the ignition, leaving the engine running, unshaken by a memory that I had grown used to, that had been squashed up inside my chest, pressing on my organs, aching when my heart worked too hard.

All those years ago, I had left on the flight to Bangkok wanting to trick my mind into blanking out the sight of the umbrella, determined to stay ignorant.

Sophie had told me it was a deer. I had decided to believe her. Over the years, it had become true. I had experienced several real-life visions of that deer hitting the windscreen. Why could Sophie not have kept it that way? Why had she ruined it by getting greedy?

I turned the radio up, so loud it vibrated through my bones, but she turned it down, quickly.

'Stay here a minute,' I said, opening my car door again. 'Just realised I forgot the Exeter mixtape in my car.'

'You've still got that?'

'Of course,' I laughed, amazed that I was able to let out a noise that resembled good humour.

But I hurried out of my seat, refusing to see her smile, refusing to witness the thrill and anticipation on her face. I couldn't bear to see her delusion.

I pressed the driver's door closed and flew outside, where the exhaust pipe chucked out huge storm clouds of carbon monoxide.

As I reached up for the cool, metal garage door, I choked on the car's emissions, on its faltering put-putting, old and poisonous.

Tears broke across my cheeks as I slammed the corrugated red door down, leaving the keys in the lock – but not locking it – dropping the car key just outside the garage door, where she might have thrown it before closing herself in.

The door rattled like thunder and I jumped back from its growl, as though it were the monster, not me.

There would be no way out for Sophie. The door was closed on our forever friendship. Forever gone.

CHAPTER THIRTY-ONE

The clatter of the garage door closing brought with it a strange new light. The bulb seemed to flicker and dim. Sophie twisted round in her seat, wondering what had happened, why they were shut in.

She called for Naomi over the noise of the radio, wound down her window, stuck her head out.

'Naomi?' she yelled, catching a gulp full of exhaust fumes, wondering where Naomi could have disappeared to. She darted out of her seat, choking, and squeezed herself around the bonnet to look for her, worrying she might have hit her head or fainted.

She looked around the car and checked under the chassis.

An old rag was lying on the workbench. She grabbed it and pressed it over her nose and mouth and ducked back into the car, sliding into the driver's seat, fumbling for the ignition. There was no key. She patted the floor around the pedals, wondering if Naomi had dropped it. The radio blasted into her eardrums, as if it had suddenly been switched on. She turned the dial to stop the noise, but she had no idea how to turn off a running engine without a key. *A ghost car*, she remembered Adam calling it. Underneath the steering wheel, she knew that there were wires to fire up an engine and to cut an engine, but she did not know where to start. Her grandfather should have taught her how.

'Naomi!' she cried, lurching out of the car to the tool bench to scrabble around for the key to the side door. If she couldn't turn the car off, she had to get out of the garage.

As her panic built, as the carbon monoxide ate away the oxygen in her red blood cells, her mind became cloudier. She began banging on the heavy solid oak of the side door, retching with each exertion, already barely able to stand. Her fists were as effective as feathers. The blood seeped through her bandage.

'Naomi! I don't have the keys! Naomi! Can you hear me?' she called out, moving to the main garage door, smashing her palms onto the painted metal, but her voice was weak. She could barely hold her arms up.

The drawers under the bench might have a tool that could prize open the garage door. The bandages on her right hand loosened as she rooted around. A screwdriver was useless, a spanner was worse. None was heavy-duty enough to break through metal or open a jammed lock. She thought of the axe in the loft, out of harm's way, and cursed her son for being so mischievous. Thinking of him made her cry. She heard Bear's distant bark and imagined Dylan trying to quieten him down. She had lied to Naomi, letting her believe he was at Adam's, knowing she would not have allowed her to leave him alone in the house at night. The image of Dylan tucked up in bed in the house, a few feet away from where she was trapped, was excruciating.

She remembered the wrench in the boot of the car. It would be her only hope, if she had the energy to use it to prize open the door.

Having crawled to the back bumper, she pulled herself up with one hand, woozily fumbling for the boot catch, feeling the scratch of Dylan's string under her fingertips. The air was thick. Delirium and confusion made every movement painstaking, surreal, as though her limbs were not attached, as though this were happening to someone else.

She popped the boot. A remnant of green thread dangled.

When she peered in, she hallucinated.

Inside, she saw a vision of Dylan's body curled up asleep with his teddies. Her hand shot out to touch this blurred form, to burst the horrifying apparition, but her fingers met with the warmth of his downy arm.

'*DYLAN!*' she screamed, curdling the poisoned smoke around her head. It took superhuman strength to lift him into her arms and her knees buckled under his weight. She slid down to the concrete floor, holding onto him with all of her dwindling strength. '*Dylan,*' she whispered, weeping over him, trying to kiss him awake. He must have snuck down from his room and out of the back door, either before Naomi arrived or while she had been talking to Naomi on the doorstep. Maybe that was why Bear had started barking. Bear had been telling her he was gone. He was gone. He was gone!

'I won't let you go!' she screamed.

His head lolled back over her arm, spikes of white-blonde hair falling the wrong way, his mouth smiling a little, opened a little, but his eyes closed, with his long white lashes pointing down his cheeks. When she felt for his pulse, she could not find it. When she put her face to his mouth, she could not feel his breath.

The toxic air bloomed. Her own breathing became laboured, her will to live became weaker, her thoughts of Naomi's betrayal breaking what was left of her spirit.

Knowing there was no way out, knowing there was nothing left, knowing that this was the end, she dragged herself and Dylan into the back seat. She lifted him, pale like an angel, into the ghost car, into her grandfather's pride and joy, where they lay together in the white clouds, where they died together; where an eye for an eye became a tooth for a tooth, where Ilene Parker might think justice had been done.

CHAPTER THIRTY-TWO

SURREY ECHO
MOTHER AND SON FOUND DEAD INSIDE GARAGE

MURDER–SUICIDE VERDICT RETURNED IN SURREY INQUEST. Sophie King, 41, gassed herself and her son, Dylan King, 8, inside a classic car in the garage adjoining her home, the inquest heard.

Emergency services were called to a woodland cottage near Farnham, Surrey just before 3 p.m. on Tuesday 20 July, where detectives made their grim discovery.

Detective Sergeant Mark Price, who found them dead after a concerned phone call from Dylan's father, Adam King, 42, said there were no signs of violence and no sign of forced entry. Post-mortem examination reports confirmed that both had died from carbon monoxide poisoning.

Surrey Coroner Arthur Carney said it was clear from friends and family that Mrs Sophie King had been suffering from a bout of severe depression following a recent separation from her husband, Adam King.

Naomi Wilson, a close friend of the deceased, told the inquest that she had been terrorised by King in the months leading up to the murder–suicide, and described how volatile King's moods had become, detailing specific incidents of King's stalking, blackmail and death threats. Wilson had tried to end their friendship repeatedly, the inquest heard.

Returning a verdict of murder–suicide, Arthur Carney described it as a 'desperate act by a mother who had been experiencing a period of intense mental distress. Their loved ones must try not to blame themselves for this terrible tragedy.'

CHAPTER THIRTY-THREE

Many years later

'Loved ones must try not blame themselves, no, no, must not, must not, must try to, remember not to,' Naomi sang to a nameless tune, sipping from her tumbler on the side table, watching the television images flicker before her. A drop of her drink spilt onto the coral sofa.

She shuffled to the kitchen to get a cloth. 'Oh no, oh no, no, no, no,' she said, returning to her spot, rubbing at the clear spill. If she didn't keep it clean, Sophie would not like it.

There was a knock at the door. She checked the time on the clock that sat above the five-bar heater in the inglenook fireplace. It was too early for visitors. Unless, unless. She checked her calendar and gasped. Always they came on her birthday. Always in the morning.

In the mirror, she saw an older person with short, tight curls and sunken cheeks and milky eyes. In her mind she remembered someone with long corkscrew curls and rosy cheeks. She pinched at her sallow skin, to bring the blood to the surface. There wasn't time to change out of her nightie.

'Hi, Mum,' Diana said, standing at the door with her bouncing curls and bonny cheeks.

Diana, my beautiful baby girl, Naomi thought.

'Happy Birthday,' she said, handing her a bulging supermarket shopping bag. 'Sorry, Izzy couldn't make it today.'

'Come in, come in.'

Naomi looked inside her bag for the vodka. There was none. She wanted to hurl the biscuits and bread across the room. Not even on her birthday! She would have to send Adam to the shops when he visited on Friday. Always Friday, Adam would bring her vodka.

Naomi returned to her worn spot on the sofa, while Diana messed around in the kitchen making tea. Always bloody tea.

Cupboards were opened and closed. She would be rifling around, checking on things, nosing into her private business.

'Everything to your liking?' Naomi barbed when Diana returned.

'I was just putting the shopping away.'

She snorted at her daughter.

'How are you, Mum?'

'Fine. Except those people. Those *people*. They make so much noise.'

'What people?'

'In the shack. They play loud music. I go over there to tell them to turn it down and they ignore me.'

'Do you want me to have a word?'

'I don't need *you* to do it for me.'

'Fine.'

Naomi knew she was hurt. That was just how she wanted it.

'Tell me about your life, Diana,' Naomi asked, looking at the television, feigning disinterest, holding her breath so that she didn't miss a syllable, eager to hear every detail, eager to know that it had not been for nothing.

Diana began to chatter, just as she had when Naomi had sat on her bed after story time when she was little. '... Josh is moving in, finally. He was funny about not earning as much as me but I told him he was being dumb. I love his work. It always makes me laugh, but Dorling Kindersley might not be publishing his next story. They say that kids only want to read horror stories these days.' She laughed and continued, 'But his illustrations are funny, which I think kids will always respond to, don't you?'

Naomi shrugged. But she agreed, relishing her daughter's opinions.

'Anyway, Izzy's driving me mad. Blake just got a promotion and they've moved into this amazing house in Shropshire and she's always asking me up there to stay, but she never comes down to London to see me and Josh. I think she thinks she's going to get mugged or something, or suffocate in my small flat. Or something,' she complained. But then she chuckled. 'It is beautiful up there, though, Mum. I wish you could see it. You know, Dad practically lives there.' And on she went.

When Diana's stories held something uncomfortable for her, Naomi rolled her mind right back to their childhoods, where she liked it to stay, where it was safe. There, Naomi could find happiness in the distant memories of smiles: flickering, faded, bliss. Never, ever would she linger in the present. In the present, she would see her life for what it was. She would see a bitter old drunk, living in the house her victim had bequeathed to her, eaten up by the irony, driven slowly insane by the sins of her past. She would see what she had destroyed, and how she had failed; and she would be too scared to die. Dying would collect up her regrets and her shame and throw them back in her face. Dying would mean it was too late. Dying would mean she had wasted her life.

So, here she was, too scared to die and too scared to live. Only intoxication could take her away into a limbo land that suspended her in neither: the pretence of peace, keeping the torture of reality at bay a little longer. Of course, it wouldn't always work. And it wouldn't ever last.

She sipped her drink and let her heavy head fall back onto the cushion. *What is done to you lives long; what you do to others lives longer. Tit for tat. Tit for tat.* Her mind sang on.

Diana's voice came through the sing-song. Or did it? Oh yes, she was there.

'Mum? Are you listening?'

'I've got a terrible headache.'

'Okay. I'll leave you to it,' she said, kissing Naomi's forehead and squeezing her hand. 'See you soon, Mum.'

As the door closed behind Diana, Naomi managed to say, 'Bye, Diana, my love,' under her breath, but Diana would not have heard.

Then another screeching voice crowded into her brain.

'Happy Birthday to you… Happy Birthday to you,' the haunting voice continued on repeat.

The smell of Sophie was present, like incense, as strong as Diana's perfume had been.

'Go away!' Naomi screamed, holding her hands to her ears.

'Never, ever,' Sophie hissed.

Her pale hair blew and her long limbs danced. And Dylan leapt at her feet, like the devil itself.

She closed her eyes and rocked back and forth and the songs became louder.

Naomi sang like a shout over Sophie's voice, 'Loved ones must not blame themselves, no, no, must not, must not, must remember not to! Loved ones must not blame themselves!'

To make her go away, she sang and sang. Sophie's melodic tones encompassed her soul, overriding any scream. Sophie was not gone. Sophie was never gone. Sophie was in her head, like Suzanne had been in Sophie's. The pain lived on inside. The echo of abandonment. The echo of neglect. The echo of abuse. The echo of rape. The echo of violence. The echo of revenge. The reverberations had spread outwards from the epicentre of Suzanne's abandonment, which had ruptured Sophie's innocence long ago, and, in turn, rumbled through Naomi's life like an aftershock. In the aftermath, Naomi's love could never have been enough for Sophie, and Sophie's love had proven too much for Naomi. Sophie had stolen from Naomi what she should have found inside herself. And more suffering had ensued. The cycle never-ending.

But Ilene Parker was dead now. And Naomi had saved her daughters. She had broken the cycle for Izzy and Diana, making sure they would live out their life without Sophie and Naomi's legacy, without the haunting of Jason Parker. For them, at least, Naomi's love had been enough. For Naomi, their happiness was plenty. Hers in exchange for theirs. It was more than enough for her.

A LETTER FROM CLARE

Dear Reader,

Thank you very much for reading *Her Closest Friend*. It still amazes me to think that I have real-life readers out there in the world. You are like distant friends!

Please keep in touch by clicking on the sign-up link below, where you'll hear about what I'll be writing next:

www.bookouture.com/clare-boyd

For a long time, I have wanted to write about friendship. Yet I could not have predicted how much disturbing material I would drag out of my brain in the process of writing on this subject. My previous books about child abuse – *Little Liar* – and suicide – *Three Secrets* – were more obvious starting places for dark storylines. But I discovered a deep well of anguish, paranoia and self-doubt in the friendship dynamics that I drew inspiration from for *Her Closest Friend*.

It is easy to consider our friends as added bonuses, extras on the periphery of family life. Some friends come and go according to our changing circumstances and some stick around, for better or worse. The more intense friendships can make their mark in wonderful or terrible ways, to leave an indelible impression on us, and even shape us as people. I realised, in the writing of this book, that the friends we bond with, and sometimes get rid of – and I don't mean by locking them in garages! – can be as influential or damaging to our well-being as family can be.

Now that I'm in my mid-forties, I have found friends who are nothing like Sophie; they have my best interests at heart. Unlike family, we can choose our friends, and thank goodness for that! I do not know what I would do without them.

If you have enjoyed *Her Closest Friend*, please do write a review, and follow me on social media. See below for details.

Another huge thank you for reading my book.

With very best wishes,
Clare

 clare.boyd.14

 @ClareBoydClark

 claresboyd

ACKNOWLEDGEMENTS

I would like to thank my agent, Broo Doherty, and my editor, Jessie Botterill: our editorial meetings are the highlight of my year.

As always, I am in awe of the energetic, forward-thinking team at Bookouture. Thanks to you all.

Major thanks go to Helen McGinn, for helping me to understand the job of wine

blogging. My characters, Naomi and Sophie, could only dream of creating a wine blog as brilliant and funny as Helen's.

I would not have been able to piece together the car accident storyline without Duncan Brown's expertise in road traffic policing. And I would not have been able to meet Duncan Brown without Maria Edwards' help and contacts. A huge thank you to both of you.

As ever, I want to thank my family and friends, who are a continual support throughout the process of writing my books.

Made in the USA
Middletown, DE
03 January 2020